THE CALL OF ANCIENT LIGHT - BOOK TWO

THE WAY OF ANCIENT POWER

BEN WOLF

A COMING OF AGE FANTASY NOVEL

PUBLISHED BY

SPLICKETY PUBLISHING GROUP

WWW.BENWOLF.COM

The Way of Ancient Power
Book Two of the Call of Ancient Light Series

Published by
Splickety Publishing Group, Inc.
www.splickety.com

Ebook ISBN: 978-1-942462-47-7
Print ISBN: 978-1-942462-48-4
Copyright © 2021 by Ben Wolf, Inc. All rights reserved.
www.BenWolf.com

Cover design by Hannah Sternjakob
https://www.hannah-sternjakob-design.com

Contact Ben Wolf directly at ben@benwolf.com for signed copies
and to schedule author appearances and speaking events.

To Carla Hoch:

You are my favorite ginger.
I hope this book has enough fight scenes for you.

Also, you may be immortal (like every other ginger),
But I'm still coming for you.

ORIGINAL MAP OF KANARAH

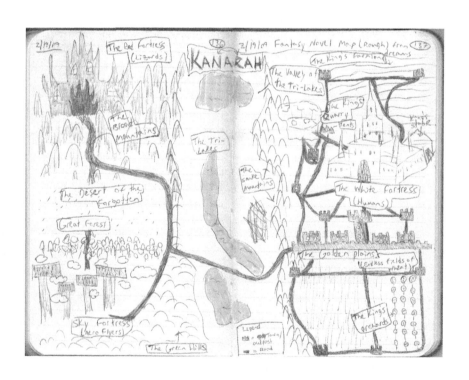

CONTENTS

PROLOGUE

L umen's eyes opened in the darkness.

He could see them, feel them.

They were much closer now.

Three travelers had set out to discover the secret to release him, and two more had joined them. Two humans, a Saurian, a Windgale, and a Wolf.

As the King had proclaimed nearly a thousand years earlier, Lumen would soon be set free.

And when he was set free, he would save Kanarah.

CHAPTER ONE

C alum ducked under a blade and drove his fist into the bandit's gut.

A follow-up swipe with his red-bladed sword felled the bandit, then Calum whirled around to block an axe to keep it from cleaving him in half.

The tip of Axel's sword burst through the axe-wielding bandit's chest from behind, and the bandit slumped to the ground atop his dead comrade.

Beyond Axel, Magnus engaged ten—literally *ten*—of the bandits on his own, and he was winning too. Easily. Now a seven-and-a-half-foot Sobek, his dark green scales had hardened to the point where steel just glanced off his skin, and he only wore his Blood Ore armor over his chest and stomach.

Magnus swung his matching Blood Ore sword in massive arcs at the men who encircled him. Though they timed their blocks and parries well, they simply couldn't withstand his strength. Every blow sent shudders throughout their bodies, and in a matter of minutes, all ten of them lay the ground, slain.

As he marveled at the sight, an arrow zipped by Calum's ear, followed by a sound like a knife piercing an apple's skin. A bandit face-planted next to him, his sword tumbling across the arid dirt that spread out for miles north and south of Trader's Pass.

"Watch your back." Lilly swooped into view, still afloat on the air with an empty bow in her left hand. Her blonde hair shone under the afternoon sun, and her blue cape shimmered and billowed with the wind. A hint of teasing colored her words, and her half-smile and mischievous blue eyes added to the effect.

Marveling at Magnus was great, but the big lizard had nothing on Lilly.

"That's what I have you for." Calum drank her in. Beautiful didn't even begin to describe her. Had they not been in a battle, Calum could have stared at her all—

A brown and gray blur knocked him to the ground. Calum repositioned his sword to run the thing through, but it had already leaped off him.

Its furry tail wagged as it pounced on an approaching bandit. A few ferocious tears and bites later, it turned back to Calum with lupine ears and keen blue eyes.

"She *just* told you to watch it. Where's your head?" Riley gave him a low growl. "You're gonna get yourself killed."

"Sorry." Calum pivoted and absorbed a hack from another bandit's sword with his own. Before Calum could counterattack, an arrow lodged in the bandit's neck, and he dropped. Calum glared at Lilly, who still hovered above him. "Hey! I had that one under control."

She just shrugged and winked at him, then she nocked another arrow.

He smiled back until he noticed Axel's steely dark-blue eyes and his sour expression. As quickly as their eyes had met, Axel refocused on the battle and downed the next bandit with one vicious swing. It reminded Calum how glad he was that he'd never be on the receiving end of one of Axel's blows.

Magnus roared and whirled around. His sword took out three more bandits in one swing, and his whiplash tail flattened another two.

Riley knifed past another bandit, skidded to a halt, then sprang toward the bandit's back. He caught the bandit's collar in his teeth and

4

slammed him to the ground. Another salvo of furious bites and tears at the bandit's throat finished him off.

Barely half a week had passed since their encounter with the Gronyxes in the underground tunnel from Kanarah City to Trader's Pass, and already trouble had found them again. Sometimes Calum wondered if their troubles would ever end, if they'd never get a real rest.

The constant trials and stress weighed on them all, but Calum kept reassuring himself it would all be worthwhile in the end. Freeing Lumen would transform Kanarah and everyone in it, and then all would be made right. The thought of it renewed Calum's resolve, and he refocused on the battle—or what was left of it, anyway.

Of the two-dozen bandits who'd initially confronted them, only three remained. Instead of surrounding Calum and the others, they were surrounded.

Still, these men were rough grizzled types accustomed to the harsh life of scavenging for whatever they could find, steal, or scrounge, either from travelers along Trader's Pass or from the expansive wasteland that stretched out as far as they eye could see.

They brandished their weapons and charged in three separate directions instead of as a group. Calum was still learning strategy from Magnus, but even he knew that was a huge tactical error. They felled the bandits with ease then stood in place and looked at each other.

"Anyone hurt?" Magnus wiped the blood from his broadsword with one of the bandits' shirts, then he sheathed it.

"I'm good, thanks to Lilly and Riley." Calum shook his head and did the same. He'd taken his red-bladed sword from a bandit in Eastern Kanarah named Tyburon. It had been his toughest one-on-one fight ever, so he'd kept the sword as a memento.

It was also a lot better than his previous sword, which was nothing but a standard weapon issued to the King's soldiers. By contrast, the red blade in his hand had a curve right at the end, near its tip, that made it especially good for slashing.

And it looked awesome, too.

"I'm fine." Axel still wore the same frown as when Calum had last looked at him.

"You sure?" Calum nodded to him and sheathed his sword. "You look frustrated."

"I said I'm *fine*," Axel insisted, now scowling at Calum. "Just sick of the constant fighting."

Even as Axel said it, Calum knew it wasn't the truth. If anything, the fighting was probably the only part of their journey along Trader's Path that Axel *did* like.

"At least you get to wear Magnus's arm and leg guards." Calum held out his arms, each with a different color and style of armor on them. Black gauntlets with steel studs in the knuckles covered his hands. "I'm still stuck with this mixed armor from the Southern Snake Brotherhood and the King's soldiers."

"Yeah, but there's no way you'd ever fit his armor. It barely fits me." Axel tapped his blue forearms with his sword. "I'm just tall enough and big enough to make it work."

"Once you tightened the straps to their max." Lilly landed beside Calum.

"Armor's overrated," Riley said. "If you're fast enough, you can avoid anything that comes at you."

"But if you don't see the blow coming, armor could save your life." Lilly re-tied her shoulder-length blonde ponytail behind her head then drummed her fingers along the pale pink armor covering her arms. "I'm fast too, but I'm keeping my armor on."

"This conversation is the very definition of frivolous." Magnus turned his head west. "We need to cover far more ground before we camp for the night, so if you intend to talk, walk at the same time."

"Shouldn't we search the bodies first?" Calum asked.

"Yes." Magnus's golden Saurian eyes narrowed at him. "But make haste."

Three bodies in, Calum found a small lightweight sword not much bigger than a dagger. He pulled it out of its sheath, waved it around a bit, and then slid it back in. Nothing fancy, but it was well balanced and seemed durable enough.

"Lilly?" he called.

She hopped into the air and glided over to him. "Yeah?"

He showed the sword to her. "Could you use this?"

"I've mostly trained to use a bow and arrow. I don't know as much about swordplay." Lilly hooked the sheath to her belt and drew the blade. She met his gaze with a glint of mischief in her blue eyes. "But I'm willing to learn."

Calum matched her smile. It had taken him awhile to get used to her being anywhere close to him. Before the Gronyx fight, and even a little bit after that, he'd get nervous, jumble his words, and start sweating whenever she got too close.

Now he could carry on a conversation with her—while still being nervous and sweating. Not much of an improvement, but an improvement all the same.

"Magnus taught me," he said. "I'm sure he'd be willing to teach you too."

Lilly tilted her head, sheathed the sword, then nodded. "I'll keep that in mind. Thanks."

Her tone had flattened a bit, but Calum didn't know why.

Over her shoulder, Axel rolled his eyes.

Did I miss something?

"I'll be more than happy to teach you to use it." Axel cast a quick glance at Calum, then he put his gloved hand on Lilly's armored shoulder. "I have a feeling you'll get the hang of it quickly."

As the revelation of Calum's ignorance dawned on him, he opened his mouth to protest, but Magnus spoke first.

"Time to move on." Magnus sniffed at the air and turned to Riley. "Do you smell that?"

He growled. "Of course I smell it."

"What?" Calum glanced between them. "What do you smell?"

"Dactyls." Riley growled again.

"What?" Axel asked.

"Flying devils. Beasts with bat wings, eagles' beaks, and bodies like humans." Magnus shook his head. "Not something we wish to run into."

"Your skin's as hard as stone, and you're worried about flying monkeys?" Axel asked.

Magnus leveled his gaze at Axel and clacked his claws on his breast-

7

plate. "Their beaks and talons can pierce Saurian skin and most armor. Only dragonscales and exceptionally rare types of metal can withstand their attacks. Unlike the sabertooth cats we faced before we found Lilly and Riley, Dactyls are intelligent, cunning hunters."

"We just took down two Gronyxes not even a week ago." Axel pointed his thumb over his shoulder. "Why should we be worried about these things?"

"First, we barely survived that. If you recall, we lost Nicolai as a result," Magnus said.

"Not much of a loss, if you ask me," Axel muttered.

Calum whacked his shoulder for the comment, and Axel promptly whacked him back, much harder. Instead of retaliating at the sting in his arm, Calum just clenched his teeth and shook his head.

Magnus eyed them both. "Second, these things can fly, they are impressively fast, and instead of two or three large ones, we would have to face dozens, or perhaps even hundreds of them. They attack in large groups.

"They eat flesh, but they prefer bone marrow, and they will crack your bones open while you still live to get it. I have witnessed what they can do firsthand, so believe me when I say that it is essential to avoid them."

Riley scanned the path ahead. "I smelled 'em when I crossed to the human side six months ago, but I didn't see any."

"So did I," Magnus said. "They did not attack me, either. They are migratory, to some extent. With autumn setting in, they are likely heading south to roost."

"We didn't run into any on my trip over with the slave traders either," Lilly said.

"How come we can't smell them?" Calum asked.

Riley raised on eyebrow. "Wolves, and to a lesser extent, Saurians, have an excellent sense of smell. Once we get a little closer, you'll smell them too. It's a scent you'll never forget."

"Why would we go closer?" Lilly glanced between Magnus and Riley. "I mean, I know we have to head west to get back to the other side of Kanarah, but—"

"They are coming toward us. I did not smell them when we started fighting the bandits, but now I do. That suggests they are headed our direction." Magnus frowned.

"They eat meat, right? Bone marrow?" Calum said. "Why don't we fall back near where we came out of the underground passage? Maybe they'll eat the bandits, and we'll be free to pass when they aren't hungry anymore."

Riley eyed Magnus. "That plan's not half bad."

"Except we'd have to backtrack three—no, almost four—days and entirely erase our forward progress along the pass," Axel said.

"Oh. Yeah. Not such a great plan after all." Riley frowned up at Calum. "No offense."

Calum shrugged. "Takes a lot more than that to offend me."

"Well, I'll keep trying, then," Riley replied.

Calum started to ask if he was being serious, but as before, Magnus spoke first.

"Worse yet, we would likely run out of food in the process, and Commander Anigo made it clear we were not to return to Kanarah City, or to Eastern Kanarah at all. We do not know how long it will take them to get here, if they even show up at all, and we also do not know if the bandits will satisfy them. If it is a larger flock, then it might all be for naught."

"You mean the puppy's nose can't tell us *everything* we need to know?" Axel quipped. "You made it sound like your snout was all-knowing."

"I told you *not* to call me that anymore." Riley growled and bared his teeth.

Axel held up his hands in mock surrender. "Just contributing to the conversation. Not that anyone cares about my opinion anyway."

"Cut it out, Axel," Calum said. "He hasn't done anything to you."

"In any case," Magnus cut in, "we cannot afford to linger here or anywhere else. We barely have enough food to make it to the other side with rationing, as it is. Backtracking now would hamstring us."

"But if we move forward, we risk having to face those things, and you said yourself that it's not something we want to do." Calum glanced between the four members of his group. "I say we fall back and hide, let them eat their fill, and then move forward once they're gone."

"I'm with Calum," Lilly said.

"Me too." Riley stepped forward. "I know it's not a sure thing that they'll be here, but I can stick around here and watch them. Then I'll report back to you guys when I know it's safe to move forward."

"That could be days. Weeks, even." Magnus shook his head. "We do not have enough food to last us that long." Magnus's golden eyes widened, and he clacked his talons against his breastplate. "Unless..."

"Oh, *great*. Where is this going?" Axel raised an eyebrow and sighed. "Unless what?"

Magnus grinned. "Unless we go fishing."

CHAPTER TWO

Calum blinked. "Huh?"

Magnus stared out over the Valley of the Tri-Lakes. "We can catch our food. The lakes are teeming with fish and other creatures fit for eating."

"I thought the lakes were off-limits." Calum's gaze followed Magnus's line of sight.

"I'm not sure about the lakes to the south and north of that one—" Magnus pointed to an expansive stretch of blue water set into the gray wasteland around it. "—but there is at least one small port town that borders the Central Lake not far from here."

"A 'port town?' You told us nothing can survive in the valley." Axel folded his arms.

"And I was not lying. You will find no vegetation or animal life in this wasteland, but the lakes can provide ample sustenance for anyone willing to brave their dangerous waters."

"It's true," Lilly said. "Some Windgales live out here as well, fishing and whatnot. There's a high demand for fresh fish back in Aeropolis."

Magnus motioned to the east with his head. "And Kanarah City has a flourishing fish market in the southwest quadrant of the city, near the entrance to Trader's Pass. They get their goods from fishermen who catch fish and transport it back to the city."

"So we can just cast a line out from the shore and catch something?" Axel asked.

"No. We will have to charter a vessel already equipped for a fishing excursion and venture into deeper waters if we mean to catch enough to sustain ourselves."

"Good thing I'm scouting." Riley glanced between Calum and Magnus. "I don't do boats."

"So you wanna go to that port town, get a boat, and spend time fishing to replenish our food reserves?" Calum asked. "Instead of heading back along the pass and taking shelter until the Dactyls pass?"

Magnus nodded. "I think it would be to our benefit. I noticed a well-trodden path a couple miles back that led toward the Central Lake. We can backtrack a little and camp there for the night."

"I saw that path, too. That should put you out of range for the Dactyls. They avoid cities, so I don't think they'd travel that far east without a good reason. And when they run across these dead bandits, they'll be occupied for awhile, anyway." Riley eyed Calum. "I say you do it. I'll meet you later on, once the Dactyls have gone away."

Calum glanced between Lilly and Axel. "You two alright with this?"

"I still think we can take 'em," Axel placed his hand on his stomach, "but I've never been fishing before, and I'm sick of not eating my fill at dinner time. I say we do it."

Lilly shrugged. "I just need to get home to my parents. If this is the way we do it safely, then I'll go along with it."

Calum grinned. If nothing else, it was a new sort of adventure, and they had to find more food if they were going to make it across the pass to free Lumen, anyway.

"Riley?" he said.

"Yeah?"

"Stay safe. Don't take any unnecessary risks. If anything happens, we'll meet up with you at the western end of Trader's Pass. Crystal?"

Riley nodded. "Clear."

"A large dead tree stands about fifty paces south from the western end of Trader's Pass," Magnus said. "You cannot miss it. If you fail to find us on the pass, meet us there."

"Yeah, I know it." Riley nodded again. "I'll be there, if I have to be."

Calum unslung a sack of food from his shoulder, only about a third full, and set it in front of Riley. "This should last you awhile if you're careful. We'll see you later."

Riley maneuvered his head through the strap and shifted it over his back. "Thanks. You be careful, too."

Magnus grinned again, the same as when he'd first proposed the idea of going fishing. "Let us go."

IN CALUM'S dream that night, Lumen's form materialized with so much brightness that Calum had to squint and shield his eyes with his hands. As before, Lumen traced a large circle with the tip of his sword, and an image focused within.

Tall red mountains, some with snowy caps, sharpened under Kanarah's golden sun. The image panned down to the base of the mountains, swooped over several red snowcapped peaks, and lowered down into a valley set between two ridges. The picture ended at a wall of red rock. A concealed door set into the wall opened like the giant mouth of a crimson beast.

"Find the Arcanum." Lumen's golden eyes glistened with fresh fire from behind his emotionless white mask. "Discover the way to set me free."

Before Calum could respond, the vision disappeared in a quick spiral.

WHEN CALUM'S EYES OPENED, Lilly was standing over him with her hands on his shoulders.

She tilted her head. "Are you alright?"

13

Even in the dim light of the campfire, she looked incredible—like an angelic being staring down at him, her hair aglow with golden light.

He nodded, immediately restored. "Yeah. I'm fine."

"Bad dream?" It was Lilly's shift to stand guard for a few hours, which meant Axel and Magnus were asleep.

"Yeah, I guess."

He still hadn't told Lilly about his commission from Lumen, delivered to him in a series of dreams since just after he'd met Magnus. In truth, he didn't know how to tell her why they were traveling to Western Kanarah.

So far, she'd been operating under the assumption they were fleeing Eastern Kanarah as fugitives for escaping the quarry and Axel's family farm, and for resisting the King's men after that. Calum hadn't corrected her, Axel wasn't about to say anything, and Magnus undoubtedly felt like it wasn't his place to speak up.

But Calum was fast reaching a point where he couldn't hide what they were doing anymore. He really liked Lilly and had come to view her as a friend—more than that, if he were honest about it—and he really wanted her to know what he was trying to do.

Another part of him was mortified at what she might say or think of him. The reality of his intentions landed just shy of outright madness—and that was how Calum viewed his mission. How would someone like Lilly view his quest? Would she believe him? Accept him?

"Tell me about it," she said with a soft grin.

Calum chuckled, sat up, and rubbed the back of his neck. *Only one way to find out.*

"You're… you're gonna think I'm crazy," he said.

She smiled and sat down next to him, closer than he'd expected. "Try me."

"Alright." Calum swallowed the lump in his throat, ignored his nerves and the sweat trickling down the middle of his back, and explained his series of dreams to her, starting with his first dream while still at the King's quarry.

Lumen had appeared to him in several successive dreams since then, each of them almost identical up until this point. A path across the

Valley of the Tri-Lakes formed in the center of Lumen's circle and then stopped at the base of the Blood Mountains, where a black hole opened like a gaping mouth.

Then, of course, this last dream seemed to get more specific as to the way to reach that opening. Lumen had called it the Arcanum, which somehow apparently held the secret to releasing him.

"So that's why we're out here in the first place." Calum let his gaze linger on her a little too long, and she turned her head away. *Stupid.*

"That's—" She bit her lip. "—different."

"Different?" Yep. She thought he was crazy. "That's all you have to say?"

She refocused on him, totally serious. "I believe you."

Calum blinked. He hadn't expected that. "You do?"

Lilly nodded. "Yeah. Why wouldn't I?"

"Because it's ridiculous. Because we're risking our lives for something we aren't even sure is real."

"No. You're risking your lives to make Kanarah a better place for everyone. That's a worthy cause, even if you fail, even if it's not real." Lilly broke eye contact with him and stared up at the stars. "Besides, I believe Lumen *is* real. I believe he can set Kanarah free."

"What makes you say that?" Calum stoked the fire with a stick, and a plume of orange and yellow embers spilled into the sky.

"When I was young, my parents taught me that he was real. It's not something I've really even questioned because I believe my parents. He's a part of Kanarah's history, and if you believe the prophecies, he's part of our future, too."

"The only things I know about Kanarah's history are what Magnus has taught me since we left the quarry." Calum tossed the stick on top of the flames and shifted a bit closer to the fire. "I didn't get much of a formal education working in a place like that."

"I bet you know more about rocks than I'll ever know," Lilly offered.

"Whoopee." Calum's voice flattened.

Lilly touched his shoulder. "Hey, I wasn't trying to make fun of you."

Calum nodded. "I know. It's just that I lost eight years of my life when the King's men killed my parents and sent me to the quarry. I

15

don't have many pleasant memories from that place. My favorite one was the day I left with Magnus."

"I'm sure it was." Lilly positioned herself so she could look directly into his eyes again. "I can't imagine what you've gone through. When Roderick and his men captured me, I didn't know what to do. I thought my life was over. I hope you take comfort knowing you saved someone from a fate just as bad as what you endured during those eight years at the quarry."

Calum managed a half-smile. "It does make me feel better when you put it that way."

Lilly beamed. "Good."

"You know, if you want to start sleeping a bit early, feel free. I'm wide awake now, so I might as well start my shift early."

"I think I might." Lilly tried to stifle a yawn but failed. "Yeah, I will. Thanks, Calum."

Calum nodded. He watched her curl up and drape her cape over herself near the fire. After a moment, he whispered her name. "Lilly?"

"Hm?" She looked up at him.

"We will get you back to your parents. I promise."

Lilly smiled again. "I know you will. And I know you'll make it to Lumen."

Calum wasn't so sure of that, but he nodded nonetheless.

A SCREECH JARRED Axel from his sleep. He drew his sword and sprang to his feet.

Morning sunlight blinded him until a dark, winged form blotted out the sun. It grew larger and larger until he couldn't see the sun at all.

The screech ripped through the air again, this time aimed right at Axel.

The winged monster was headed straight for him.

He raised his sword.

CHAPTER THREE

Red metal flashed, and the flying beast smacked into the rocks next to him in two halves leaking glowing purple blood.

Axel turned his head and saw Calum standing next to him, sword in hand, its red blade streaked with more of the same purple goo.

Axel scowled as he tried to calm his hammering heartbeat. "Guess I can't yell at you for not paying attention on your watch, can I?"

"Nope." Calum shook his head. "Next time, don't freeze up. I may not be there to save you."

Axel tried to say something back, but Magnus spoke first.

"We must flee. Now." Magnus motioned toward the path. "Dactyls can smell one of their own dead from miles away. They are doubtless headed for us right now. Calum, clean off your sword as best you can while we walk, and leave the rag behind. Their blood gives off a pheromone that attracts other Dactyls."

"Gives off a what?" Axel jammed his supplies into his bag, sheathed his sword, and then started to help Lilly pack, even though she really didn't need his help. But it was an excuse to get closer to her, and Axel didn't want to pass it up.

"Pheromone. It is like a scent, only much more potent. Only Dactyls can sense it."

"Watch out!" Lilly drew an arrow from her quiver and launched it into the sky. Another Dactyl screeched and plummeted to the ground right on top of their dwindling campfire.

Axel finished it off with one vicious swing at its neck, and it lay there, crackling and crisping atop the hot coals. The stench hit his nostrils then, and he almost retched all over the ground.

"Ugh. They really do stink." He buried his nose in the crook of his elbow and backed away from the dead beast.

The Dactyl had expansive wings, plus four additional limbs—two arms and two legs. Pale green skin covered its human-like body, but the resemblance stopped there.

It had a huge charcoal-gray beak in place of its mouth. Talons tipped each of its three toes, its three long fingers and one thumb on each hand, and on the tip of its tail, not unlike the spike on the end of Magnus's tail, except smaller.

The glow in its white eyes faded as more purple blood leaked from its severed head.

"Quit staring and clean off your sword, Axel," Magnus growled.

Axel unslung his pack and dug his hand into it. "Fragile birds, aren't they?"

"Make no mistake—if one of them gets ahold of you, you'll form quite the contrary opinion within a matter of seconds, if not less." Magnus started down the path. "Follow me toward the lake. Calum, bring up the rear, and make sure you watch our backs."

"Got it."

Lilly took to the sky. "I'll scout from here."

"No," Magnus waved her back down. "Stay low, with us. If they see you, it will only attract more of them."

She glided back and landed behind him. "Alright."

Axel wiped the edge of his sword with a piece of fabric he'd been saving in case someone needed a bandage, then he dropped it behind him as they ran. "I thought they attacked in groups. Dozens. *Hundreds*, you said."

Magnus didn't turn back, but Axel could hear him anyway. "We are fortunate there were not more. Just keep moving."

"There's one behind us," Calum called from the rear. "Two behind us."

Maybe they weren't so lucky after all.

"Keep moving," Magnus said. "We need to put distance between us and them. Lilly, can you shoot them down?"

"My pleasure." She nocked another arrow and took to the sky, but stayed low.

Axel refocused on following Magnus. The view wasn't nearly as good as when he'd trailed behind Lilly, but at least Magnus could get them somewhere safe.

Two bone-snapping crashes sounded behind them in quick succession. Lilly's voice followed. "We're clear."

Does she ever miss?

Lilly swooped down behind Magnus and followed him like before, and Axel's view improved once again.

He smiled.

TO CALUM'S RELIEF, Magnus's port town materialized on the horizon half a day later. After the first four Dactyls, they'd kept up their quickened pace for far longer than Calum thought he would last. Now, even at a walking pace, every step felt like a new and brutal punishment, both on his lungs and his aching feet.

"You don't think they got Riley, do you?" Calum walked side-by-side with Axel and Lilly while Magnus led.

Axel shrugged. "I don't know. Those things didn't seem all that dangerous to me, but I guess with a few dozen it could get pretty rough."

Calum rolled his eyes at Axel's posturing. "Yeah, but Riley's fast and stealthy, right? He probably made it past them, don't you think?"

"Like I said, I don't know," Axel repeated. "I can imagine plenty of scenarios where having a thief would be useful, so I hope he made it."

"I'm sure he's fine, Calum." Lilly put her hand on his armored shoulder, and he liked it. "He's a grown Wolf. He can take care of himself."

19

"Yeah. We just need to take care of ourselves now." Axel called ahead to Magnus, "You sure this is the right place?"

"Do you see any other signs of civilization around here?"

"No."

"Then I am sure."

A small wooden sign stuck in the arid ground in front of the town read "Sharkville" in scratchy letters marked with faded ink. Several months ago, Calum wouldn't have been able to read it, but Magnus had taught both Axel and him the alphabet and how to use it over the course of their journey.

Why they'd named it Sharkville, Calum couldn't say. Whatever a shark or a ville was, he didn't know, so it seemed like a nothing-word to him—just the name of the town.

Sharkville itself resembled the surrounding landscape: gray, unimpressive, and dull. A few of the buildings were large enough to constitute warehouses, but most of them barely rose above the ground on which they stood. Gray wood, occasionally patched with green mildew, made each structure in the town look like every other.

Beyond Sharkville itself lay the Central Lake, glistening and blue under the sunshine. It extended as far as the eye could see, and for some reason, the sheer breadth of it gave Calum chills.

Magnus motioned to them with his head. "Come. Let us find a vessel to charter."

A sprawling dock, also made of that same gray wood, lined the shore. Despite space for several dozen ships, only one—more of a large boat, really—floated in the waters adjacent to the dock.

"Doesn't look like we've got many options," Axel muttered.

Where Kanarah City's streets had seemed almost overcrowded to Calum, Sharkville's population either preferred to remain indoors or just didn't exist in the first place. No children played in the alleys. No merchants peddled goods from carts. No soldiers stood guard at the street corners. No one at all was outside, and none of the buildings had windows of any sort.

A weatherworn sign that hung from one of the buildings bore an image of a fish caught in a net with the word "Fishig" next to it.

"Wait here." Magnus clasped his hand on the wooden doorknob. "I will go inside and try to find out what I can."

Moments later, the door under the Fishig sign swung open again and smacked against the wooden wall.

Magnus stood in the doorway, beckoning them forward. "Come inside."

The inside of the building amounted to one room with a bookshelf, a bed, and a fat bearded man seated at a table. A big double-edged battle-axe leaned against the table leg on the man's right side, and he puffed on a pipe in his left hand.

The smoky-sweet smell of the tobacco reminded Calum of his father, who had also smoked a pipe long ago. How he'd remembered that so many years later, Calum did not know.

"Gill, here, is in charge of the docks," Magnus said. "He is willing to allow us to charter a vessel."

A man in a fishing town in charge of chartered vessels named Gill. What are the odds? Calum grinned.

Gill motioned to the chair on the opposite side of the table from where he sat.

Calum turned back to Magnus, who nodded. Behind him, Axel stood next to Lilly, closer than Calum would've liked, but in the small space, he supposed it was unavoidable.

Calum sat in the chair and faced Gill, who pulled a scrap of paper from his lap and flattened it out on the table.

He picked up a quill from the desk and dabbed it into the inkwell. "How long you gon' be fishin'?"

"Uh—" Calum looked back at Magnus, who held up three long fingers. "Three days?"

"Weeks," Magnus said. "Three weeks."

"That long?" Calum's eyebrows rose.

Gill chuckled and scribbled on his paper. "That's nothin'. Mos' our charters las' six months or longer."

"Oh." Calum faced him. "Well, three weeks, then."

"Heard you the firs' time, kid." Gill's voice flattened but he kept scribbling. "How many crew members you bringin' along?"

21

"Four, including me."

"Bait?"

Calum blinked. "What?"

"You bring yo' own bait, or you nee' some?"

"Uh—" Calum looked back at Magnus again.

"We need some," Magnus said. "Enough for a week. We'll make do after that."

Gill nodded then scribbled some more. "Got yo' own nets 'n lines?"

"No." Calum shook his head.

More scribbling, then Gill blew a puff of smoke from his pipe above Calum's head. "You all nev' done this befo', have you?"

"No."

"You wan' fishin' lessons too? Or a guide?"

Calum opened his mouth to speak, but Magnus beat him to it.

"No, but thank you."

Gill stared at him, then his quill danced some more. Then he set the quill down and spun the paper around to Calum. "What you think?"

There, before Calum, lay a drawing of some sort of bird—at least from what he could tell, anyway. He hadn't been sure what to expect, but a lousy piece of artwork wasn't on the list. "Very nice."

Gill laughed. It sounded like he'd *swallowed* a bird and its bones had lodged somewhere between his throat and his chest. "It's terrible, an' we bo' know it."

Calum raised his eyebrows, filled with uncertainty. "Alright…?"

"You got yo'seff a boat, kid, but I nee' somethin' to kee' fo' collateral 'n somethin' to pay fo' the charter isseff."

That might be a problem. "We don't have anyth—"

Magnus dropped a leather pouch on the table. "This should cover both."

Before Calum could respond, Gill snatched the pouch from the table and dumped out its contents. When shimmering gemstones in a variety of colors spilled across the table. Calum's jaw clenched. Magnus must've collected some of the stones from Nicolai's body after the Gronyx killed him back in the tunnel.

Gill extended his hand. "Deal."

Calum stared at the gems and sighed. He hadn't known Nicolai for long, but using his remains this way soured his stomach.

Calum exhaled a long breath and shook Gill's hand. "Deal."

Gill smiled, then he stood up and grabbed his battle-axe by the handle. "Follow me. I'll show you to yo' floater."

As Gill walked out the back door behind his desk, Calum stood and nudged Magnus. "Where'd you get those?"

"You know where I got them."

"You sure we should be using Nicolai's crystalized remains to pay for this?"

"He gave his life to save you in that tunnel. He would have wanted this, too." Magnus placed a hand on Calum's shoulder. "Besides, there is no other way."

Calum clenched his teeth, but nodded.

"Hey." Axel waved at them from the back door and pointed to the sign above his head. "Come on. I want to go 'fishig.'"

Lilly smacked his shoulder. "Don't be so obnoxious."

Outside, Gill's jovial persona reverted back to the solemn presence he'd displayed when Calum first sat down at his table. His eyes searched the skies and scanned the shoreline, and his knuckles whitened as he gripped his battle-axe.

Sure enough, Gill led them to the only ship—boat—docked there. The words *Baroness of Destiny* adorned the ship's hull. "She all yo's for three wee's. Bait's arready isside, same's the nets 'n lines 'n other s'pplies. Have fun."

Gill glanced over the lake again then started back toward the town with his sack of gems in one hand, his battle-axe in the other, and his pipe in his mouth.

"Dumbest name for a ship I've ever heard," Axel said once Gill was out of sight.

"And how many ships did you encounter in your years on your family farm?" Magnus asked.

Axel scowled at him. "It's still a dumb name."

The boat could certainly accommodate four people, but from its appearance, Calum didn't know how it managed to stay afloat. Black patches the size of human skulls dotted its gray hull, and a network of dark cracks worked from the ship's bow down to the water line. A mast, twenty feet tall with a patchwork sail, towered from the center of the boat.

Despite the boat's small size, the hull seemed thick enough that there could've been a small cabin inside. The main deck looked as if a whirlwind had tossed a bunch of barrels, ropes, and tools around.

Not that Calum knew anything about sailing or fishing or what most of that stuff was supposed to be used for, but still… Burtis never would've allowed the quarry's toolshed to get this messy. Not in a thousand years.

Calum knelt down for a closer look at the burgundy-brown marks that stretched across almost the entire deck. "What are these streaks?"

Magnus growled. "Blood."

CHAPTER FOUR

"What?" Calum straightened up. "Whose blood is it?"

"I have a bad feeling about this." Magnus shook his head. "Perhaps we should not take this boat out after all."

"Really?" Axel raised his hands and slapped the sides of his hips with a huff. "You dragged us all the way out here, and now you don't even want to go fishing?"

"I think you mean 'fishig,' Axel," Lilly interjected with a smirk. Then she winked at Calum, who matched her with a sly grin of his own.

"Funny," Axel said, still frowning. "But I'm serious. Are we doing this or not?"

"Where do you think all this blood came from, Axel?" Magnus asked. "Something attacked the ship and probably killed the crew. You saw the dire condition of the hull."

"Then how did Gill end up with the ship?" Axel jammed his fists into his hips.

"Perhaps some of them made it back, but some of them obviously did not." Magnus kicked a rope aside, revealing the largest dark red spot on the deck they'd found thus far. "This is a *lot* of blood."

"How do you know they didn't kill whatever attacked them? Maybe that's where the blood came from. Maybe they cleaned the fish they caught and that's where the blood came from."

"Then where are they?" Calum asked.

"I don't know." Axel shrugged. "Probably already left for Kanarah City, or they crossed to the other side to sell their catches."

"Or they are dead." Magnus stared at Axel, who set his jaw.

"Either way, we're low on food, and we're already here," Lilly said. "Many of the fish in this lake are considered delicacies in Aeropolis, and the fact that the ship made it back at all, regardless of whatever happened, is a good sign. I think we should go."

"I'm with Lilly." Axel folded his arms.

Magnus looked at Calum. "It is your decision to make."

Calum met each of their eyes. He didn't love that he had to make the call, but ever since Magnus had declared him leader of their group, it had fallen to him.

In any case, the reality of the situation was sobering: either they risked starvation while trying to cross the rest of the way to Western Kanarah, or they risked starvation while trying to catch fish out on the lake.

At least with the latter option, they would be doing something to try to change their fates.

"I don't think we have a choice at this point," Calum said. "We need to risk it. We're going fishing."

———

HIGH ABOVE THE SHIP, Lilly hovered on watch, her eyes scanning the endless waters both for schools of fish and any signs of trouble. Thus far, the waters and the skies had remained calm and clear except for a few patches of clouds. On the whole, it made for a sunny and pleasant autumn day.

Below her, Calum, Axel, and Magnus lowered the ship's nets over the side of the *Baroness of Destiny*, which now floated several miles out from the shore.

Within two hours, they managed to haul in a couple dozen fish, and

Lilly dropped down for a landing. When Magnus showed them how to clean the fish with a knife, the foul stench of fish guts hit Lilly's nose.

"Now the only thing we gotta do is cook these before we eat 'em." Axel scanned the ship's deck. "But I don't know where we can safely set a fire aboard the ship."

Magnus smirked and stuffed a whole fish the size of a man's forearm into his mouth—scales, bones, head, and all. The sight of it shocked Lilly, but only for a moment. After all, he was just behaving like a Saurian.

Axel wrinkled his nose. "Unless you're a giant lizard, apparently."

"Let me see your knife," Lilly said.

"Huh?" Axel looked at her. "Why?"

"You don't have to cook the fish to eat it."

Calum glanced at Axel and then at Lilly. "How do you figure?"

"We eat it raw all the time in Aeropolis. You just have to prepare it the right way." Lilly reached toward Axel. "May I use your knife, please?"

Axel handed it to her, and she filleted one of the larger fish and delicately separated the scales from its flesh.

When she finished, she held the glistening orange filet in her bare hand. Not as good as a professional cook might've done, but not bad, either. "Who wants it?"

"How about *you* eat it first?" Axel motioned to her with his head.

Magnus chomped into another fish, this one still writhing in his hand. A second bite and it disappeared down his throat.

Lilly shrugged and bit off a sizable bite of the filet. It didn't taste quite as good as when the chefs prepared it for her back home, but it filled her belly all the same. "See? It's good. A little squishy and weird the first time you try it, but otherwise it's good."

Calum extended his hand. "I'll try it."

"Give me half, will you?" Axel held his hand out too, and Calum handed him his portion.

They both popped the fish into their mouths and chewed, then swallowed. Lilly grinned as their faces twisted with disgust, but they gradually softened to guarded curiosity.

She glanced between the two of them. "What do you think?"

"Not bad," Calum replied.

Axel swallowed his bite and stuck out his tongue. "I think I'm gonna figure out how to cook it before I eat any more."

Lilly chuckled and nodded. "It's not for everyone. Usually, you're supposed to eat it with some other ingredients too, and they can really improve the taste."

"*That* I believe," Axel said.

"I'm heading back up to scout some more," Lilly said. "Axel, if you figure out how to cook the fish on board, signal me."

He nodded. "Will do. Calum can keep cleaning the fish while I handle that."

"What?" Calum tilted his head. "That's not fair."

Magnus devoured another fish whole.

Axel shook his head. "And you can just keep eating them raw, I guess."

"Gladly." Magnus smiled and patted his armored belly.

Lilly gave Calum another look. Their eyes met, and drops of molten excitement dripped into her gut. She had to look away.

She sprang into the air, contemplating how and why Calum made her feel that way as the wind rippled through her cape.

They'd been friends ever since they'd helped her escape the slave traders. After that, as she'd gotten to know him, she'd formed a bond with him—closer than she'd have expected in such a short time, but nothing sky-shattering.

Still, she couldn't deny the feelings that soared through her body when their eyes met for too long. She'd come to love his blue eyes; they reminded her of the sky, a place where she felt totally free.

Perhaps that was the answer behind it all: when she was around Calum, she felt truly free.

Within seconds, she ascended fifty feet above the ship's mast. Down below, Axel and Calum continued arguing who would try to cook the fish and who would clean them. She shook her head at them with a smile.

In truth, they were both great guys. Axel was definitely the more outspoken and confident of the two, but Calum—well, there was just something about him. Something different. Something—

A dark form broke the golden horizon to the north of the ship. Lilly squinted at it, but it was too far away to see. Even so, she could tell it had to be large, given how big it seemed even from such a distance.

She swooped down in a wide arc and landed on the deck just behind Axel. He jumped and whirled around to face her.

"What'd you sneak up on me for?" He glowered at her.

Lilly didn't bother apologizing. "There's something on the horizon to the north."

Magnus, Calum, and Axel redirected their attention toward what she'd seen.

"I don't see anything," Calum said.

Axel shielded the sunlight from his eyes with his left hand and leaned over the edge of the boat. "I don't see anything."

"It's there," Lilly said. "I saw it from the air, but I couldn't make out what it was."

"I see it. It is quite far away," Magnus said. "But I have better vision than humans do."

Calum turned to her. "Can you get a closer look at it?"

"Of course." Lilly jumped up to the railing that lined the edge of the boat, leaped into the air, and zipped into the sky toward the form. Almost three minutes later, the form sharpened into the shape of a ship, a mammoth compared to the *Baroness of Destiny*.

It had black sails.

Lilly cursed under her breath, then she repeated it aloud.

She pivoted in midair and swooped back toward their boat faster than she'd left. By submitting to gravity's pull, she picked up incredible speed as she approached the water's surface. Just before she would have impacted the water, she pulled up and shot toward the boat like one of her arrows screaming through the air.

She made it back in less than a minute thanks to her fancy flying. The soles of her boots touched down on the boat's deck between Axel and Calum.

"What is it?" Magnus asked.

"Pirates. We need to get out of here now."

Axel and Calum looked at each other, then Calum squinted at her. "Pirates?"

Lilly tilted her head and her mouth hung open.

"They are identical to bandits, only they live on water and have ships," Magnus explained. "The difference is that they have an incredible advantage on the water. This is their home, and we are but strangers. Lilly is right. We need to get out of here."

"Hey, if they're bandits, I say we take 'em on. Sounds like fun. Fishing's kinda boring anyway." Axel glanced between the three of them, then centered on Magnus. "Plus, we've got you as a Sobek now. What have we got to lose?"

Lilly stared at him. Someday, Axel's confidence was going to get him in trouble. Part of Lilly hoped she'd be there to see it, and another part of her really hoped she wouldn't.

"Our lives." Magnus leveled his gaze at Axel. "You cannot go through this world fighting everyone you dislike."

"I guess we see things differently, Scales." Axel folded his arms.

"Furthermore, we lack the sailing ability and know-how to fend them off," Magnus continued. "My comprehension of water-based combat is nominal at best. If they sink this ship while we are still on it, we stand no chance of surviving, especially in these waters."

"We're also probably outnumbered, as usual," Calum added.

Axel shook his head. "I still say we should fight."

"And I say we leave. Head back to shore." Calum started toward the mast. "Which of these ropes does what again?"

Magnus's voice hardened. "Calum is right. We have enough trouble as it is without having to deal with pirates, too."

Axel sighed. "Fine. I'll get on the wheel."

Lilly heard their conversation, but her eyes had focused on the approaching ship. "Hurry. They're getting closer."

Magnus followed her line of sight. "They are approaching fast. Does this vessel have any oars?"

"Now you think you're gonna row us outta here?" Axel scoffed from behind the wheel.

"That must be how they are catching up to us," Magnus said. "The wind is too light to account for their speed."

Lilly shook her head. "What do you need me to do to help?"

Magnus pointed toward the top of the mast. "Fly up and unfurl the sails. You can get up there faster than we can, and even a little wind is better than none."

She zipped into the air and loosed the sails in seconds, and Calum continued to work beneath her. The modest wind caught the broad fabric, and within a minute, the boat began to carve through the water away from the pirates.

"Turn starboard," Magnus called to Axel. "Hard starboard. Away from their ship."

Axel tilted his head and held out one of his arms. "What?"

"To the *right*. Do it now."

"Why didn't you just say that?" Axel cranked the wheel.

Though the *Baroness of Destiny* began to pick up speed, the pirate ship still gained on them. Lilly landed next to Magnus and watched as the pirate ship loomed ever larger.

"We are not going to make it." Magnus shook his head. "They are too fast."

"What do we do?" Lilly asked.

Magnus stared down at her. "You should fly away. Get to safety. There is no reason you should have to endure the forthcoming bloodshed."

"Not a chance. You three saved my life. I'm fighting with you." Lilly slung her quiver and bow over her shoulder and unsheathed her new sword.

"I suspected you would say that." He turned to face Axel. "It looks like your wish is granted, Axel. Ready your weapons. You too, Calum."

Axel smirked and drew his sword. "Alright. Let's do this."

In minutes, the pirate ship closed within several hundred yards of their boat. That's when the attack began. Six Windgales with sabers flew ahead of the pirate ship and swooped toward the *Baroness of Destiny*.

Lilly shot straight up into the sky to try to draw them away, but only two of them followed her. The other four continued toward the *Baroness of Destiny*.

The two Windgales were quick and lithe, but she was quicker. She darted around the air and ducked under their saber slashes, all while wielding her own blade. Finally, she could properly test the bit of sword training she'd done since the fight with the bandits.

After awhile, the two Windgales stopped attacking and just circled her in the sky. Then, in a coordinated effort, they closed in on her and swung their swords. With a smirk she plunged toward the waters below, and the Windgales chased her.

As before, she pulled up at the last instant, only this time the tip of her left boot caressed the water in the process. Behind her a splash sounded. She stole a glance and saw a cape and some flailing limbs in the water. Impacting the water at that speed would be almost as bone-shattering as hitting solid ground.

A saber lashed at her from the right. Had she not already had her sword out to block the blow, it could have killed her or knocked her into the water, which was almost equally as dangerous.

She traded sloppy blows with the remaining Windgale, who seemed to have even less experience with a blade than she. Lilly adjusted her trajectory as she dueled with the Windgale, mostly dodging or avoiding his swings but parrying a few as best as she could manage for not knowing how to sword-fight.

The actual fight didn't matter, though. If she could keep his focus on her and not where they were headed—

The Windgale swiped at Lilly's head.

Perfect. She ducked under it then blasted upward in time to avoid colliding with the *Baroness of Destiny*'s hull. The Windgale didn't.

A sickening *thud* reached Lilly's ears from below, followed by a faint splash. He wouldn't recover from that.

TOGETHER WITH AXEL AND MAGNUS, Calum handled the other four Windgales, but not without difficulty.

The Windgales weren't more capable fighters—they were just quicker. A *lot* quicker, which made them hard to hit. Calum regretted not taking the opportunity to spar with Lilly more often.

Even so, he found success in baiting them to come after him, and once they did, he'd dodge the blow and Axel, positioned behind him, would take a swing at the Windgale. They downed two of them that way.

Magnus, on the other hand, didn't employ any such trickery. He simply waited for them to attack, and then he let them. Their puny swords deflected off his scales or off his breastplate, and on their follow-up swing, he would grab one of their limbs and slam them against the deck. Even though he didn't need to, Magnus followed each slam with a final blow from his sword.

Calum had to smile—until he realized what was coming next.

By the time the trio defeated the four Windgales, the pirate ship had pulled alongside the boat. Humans clad in dark clothing swung on ropes from the pirate ship's towering masts and landed on the *Baroness of Destiny*'s deck. More Windgales dropped aboard the boat from the sky, and even a handful of Saurians extended long wooden planks from the pirate ship to the side of the *Baroness of Destiny*.

Magnus, Calum, and Axel stood back-to-back, their swords ready, as the pirates swarmed aboard the boat. Within moments, the pirates had them totally surrounded.

"Give up yar weapons," a voice growled from behind the half-dozen Saurians who'd stepped across the planks.

From among them, a hulking, muscular form emerged, covered with dark-brown fur. A Wolf of some sort, but he walked upright and wore a burgundy wide-brimmed hat. A big white feather stuck out from the black ribbon that wrapped around the hat above its brim. He also wore a long black cape that billowed behind him in the wind.

"I said to give up yar weapons." The Wolf's vibrant amber eyes glistened under the brim of his hat. "Or we'll be takin' them from ye, along with yar lives."

Magnus stepped forward, his colossal broadsword still in-hand. "I do not fear you or any Werewolf. You may be faster than me, but neither you nor your crew can penetrate my skin or out-muscle me. Now get off our ship."

The Werewolf shook his head. "So's it may be, none of us can *individually* overpower ye or do ye much harm, but ye also be outnumbered three fives to one."

Something *thunked* above their heads.

The Werewolf jerked his hand upright and clamped his fist shut. A thin wooden shaft vibrated in his hand for an instant, then it stopped moving altogether, its arrowhead lingering about three inches from his head.

Calum chanced a look up. Lilly hovered above them, her mouth open and eyes wide. She still held her bow in front of her body as if taking aim again, but she hadn't nocked a new arrow.

The Werewolf tossed the arrow aside and shook his finger at her. "Ye be havin' to do better'an that to best the likes o' me, m'dear."

Magnus lunged forward and lashed his sword at the Werewolf, and the surrounding pirates converged on Calum and Axel while a few Windgales flew up to engage Lilly.

Calum swung his weapon with fervor and felled a few of the pirates, but it didn't take long for their numbers to overwhelm him. He took a few punches to his face and gut, then someone batted his sword from his hands.

Two burly human pirates wrapped up his arms and pinned him to the deck. Since leaving the quarry, Calum had gotten somewhat stronger, but not nearly enough to pull free of their grasp.

Axel fared a little better, but not by much. He broke free from the human pirates who initially held onto him and leveled one of them with a haymaker, but two of the Saurians grabbed him from behind. Though they'd anchored his arms in place, even they struggled to hang onto him.

Magnus's first three swings failed to connect with the Werewolf who, when moving to avoid Magnus's attacks, resembled a dark blur to Calum. Three Saurians came at Magnus from behind and tried to restrain him, but he threw them off as if they weighed nothing.

When he turned back, Magnus caught a swipe to his face from the

Werewolf's claws, which left four shallow cuts on the side of his snout. Magnus recoiled a half step then retaliated with a swat of his own, but the Werewolf easily ducked under it. One of the Saurians recovered and grabbed Magnus from behind again.

"I don't have to kill ye to beat ye," the Werewolf said. "I've other fine options to attain victory at me disposal."

Magnus reached over his shoulder, grabbed the Saurian's arm, and slammed him down in front of him. He raised his sword to finish the Saurian off, but the other two Saurians grabbed his arms again, stalling him just long enough.

Calum's heart seized in his chest as the Werewolf charged forward and drove his shoulder into Magnus's gut.

Magnus's footing faltered, and he tipped backward over the edge of the boat. Along with the two Saurians, he fell into the water below.

LAKE WATER SMOTHERED Magnus's senses. It filled his mouth, his nostrils, and his lungs. His eyes opened and he saw sunlight above him.

Sword in-hand, he kicked and clawed toward it, desperate for air. His armor weighed on him more than usual, and instead of being his ally, it continued to try to pull him down to the dark depths of the lake.

Had he taken a solid breath before he'd hit the water, he could have stayed under for at least ten minutes, and that was from when he'd tried it as a Saurian. As a Sobek, it probably would've been longer.

Despite his armor, his head finally surfaced, and he coughed out the excess water. Sweet air took its place and his ears opened.

"—agnus!" Calum's voice sounded from above. "Magnus! Look out!"

A hand grabbed his shoulder and pushed him underwater again. One of the Saurians.

Magnus flailed and broke free, then he resurfaced. A hard whip of his tail propelled him away from the Saurian, but also away from the boat. He glanced back.

The Saurian swam after him, but an arrow plunged into the top of his shoulder, and he stopped with a snarl.

Above Magnus, Lilly floated thirty feet above the water and twenty feet out from the boat. She nocked another arrow.

"After her!" The Werewolf pointed at Lilly, and three Windgale pirates darted into the sky.

Lilly twisted in the air and loosed her next arrow. It lodged in the forehead of one of the Windgale pirates, and he crashed down into the water about thirty feet from Magnus's position.

"Get away, Lilly!" Magnus hollered. "Fly away!"

She gave him a nod and shot into the clouds overhead.

The Saurian in the water ripped the arrow from his shoulder and started toward Magnus again. Blood pulsed from the wound, and along with the dead Windgale, the otherwise clear blue water around Magnus had accumulated a cloudy reddish tint.

Another set of hands latched onto Magnus's right arm and tried to wrest the sword from his iron grip. The second Saurian.

Magnus wrenched his arm away, launched himself up out of the water with a forceful thrust of his arms, legs, and tail, and he swung his sword down at the second Saurian.

The second Saurian dodged the blow and swam a few feet away from Magnus, and the Saurian behind Magnus grabbed his left arm. The second Saurian clamped onto Magnus's right arm as he raised his sword to finish off the first Saurian.

He sucked in a sharp but deep breath as they pulled him underwater. Combined with the weight of his armor, their combined strength managed to subdue him, even if only temporarily.

These pirates were no doubt accustomed to swimming in the deep waters of the Central Lake and had proven far more adept at it than Magnus was, but they wouldn't drown him. He refused to die here, in this way. He had too much unfinished business to resolve.

As Magnus strained against them, one of them released his arm, but not from anything Magnus did to twist free. When Magnus looked, the Saurian was gone, replaced by a large cloud of red.

Oh, no...

Magnus broke free from the other Saurian and surfaced again. As

36

Magnus filled his lungs to capacity, Calum's shouts filled his ears again in another warning.

But Magnus already knew what had happened to the other Saurian, and he'd abandoned any thoughts of righting the wrongs inflicted upon him and his family in Reptilius. Instead, only one motivation drove him: survive.

But was it already too late? Not if he could get back aboard the *Baroness of Destiny* quickly enough to avoid the same fate.

The other Saurian grabbed and yanked on his right arm again, and Magnus's grip on his sword faltered. It dropped from his hand into the water. He jerked free and torpedoed down after it, his tail and all four limbs lashing at the cool water with full fury.

He had to get that sword before it disappeared forever.

The Saurian kept pace with him and grabbed Magnus's tail, but just as soon as grabbed on, he let go. A shadow passed over Magnus, and a bubbling roar bellowed through the water, then abruptly ceased.

Magnus didn't have to look back. He knew the Saurian was already dead.

The sword knifed down, down, down through the water, but Magnus chased it nonetheless, even as the waters grew murkier, darker. This time, the added weight of his armor was working *for* him as he descended into the depths.

Yet even as he chased his sword, the primal animalistic part of his brain crackled with warnings, threatening to override his calm and make him panic. Whatever had gotten the other two Saurians now chased him. He could sense it behind him, drawing closer and closer.

Magnus resisted the urge to flee, resisted the urge to abandon his sword to the depths. It was his only chance of defending himself. His only chance of staying alive.

His hardened scales and armor would do him little good against one of the fabled beasts that made its home in this lake, especially one big enough that it only left a cloud of blood in the water in the wake of its attack on the first Saurian.

Magnus kicked and whipped his tail with all his might until his fingers coiled around the sword's silver hilt. He tightened his grip, then he whirled around in the water to face the monster.

There was nothing there.

LILLY PLOWED through the nearest white cloud. Normally, she'd savor the puffs of water vapor that cooled her cheeks under the sun, but with two Windgale pirates not far behind, she didn't have time to idle. As quickly as she entered the cloud, she dropped out of it, then she curved up and into another one.

The Windgales chased her just as she figured they would: they followed the trail she carved through the clouds and didn't bother to try to cut her off or try anything else. Did they expect her to tire out? Or run out of ideas and give up?

Whatever they thought, they were wrong. She hadn't been kidnapped by slave traders, escaped, and survived an encounter with not one but *two* Gronyxes to be brought down by a pair of idiot Windgale pirates.

Again using gravity's pull to her advantage, she looped through the air with incredible speed and reentered the cloud from which she'd just exited. She drew her sword, waited a beat, then swung the instant she saw a dark form flicker toward her from inside the cloud.

Her blade connected just below a stunned face, and the Windgale pirate dropped out of the cloud, his arms and legs limp.

One down, one to go.

MAGNUS'S HEAD SWIVELED, but he couldn't see anything around him, partially due to the darker, deeper waters in which he floated. High above him, the sunlight amounted to little more than a pale orb, barely visible.

No reason to stay here any longer than he had to. Wherever the thing had gone didn't matter. The lake was home to dozens, hundreds—

even *thousands* of other creatures both big and brutal enough to take him out.

The two vessels, now comparable in size to a big leaf next to a small leaf, floated on the surface. Magnus's tail swished back into action and he fought against his armor as he began to ascend again until his head broke through the surface.

"Magnus!" This time it was Axel's voice calling as Magnus inhaled a deep and wondrous breath.

Magnus wanted to respond, but his eyes locked on the Werewolf captain, who stared back at him.

"Like I said..." The Werewolf smirked. "*I don't have to kill ye to beat ye.*"

Next to the Werewolf, Calum's eyes widened. He opened his mouth to scream, but his voice disappeared against the deafening thunder of water that surged at Magnus from his left.

His sword ready, Magnus braced himself for the blow as a dark finned form emerged from the swell. Dozens of spearhead-sized teeth lined its gaping mouth, all of them aimed at Magnus.

He swung his blade just as the beast hit him, and then everything went black.

CHAPTER FIVE

Calum's scream died in his throat.

Magnus was gone. Instead, a black dorsal fin and matching tail thrashed in the bloodied water, then it all disappeared beneath the lake's rippling surface.

"You brigand!" Axel strained against his Saurian captors and almost tore free until one of them punched him in his stomach. He doubled over and gasped in between curses.

Calum wanted to try to break free as well, but he knew there was no use. Even after taking down a few of the pirates before they got ahold of Axel and him, he knew they couldn't possibly overcome the rest of them, not without Magnus.

Magnus is... gone.

The image of the giant fish launching out of the water toward Magnus, its ferocious teeth bared, and pummeling his body below the water's surface twisted Calum's gut. All of his memories with Magnus, everything they'd endured and survived together—it all faded to darkness against the horror of Magnus's death.

When the Werewolf's dark-brown hind paws stepped into view, Calum realized he'd let his head droop. He raised his head with defiance on his mind.

The Werewolf smirked. "Ye've got a lot o' spirit. Ye contain it inside, unlike yar comrade here, who lets it lead 'im to shipwreck. Can't help but wonder what'll happen when ye finally loose your terrible fury. Will ye be able to control yarself?"

"I'm *not* your friend." Calum's jaw hardened. "You murdered Magnus."

The Werewolf waved his hand in front of his chest and shook his head. "I did no such thing. Ye saw what happened to 'im yarself. A shark got 'im."

Calum recalled the name of the meager town where they'd set sail: Sharkville. It had been a warning of sorts, but he hadn't known to heed it at the time.

Indignant, he said, "*You* knocked him overboard."

"Had he surrendered, he would surely still breathe this fragrant lake air. The Overlord has exacted justice upon 'im, and I shall not question it." The Werewolf leaned so close that Calum could smell the stink of fish on his breath. "Now what be yar name?"

"What do you care? Go on and kill us already. Get it over with."

The Werewolf straightened up and tilted his head. "Who said anything about killin' ye? Young 'n healthy, ye be. I'm making ye a part o' mie crew."

"We don't want to be part of your crew." Axel stood up and kept straining against the Saurians who held him in place. "So let us go."

"Is he always so demandin'?" The Werewolf pointed at Axel with his thumb. Part of Calum wanted to say yes, but he bit his tongue. "Ye don't have a choice."

"You can't *make* us join your crew," Axel said.

"Aye, but I can, an' I will," the Werewolf countered. "I don't have to kill ye, and I don't have to let ye go. Like I said: ye don't have a choice."

Axel spat on the deck near the Werewolf's feet, which earned him a backhanded smack from the Werewolf's thick paw.

"What be yar name, boy?" the Werewolf asked.

Axel glared at him. "Axel. Remember it when you're laying at my feet, begging for mercy."

The Werewolf chuckled. "Yar sense of humor is palpable."

41

"I'm not joking."

"Nor am I, boy." The Werewolf stepped back to Calum. "And ye be called...?"

"Calum."

The Werewolf nodded. "I be Brink, cap'n o' the pirate ship *Malice*. Welcome to me crew."

BY now Lilly had to have lost the other Windgale pirate. He'd stopped following her, and she'd stopped popping in and out of clouds.

Still, if she'd learned anything from getting captured by Roderick and his men that first time, it was to never let her guard down in the vicinity of danger.

Perhaps the Windgale had given up and flown back to his ship, or perhaps he was hiding in one of the clouds, waiting for her to fly past and then ambush her. Either way, she'd behave like he was still out there, hunting her.

Hovering near the clouds had lost its advantages, so she dropped down to about ten feet above the water level and took a moment to regain her bearings. She'd flown northwest from the ships once Magnus told her to fly away, and she'd gone so far that now the ships were out of sight.

No matter—she'd find her way back to her friends, and she'd find a way to rescue them, just as they'd done for her.

Lilly maintained her ten-foot altitude as she headed back the direction she'd come, more or less. Every so often she'd glance down at the water and see her shadow tracing her route along the water. If another one showed up behind her or in front of her, she'd know she wasn't alone.

After a few minutes of constant flight, she stopped and scanned the waters. Still no ships in sight. Was she going the right way? Perhaps a higher altitude, while more dangerous, would give a better view of the surrounding waterscape.

As she climbed higher, something whistled on her right side.

42

She brandished her sword in time to fend off a savage attack from the Windgale pirate, but the force of his blow sent her careening down toward the water. She righted herself about twenty feet above the surf and dodged the pirate's next attack.

He blazed past her, but her body jerked down after him. His left hand had latched onto the corner of her cape, and he yanked her toward him.

Lilly reacted blade-first. Her weapon clanged against his, but this Windgale fought with more skill than the others. He deflected her next swing, clamped down on her right wrist with his left hand, then jabbed his sword at her gut.

She twisted her body out of the way just in time, then she caught the wrist of his sword hand with her left hand just as he'd done to her.

He glowered at her with bloodshot brown eyes and a snarl churning his scarred face. His cape billowed behind him, black like the sails of the pirate ship.

Lilly's hold didn't last long. He was stronger—much stronger. He wrenched free and lashed his chipped cutlass sword at her midsection.

She kicked both her feet up over her head, and his sword severed only the air. She rotated her wrist hard, breaking his grip. An errant slash at his hand only managed to carve a small cut into his palm.

He growled and charged. His arms wrapped around her waist, and from ten feet up, they slammed into the water—the one place she didn't want to be.

Everything blurred under the water, and her lungs begged for air. Panic threatened to overwhelm her. She'd swum before—certainly as a child and for fun—but she'd never engaged in water-based combat. Staying above the water had been her preference, but now she had no choice.

He still held onto her, and no matter how she thrashed, he refused to let go. Even when she dug the heel of her boot into his shin, he refused to release her. With no other options, she lurched forward, toward his scarred face, and sank her desperate teeth into his nose.

Blood erupted from the wound, and he released her to clench at the new scars she'd given him. Finally, she swam up to the surface.

Air expanded her lungs as she treaded water. Swimming wasn't like flying—it was so much harder. Her body felt as if it weighed five times as much as usual.

She pushed against the water to boost herself into the air so she could fly again, but as soon as she took flight, the pirate grabbed her cape again and hauled her back down into the water.

This time his hand clamped onto her hair and he held her underwater, facing away from him. She kicked and struggled and maneuvered, but she couldn't break free. Her body ached, and her lungs expelled the last of the air she'd sucked in before going under.

She shifted her grip so her sword pointed back at him, but he clamped onto her wrist and kept her from stabbing at him. Her left hand found his, and she dug her fingernails into his knuckles, drawing more blood, but he still didn't let go.

No matter what she did or tried, his grip continued to hold her in place.

The air in her lungs turned toxic. She needed to breathe.

But the pirate refused to budge.

This is it, she realized. She would die in the lake, at the hands of some common pirate. She'd never see her parents, her home, or her people again. *It's over.*

Lilly closed her eyes and prepared for the water to fill her anxious lungs.

Vertigo flipped her upside down and sent her spiraling through the water. The pirate had completely let go of her—both her hair and her wrist. She clambered for the surface and found it with a gasp and a lot of sputtering.

The pirate wasn't anywhere to be seen.

She jumped out of the water and ascended five feet into the air again, her sword ready, her eyes searching everywhere.

The pirate burst out of the water a second later, flying right at her with an expression of terror etched into his scarred bloody face, but before he could reach her, a massive black mouth full of huge pointed teeth chomped shut on his legs.

Lilly's eyes widened.

The pirate screamed.

The jaws opened again, and the rest of the pirate dropped inside the monster's gullet, but the monster didn't stop coming at her. Its lifeless black eyes rolled back into its wide head as its jaws opened even wider, greedy to taste her flesh next

Lilly recoiled and rolled to her left, and something solid smacked against her back. She hit the water again. She must've drifted too low, and now she was back in the waves, treading water.

And the monster was coming for her next.

A black dorsal fin pierced the surface, circled back, and raced toward her.

Lilly thrust herself out of the water and took to the sky as the monster leaped at her. Its angled nose smacked the sides of her boots and threw her off her trajectory, but she managed to stay in the air this time.

The creature smacked back down into the water as she flew higher and higher until she hovered a hundred feet above the waterline. Its dorsal fin circled a red spot in the water a few more times, then it finally submerged and didn't reappear.

Drenched, startled, and somehow still holding her sword, Lilly shut her eyes and logged a silent prayer of thanks to the Overlord. She sheathed her sword, gripped her cape in her hands, and twisted it until most of the water squeezed out, then she did the same thing to her hair. She could air dry the rest of herself with a few acrobatic spirals at higher altitudes later on.

Somehow, her bowstring hadn't snapped amid all the fighting and thrashing, so her bow was still slung over her shoulder. She still had all of her remaining arrows in her quiver, too—everything she hadn't already fired, anyway. It was designed specifically for Windgales so the arrows wouldn't fall out during loops and stunts. Apparently, it held up in water, too.

Good enough for now.

She had to get back to the boat to see what had happened to her friends. Lilly zipped upward, set her altitude to just below the clouds and plenty high above the water, and she headed southeast.

45

Fifteen minutes later, she found their boat, now empty and capsized. The bait and some of the equipment floated in crates in the water, and some of the fish still wriggled in the nets now strewn overboard while more of those huge black water monsters circled and occasionally nipped at the nets.

She counted at least three dorsal fins in close proximity to the boat—more than enough to keep her from descending too low, especially after her last close encounter with the beasts.

The pirate ship was gone, out of sight.

The last she'd seen of them, Magnus was in the water, and Calum and Axel were captured. She couldn't do anything about Magnus—either he'd made it or not—but if the pirates had taken Calum and Axel back to their ship, maybe there was still a chance to help them.

A voice inside her mind urged her to continue the journey back to Aeropolis alone, but her heart wouldn't abide it. If there was even a chance her friends were still alive, she had to do everything possible to save them.

Either way, she would know as soon as she found that pirate ship.

CHAPTER SIX

P ain split Calum's back. Krogan, a scar-faced Saurian and first mate aboard the *Malice*, drew his hand back for another lash. The whip seared into Calum's flesh like a hot poker. He ground his teeth and dropped to his hands and knees.

"Hey, cut it out." From the tone of Axel's voice, Calum knew he was going to do something stupid. "You wanna whip someone, whip me."

Yep. Stupid.

The whip cracked again, and Axel landed on the deck next to Calum with a red laceration that stretched from just below his left eye down his cheek. Blood oozed from the fresh wound.

"I can take a beating, Axel," Calum whispered to him. "I had more than my share at the quarry."

"Doesn't mean you should have to take any more." Krogan's whip cracked again, and Axel winced.

"Doesn't mean you should take them for me, either."

"While you're down there, start scrubbin' the deck." Krogan grunted. "Wanna see my pretty green face in its reflection within the hour."

Krogan tossed two coarse scrub brushes in front of them, and a burly human pirate set down a sudsy bucket within their reach.

Right after Calum and Axel boarded the *Malice*, the pirates stripped them of their armor and confiscated their weapons. Another pirate took the remainder of their equipment and supplies away, and Krogan promptly put them to work.

Even in spite of their situation, Calum had to note the irony: Krogan, a Saurian, was whipping him in order to force him to perform manual labor, just as Calum had been ordered to whip Magnus back at the quarry. Funny how things turned out sometimes.

Fire flared along Calum's back again.

"I said *start scrubbin'*," Krogan roared.

Calum picked up the brush, dunked it into the bucket, and jammed it against the deck.

BY NIGHTFALL, Lilly still hadn't found the pirate ship, and all her flying was beginning to wear on her. She'd begun to lose hope when she noticed an orange flicker down on the water, probably a couple miles away.

As she closed in on the sight, she recognized those familiar black sails under the moonlight and the deck of a pirate ship alive with multiple oil lamps.

If only Axel had found one of those aboard their now-sunken boat, perhaps he could've found a way to cook his fish with it, she mused, then she refocused on the task ahead.

"Got you," she muttered.

Yes, she'd found the ship, but what was she supposed to do now?

THE LOCK in the cell door clunked into place with a quarter-turn of the skeleton key, one of about a half-dozen lookalikes that hung from Krogan's belt on an iron key ring.

Axel had noted it the instant he saw Krogan. The Saurian always wore it on his right side, at least so far, and he knew it unhooked from Krogan's belt a certain way, or it wouldn't come off at all.

Important information to know and remember for later on. But at the moment, Axel faced more pressing concerns, like his own exhaustion, the lingering sting from Krogan's whiplashes, and the six disgruntled prisoners with whom he and Calum currently shared a ten-by-ten cell.

"Evening," he said with a nod.

None of them responded, but Calum nodded to them as well.

"I'm Calum," he said. "This is Axel. We're, uh—we're new."

"How do things usually go at night around here?" Axel's gaze flitted between the hardened faces in his cell to those of the prisoners in the adjacent cell.

No one said a word, but no one broke eye contact either.

Axel clapped his hands and waved. "Hello? Anyone? All your tongues get cut out or something?"

"Why don't you two just shut up?" came a voice from the back of the cell.

Axel squinted. Only one lantern burned under the deck, and it didn't give off a whole lot of light through its clouded glass panes. "Who said that?"

A massive human form arose from against the back wall of the ship and stepped into the light. Big guy, a good four inches taller than Axel, and broader, too. Short, scruffy hair crowned his head and stubble dotted his round chin. Bitterness oozed from in his brown eyes under a furrowed brow.

"I did," he said.

"You got a name?" Axel stepped toward him. Big or not, he'd stand toe-to-toe with the brute if it meant he and Calum would be safe among the prisoners. Maybe they could even organize an escape attempt and convince these losers to help.

"Yurgev."

"Well, *Yurgev*, I asked a question." Axel kept his hands at his sides in case Yurgev tried anything. Magnus—may the Overlord guide his soul to peace—had taught him to always be ready for a fight whether it looked likely or not. "When I ask questions, I expect answers. Crystal?"

Yurgev leaned forward. "And I told you to *shut up*. When I tell someone to shut up, I expect them to *shut up*. Crystal?"

Axel clenched his fists. If Yurgev wanted to play it this way, he would happily oblige. "I'll show you what's *crystal*."

Calum stepped between them. "Easy, guys. No need to—"

Yurgev shoved Calum against the bars adjacent to the other cell, which rattled from the impact.

It was all the excuse Axel needed to get to work.

He drove his left fist into Yurgev's gut, then his right cracked against Yurgev's chin.

Around them, the other prisoners whooped and hollered, both cheering Yurgev on and scrambling to get away from the fight itself.

Yurgev staggered back a half step, then he swung at Axel. Had it connected, the blow might've knocked Axel into another world, but he ducked under the punch, threw a sharp jab into Yurgev's stomach, then delivered a stunning uppercut to Yurgev's nose.

He dropped to the floor, stunned. Axel started to head toward him but Calum pulled him back when the other five prisoners, all with rage in their eyes and clenched fists, stepped between them and Yurgev.

"What did you just get us into?" Calum muttered.

"Nothin' we can't handle." Axel rubbed his sore right fist. Punching idiots hurt more without his armored gauntlets on.

The other five prisoners in the cell stalked toward them.

"*Hey.*" A low growl split the tension. Krogan's taloned green feet descended below deck until he stood at the base of the stairs. "What's all the ruckus?"

Axel started to say something, but Krogan held up his hand.

"I'm puttin' you two in a different cell. You cause any more trouble, I'll get my whip back out." Krogan unlocked the cell and hauled them both out, then he thrust them into the adjacent cell. "Play nice. You'll be very, very sorry if I gotta come back down here tonight."

Axel watched him lock the cell with a different skeleton key than the previous cell—or at least he thought it was a different one—then he hooked his keys back onto his belt in the same way, same side as before. Consistency was good.

As Krogan clomped back up the stairs, Axel scanned the eyes of the eight men who'd already occupied the cell before he and Calum got here. Instead of anger, Axel found distress, dismay, and surprise. In some ways he preferred anger, as he could more easily channel it into action, but depression could work too.

He smiled at them. "So how are *you* guys doing tonight?"

"Thought I told you to *shut up*."

Axel turned back and stared at Yurgev, whose bloody face pressed against the shared bars of the cells. "And I thought by now you would've learned what happens when you try to order me around."

"This isn't over." Yurgev shook his head and spat on the floor. "Not even close."

Axel stared steel at him until he retracted back into the darkness of his cell. Part of him wanted to say something keen in response, but another part of him believed the rage in Yurgev's eyes.

As much as he'd won the fight—decisively—Axel couldn't help but wonder if he'd started something too big for him to finish.

LILLY SWOOPED in low and hovered only fifteen feet from the surface of the water, hopefully high enough that no other marine life would try to come after her but low enough that the pirates wouldn't see her approaching.

When she reached the back of the ship, she perched her toes on a small ledge about seven feet below some windows, presumably belonging to the captain's quarters. If she could get on board, find that Werewolf, and kill him, then perhaps she could frighten or force the rest of the crew to release her friends.

She didn't know much about pirates, but perhaps they operated on a ruling structure like that of the Wolf tribes—whoever held the most power was in charge. Given the ship's Werewolf captain, that could be the case.

With her hands locked onto the windowsill, she pulled herself up for a look inside. Though the glass was foggy and dirty, she could still see clearly enough.

Four candles on a table in the center of the room cast an orange light on a bed, the table itself, the door, and two chairs, in one of which the Werewolf sat facing her. He still wore his hat and cape, but his head was down, and he was writing in a large book of some sort with a feather quill. Perfect.

Lilly lowered herself, stepped to the side, and then floated up toward the back of the ship so the Werewolf couldn't see her through the window. She peered between two rungs of a railing.

Two pirates stood at the wheel, both humans, both facing away from her. High above, in the crow's nest, two others gazed out across the moonlit waters with the aid of brass telescopes. Four pirates in total, two of them perched thirty feet higher in the air. Maybe she could ignore the crow's nest for now.

She dropped her altitude and curled around to the side of the ship, her eyes level again just below the railing so she could peek through with less chance of being seen.

A few more pirates milled about on the main deck, but apparently most of them had gone to sleep or at least had ventured below deck. Back toward the rear of the ship, Lilly noticed a door under the wheel. Probably the captain's quarters.

Now how do I get past two men at the wheel, a half dozen pirates on the deck, and two in the crow's nest? She headed back to the rear of the ship with the beginning of a plan in mind.

From just below the railing, she whistled loud enough for the two men at the wheel to hear her. They didn't move.

The second time she did it, they both glanced over their shoulders but stayed put. On Lilly's third whistle the one not steering the ship turned and headed toward the railing.

Lilly zipped around the side of the boat as he approached and flew up into the air. After a quick check on the pirate at the wheel, she landed on the deck in silence behind the pirate she'd lured to the edge.

As the pirate leaned over the railing, searching the churning waters below, Lilly made her move. She grabbed his ankles, and with all her strength she pulled up. The pirate pitched over the railing down into the frothy trail in the dark waters below.

He yelped on the way down.

Lilly mentally chastised herself. Too sloppy. Now she had to make up for it.

With no time to spare, Lilly darted toward the man on the wheel. When he'd fully turned around to investigate the sound, Lilly plunged her sword into his chest and clamped her left hand over his mouth.

His frightened eyes glazed over and he slumped to the deck. She twisted him around and hefted him up against the wheel. It didn't look great, and blood was practically raining out of his chest, but it should buy her a little extra time if she needed it.

Six pirates on deck, and two in the crow's nest. She could have tried to find a way to take the rest of them out, but even with her speed they'd probably notice her. It just wasn't worth the risk.

Instead of bothering with them, she dropped down by the captain's door and opened it in silence.

She was inside.

There before her, not ten feet away, the Werewolf sat in his chair, head down, hat on, his cape draped over the back of the chair, just like she'd seen him five minutes earlier. Her sword still in-hand, she left her feet and hovered toward him.

As Lilly approached, she noted that four candles still burned in front of him, and his book still lay sprawled open before him, but he wasn't moving. Must be deep in thought, or—

She gasped. *No!*

From her right, a dark blur launched toward her.

CHAPTER SEVEN

The sword in her hand clattered across the floor, and so did she. Even though she wore armor, every inch of her body still hurt. Lilly reached for her weapon, but it wasn't there anymore.

A furry paw pulled her to her feet by her collar, and cool steel pressed against her neck. "Not bad, m'dear. Not bad at all—but not good enough, either."

Lilly struggled against his grip, but between his strength and her own sword at her throat, she stopped quickly.

"I really be impressed. Ye musta been trained to fight somewhere. An' yar armor—it be so pristine, so high-end. Ye must be a well-connected, *wealthy* Windgale."

Lilly didn't respond. She just glared at him.

"Not gonna tell me who ye be? Here, I'll start. Captain Brink. Ye're aboard the *Malice*, me pirate ship. Now go ahead. It be yar turn."

"Do you have my friends?" Lilly asked through gritted teeth.

Brink smiled at her. "As a matter o' fact, I do. Well, two o' them anyway. Yar Sobek friend—Magnus, wasn'it? He met an unfortunate end thanks to a fierce encounter with a lake shark. Overlord's sovereign justice, I reckon."

Lilly clenched her eyes shut. She would've been devastated had any of them died, but of the three, Magnus had truly saved her when she'd needed it most.

Though Calum and Axel had stumbled upon her in the wheat field, it was Magnus who had cared for her, bound her wounded shoulder, and set her at ease. It was Magnus who personally made sure that Roderick, the man who'd captured her for slavery, would never come for her again.

Lilly longed for her protector, and she fought to resist the tears stinging the corners of her eyes. They trickled down her cheeks anyway.

"For conversation's sake, ye only made one mistake in trying to get to me. That one mistake be why I've got a sword to yar throat instead o' lying on the floor with this same blade stuck in me back." Brink tilted his head. "Do ye care to know what your mistake was?"

Lilly shuddered, sniffled, and raised her eyes to meet Brink's. "Enlighten me."

"Yar mistake was comin' to get me. Ye shoulda waited for me to come to ye. I knew ye were comin' the instant ye twisted my doorknob. Everyone else aboard knocks. Only people who wish harm upon me come in without knockin'. Soon's I heard the door, I positioned my decoy and disappeared." Brink smiled at her. "Had ye been more patient, ye coulda killed me. Maybe."

"I'm done talking to you," Lilly asserted. "Just kill me already and be done with it."

Brink sighed. "Why does everyone think I'm gonna kill 'em? I'm not gonna kill ye. I'm makin' ye part o' me crew."

"And if I don't—"

"Trust me. You've no other choice, m'dear." Without breaking eye contact, Brink turned his head slightly and called out, "Krogan?"

Not long after, a knock sounded on the door.

Brink smiled at Lilly. "See? They know to knock."

Lilly rolled her eyes.

"Come in."

One of the biggest Saurians she'd ever seen stepped inside the cabin. He would've rivaled Magnus in size before Magnus became a Sobek, and his scaly face bore all sorts of scars. Lilly decided it must be a sort of rite of passage for a pirate.

"New catch, Krogan." Brink nodded to him, and he walked over. "Strip 'er down to 'er skivvies, an' make sure ye take off 'er cape so she can't fly away. Put it all with the rest o' the armor and weapons in me closet, then take 'er down to the brig and put 'er with the others."

"Aye, sir." Krogan nodded and unfastened Lilly's cape from her shoulder armor. Only then did Brink release his grip on her and lower the sword.

Brink stepped back and smirked at Lilly. "I hope ye enjoy yar stay aboard the *Malice*."

Lilly just glared at him.

CALUM STOPPED LISTENING to Axel talking with the prisoners in their cell when he noticed a shapely female form descending down the staircase.

She wore nothing but boots, skintight white armor lining that covered her from the waist down to her mid-thighs, and a matching upper lining, stained dark-brown near her left shoulder. The top defined her chest and shoulders but left her arms and stomach bare.

Long blonde hair hung down below her shoulders, and her blue eyes sparkled with relief when they met Calum's.

Overjoyed, he swatted Axel on his shoulder.

"What?" Axel snapped.

"Lilly." Calum pointed out of the cell.

Axel blinked, looked her up and down, then blinked again. "What's she doing here?"

Calum shrugged. Had she been captured? Given herself up?

Krogan started toward their cell and unlocked it, but instead of putting Lilly in with them, he ordered Calum and Axel out. Then he opened another cell across from theirs and swapped the four prisoners inside with Calum and Axel, and he shoved Lilly inside as well and locked both cells.

From their original cell, Yurgev and the other prisoners locked in with him leered at Lilly. One of them whistled at her, and Krogan whirled around and whacked the bars with his forearm. Everyone inside backed away.

Starting with their cell and ending at Calum's, Krogan panned his finger across all the cells. "The next prisoner I hear before sunrise gets keelhauled. Crystal?"

Calum had no idea what that meant, but they'd made enough fuss for one night. Now that Lilly was with them, Calum would rest easier.

Once Krogan disappeared back up the stairs, Calum turned toward Lilly and started to speak to her, but she flung herself at him and wrapped him in fierce hug. It startled him at first, but he quickly returned it.

He had to admit, he loved every second of it—the warmth of her lithe body against his, the faint scent of flowers on her skin... It was incredible. And she'd singled him out, specifically for—

Lilly abruptly let go and flung herself at Axel next, wrapping him in the exact same embrace she'd just shared with Calum.

The sequence left Calum confused and frustrated—but mostly confused.

When Lilly released Axel, she took hold of one of each of their hands in hers.

"Is it true?" she whispered, desperation and fear in her blue eyes. "About Magnus? Tell me it's not true."

Calum's heart tore in half all over again. Both he and Axel gave solemn nods.

Lilly's posture crumbled, and she stared down at the floor with empty eyes for a long moment.

Finally, she said, "I'm sorry."

Axel shook his head. "Why are you sorry? You didn't get him killed."

Though Calum wondered what Axel meant by that, the last thing he wanted was to start another argument, so he let it go. "He did every-thing he could to save us, but a shark—that's what those big black fish with all the teeth are called—a shark got him."

Lilly gave a solemn nod, and the three of them continued to stand there.

"We should get some rest," Calum said. "They worked us like dogs today. I have no doubt they're gonna do it again tomorrow."

The three of them sat down together, leaned up against the back wall of the cell, and stared at the bars until they couldn't anymore.

Not long after, the anchors tied to Calum's eyelids dropped, and blackness flooded his mind.

———

BLINDING light burned Calum's eyes, but this time he couldn't even lift his hands to block it. Lumen stood before him, his sword shimmering in his hand.

"Do not be discouraged. Your victory is at hand. You will find me, you will free me, and together we will reclaim Kanarah for its people." Lumen extended his open hand toward Calum. "Rise, Calum."

Calum hesitated at first, but gripped Lumen's hand with his. A jolt raised him to his feet and vibrated through his entire body, and then Lumen vanished.

———

WHEN CALUM AWAKENED from his dream, he found himself standing in the cell. Axel's body still lay sprawled across the cell floor, motionless, and Lilly lay with her head on Axel's shoulder, though it looked like Axel had no idea she was laying that way.

The sight sent pangs of hurt and jealousy through Calum's chest, but he realized that if she'd been laying on his shoulder instead, he probably would've scared her half to death with how quickly he'd just woken from his dream.

Lumen had visited Calum's dreams again, it seemed he had physically *pulled* Calum to his feet. And that jolt—had Lumen done something to him? Had Calum somehow been healed of the lashes he'd taken from Krogan?

Calum spread his arms out, and the dull sting of partially sealed wounds crackled across his back. He grunted.

Nope. Not healed.

Worse than that was Lumen's message: How could Lumen claim that Calum's victory was near while they were locked in a cage, trapped on this pirate ship indefinitely, now with six more enemies than they'd had before last night? In their current weakened condition, what chance did they have for escape?

"Someone else will have to let you out," Calum muttered. "We're not going anywhere."

He leaned against the bars and his gaze landed on Lilly again. Beautiful, but shaken by Magnus's death. Strong, yet fragile. Stuck or otherwise, being with her was worth every lash he took from Krogan.

She stirred, and her eyes opened. When she saw him she tensed at first, then, realizing she was on Axel's shoulder, sat up. "Calum?"

He nodded. "Yeah?"

"You look…" She studied him. "Are you alright?"

Calum shook his head and leaned against the bars. "No. And yes. I feel terrible about Magnus, but at least you're safe."

Lilly stood up and stepped toward him. She reached out and cupped his jaw with her hand. "Calum, I'm so sorry."

He closed his eyes and reveled in her touch, though he tried not to read into it. He wanted to take her hand in his, but his heart wouldn't let him. He couldn't trust himself to know how to behave at the moment. He didn't know what he wanted or what she wanted, and even if he did, they were still locked in a cell in the belly of a pirate ship.

"It's not your fault."

"I know," she said. "But I tried to save you, and I only made things worse."

While that was true, Calum didn't care. "You did what you thought was best. I can't fault you for that."

She shook her head.

"Besides, we're all together again," he said. "We can watch out for each other from now on."

"Except for Magnus. He's gone."

Calum sighed. His back ached, but the reminder of Magnus's demise shredded his heart all over again. First his parents, then Nicolai. Now Magnus. He slumped down against the bars and buried his head in his hands. He was running out of people to lose.

Lilly knelt down next to him and put her hand on his shoulder. "I'm sorry, Calum."

"I don't know what we're gonna do without him. He knew so much. He was so strong. He taught me everything I know about fighting. He taught me to read and write. He was my best friend."

Calum wished he could stop the tears from streaming down his face, wished he could keep his voice from shuddering.

He glanced at Lilly and gave a sad chuckle. "You must think I'm weak."

She shook her head. "Not at all. There's nothing wrong with crying when you're sad."

Calum scoffed. "Axel wouldn't cry."

"Maybe not, but Axel—" She turned and glanced back at him. He still lay there, arms and legs extended, taking long deep breaths with his eyes closed. "Axel is different than you. You've got a kind soul, Calum. It's what I love most about you."

Love? Calum blinked at her. "You... what?"

"I, uh—" Lilly looked away. "Nothing. Nevermind."

"No, I heard what you said." He *had* heard it... hadn't he? "What do you mean?"

"Nothing." She shook her head. "It's nothing."

Calum wanted to say something else, but Axel moaned and rolled over on his side.

"I feel terrible." He moaned again.

Lilly stood and put some distance between herself and Calum. The action filled Calum with even more confusion than before, especially since she'd said what she'd said. How was he supposed to make sense of any of this when everything kept changing?

"Everything hurts." Axel's words slurred. His eyes cracked open and he looked at Lilly. "You alright?"

She smiled and nodded. "I'm fine."

60

When Lilly glanced back at Calum and showed him that same smile, he managed to send one back at her. Forget Lumen in all his splendor —*she* was the most amazing being he'd ever seen.

Footsteps sounded behind Calum, and Lilly's countenance changed. She stood up and backed away from Axel, her eyes fixed on the newcomer.

Calum twisted his torso and craned his neck—both of which hurt— to get a look.

Captain Brink stood before their cell with Krogan and two other Saurians behind him.

"Mornin'," he said.

Calum scooted away from the bars and stood, as did Axel.

Brink approached the bars. His lupine snout twitched, and his nostrils flared. "I take it neither of ye gentlemen feel well this mornin'?"

Calum glanced at Axel, whose posture straightened, even though it must have racked every inch of his back to do so. Calum had nothing to prove, so he stayed hunched over.

"I regret that Krogan decided to put ye in with that bunch over there." Brink motioned toward the men in Yurgev's cell, all of whom now glared at them through the bars with bitter eyes alongside Yurgev's bruised face. "But what's done be done. Krogan has forced my hand, and so have you."

Lilly's hand touched Calum's shoulder. Any other day it would have felt good, but not after last night's events.

Brink nodded to Krogan, who stepped toward their cell with his keys out. "I'm afraid, in this case, it be in the ship's best interest to terminate yar stay with us."

"Over a little scrap?" Calum protested. "Are you serious?"

"We didn't even start that fight." Axel pointed at Yurgev's cell. "They did."

Brink held up his hand and shook his head. "I've made me decision. Can't tolerate fightin' amongst the crew. There be six o' them and three o' you. Simple math, really."

Calum's fists clenched. He wasn't just going to give in. Even though he had no hope of overpowering three Saurians and a Werewolf with just his fists, he'd already decided to fight every step of the way.

"What are you going to do to us?" Lilly asked.

Krogan inserted the skeleton key into the cell's lock and smirked at Calum.

"I be a merciful master." Brink brushed some hairs off his cape. "We're gonna toss ye overboard, an' ye can take yar chances in the lake. The Overlord will decide yar fates."

Axel stepped toward the cell door with his fists balled tight. "That's a death sentence, and you know it."

Krogan twisted the key and the lock disengaged. Calum wanted to charge the cell door and knock him on his back right then and there, but he knew that tactic wouldn't get him anywhere, so he waited.

Brink shrugged. "When ye're a pirate, that be as merciful as it gets, friend."

One glance at Axel's eyes told Calum he was considering an attack on Krogan, but his posture betrayed the reality of their shared situation. Resistance just meant they'd be more tired and more injured when it came time to swim for their lives.

Krogan hooked his keys on his belt, removed his whip from the opposite hip, and pulled the cell door open, his eyes fixed on Axel. "C'mon, now. Don't give me any trouble, and I won't give it back to you twicelike."

Axel set his jaw and didn't move.

A loud thud sounded from behind Brink. A contorted human body tumbled down the stairs, and both Brink and Krogan whirled around.

Something thudded on the deck over their heads. Men screamed, and metal clashed.

"Lock that cell, Krogan!" Brink growled and charged up the stairs, but his furry form promptly tumbled back down and crashed onto the floor. He cursed, hopped to his feet, and bared his jagged white teeth.

"Cap'n?" Krogan slammed the cell door shut and locked it. "You alright?"

Brink waved his arm and shifted the cape off his shoulders so it hung along his back. "Of course I be alright. Rally the men. We need to mount a resistance *immediately.*"

Calum glanced at Axel, who shrugged. Lilly did the same. Whatever it was, it was bad for the pirates, so hopefully it was good for them—if they could get out of this cell.

Another thud sounded, this time above their cell. Two more thuds in quick succession followed. Krogan charged up the stairs.

"What in the Overlord's name is going on?" Lilly asked.

Calum scanned the ceiling, but it gave him no answers. "More pirates?"

A roar sounded above them, then Krogan tumbled down the stairs just as Brink had. He landed face-up in front of his captain with a large broadsword protruding from his chest.

A familiar broadsword, one with a blue blade and a silver hilt, far too large for most humans to wield.

Calum's breath caught in his throat. *Impossible.*

Dark-green feet, legs, and a strong, scaled torso covered by a Blood Ore blue breastplate descended into the brig. A dark-green hand wrenched the broadsword from Krogan's chest.

Magnus stood at the base of the stairs, glaring at Brink with all the fury in the world.

CHAPTER EIGHT

As soon as Magnus swung his sword, the Werewolf snarled, dodged the blow, and disappeared into the plentiful shadows below decks. All that remained of his presence were his black hat and cape.

Magnus growled. He should have drawn the Werewolf up to the ship's deck, where the sun now shined, instead.

"Magnus?" Calum called. "Is it really you?"

Magnus held up his hand. "Stay clear of the bars. This Werewolf and I have a score to settle."

"Brink," the Werewolf said. "Cap'n Brink. We be old friends now, *Magnus.*"

A dark blur ratcheted out of the shadows and past Magnus. He whipped his sword at Brink but missed. The solitary lamp in the brig dropped to the floor and shattered, and its flame extinguished.

Even in the lack of light, Magnus could see well enough to locate the cell keys on the dead Saurian's belt. He snatched them into his left hand and clamped his fingers around them. If Brink got ahold of those keys, or if he had his own set, he might be able to get inside the cell and kill the others before Magnus had a chance to do anything about it.

He snapped the metal key ring with his fingers and tossed them up the stairs and out onto the main deck. It meant his friends would stay locked up, but against a foe as dangerous as Brink, they would be far safer that way.

"Your crew is dead, Brink." Magnus's head swiveled in the darkness. "All of them."

Behind him, the hatch at the top of the stairs smacked shut. He lashed his sword at the sound but failed to hit anything.

"We can stay down here for eternity if you wish, but we both know how this ends: you scratch me up, perhaps bite me a few times. It will hurt, but I will heal. Quickly.

"Then, at some point, I will catch you as you run past. Maybe clip you with my sword. I will eventually find you in the darkness, and I will kill you. You will pay for enslaving my friends and for hurling me into the lake."

A growl reverberated throughout the brig. Something chomped down on his shoulder, and pressure stung Magnus's nerves. He winced and jerked forward. Brink rolled over his head and disappeared into the darkness again with another growl.

"Go ahead. Get as frustrated as you wish." Magnus shook his head and dabbed at the blood that oozed from his shoulder. Nothing the veromine in his body couldn't repair in a matter of hours.

Still, knowing that Werewolf teeth and talons could penetrate his scales didn't set him any more at ease. He hadn't learned that back in Reptilius.

"You have nothing left, except your ship and your life, and I will not allow you to take anything else from my friends or me."

A half-howl, half-laugh echoed throughout the brig. "That's what ye think."

Wood snapped to Magnus's left.

"He's punching through the ship's hull!" Axel yelled. "Right here between the cells!"

Magnus charged toward the spot, but a blast of lake water sprayed his face.

More howling-laughter. "I hope ye be ready for another plunge in the brine, Magnus."

Magnus jabbed his sword into the gap between the cells but only struck solid wood. Brink had snuck past him again.

Water began to collect at Magnus's feet. "You really intend to sink your own ship out of spite?"

Brink laughed again from somewhere in the shadows. "If it means ye and yar friends go down with it, then aye. I can replace me ship. Can ye replace yar friends?"

Magnus glanced back at the trio, all of whom wore worried expressions.

"They will not go down with your ship," Magnus assured both them and Brink.

"A chance not, but they die the moment ye let 'em out. Or they drown. Yar choice."

Magnus scowled at the darkness. He needed to take action—extreme action—to reclaim control of this situation. And there was only one way to do that.

He sheathed his sword, raised his arms into the air, and intertwined his fingers. In one mighty blow, he smashed through the brig's wooden floor. Underneath, he recognized familiar gray wood—the hull. Another comparable blow gashed a hole into the ship's hull, and more lake water splashed up into his face.

"What are you doing?" Axel gripped the cell bars, frantic at the water swirling around his knees. "You're gonna drown us!"

Magnus faced him. "Trust me."

The water level rose to Magnus's thighs. Brink launched toward him from the shadows and knocked him to the floor, then vanished again.

The prisoners in the other cells rattled their bars and shouted as the water rose to their waistlines. So much for listening for Brink's next attack.

"You'd better do something quickly, Magnus—" The water had already reached to Calum's chest, yet his voice remained surprisingly calm. "—or we're gonna drown in here."

Magnus clenched his teeth until he noticed a splash in between the cells where Brink had punched the first hole in the hull. A furry brown tail disappeared under the water. The captain had abandoned his ship.

Amid the rising water and shouts of the prisoners, Calum, Axel, and Lilly gripped the cell bars and floated with just their heads above the water line, but they didn't have much space left to get air.

Magnus dove into the water as it rose almost to his neck. He zipped toward their cell, and instead of fiddling with the keys in the lock, he grabbed two of the bars. With one yank he ripped them out, creating a wide opening for them to escape.

Lilly swam out first, followed by Axel and then Calum. When Calum surfaced above the water again he said, "You have to get the other prisoners out."

Before Magnus could respond, Axel floated over. "No way. Half of them tried to fight us. We're not freeing them."

Calum shook his head, indignant. "They're all here against their wills. We need to let them out, and at least give them a chance at freedom. You wouldn't want to die in a cage in a sinking ship."

"They deserve whatever they get." Axel glared at him. "We let 'em out, and they'll come after us again. Lilly, too."

"Then we'll stop them again, like we did last time, only now we have Magnus back. With him around, she's safe, and so are we."

"And I can take care of myself," Lilly added, though of the three, her anxious water-treading and shuddering voice demonstrated the most anxiety about the possibility of drowning.

Calum refocused in Magnus. "We'll work on getting the hatch open. Get them out."

Magnus nodded and dove into the water again. Within moments he wrenched the cell doors from their hinges, and the prisoners spilled out after him. When he made it back to his friends, he realized they hadn't yet gotten the hatch at the top of the stairs open, and now the brig was totally submerged.

They were trapped with no air.

Magnus positioned himself under the hatch with his back against it and his feet on the stairs. He heaved against the wood above, and it snapped from the pressure. Sunlight streamed into the brig, and the prisoners began to scramble out.

Again, Lilly went first, and then Axel and Calum, followed by the rest of the prisoners, and Magnus brought up the rear.

WATER EQUALIZED EVERYTHING.

It had almost drowned all of them, including Lilly's friends and the other prisoners from below. Lilly kept an eye on the ones who'd come to blows with Calum and Axel especially, but the big guy, Yurgev, wasn't among them. Had he drowned before he could make it out in time?

"Everyone to the lifeboats," Magnus said. "Divide as evenly as you can."

Lilly grabbed Calum's wrist before he could leave. "I know where our armor and weapons are. If we hurry, we still have time to get to them."

Calum nodded, then told Axel their plan.

"Go on, then. Magnus and I will handle things here. And *hurry*." Axel began to work on one of the ropes that secured the nearest lifeboat to the ship.

Lilly led Calum up to Captain Brink's quarters. The curtains at the window were drawn shut, and none of the candles on the desk were lit.

The ship pitched to the right under them and Calum caught Lilly in his arms. He promptly set her back on her own two feet, saying, "Sorry."

The way he said it made her think he was apologizing for something else entirely.

"I'm the one who should be sorry." She hoped he would understand her meaning. "Come on. Our armor and weapons are in the captain's closet."

Calum pulled the door open. Sure enough, a pile of armor parts and weapons lay inside with Lilly's armor on top. Calum handed her a few pieces and then dug for his own.

"Good to get this stuff back again." Lilly stepped into her leg armor. "I felt exposed without it."

"You *were* exposed without it, almost entirely." Calum slid on his breastplate then picked up one of his greaves.

"You didn't seem to mind." While Lilly fastened her own breastplate over her undergarments, she stared at him to gauge his response.

He glanced at her then broke eye contact. "I—uh—"

Lilly stifled a smile and slung her cape over her shoulders. "You don't have to be embarrassed, Calum. You weren't dressed in much more than me."

Calum slipped on his gauntlets and brandished his red-bladed sword. "I think we'd better get going."

The cabin door shut and the room plunged into darkness. A man's heavy breathing sounded, and a large shadow advanced toward them, holding a gleaming blade.

"Stand back, Lilly." Calum extended his arm and physically pushed her back. "It's Yurgev."

He hadn't drowned after all.

Metal clanged against Calum's blade, then twice more in quick succession. How Calum had even seen to defend against them, Lilly didn't know. She backed away from the fracas toward the curtains.

"I'm gonna kill you first," Yurgev said to Calum. "And then I'm gonna move on to your little girlfriend."

Lilly's jaw hardened, and she drew her sword. Her bow was still in the captain's closet. She regretted not grabbing it first, but now it was too late. She'd had to make do with her sword.

As she pulled the curtain open to drench the space with more light, she noticed a stream of water trickling toward her from under the cabin door. They didn't have much time.

Calum blocked a savage blow from Yurgev and staggered back toward Lilly.

She stepped to his side and nudged him. "We're doing this together."

Calum nodded. He leveled his sword.

The ship pitched to the left, and all three of them lost their footing. Lilly recovered first because she took to the air, but Yurgev wasn't far behind her. He jabbed his sword at her and missed, then he swung it again. The blade should have connected with Lilly's sword, but it never made it that far.

From the shadows, a dark blur slashed at Yurgev. He dropped, his throat split open, facedown on the water-covered floor. His blood tinted the water red.

Now Captain Brink stood before them, his amber eyes burning with revenge.

CHAPTER NINE

L illy ran through the list of possibilities in her head, but in the end, the simplest explanation also made the most sense: Brink must've swum around to the side of the boat and somehow found a way back inside his quarters.

It didn't matter how—what mattered was that if they wanted to get off the ship alive, they'd have to get past Brink.

Lilly shot toward him.

"Lilly, no!" Calum reached for her, but she zipped past him.

With one swing of his arm, Brink sent her careening into the wall. Her body smacked against it, and she slumped down to the water-covered floor. The blow might've killed her if not for her armor.

She didn't move, except to grope for her sword, now hidden somewhere under the ever-rising water.

Then Brink charged Calum, who barely dodged his first attack but fell under his second. Calum slapped the water in search for his sword, but Brink kicked his ribs. He rolled over on his side, his teeth bared.

Brink turned back and started toward Lilly. "Ye, m'dear, be the reason me ship is goin' down. I should've killed ye last night when ye asked."

Lilly tried to back away, but the cabin wall kept her from moving anywhere. As she did, her hand brushed against something under the water.

Brink stalked nearer. "I think, for me next ship, I won't be takin' anymore slaves. I'll just kill 'em from the start. I guess in this age a pirate cap'n needs to be more ruthless to maintain order. I shall not repeat this mistake."

Lilly's fingers coiled around the hilt of her sword. She didn't dare glance at it for fear of giving it away.

As Brink raised his claws to strike, Lilly lifted her sword out of the water and sprang forward. The blade pierced deep into Brink's chest, and he dropped onto his back with his eyes wide and mouth open.

Lilly stood over him as water splashed over his astonished face. "I waited for you to come to me this time. Thanks for the advice. It worked."

Brink coughed, and then he lay back in the water. His amber eyes shut for good.

The cabin door burst open, and a cascade of water streamed inside. Lilly wrenched her sword from Brink's chest and pulled Calum to his feet. "Come on. We have to grab the rest and get out of here."

The ship pitched toward its stern, and they slid toward the cabin's windows, now submerged in lake water. Calum recovered his sword, sheathed it, and together with Lilly he darted over to the closet. They collected Axel's armor in a sack, she grabbed her bow and arrows, and they clawed their way back up to the door.

Lilly made it out first, and Calum followed with the sack slung over his shoulder. He found a grip on the outside of the doorframe and began to pull himself out of the captain's quarters, but the ship pitched again, this time so far that its bow pointed straight up into the sky.

The sack of armor slipped, but Calum snatched it before it could fall into the whirlpool below. Now he dangled over the watery chasm below with his right hand clamped onto the doorframe and the sack of armor hanging from his other hand.

He looked up at Lilly, who reached down to help him.

A loud crash sounded below Calum, and the entire ship shuddered.

The cabin windows shattered, and the edge of Brink's table disappeared in the water rushing up to meet them.

"Take my hand, Calum!" she shouted over the ship's groans and the roiling, churning water below.

As she continued to reach toward him, a massive dark form materialized in the rising waters below. A black fin emerged from the water's furious surface and circled underneath Calum.

A shark.

"Drop the armor and grab my hand!" Lilly pressed her chest against the doorframe and reached even farther down toward him. She couldn't lose him.

Calum's face tightened with strain, and he hefted the bag up to her instead. Lilly grabbed it and slung it over her shoulder, then she reached down with her other hand. Just as Calum's grip slipped from the doorframe, Lilly caught him by his wrist.

He yelped, but he clasped his fingers around her wrist as well and anchored his free hand on the door frame again.

The shark spiraled closer, and the froth lapped at the bottoms of Calum's boots.

"Help me!" Lilly yelled at him. She yanked and pulled and used her flight to help with the strain, and Calum strained along with her.

Gaping jaws and spearhead teeth burst from the water below and chomped shut just beneath Calum's right foot as he made it above the doorframe. When Lilly looked down again the shark had clamped its jaws on Brink's body, and then it disappeared into the angry waters.

As Calum stood to his feet, Lilly glared at him. "Why didn't you just drop the armor?"

"Axel would've killed me if I didn't get it back for him." Calum shrugged.

Lilly rolled her eyes. "Come on. This ship is going down fast."

"I can't go into that water," Calum told her in calm tones. He hardly seemed worried about it. "My armor's too heavy, and I'm too exhausted and weak to keep my head above the water for long. I'll sink."

Calum grabbed the railing above his head, which, when the ship had been floating, lined the staircase that led up to the wheel and the captain's quarters. He pulled himself over it.

"Take the armor and get outta here," he continued, equally as placid. "I'll climb up higher to give the lifeboat a chance to circle near me."

Lilly took to the air, even though his plan baffled her. If he could fly like she could, then maybe it would work, but he couldn't. "How are you going to get to the lifeboat without getting into the water?"

"I'll swing over." He grabbed a rope and pulled himself off the rail toward the first of the masts. "If you hurry, you can drop that off and get back to help me."

Lilly nodded and sped off. She wouldn't let him die. It wasn't an option she'd even consider. She landed on Magnus's lifeboat and dropped the bag next to Axel. Both of them looked at her.

"We worried you were dead," Magnus said. "What happened? Where is Calum?"

"Long story." Lilly sprang back into the air. "Just get the boat as close to the ship as you can without letting it take you under. Hurry."

She darted back toward Calum.

WITH EACH TUG on the network of ropes that hung from the masts, Calum's body raged against him. Exhaustion and a lack of food plagued him. He felt weak, yet determined.

But if he let go, or if he slipped, he was as good as dead. So he kept going.

The ship's black sails tore loose and whipped past him as he climbed higher. Something above him snapped. A barrel from the ship's bow plummeted toward him.

He leaped clear, his arms outstretched, and he grabbed a rope with greedy fingers. It tightened, and he swung out of the barrel's path.

The ship seemed to be sinking faster. As soon as he swung back to the second mast, water licked his heels. Water meant sharks.

Maybe Magnus could survive one, but Calum didn't stand a chance. He had to get above the third mast, grab a rope, and then try to swing out over the water. Hopefully there'd be a lifeboat nearby, if not underneath him, by then.

Calum jumped up and clamped his fingers around an iron ring mounted to the third mast. His arms protested when he tried to pull himself up, but they did the job. He managed to grab one of the ropes just above the mast, and—

He dropped. Water smothered him. The rope was loose.

He surfaced and pulled on the rope still in his hand, silently praying it would catch on something, but the opposite end dropped into the water next to him. He had to get out of there.

Too late. A black fin cut through the surf toward him.

Calum scrambled and splashed, but couldn't get ahold of anything, and his armor kept trying to tug him ever downward toward a different kind of demise.

The shark zoomed closer, growing larger and larger as it approached. Its gigantic jaws broke through the water and spread wide to receive him.

Before the beast could reach Calum, the shark's jaws clamped shut, but it still collided with him. The impact spun him in the water as if he weighed nothing, and he sank down low, confused and trying to find the surface. Something red in the water blinded him, and his armor pulled him down fast. He flailed his arms.

It was blood. Was it his? He didn't feel wounded, but that didn't mean he was whole.

Something fastened on his wrist. Shark teeth, but much softer and more forgiving than he'd expected, dragged him toward the surface.

Not shark teeth—*fingers*.

The instant Calum's head broke through the water he gasped, and precious air flooded his lungs. His entire body left the water, and the sinking ship shrank beneath him. Then it rushed up to meet him once more. On the way down, he grabbed a rope on the third mast and held on to keep from plunging back into the water.

He looked down. All his limbs seemed to be intact, and he didn't see or feel any blood gushing out of his body.

When he looked up, he saw Lilly hovering just above him. She held her bow in one hand and beckoned him toward her with her other.

Had she *shot* the shark? That would explain the blood in the water.

"Wake up, Calum!" She motioned toward the lifeboat behind her, occupied by Magnus and Axel, who rowed furiously to stay out of the whirlpool created by the sinking pirate ship. "Swing over!"

Beneath him, the water continued to consume the *Malice*. The shark's head resurfaced, but something long and narrow was sticking out of its right eye.

An arrow.

Lilly *had* shot the shark. In its eye, no less.

Calum marveled at it. *Incredible.*

"Calum, now!" Magnus roared from the lifeboat.

Calum snapped back into the present. He kicked his feet back toward the mast and landed on one of the sail rods that extended from the mast itself.

He found a new rope to grab, and then he pushed off the sail rod with all his remaining strength and swung toward the lifeboat. But even with all his momentum, he'd never make it all the way to the lifeboat—it was too far.

When Calum released the rope, hoping for a well-timed release to get him as close as possible, Lilly grabbed onto his wrist with both hands and dropped toward the lifeboat right along with him. Her flying thrust helped him traverse the extra distance between the *Malice* and the lifeboat, and they fell into Axel and Magnus's open arms.

The lifeboat rocked so much that it almost tipped over, but it stayed upright.

Calum pushed himself up, amazed that he'd even made it into the lifeboat. Twenty yards away, the ship sank deeper and deeper until it disappeared under the water entirely.

"There she goes," Axel said, back to rowing along with Magnus. In all the commotion, he hadn't yet put his armor back on, so he once again resembled the farm boy Calum used to know back from his days in the quarry, rather than a budding warrior, strong and powerful.

Calum turned to Lilly, who also sat up. "Why didn't you just pull me to the lifeboat in the first place?"

"I can only fly with as much weight as I could carry on the ground." She smiled at him. "But I can redirect heavier things with my momentum, which is how I got us into the boat."

Axel whistled. "Can all Windgales do that?"

"Sure, they're capable, but not all of them know how. I've had special training."

"Thank the Overlord for that." Calum lay back down in the lifeboat, closed his eyes, and exhaled a long, painful breath. Everything hurt. *Everything.* He opened his eyes again and looked at Axel and Magnus. "How many prisoners survived?"

"Another three lifeboats, including one with the five men who tried to attack us, all big enough to hold about twenty men, but most of them are only half-full with limited supplies." Axel glowered at them over his shoulder then turned back.

"Speaking of which, we have seen no sign of either the man Axel called Yurgev or Captain Brink. Do you know what happened to them?" Magnus asked.

"Dead. Both of them." Even talking seemed to sap Calum of his energy. He wanted to closer his eyes again and rest, but he couldn't. Not yet.

"What happened?" Axel leaned forward and rubbed his lower back with his hand.

Calum motioned to Lilly so she could talk for the both of them. He couldn't make his mouth form words. He needed just a little more rest, so he lay back again and stared up at the blue sky above.

"Yurgev ambushed us while we were getting our armor back," she said. "Calum fought him off for awhile until Brink showed up. He killed Yurgev, then came for us. I put my sword through his chest when he wasn't expecting it, and he died. Last time I saw him, he was wedged between a shark's jaws."

With renewed energy, Calum sat up to look at Lilly, and his view greatly improved.

"Impressive. Brink was no ordinary foe." Magnus smiled. "Well done, Lilly."

"I never would've had a chance had Calum not held off Yurgev for so long." Lilly showed Calum a smile that totally eased his exhaustion for an instant, and then it returned full-force. "He was incredible."

"You wanna talk about incredible? Calum, did you see that *unbelievable* shot Lilly made to save you?" Axel whacked Calum's shoulder, probably on purpose. The blow disrupted most of the progress Calum had made through resting.

Calum ground his teeth and shook his head. "Only the result."

"She hit the shark right in its *eye*." Axel chuckled and turned to Lilly. "How does that even happen? How are you so accurate all the time?"

Lilly shrugged. "I've had a lot of practice. I started learning when I was four years old, and I've been shooting ever since."

"More 'special training?'" Axel asked.

She grinned at him. "Exactly."

Calum lay back in the boat again and exhaled a relived sigh. "So what do we do now?"

Magnus peered over the side of the lifeboat. "The sharks are circling the wreckage, probably picking at the dead bodies that were on board the ship. I expect they'll leave us alone for awhile, but all the same, I'd like to row toward shore immediately."

"Which way do we go?" Axel asked. "It all looks the same to me."

"South." The voice came from behind Magnus, but there was no one else on the boat.

Calum sat up too quickly, and this time his head throbbed as punishment. One of the lifeboats full of prisoners floated toward them. Calum recognized them as the mellow prisoners from the other cell while he and Axel—well, only Axel—fought off Yurgev.

"Head south from here." The man speaking had a long gray beard and matching hair, except for a bald spot on his head, and he wore gray rags about the same color as the *Baroness of Destiny* had been. His sharp, blue-green eyes resembled the color of the lake water on which they all floated. "Sharkville is south of here."

"He is right," Magnus said. "But with the sun overhead I cannot tell which direction is south. I got turned around after I boarded the ship, and now it is noon, or close to it."

The bearded man extended his hand and pointed to his left. "It's that-a-way."

"How do you know?" Magnus asked.

"When you've been sailin' these waters as many years as I have, you just know." The bearded man glanced at the young man next to him in the boat, who stared at Calum. "This here's my son, Jacobus, or Jake for short. I'm Puolo. Used to captain a fishin' vessel 'bout the size of that pirate ship before they found us and took most of us captive."

"Pleasure to meet you both." Calum marshaled enough strength to introduce his companions. "And thank you for not trying to kill us."

Puolo waved his hand. "You set us free. If anything, we should be thanking you, and we certainly do."

He bowed to Magnus, who returned the bow with one of his own.

Axel cleared his throat. "Anyway, how far do you think it is back to Sharkville?"

"A solid day, at least. Could be a day and a half." Puolo added, "Depends how fast you row."

"Hopefully we grabbed enough food to sustain us until then." Axel rummaged through a burlap bag in the boat with them. "There's not much in here."

"Pirates typically aren't fishermen. They survive by plunderin' and tradin'," Jake said. "We're lucky we found anythin' at all."

"We grabbed some basic fishin' equipment and some bait they took from your vessel yesterday, though." Puolo held up a harpoon. "We can do some fishing and see if we can supplement our supply. The only thing we got to worry about is rowing away from these sharks before they decide to…"

It all sounded great to Calum, but his body still weighed him down, and his eyelids drooped low. How Axel even could tolerate being awake, Calum didn't know, but now that they'd escaped harm, Calum couldn't fight his fatigue anymore.

As the others continued to talk, he lay back in the lifeboat and let the motion of the water slapping against the hull rock him to sleep.

A SMACK on the wood under Calum's head jarred him from his sleep. He jerked upright, and his body reverberated with dull pain. He sucked in a sharp breath.

"Are you alright?" Magnus asked from somewhere behind him.

The boat rocked against the waves under a starry moonlit sky. Calum stretched his limbs and his back but the tension only sharpened his misery. "Yeah. I'll be alright."

He turned to face Magnus, who sat in the center of the boat. He held an oar in each hand and rowed against the black surf in a steady rhythm. Farther behind him, the other three lifeboats chased his wake, two on the left and one on the right.

"How long have you been rowing?"

"All day," Magnus said. "Do not fret, though. I take pride that I am the only one rowing this lifeboat, yet we still lead all the others, each of which has at least six men rowing."

Calum smiled at him, fully contented. Magnus had survived, he'd saved them, and now they were all reunited, more or less unharmed. "I'm glad we didn't lose you, Magnus."

"Even if you had, I am certain someone else would have rowed in my stead."

Calum chuckled. "That's not what I meant, and you know it."

Now Magnus grinned. "Yes, I know."

"My body is—" Calum twisted his torso and a chorus of cracks and pops sounded. He didn't feel quite as exhausted as before, but the aches of all the strain he'd endured over the last few days still lingered. "—killing me. I just don't know how Axel does it sometimes."

"Even if he will not show it, Axel is just as beat as you are." Magnus must have noticed Calum's eyes scanning the back half of the lifeboat. "He is sleeping back there."

"Where's Lilly?"

"She's back there too, also sleeping."

Calum swallowed. "Together?"

Magnus smirked. "No. Near each other, but not together. It is not quite cold enough for Axel to use body heat as an excuse to draw close to her. Or at least not cold enough that she would agree to it."

Calum nodded, and Magnus chuckled.

"What are you laughing at?" Calum asked.

"I find humans much more entertaining now that I am not enslaved by them." His oars lifted out of the water and then dug back in almost parallel to where Calum was sitting. "Specifically, you and Axel."

"What do you mean?"

"Ever since the moment you discovered Lilly, neither of you have been able to restrain yourselves. You both posture like colorful birds displaying your finest plumage, you take risks you would not otherwise take, and you go at each others' throats whenever you think it will give you an advantage." Magnus snorted and carved another swath into the water with his oars. "I find it amusing."

Calum frowned at him. "I haven't done any of those things."

Have I? he wondered.

Magnus stopped rowing, tilted his head, and huffed through his nostrils.

"Alright." Calum bit his lip. "Maybe I've done *some* of those things."

"That is putting it mildly." Magnus started rowing again. "I could point out several instances where one or both of you went a bit overboard on her behalf."

"If I remember correctly, *you're* the one who went overboard," Calum countered with a smirk.

Magnus shook his head. "You jumped ship more recently than I did."

"That's because it was *sinking*." Calum pointed at him. "You fell off."

"I was *forced* off and nearly eaten by a shark, thank you very much." Magnus grunted. "Perhaps we should just drop the subject."

"I never did hear how you got away from that shark. What happened?"

"When it came at me, I stabbed it through the roof of its mouth and into its head. The blood in the water was the shark's, not mine." Magnus huffed again. "Believe it or not, that was the easy part of what I had to deal with."

Calum raised his eyebrows.

"The blood in the water must have attracted other sharks, because half a dozen others showed up within minutes of killing that one. I managed to escape while they fed on their kin, but by then the ship had already started to sail away. I swam after it until it slowed to a cruising speed, but by then it was already a day later."

"You swam after us for an *entire day?*"

Magnus let the oars go slack again and he shrugged. "You are my friends. I could not let you perish on that pirate ship."

A smile cracked Calum's lips. "If it wasn't for you, we would have. Brink was gonna kill us right when you showed up."

Magnus began to row again. "I heard as much from Axel and Lilly this afternoon."

Something smacked the wood under Calum's feet and the whole lifeboat pitched to one side. He looked at Magnus.

"Sharks again," he explained. "They bump against the bottoms or sides of the boat from time to time. I imagine they are testing for weaknesses."

"Can they break through the hull?" Calum did *not* want to deal with any more lake creatures if he didn't have to.

"The wood is stout, but I cannot say. They are imposing monsters. Easily the size of one of these boats. Maybe bigger. Even if they cannot break through, they could certainly tip the boats over with ease." Magnus sighed. "I would like to tell you with certainty that we will make it back to Sharkville, but I cannot."

Calum exhaled a long silent breath through his nostrils. The thought of ending up back in the water with one of those monstrosities again sent shudders from his spine down to his fingertips. For now, all he could do was put his trust in Magnus, the Overlord, and Lumen to see them through.

"I understand."

"Are you hungry?" Magnus motioned toward Calum with his head. "Search that bag next to you. You should be able to find something to satisfy your stomach for awhile."

As if on cue, a low rumble vibrated through Calum's gut. "Yeah. Have you eaten?"

Magnus didn't answer right away. "I will be alright."

Calum's shoulders drooped. "Magnus, you need to eat, too."

"The way I see it, I still owe you for that chicken quarter you brought me that night when I was chained to that post at the quarry camp." Magnus smiled. "I am happy to sacrifice so you may be satisfied. Besides, I think I swallowed a fish or two when I was swimming after the pirate ship. I should be good for awhile."

"If you say so." Calum sighed. "But you don't owe me anything. If anything, I owe you for saving me. Again."

Magnus shook his head. "As I have said before, we are friends, Calum. Friends owe each other nothing. Attempting to keep track is pointless because we will always owe each other, mutually. It is the Law of Debt in its purest, perfected form: we are indebted to each other forever."

"I know what you mean."

A dark sphere tumbled out of the bag and plunked on the wooden floor. Calum picked it up. An apple, bruised everywhere, but not rotten. Not long until it would begin to rot, though, either. He could eat that without feeling guilty.

Two pieces of stale bread, a small, dried-out piece of smoked fish, and that apple later, Calum lay back down and stared up at the stars. As he drifted back to sleep, he wished Lilly was sleeping "near" him instead of Axel.

He pushed the thought from his mind and closed his eyes once again.

"CALUM, WAKE UP!" Lilly's voice cut through the blackness that blanketed Calum's vision, and morning sunlight flooded his eyes.

He sat up abruptly again, and again his body reminded him to stop doing that. "What's going on?"

"Something's coming." Her voice rang hollow with fear.

Calum scanned the surrounding waters and saw nothing aside from the other lifeboats following theirs. "What? Where are they?"

"No, not more pirates." Lilly's eyes widened. "Something in the water."

Behind her, both Magnus and Axel, who now wore his armor again, rowed twice as fast as Magnus had last night. Determination—and hefty a dose of terror—etched into their expressions.

Whatever this was, it was bad.

Calum faced the lifeboat's stern and scanned the water. Three large black silhouettes followed them. "More sharks?"

Lilly shook her head. "Worse. Much worse."

"How do you know?"

"I was scouting around, and I saw it. A gigantic dark form under the water, headed toward us from behind." Lilly stared at him. "We're in trouble."

Calum glanced into the water behind the boat again. The three shark silhouettes weren't anywhere to be found. Definitely not a good sign.

"Do you know what it is?" Calum asked Magnus, who continued to row with purpose.

"Not for sure..." His oars carved into the water, and he spoke between rows. "...but it is probably... a Jyrak."

Calum blinked. "A what?"

"No." Lilly shook her head. "Jyraks don't exist. They're a myth."

"Then what do you think... you saw in the water?" Magnus pressed.

Lilly gave no answer.

"Huh?" Calum glanced between them.

"Jyraks." Magnus didn't stop his furious rowing. "Monstrous lake creatures... definitely not a myth."

Lilly shook her head. "No one has ever seen one and lived to tell about it."

"No one that *you* have heard of." Magnus dug his oars into the water three times before he continued. "My father saw one once... in this very lake."

Lilly started to say something, but a rumble sounded from behind her and Calum. They both turned.

From the water emerged a dark scaled monstrosity of gigantic proportions, seemingly at half-speed. A long neck lifted a colossal head from the water, complete with jagged bronze teeth and a dark red tongue.

Spikes adorned its head and two large horns jutted out from just behind its glowing, pupil-less yellow eyes. The Jyrak's massive arms raised out of the water, also laden with spikes. Black talons tipped each of the four webbed fingers on its hands.

A droning roar split the air as the Jyrak slowly rose to its full height. It had to be the biggest creature in existence. Calum couldn't imagine how anything could be larger—and he was having difficulty even believing the Jyrak was real.

Then it started toward them.

Magnus stopped rowing. "We are in trouble."

CHAPTER TEN

Calum pointed to the sky. "Lilly, get in the air now. Head south. Find out how far we are from land. And take the food with you. If our boat goes down, we can't risk losing that food."

Lilly nodded and took to the sky with the sack of food over her shoulder.

"Axel and Magnus," Calum said. "We need to row. We gotta try to get away from it."

"You direct us," Magnus ordered. "We will handle the rowing. We need your eyes and your focus."

Calum nodded, and the two of them began to row again in a furious rhythm.

The Jyrak droned another roar again and started after them.

Calum glanced back at the other lifeboats. He had to keep track of their progress forward and everything that was happening behind them.

In their boat, Puolo and Jake tried to keep pace, but even with several men rowing, they had a hard time keeping up with Magnus and Axel. A third lifeboat chased theirs, but the fourth, the one with Yurgev's friends, cut hard to the right.

Fine. If they wanted to split off from the group, so be it. Calum would use it to his advantage. He leaned back. "Magnus, Axel—hard left."

Their lifeboat angled left and sliced through the water away from the Jyrak. To Calum's relief, it glanced between its two options, then it turned toward the prisoners' boat.

"Row harder!" Calum yelled. Though the Jyrak had chosen to pursue the other boat, that didn't mean Calum's and the other boats were in the clear. But at least they could gain some distance from it in the meantime.

Their boat sped forward, more due to Magnus's efforts than Axel's. Each row on his part seemed to nearly lift the small boat out of the water, almost as if they were leaping forward instead of cruising along the water.

Calum glanced back again.

The Jyrak closed the distance to the prisoners' lifeboat in two colossal steps and reached for it. The men below screamed as its humongous hand grasped their lifeboat like a toy. Two of them squelched between its fingers and fell a hundred feet to the water below, but the others disappeared into the Jyrak's deadly mouth along with the fragmented boat.

The sight horrified Calum. Yes, those men had meant Axel and him harm, but seeing them eaten by this monster shook Calum to his core.

"Calum, get down!" Axel yelled from behind him.

Calum's head swiveled forward in time to see the Jyrak's gigantic tail swinging toward them. He ducked as low as he could, and the tail swept over their lifeboat with only a few feet to spare, then it smashed into the water in front of Puolo's lifeboat. The waves launched the lifeboats in opposite directions and capsized Puolo's lifeboat.

Calum pointed at them. "Circle back and pick them up!"

Axel shook his head and kept rowing. "We can't save them and still be able to escape."

"Axel is right," Magnus called over the noise. "We must continue forward. One of the other lifeboats is already heading toward the survivors to pick them up."

Calum didn't like the idea of leaving anyone behind, but the others seemed to have the situation handled, so he just nodded.

Behind them, the Jyrak slowly turned its attention toward the other lifeboats with another droning roar, and the lifeboat behind Puolo's helped some of the stragglers in the water into their boat, including Jake.

Puolo didn't climb in. Somehow, he managed to flip his lifeboat back over, and he clambered inside. He snatched a pair of oars floating nearby and rowed with fury toward the Jyrak.

Jake hollered and reached for him from the other lifeboat, but his comrades wouldn't let him dive back in to go after his father. Puolo waved and shouted something Calum couldn't make out, then he ground his oars into the surf.

Calum's lifeboat lurched forward again, and he dropped onto his side. When he made it back up, he saw Jake's lifeboat chasing after theirs and making decent time with the extra hands rowing.

All the while, Puolo's lifeboat raced toward the Jyrak. Once Puolo came within range, he waved his arms and yelled.

The Jyrak reared its head back with another droning roar and slammed his hand down on Puolo's lifeboat, smashing it to pieces. Puolo disappeared under the surf and never resurfaced.

Calum cringed. By stalling the Jyrak, Puolo might have just saved them all, but it had cost him his life.

Lilly swooped in close and kept pace with their lifeboat as Magnus and Axel continued to row. She shouted, "There's land in sight! You're almost there."

Calum shielded his eyes from the sunlight and gazed south. Sure enough, he saw dry land in the distance, and hope filled his chest.

"We can make it," he said to Magnus and Axel. To Lilly, he called, "Now get back to shore before that thing gets you."

She nodded and zipped away with the sack of food still on her back.

They cruised along the water at a good speed, but when Calum looked back, he realized they'd separated from the second lifeboat too much, which was also heading toward the shore, albeit at a different angle.

Worse yet, the Jyrak was coming after Calum's boat now.

In four enormous steps, it closed the distance to them and reached down for their boat. It would have grabbed them in its first grasp had the water swell from its steps not pushed them just out of range again.

If Calum hadn't totally believed in the Overlord before, it didn't matter now—he called out to Him just the same.

Real or not, the Overlord didn't stop the Jyrak's next swipe. Its taloned fingers knifed down toward them.

"Bail out!" Magnus shouted.

Calum, Axel, and Magnus dove into the water just before the Jyrak's hand pulverized the lifeboat. When Calum surfaced, he saw Axel clawing at the water toward Magnus, who had surfaced several yards ahead of his position.

Calum swam the same direction with every ounce of energy he had left. As before, his armor threatened to sink him, but he'd regained enough energy to keep his head above water for the time being. Even so, he couldn't keep it up forever, so he swam toward a long piece of curved wood, almost big enough to lie on, floating nearby.

As the Jyrak smashed the boat, its tail whipped around behind it again. The tail's velocity created a swell that pushed Jake's lifeboat back toward them. Calum saw the swell approaching and grabbed onto the large piece of his broken lifeboat.

As the swell hit, Calum kicked his legs to propel himself higher out of the water. He positioned the flattest part of the lifeboat against the water and let the cascade carry him toward the shore on his belly. A rush of excitement filled his chest, and he almost whooped as the waves ferried him along.

The same wave plowed into Axel and Magnus, and Calum zipped past where they had just been. He considered waving at them as he cruised by, but he decided it was more important to hang on instead.

The wave died slowly, and it deposited Calum in the water only about three quarters of the way back to shore. Jake's lifeboat actually ended up closer to shore than he did. He held onto his board and craned his head back for a look.

Axel's head popped up from the water about twenty yards behind him, and Magnus's did as well, but about five yards closer. Another man's head surfaced near Axel.

It was one of the two prisoners from Yurgev's cell who hadn't been eaten. He launched toward Axel and pushed him under the water, then swam toward the shoreline.

A hand emerged from the surf behind the prisoner's head and yanked him under the water, then Axel popped back up. He jerked backward and the prisoner surfaced again, only to get Axel's fist in his face.

Their struggle continued, and they traded off who went under the water and who got to breathe as the Jyrak reached down toward them.

"*Axel!*" Calum yelled.

Axel looked at him, and the prisoner dunked him under the water again. As the Jyrak's arm dropped down, the prisoner held a flailing Axel under the water. When the Jyrak's shadow passed over him, the prisoner's angry face went blank, and his eyes widened.

The Jyrak's hand pummeled the prisoner. When the Jyrak drew its hand out of the water, Calum could barely see the prisoner between its fingers, and Axel hung from the Jyrak's hand by his left arm.

Though he tried to pull free, he couldn't. He was stuck.

THE WATER below Axel dropped away, and his left shoulder socket burned with strain. He swore and cursed, but he couldn't get free. Above him, the prisoner's blood mingled with the lake water dripping from the Jyrak's massive hand, and his bare foot protruded just above the webbing between two of the Jyrak's fingers.

Axel twisted his body and tried to get out, but it didn't work. The Jyrak's sprawling chest passed by and gave way to its neck as Axel rose higher and higher. It wouldn't be long until its bronze teeth came into view.

The shouts of his friends sounded from below, now as distant as when his mother used to call to him from across their field to come home for dinner. He should never have left his farm.

At this point, even if he could get free from the Jyrak's grip, the fall to the water below would kill him, but Axel drew his sword from his belt nonetheless. If he were going to die, he'd cut off a chunk of the Jyrak's tongue on his way. Then he'd give it the worst stomachache in Jyrak history.

Before Axel's eyes, bronze teeth, each of them pointed and longer than he was tall, separated. A forked tongue emerged from behind them and licked the air. The Jyrak's jaws opened wide, ready to receive him, and a blast of hot air that reeked of death washed over him.

Terror gripped Axel's entire body, but he refused to succumb to it. Instead, he got angry. The mismatch of one little human with a sword against a beast of this size was enough to infuriate him. It wasn't fair, and he was going to make sure the Jyrak knew it.

Axel timed his swing as best as he could, but the Jyrak thrust him almost directly into its throat. Axel's sword clanged off its teeth, and he fell onto his side.

Next to Axel, the prisoner's mangled body crunched between the Jyrak's bronze teeth. The Jyrak's jaws closed, and darkness replaced the sunlight.

HORROR SATURATED CALUM'S CHEST. Axel was gone, devoured by the Jyrak along with the prisoner. He couldn't believe it had happened, even despite seeing it with his own eyes.

Something latched onto Calum's shoulder with so much force that his head almost submerged under the water. Magnus's hand.

"We must get to shore before it comes for us next." Magnus's voice rang with tones of sadness and anger, but mostly with urgency. "We can do nothing for him now. Come on."

Calum hated that Magnus was right, but he couldn't deny it. He clenched his teeth and dug into the surf with his tired arms.

THE PUTRID STENCH of decay and rotten flesh burned Axel's nostrils. The

91

Jyrak's tongue slapped him against the roof of its mouth and toward its throat, but he dug the fingers of his left hand into its squishy flesh.

He maneuvered his sword and jammed the point into the Jyrak's gums at the base of the right side of its bronze teeth. Glowing orange blood spurted onto his face and armor. It tingled like warm liquid metal in his mouth, and he spat it out.

The Jyrak jerked, and its mouth opened wide in a deafening roar that knocked Axel onto his back. Still, this was his chance to get out. His only chance.

Axel recovered his footing and stumbled toward the spot where he'd stabbed the Jyrak's gums. He gripped the point of one of the shorter teeth with his free hand to steady himself and peered out across the vast expanse of water hundreds of feet below him, and the first hint of fresh air he'd inhaled in what felt like an eternity hit his lungs.

It was a surreal sight—towering more than a hundred feet over an expanse of perfectly blue water on a beautiful autumn day. The waters glistened under the sunlight, and a few clouds drifted lazily in the blue sky.

And all of it was framed by an enormous set of jagged bronze teeth.

The Jyrak's jaw began to shut.

Axel had no choice.

Still gripping his sword, he dashed forward and flung himself over the bottom row of teeth, just before the top row slammed down behind him.

Axel fell, and he screamed into the ether.

LILLY'S HEART had dropped into her churning stomach when Axel disappeared inside the Jyrak's mouth. She hovered well out of its reach and hung her head. Axel was gone.

A bloodcurdling cry for help snapped her attention back toward the Jyrak. A dark human form adorned with familiar blue armor on his arms and legs dropped from its mouth.

Axel... was *not* gone!

She abandoned the bag of food on the shore and exploded toward him at full speed. Based on her trajectory and his, Lilly aimed to reach him by the time he fell about halfway from the Jyrak's mouth to the water—provided the Jyrak didn't get him first. It had already locked its vision onto him and began to move its hand to catch him.

Not if I can do something about it.

Lilly swooped in to intercept Axel. He yelled until the moment her hand latched onto his left wrist, and then he stared up at her with astonished eyes.

Beyond him, the Jyrak's hand whipped toward them.

"Hold on!" Lilly yanked him to her left, and they dropped below the Jyrak's hand by inches.

"We're still falling!" Axel shouted as he managed to sheathe his sword.

Lilly ground her teeth and pulled against the air, but they continued to fall anyway. She couldn't lift him, but that wasn't the only way to get them both to safety. "You weigh... a *lot* more than Calum!"

Layers of dark scales passed them by as they plummeted toward the water below. Lilly focused all of her force into Axel, and their trajectory shifted, but not enough. She had to level them out or they'd both die upon impact.

Then the Jyrak's tail rose from the water and lashed toward them. Lilly couldn't lift him higher, above it, and if she tried to drop below it, Axel's weight might throw off any hope of her gliding them to safety.

"When you get close enough, let me go," Axel yelled amid the wind rushing past them. "I'll skid right off its tail, and you can pick me up again and redirect my momentum like you did to Calum."

"It won't—"

"If it doesn't, then I'm dead anyway!" Axel shouted. "I trust you."

When the tail got close enough, Lilly released Axel like he wanted. His body smacked hard against the tail, and his armor scraped the scales for a few seconds, then he dropped off the other side, no longer screaming.

Lilly spun under the tail and caught him by his ankle as he fell. She might as well have been trying to carry Magnus.

"Axel?" she called down to him, but she got no response. *"Axel!"*

He was either dead or unconscious. Either way, Lilly was on her own.

With all her strength and focus she pushed perpendicular to the shoreline, away from the Jyrak. The blue water jumped up to meet them. They were going to crash, and she couldn't prevent it. She couldn't pull Axel up.

When she let him go, Axel's body flew parallel to the water for just a moment before it crashed into the surf. She angled up as hard as she could, but it was too late.

She hit the water and skipped along the surface until she finally slowed down enough to sink. Water smothered her senses, and then it consumed her completely.

CHAPTER ELEVEN

When he saw Lilly hit the water, Calum knew she was in trouble. He'd seen Axel fall from the Jyrak's mouth—somehow—and then Lilly managed to get him away from it. Calum broke his swim back to shore and doubled back toward her.

She landed in the water about twenty feet to his left and then skidded another ten or so feet toward the shoreline. Thanks to his piece of the lifeboat, Calum made it to her within three seconds of her head disappearing under the water.

He reached down and flailed to find her, prepared to dive in if he couldn't, but his hand found hers before she sank too deep. He grabbed ahold of her wrist and hauled her up and onto the piece of the lifeboat.

A huge form knifed past him in the water, and Calum caught a gleam of iridescent blue under the sunlight—Magnus. He was heading for Axel.

Calum positioned Lilly on the piece of the lifeboat, got in front of it, and pulled it as he swam toward the surface. He had to get her to shore before he could check on her. It didn't take long for Magnus to catch up with him.

"Save yourself," Magnus said as he hefted Axel onto the curved piece of wood alongside Lilly. "I will get Axel and Lilly to shore."

Calum nodded and relinquished the makeshift life raft to him.

"Swim fast. It is still coming." Magnus cruised forward, hauling Axel and Lilly behind him.

Sure enough, the Jyrak plowed through the surf toward them, still upright, and, if possible, angrier-looking than before.

Calum didn't dawdle. He dove under the water and kicked his legs with fury until something propelled him up out of the water. The force of it sent him tumbling end-over-end in the surf.

When he finally resurfaced and cleared the water from his nostrils, Calum was facing the Jyrak, which towered over him. It pulled its hand out of the water no more than twenty yards from Calum and raised it to its chest.

Calum turned and dug his arms into the water. His legs launched him forward a few feet when he kicked, but he still wasn't making much progress. Terror powered every one of his desperate strokes, and he gritted his teeth.

He glanced over his shoulder and saw the Jyrak's hand plummeting toward him. He kicked harder and screamed.

The hand hit the water just behind Calum's feet and created a swell that carried Calum toward the shoreline. When the swell finally died down, Calum's boots scraped against the dirt at bottom of the lake. He sprang off the lake's floor and continued to claw toward the shore.

Magnus met him there and took hold of his wrist like a father escorting a child, but Calum didn't resist. Together they ran through the shallows.

Behind them the Jyrak roared, but it didn't pursue them any farther. Instead, it turned away and receded into the depths of the lake once again.

Calum exhaled a sigh of relief until he noticed Axel and Lilly lying on the shoreline, motionless, surrounded by Jake and his friends. He ignored his waterlogged boots and armor and ran over to them with Magnus close behind.

When he got closer, he noticed a man on top of Lilly. "Hey!"

Jake stepped into his path and stopped Calum before he could bash the guy's head in. "It's alright, Calum. He's helpin'."

It looked like the man was trying to take advantage of her—sort of. His left palm rested on the back of his right hand, and the heel of his right hand pressed into the center of Lilly's armored chest. He pumped on her chest five times, then leaned over and put his mouth on hers.

Calum sprang forward, but Jake reeled him back in.

"Let 'im work, Calum." For as wiry as he was, Jake managed to anchor Calum's arms in place. "He's gonna save her life."

"He'd better." Calum's tone surprised even him. It sounded like something Axel would say.

Lilly coughed and sputtered, and the man helped her onto her side. She hacked, and water trickled out of her mouth into the wet, gray sand below.

Calum's heart fluttered when her eyes met his. His relief at seeing the Jyrak descend back into the lake was nothing compared to this.

He twisted out of Jake's grip, ran to Lilly, and skidded to a halt on his knees next to her. He wrapped her in his arms and whispered into her ear. "I'm so glad you're alright."

She half-laughed, half-coughed, and returned his embrace for a moment, then she pulled away from him. Her head swiveled, and in a raspy voice, she asked, "Where's Axel?"

Calum blinked. He'd almost lost her, and she was asking about Axel?

Lilly's gaze fell on Axel, who lay next to her. The same man who'd helped her now leaned over Axel and pumped his chest the same as he had for her.

She covered her mouth. "Oh, no..."

It seemed like hours elapsed as the man worked on Axel. With every passing moment, Calum worried more and more for his friend, and Lilly clutched his hand in hers.

Then Axel's eyes finally opened. He coughed his lungs clear of lake water just as Lilly had, and he rolled onto his stomach with a moan.

Next to Calum, Lilly released her grip on his hand, sighed, and lay on her back. Just when Calum decided to get up, Lilly grabbed his hand again and smiled at him. "Thank you."

Calum couldn't restrain a smile of his own. He nodded and squeezed her hand in return.

Jake and Magnus stood over them. Magnus set the bag of food Lilly had rescued next to Calum and nodded toward the Jyrak, which had now fully disappeared into the Lake. "It does not appear the Jyrak means to follow us on land. After some rest, we should be safe to return to Sharkville."

Calum nodded.

Axel moaned again. Lilly gave a weak giggle, then she sighed. They had made it.

THEY REACHED Sharkville within a few hours of walking, and by that evening they made it back to Trader's Pass. It was there that Jake and his friends elected to part ways with Calum's group.

"We're headin' for Kanarah City," Jake had said. "My father had lots of friends in the fishin' industry there. They'll help me out with a new ship. We're gonna rebuild our crew and start fishin' again in the lake as soon as we can get the ship out there.

"Now that Brink is gone, the waters will be a lot safer, so thank you for that," he continued. "You ever need anythin', you let me know. We owe you our lives."

Calum nodded. "None of us would be here if it weren't for your father."

Jake gave a solemn nod. "I regret his death, but I understand why he did it. Your words honor 'im. Thank you."

Jake motioned toward one of the men standing behind him, and the man brought forward a sack bulging with food.

"I know it's not much, but our journey's far shorter than yours. Please take this." He offered the bag to Calum, who took it. "It's mostly dried or smoked fish. Nothin' fancy, but it should keep you goin'."

"Much appreciated," Calum said. "Thank you, and stay safe out there."

Calum extended his hand, and Jake shook it.

The two groups parted ways near where Calum and Lilly had killed the Dactyls and headed in opposite directions.

Several days and nights later, Calum, Axel, Lilly, and Magnus arrived at the western end of Trader's Pass hungry but alive. With the additional food given to them by Jake and his friends, they'd run out of rations only two days earlier. Thus far, the worst part about it had been Axel's complaining.

The moment they stepped into Western Kanarah, Lilly's smile widened. "It's good to be home."

Calum glanced at Magnus, whose face showed only quiet anger. Unlike Lilly, Magnus didn't seem happy to be back.

"So how do we find Riley?" Axel asked.

Calum turned to Magnus. "I've never been here before. Are we in the right place?"

"The dead tree is over there." Magnus pointed to a tall leafless tree to the south. Its body had turned a weatherworn charcoal gray. "We will wait for Riley there, as we discussed."

"If he doesn't show up within a few hours, then we should move on." Lilly scanned the skies. "We're near Raven's Brood territory."

Axel sighed and rubbed his forehead. "I take it that's a bad thing?"

Lilly nodded. "They're Windgale insurgents. They want to overthrow the Premier of the Sky Realm and establish their own alternate government. If they catch us in an open space like this, we're in trouble, so we shouldn't stay long."

They sat under the dead tree for an hour. In that time Calum took in the terrain around them. All in all, it didn't seem too different from the eastern half of Kanarah: both had trees and forests, dirt and rocks, and mountains in the distance.

Yet something about the western half set him at ease, even in spite of the potential threat of the Raven's Brood. Perhaps it was the lack of humans in this half—or more precisely, the lack of the King's influence and his soldiers. With no one in the King's employ chasing them, Calum felt free in an all-new way.

Lilly pointed along a road that headed southwest. "If you follow that road, you'll end up at the base of Aeropolis, where I live."

Calum nodded. "What about the one that heads north?"

"That leads to the Desert of the Forgotten, and then to the Blood

Mountains and Reptilius, where Magnus is from." Lilly nodded toward Magnus.

Magnus's face hardened into a scowl.

"How far is it from here to Aeropolis?" Axel asked.

"I usually fly there, so I'm not sure how long it takes on foot. From the air it takes about a day at a steady pace, with a couple of stops for rest." Lilly leaned forward, shifted her quiver onto her lap, then leaned back against the tree again. She brushed her fingers through the fletching on her arrows.

Magnus squinted at the tree line. "Perhaps Riley ran into the Raven's Brood and had to take cover. That forest would be a good place to avoid them, and it is a type of terrain he is already familiar with."

"Makes sense," Axel said. "Maybe someone should go and—"

Lilly collided with him at nearly full speed and tackled him backward onto the ground.

Before Calum could question her action, a dark form slammed a sword into the earth where Axel had been sitting, then it zipped away just as fast.

Axel shoved Lilly away. "What in the—"

"Get down!" Magnus roared.

Calum dropped low and watched as three Windgales in dark armor flew at Magnus.

The first one lashed at Magnus with his sword, but the blow just bounced off Magnus's scaly shoulder. Magnus grabbed the attacker's ankle with his opposing hand and swung him at the second Windgale as if he weighed nothing. They smacked together and dropped to the dirt at Magnus's feet.

The third swung his sword at Magnus's head, but he ducked under the blow, latched onto the Windgale's cape with his hand, and slammed him against the dead tree face-first. He too fell to the ground, motionless.

Calum jumped to his feet and drew his sword, along with Axel. Lilly nocked an arrow in her bow and stepped up beside them.

At least fifty Windgales, all clad in dark armor, landed all around them. A black bird outlined in red emblazoned their breastplates, and each of them wore a black-and-red cape with the same image embroidered on the back.

The Raven's Brood.

CHAPTER TWELVE

The last of the Raven's Brood landed in front of Lilly, and she immediately recognized him as their leader, Condor. He wore charcoal armor with the same raven on his chest, only it was all black. Instead of red accents on his armor like that of the rest of the Raven's Brood, they were black, and he wore no cape.

She remembered seeing him at the Sky Fortress several times before but hadn't remembered how handsome he was—tall and trim with black hair and sharp cheekbones. A pronounced scar ran from the outer edge of his left eyebrow to the top of his cheek. If anything, the scar intensified his cunning blue eyes and gave him an ominous appearance.

Too bad he chose the betrayer's path.

"Welcome to Western Kanarah. I am Condor, leader of the Raven's Brood." Condor focused on Lilly for a long moment, scrutinizing her and her armor. Then he placed his hands on his chest with his thumbs up, wrists crossed, and fingers extended over the wings of the raven on his breastplate, and he gave a slight nod.

"We're just passing through." Calum stepped forward without lowering his sword. "We don't want any trouble."

Condor smirked. His voice took on a casual tone. "Nor do we. But you've already harmed three of my men. And, unfortunately, that means there's a price to be paid."

"We just want to go our own way," Calum said. "We have nothing to give you anyway, even if we wanted to."

Condor nodded at Magnus. "That's quite a bulge in that pouch hanging from the side of your belt. You're certain you don't have anything of value?"

Magnus drew his hulking broadsword from its sheath. "Nothing I intend to hand over to you."

"Well then, it seems we're in a predicament, aren't we?" Condor eyed Lilly again, and another smirk formed on his lips. "I'll take her."

Axel pushed between Condor and Calum. "I'll die before that happens."

"What are you, a farm boy with a sword?" Condor chuckled and sighed. "Look, I'm happy to oblige you, but—"

Axel sprang forward and lashed his sword, but Condor took to the air the instant Axel began his advance.

Axel stared up at him, bewildered. "How is he flying without a cape?"

Magnus grabbed Axel's shoulder and yanked him back toward the group. "He's a Wisp. A promoted Windgale. He no longer needs a cape to fly."

Axel twisted free from Magnus's grip and glared at Condor, who hovered about ten feet off the ground with a grin on his face.

"He's also faster than any of us," Lilly said. "Significantly faster."

"We'll see about that." Axel shifted his sword and stepped forward.

"No." Magnus pulled him back again. "We must proceed with caution, not the reckless abandon you subscribe to. If you wish to get out of here, we must fight intelligently."

"The Sobek is right, Farm Boy." Condor's right hand rested on the pommel of his sword, which still hung from his belt in its sheath. "Except for the part about getting outta here. Like I said, we'll let you pass if you give up the girl."

Calum leaned close to Lilly. "Everyone seems to want you."

She huffed. Calum was more right than he even realized. She muttered, "Believe me, I wish that wasn't the case."

"Well?" Condor tapped his pommel with his fingers and descended to the ground well out of Axel's reach. As his feet touched the path, he asked, "What's your decision?"

In one fluid motion, one Lilly had practiced thousands of times, she raised her bow, drew back her arrow, took aim, and let it fly at Condor's chest. Armor or otherwise, the arrow would at least wound him and hopefully—

Condor sidestepped the arrow as if he'd seen it coming and had a full minute to avoid it.

Instead, the arrow struck the shoulder of a Windgale behind Condor, who yelped. The Windgales around him tensed up and raised their swords, but Condor gave a whoop, and they settled back into their positions.

Lilly's gaze narrowed and her mouth opened. She'd never seen anyone dodge an arrow like that before. Then again, Condor had been the youngest Captain of the Royal Guard before he rebelled and tried to assassinate the Premier. No doubt his speed and prowess had accelerated his rise to authority.

Condor extended his index finger at her and waved it. "Not very nice of you, my dear. Didn't your parents teach you any manners?"

Lilly's jaw hardened.

"Last chance." Condor's fingers curled around the hilt of his sword, but he still didn't draw it from its sheath. "What's your play?"

"We're not handing her over," Calum said.

Condor's sword flashed as he launched toward Calum, but Magnus pulled him back and absorbed the blow on his breastplate. The next two slashes skidded off his scaled arms before Magnus could even bring his sword up. Then Condor kicked his heel into the bottom of Magnus's chin, and he staggered back.

"Run for the trees!" Magnus yelled once he recovered. He swung his sword in a wide arc around him. Condor darted out of the way, but Magnus felled two approaching Windgales with his swing.

Lilly knew she couldn't help Axel and Calum from the ground, so she took to the air, even as they called after her. "Just run! I'll cover—"

A Windgale collided with her from the side and sent her careening through the air. She righted herself, drew another arrow, and shot him down. Another Windgale lashed his sword from above her. She reacted and blocked the attack with her bow, but the blade severed its string in the process.

Lilly whipped her right leg at the Windgale's face. Her shin slammed into the side of his head, knocking him from the sky. Lilly drew her sword with her right hand and wielded her unstrung bow in her left. She zipped higher into the sky and glanced behind her as she flew.

A dozen Windgales chased after her, two-dozen went after Axel and Calum, and the rest stayed with Condor to fight Magnus, who now ran after them toward the forest. So much for trying to cover them.

She angled down and spiraled toward the ground with the Windgales close behind.

AXEL COULD BARELY RUN for all the Windgales he had to kill along the way. They kept dropping in front of him, so he kept hacking them down or avoiding them as he and Calum raced toward the forest.

Something struck his back. He toppled forward in the tall grass and skidded to a halt on his chest. Axel whirled around in time to skewer a Windgale who dropped down at him with his sword raised high, primed to deliver a killing blow. Axel grinned until a second Windgale emerged from overhead.

He tried to pull his sword free of the first Windgale in time, but by the time he managed it, the second Wingale was already on top of him.

Had Calum not sprung from the tall grass and cut him down, the second Windgale would've killed Axel with his first swing. Calum reached down and pulled Axel to his feet. "What are you just laying around for?"

"Ha, ha," Axel said. "Not funny."

A dark blur materialized behind Calum. Axel yanked on Calum's arm, pulling him forward, and jabbed his sword at the next Wingdale. The blade lodged in the Windgale's throat, and he fell flat on his face.

Calum nodded to Axel, and they kept running.

Magnus batted Windgales away as he ran. On occasion, they managed to trip him up, but by far his biggest concern was Condor.

He was not only faster than the rest of the Raven's Brood but also stronger and an extremely skilled fighter. For every swing Magnus managed, Condor threw six or seven attacks back at him.

Worse still, Magnus hadn't landed a single blow on him. Every one of his hacks either missed Condor and hit a different Windgale, or missed everything entirely. At least their puny steel swords couldn't pierce his scales, and as long as he wore his breastplate, they couldn't cut into his soft underbelly.

Far ahead, Magnus saw Axel and Calum cross into the forest. They'd find some cover there, but the numbers still favored the Windgales. They had to work together to get out of this alive.

Then Condor abandoned his onslaught and instead shot into the sky, leaving about six Windgales to pester Magnus while he ran.

When Condor didn't return, Magnus realized he was going after Lilly.

And Magnus couldn't do anything to stop him.

Lilly knew she ought to slow down before she hit the top of the forest canopy, but she didn't. The Windgales pursuing her weren't going to slow down, and that meant she couldn't, either.

She hit what looked like an opening at about half of her top speed and wove down through a network of leafy branches. They clawed at her face and hair and smacked against her shoulders as she descended toward the forest floor.

By the time she cleared the canopy, she was no longer flying, but falling. A large prickly bush cushioned her body weight and dumped her onto the forest floor where she lay sprawled on her back for a moment, until a dozen dark forms crashed through the canopy and thudded against the ground around her.

Lilly sprang to her feet and gripped her sword and bow tighter. Half of the Windgales weren't moving, but the other six slowly stood to their feet. One darted toward her and swung his sword.

It clanged against her bow, and she ran him through with her blade. As he fell, two more Windgales shot forward. Lilly ducked under one swing and parried the second with her bow, then slashed the back of the first Windgale's knee. He tumbled to the ground, clutching at his wound.

The other Windgale chopped at her again, and she parried the attack with her sword. She whipped her bow at his head, but he blocked it with his armored forearm and smirked at her—until she drove her boot into his groin. He doubled over next to his friend, and she dispatched them both with two quick swings of her sword.

Though six of the Windgales still lay unconscious on the forest floor, covered in scrapes and scratches from the trees they'd crashed through trying to follow her, the three conscious Windgales launched into the fray, weapons brandished.

For Lilly, taking on one Windgale opponent at a time was reasonable, and two was pushing it. Three wasn't something she even wanted to attempt, at least not without her bow. If she meant to get away from the Raven's Brood, she had to use the forest to her advantage.

She leaped into the air and threaded through the thick trees with the Windgales close behind.

As Axel and Calum reached the trees, the Windgales pursued them, still flying. He'd expected them to slow down some, but they flew into the forest with the kind of gusto he usually employed when he fought enemies.

"Take lots of sharp turns," Calum called to Axel. "Let the forest do the work for you."

"I know," Axel yelled back. *Obviously.*

Axel stole a quick glance over his shoulder as he ran. One of the Windgales was closing in on him with his sword extended, and fast.

Ahead of Axel, a thick branch hung just above his reach. He leaped for it, grabbed ahold, and kicked his feet up.

The Windgale behind him couldn't alter his flight path in time and zoomed under Axel's legs, and as he looked back at Axel, he smacked into the next tree at almost full speed.

Axel smirked and dropped back down to his feet.

Another Windgale zipped toward him from his left side and almost took off Axel's head with his sword, but Axel noticed in time to duck under the swing. The Windgale swung again, but Axel blocked with his sword and drove his fist into the Windgale's gut.

With the Windgale doubled over, Axel grabbed a handful of his cape and whipped him against the nearest tree. The Windgale's body cracked against the trunk, and he fell to the ground, limp.

They were quick, but lightweight, too. Kind of fun to toss 'em around just like Magnus had before the rest of them showed up.

A third Windgale cut through the canopy at him. He hopped back, and when the Windgale tried to correct his trajectory, he crashed into the tree branch that Axel had just grabbed to avoid the first Windgale.

Quick, lightweight, and apparently not too bright. Either that, or they didn't have good combat training.

The third Windgale tumbled to the ground and struggled to get back to his feet, but the pommel of Axel's sword laid him out flat.

This wasn't just kind of fun, Axel decided. He was having a blast.

CALUM RECOGNIZED the smirk on Axel's face even from twenty yards away and while dodging a haphazard swing from one of the Windgales.

He drove the tip of his sword through the Windgale's armor and into his chest, and then he ripped it out to block another blow from another Windgale. Magnus had been right—the trees had negated the Raven's Brood's advantage from a combat perspective, though the Windgales still had the numbers in their favor.

A trio of Windgales hovered toward Calum with more caution this time, but the sound of wood snapping cracked from behind them.

Magnus burst from the trees with a roar. He grabbed two of the Windgales by their capes and slammed them together, sandwiching the third Windgale in the middle. All three of them dropped.

Calum couldn't stifle a grin of his own. "Nice."

Magnus's face betrayed no such amusement. "Condor went after Lilly."

Calum's mirth fizzled, and his heart shuddered. "Which way?"

"Follow me."

LILLY HAD LOST two of the three Windgales in the forest, but the third managed to keep pace with her without colliding into any of the trees or branches. She'd taken more than a few close knocks herself, but she'd made it this far with only a few small cuts on her face and scrapes on her armored legs, arms, and torso.

She looped up toward the canopy and slowed her ascent enough to grab onto a branch. She pulled it up with her, and as soon as the Windgale came into view beneath her, she released her grip. Tension whipped the branch at the Windgale and it smacked him out of the air.

He dropped down to the forest floor, and Lilly followed him. She landed ten feet away and started toward him. As Lilly raised her sword to finish him off, the Windgale lashed his leg and swept her off her feet. Her back hit the forest floor and pushed the air out of her lungs, and her sword and bow tumbled out of her fingers.

Before she could recover, the Windgale stood over her, his wild eyes raging amid his bloodied face. He held his sword over his head. Just when Lilly thought it was all over, a dark streak flashed behind the Windgale's head, followed by a dull *thunk*. He dropped to the dirt face-first.

In his place stood Condor.

CHAPTER THIRTEEN

"There's something oddly familiar about you." Condor stepped past the Windgale and slowly approached her with his sword down. "Have we met before?"

Lilly glanced at her sword. Still out of reach, but Condor might be far enough away for her to get it in time. Maybe.

"I asked you a question, love."

"I'm not your 'love.'" Lilly glared at him.

"But I *do* know you from somewhere, don't I?" Condor asked. "From back when I was still allowed in Aeropolis, right?"

Lilly clenched her jaw. The less Condor knew about her, the better off she was...

Unless he already knew too much.

"In fact, I believe I've seen you in the Sky Fortress itself." He rubbed his chin. "Perhaps you worked there as a servant to the Premier's family?"

"Yes." Lilly feigned frustration. He was close to the truth. Too close. "That's it."

Condor grinned and nodded. His tone remained casual and conversational, despite the sword in his hand. "Born into your caste, just like me. Just like all Windgales."

"That's how it is." Lilly eyed her sword again. Without it, she stood no chance of beating him. With it, her odds improved only marginally, but it was better than nothing.

"Go ahead. Take it up. I won't try to stop you." Condor motioned toward it with his own sword. "Wouldn't be a fair fight while you're unarmed."

Lilly didn't hesitate. She zipped over to the sword and gripped it in her right hand.

"Then again, your prowess *is* impressive." Condor squinted at her. "Especially for a servant girl."

A lump arose in Lilly's throat. Did he know?

"And your armor—far too fancy for any normal servant girl. Perhaps you found it." Condor chuckled. "No, no. You *stole* it. Even better, right?"

Lilly exhaled a long breath through her nose and glared at him again. He was playing mind games on her, trying to throw her off.

"But we both know you're no servant girl, and you're certainly no thief. We both know the truth." Condor smiled and tilted his head to the side. "We both know who you *really* are."

Lilly's body moved before her mind caught up. She hurtled forward on wings of air and lashed her sword at Condor's chest, but he side-stepped and somehow sent her spiraling to the ground, all without even raising his sword.

Condor waved his finger at her as he had back when she'd shot the arrow at him. "Not very ladylike of you."

She should've known better than to attack him. Even with the sword in her hands, and even with the meager training she'd received from Magnus, Axel, and Calum over the last several weeks, what hope did she have of winning? Condor was too fast, too skilled as a fighter.

"Your skill with the bow is undeniable. Did General Balena train you himself?" Condor watched her stand up. "It was a suitable choice, given your station. Keeps you away from immediate danger. The drawback, of course, is that when it comes to close combat, your options are limited."

Lilly bit her tongue. No need to affirm his questions. Every bit of information she gave him would work against her in the future, one way or another. She longed for a functioning bow.

111

"Would you care for a lesson now?" Condor asked. "I'd be happy to teach you some techniques."

Lilly sprang into the air and dove toward him, blade first. This time, Condor batted her sword away with his blade and stepped aside. She skidded to a halt on her feet and zipped toward him again. Their blades played for a moment, and Lilly thought she was doing well—until Condor disarmed her.

He dropped the blade at his side and gave her a modest grin.

Lilly staggered back, surprised, furious, and empty-handed. She took to the air, but Condor grabbed her cape and yanked her down. Two hard strikes, one to her head and another to her leg knocked her to the ground.

She lay there in pain, stunned, but aware enough to realize she'd landed within reach of her sword.

Condor stood over her. "I had hoped to use you as leverage against the Premier, but I'm not sure you'll cooperate, so I'm giving you a choice: come with me willingly, or die."

Through her haze, Lilly scooped her sword off the ground and jabbed it at Condor's ankle, but it didn't do any good. He simply stepped over her feeble attack and put his foot on her wrist until she released her grip, then he kicked her sword away.

"I take it that's your answer?"

Lilly gave him a glare before she lay back again and exhaled a long breath. "I'm not helping you with anything."

"Such a waste." Condor sighed and shook his head, then he raised his sword.

Lilly clenched her teeth, stared at Condor, and waited for the blow to come.

It never did.

Condor lowered his sword and smiled at her. "You didn't really think I was going to do it, did you?"

Before Lilly could answer, a dark blur burst from the woods to her left, collided with Condor, and knocked him to the ground. Condor's sword clanged against a nearby tree, and the two forms tumbled along the forest floor in a flurry of charcoal armor and gray-brown fur.

Riley.

He pinned Condor to the ground with his forepaws and clamped his jaws onto Condor's left wrist. Condor yelled, then he drove his right fist into the side of Riley's head.

Riley yelped, and he released his grip on Condor, who zipped through the air toward his sword. He grasped it in his hand and whirled around, but Riley had already closed the distance and leaped at him. Riley knocked Condor onto his back again, but this time his jaws gripped Condor's right hand—his sword hand.

Lilly rose to her feet, rubbed her head, and picked up her sword amid the growls and curses. As she began to approach the skirmish, she watched Condor shift his sword to his left hand and angle it toward Riley.

"No!" Lilly shouted. She wanted to stop it from happening, but she couldn't possibly have gotten there in time.

The tip of the blade pierced Riley's fur just behind his right shoulder, and he yelped. Then Condor's sword knifed even deeper into Riley's torso.

CHAPTER FOURTEEN

Riley jerked away from Condor and staggered back with a noticeable limp, both growling and whimpering.

"Bad Wolf." Condor pushed himself up to his feet and switched his sword to his right hand again, despite the blood dripping from it. He started toward Riley again. "Bad, bad Wolf."

Riley snarled and narrowed his blue eyes at Condor. Lilly didn't know how he was even still alive, but somehow Riley shifted his weight back on his hind legs, ready to spring forward.

A mass of green plowed into Condor from the right. The impact sent him tumbling through the air, and he smacked against a thick tree then landed facedown in the dirt. He started to get up but Magnus grabbed him by his throat and pinned him against the tree.

"Try to fly away now, bird." Magnus hissed at him and cocked his arm.

"Don't!" Lilly yelled.

Magnus swiveled his head toward her and glared, but held his arm in place.

"If we bring him to the Sky Fortress, we'll—"

"He stabbed Riley. He is too dangerous to be left alive," Magnus said.

Condor clutched Magnus's wrist and squirmed in his grasp, but he couldn't escape.

"No, Magnus. Don't kill him." Lilly shook her head and started toward him, but her head still swam from Condor's blow. She stopped short and steadied herself. "He's extremely valuable to the Premier. We can use that to our advantage."

Magnus hesitated, then he lowered his other arm. "You had better be right."

Calum and Axel burst from the trees, their swords at the ready.

"There are more of them chasing us," Calum said between breaths. "We need to go deeper into the woods or they're gonna—"

Riley loosed a canine whimper and dropped onto his side. Blood trickled down the side of his right foreleg.

"Riley?" Calum ran over to him and skidded to a halt on his knees. "By the Overlord, what happened to you?"

A pair of Windgales shot out from the trees at Axel. He ducked under the first one's slash and batted the second Windgale to the ground with his sword. The first Windgale stopped short when he saw Condor in Magnus's hand.

"Tell your brood to stop the attack," Magnus said to the Windgale. "Or Condor dies."

The Windgale scowled at Magnus, then he shot up through the trees.

"They won't stop attacking unless I give the order." Condor twisted in Magnus's grip again. "They'll keep coming until they kill you and free me. We are united in our cause by blood, and we will not relent until—"

"Everyone in Aeropolis knows you're the only thing holding the Raven's Brood together," Lilly said.

She started toward them again, but her head rebelled with a spike of pain that left her dizzy. She exhaled a long breath with her eyes closed. When she regained her equilibrium again, she started toward Condor.

"You started an insurrection and tried to assassinate the Premier so you could succeed him, and when you failed, you took the survivors with you, but everyone in the Sky Fortress knows you're the only Wisp, the only real fighter out here."

Condor's dark eyebrows arched down. "You were only a child when

115

it happened, and all you know is what you've been told. I suppose I can't fault you for not knowing the truth."

Riley whimpered again.

Calum shook his head as he pulled off his gauntlets. "Guys, Riley's in bad shape here. He needs help, and I don't even know where to start."

"Put pressure on his wound. Try to stop the bleeding," Magnus said. "Lilly, go over and help Calum, and Calum, come over here with Axel to hold Condor while I tend to Riley."

"Lilly, what happened to your face?" Axel stopped his advance toward Condor and instead walked closer to her, his sword still out. "Did he hit you?"

"Axel, don't—"

Axel's gaze locked on Condor, and his face crumpled with anger. "I'm gonna cut his feather-flyin' head off."

He stormed toward Condor with bloodlust in his eyes.

"You will *not*." Magnus pointed a thick, green finger at Axel. "Lilly wants him alive to present to the Premier."

"What do you mean, 'present him to the Premier?'" Axel shouted. "He stabbed Riley and tried to kill Lilly. Look at the mark he left on her face!"

Lilly touched her cheek where Condor had struck her. It felt tender and warm to her touch—definitely a nasty bruise. "It's not bad. It won't—"

"He's dead. I'm not negotiating this time." Axel didn't stop his advance toward Condor.

Magnus whirled around and pinned Condor to the ground in front of Axel, who stopped short. Magnus hissed, then growled, "You are *not* killing him."

"He hit Lilly. I'm gonna kill him, even if that means I gotta go through you to do it."

Axel advanced again and raised his sword. Condor looked up at him from the ground, almost grinning.

"*Stop.*" Magnus's voice reverberated off the trees, and Axel halted again. "You gain *nothing* by killing this man, either in Lilly's eyes or in anyone else's."

"Guys?" Calum's voice tanged with urgency. "There's a lot of blood, and his breathing is slowing down. I—I think we're losing Riley."

Magnus locked eyes with Axel. "You need to hold Condor down with Calum so I can tend to Riley before it's too late."

"You wanna save the Wolf? Then let me kill Condor." Axel's tone matched his steely expression. "Or they can both die, for all I care."

"Axel!" Calum shouted. Blood oozed between the fingers

Lilly couldn't believe Axel had just said that. How could he be so cold?

"Make your decision, Magnus."

"Axel, don't do this," Lilly said. "I don't want this! Please—we need to save Riley!"

Axel frowned at her. "Condor needs to die."

Magnus glanced at Calum, who shook his head. "Then you leave me no choice."

Axel's eyes widened as Magnus sprang forward with Condor still in-hand. Before Axel could so much as raise his sword, Magnus drove his fist into Axel's forehead. He withered to the ground, unconscious.

"Magnus!" Calum yelled. "What are you doing?"

Magnus held Condor up in front of him and delivered a comparable blow to his head, and he too passed out. When Magnus released his grip, Condor slumped to the ground.

Magnus pointed at Lilly. "Watch them. If either of them wake up, tell me right away."

Lilly nodded, still shocked at Magnus's blow to Axel, though she couldn't rightly say it was an overreaction—not when Riley's life was on the line.

When Magnus made it to Riley, Calum stepped aside.

"I can't believe you did that," Calum said, more shock than anger in his voice.

"What would you have done differently?" Magnus pressed his hand against Riley's wound.

"I—" Calum bit his lip. "I don't know."

"Get me something I can use to bandage this wound, and hurry,"

Magnus ordered. "His breathing is very labored, and he has lost consciousness."

Calum returned with one of the dead Windgale's capes.

Magnus frowned. "This fabric is not ideal, but it will have to do. Tear it into strips for me."

Axel and Condor lay next to each other at Lilly's feet, both out cold. She'd come to recognize Axel's attraction toward her, but he'd gone too far this time. Where Calum would elect to show mercy, Axel's responses always skewed toward payback or even outright revenge.

From the pouch on his belt Magnus pulled the vial of veromine he'd used on Lilly's shoulder when they'd found her unconscious in the Golden Plains.

With great care, he dripped three delicate orange drops into Riley's wound. Magnus paused, leaned closer, and then he dumped the rest of the vial into the wound. Afterward, he wrapped the strips of cape around Riley's torso several times to cover it.

"The veromine will protect his wound from infection and aid in healing it, but he is still in serious trouble." Magnus tied the ends of the strips together under Riley's belly. "He may have already lost too much blood, and if Condor's sword hit any of his vital organs, we may be too late. We have to get him help, and soon. We have to get him to Aeropolis."

"Before the Raven's Brood attacked us you said we were a day and a half away. Does he have that long?"

"No." Magnus shook his head. "But if we hurry, we will arrive sooner. He may have a chance."

Lilly pressed her fingers against the cut on her face. The whole area stung, but she couldn't focus on that now. "I know the way. Calum, can you help me round up as many of these Raven's Brood capes as we can? The Premier will want to know how many we defeated."

Calum looked at Magnus, who nodded. "Sure, I can help."

"I will stay with Riley and these two." Magnus squinted at Axel. "I expect Axel will awaken soon. I did not hit him that hard."

WHILE CALUM DIDN'T like how Magnus's solution for traveling with a flight-capable prisoner had played out, he couldn't deny its effectiveness.

Magnus carried Riley, still unconscious, in his arms as they rushed toward Aeropolis, while Calum and a surly unarmed Axel walked on either side of Condor, to whom they were both tied. Lilly hovered behind them with her sword out, ready to cut Condor down if he tried anything.

Cords tied in tight knots restrained Condor's wrists behind his back, and a rope stretched between his ankles, both of which were tied so he could only jog at best. Another rope looped between his back and over the front of his elbows.

One end was tied to Calum's belt, and the other was tied to Axel's belt. That way, if he tried to fly away, he'd have to carry Calum and Axel with him.

They had stripped Condor's armor from him and left it in the forest along with his sword. Now the only thing that indicated he was a member of the Raven's Brood at all was a necklace made of delicate silver chain with a black-and-red raven pendant hanging from it.

They trudged ahead and pressed onward throughout the night, stopping for only minutes to eat and shift loads around. Calum bore both the extra burden of carrying Axel's sword and a sack stuffed full of the Raven's Brood capes that he and Lilly had collected.

Given their quickened speed and not stopping overnight, the day-and-a-half trip to Aeropolis only took a day. Even so, Calum worried they still might be too late to help Riley. He was still alive, albeit only barely, but he hadn't woken up since he'd lost consciousness back in the woods.

Soon the Windgale city of Aeropolis towered overhead, but even from a distance Calum could only see glimpses of something sparkling from among the clouds. A network of thick gray pillars lofted the city far out of reach of anyone who lacked flight ability.

As a means of defense, it was ingenious in its simplicity. If the Windgales had enemies, they would have to learn to fly before they could mount a successful attack, or they'd have to possess a power capable of taking down the pillars that held the city up.

But Calum couldn't conceive of anything that powerful, except perhaps Lumen, and even then, Calum didn't know for sure what Lumen was capable of. They'd only ever interacted in dreams.

"So... how are we supposed to get up there?" Axel asked, his voice flat but still edged with fury.

"There's a lift that lowers to ground level three times a day for merchants and travelers," Lilly replied.

"When are the three times?" Calum asked.

"Once in the early morning, another around midday, and once more in the evening, but we already missed the morning lift."

"We do not have time to wait for the lift. Riley's condition is still deteriorating." Magnus glared at Condor, who rolled his eyes. "Is there something we can do about that?"

Lilly shook her head. "We can talk to the guard at the lift and ask him, but they rarely make exceptions. Premier's orders."

Condor huffed.

"You got somethin' to say?" Axel turned to him, his fury partially renewed.

"Not in the least, Farm Boy." Condor shook his head and stared up at the clouds shielding the bottom of Aeropolis from view.

Axel positioned himself in front of Condor and leaned forward. "Good. You don't speak unless we speak to you. And stop calling me 'Farm Boy.' I haven't worked on a farm for a long time now. Crystal?"

Condor lowered his gaze to Axel's eyes. "You talk pretty big for a Farm Boy whose hands are tied behind his back."

"Stop it, you two," Calum said.

Axel leaned even closer to Condor. "Just wait until my hands are untied. Then you'll see what this Farm Boy can—"

Condor bashed his forehead into Axel's nose, then he jumped into the air and kicked both of his feet at Axel's chest. Axel landed on his back in the dirt and before Calum could subdue him, Condor zipped into the sky with his limbs still bound.

CHAPTER FIFTEEN

Calum yanked on the rope, but Condor was too strong. He pulled Calum off his feet, and the rope slipped through his fingers. Had the rope not been tied to Calum's and Axel's belts, Condor would've escaped.

From his vantage point on the ground, Calum saw Lilly take to the sky and lash her sword at Condor. He easily dodged the blow, and the tension in the rope jerked Calum onto his stomach. Two green, scaly feet planted just in front of Calum's face.

Calum rolled over, and Magnus grasped the rope and give it a sharp yank. Condor dropped from the sky, and his back smacked against the dirt. Calum drew his sword, scrambled over to Condor, and pressed the blade against his neck.

"Don't move."

"Wouldn't dream of it." Condor coughed and grunted, but didn't resist.

Lilly landed next to Riley, who lay on the ground, still unconscious but drawing shallow breaths.

"I'm gonna *kill* you," Axel growled. Blood oozed from his nose and down his chin as he stormed over to Condor.

Magnus clamped his hand on the front collar of Axel's breastplate and held him in place. "No, you will not."

"Get your hand off me." Axel twisted free from Magnus's grip, his arms still bound. "You knocked me out, took my sword, and tied me up like a prisoner to spare *his* life. You have no right to—"

"I did what was necessary at the time," Magnus growled. "If you expect an apology, prepare yourself for an eternity of waiting."

"Someday, Magnus," Axel warned. "Someday you won't be able to push me around."

Magnus grabbed Axel by his shoulders and pulled him close. In low, even tones, he said, "You were willing to sacrifice Riley's life to kill Condor. Would you sacrifice my life? Lilly's life? Calum's life? Your *own* life?"

Axel's jaw hardened, but to his credit, he didn't reply.

"You said I had no right to do to you what I did. I could have just killed you instead, and then you would not have had the *privilege* of enduring this conversation with me." Magnus's golden eyes blinked. "*You* have no right to wager others' lives for your own personal gain or to satisfy your own impulses. Someday someone might try to sacrifice *you* on a whim. We will see then how you react to it."

"Guys, we really need to get Riley help more than we need to argue," Lilly said.

Magnus released his grip on Axel and returned to retrieve Riley. He asked Lilly, "Can you get us up there?"

Lilly exhaled a long sigh and stared up at the Aeropolis. "I can try. Follow me."

Calum pulled Condor up to his feet and checked his bonds. He smacked Axel on the back of his left shoulder in a gesture of camaraderie, but Axel shrugged away from him. Calum decided to leave him alone for the time being.

Together, the bound trio hurried after Lilly and Magnus toward the base of the foremost pillar. As they approached, Calum noticed a long line of people.

"Lilly?" he called. "Are all those people trying to get up to Aeropolis?"

She nodded as she walked. "Most of them are poor, destitute

Windgales who don't have capes and can't fly up to the city. This road is lined with beggars and the occasional thief, so watch yourselves."

The closer they got to the base of the pillar, the more people materialized ahead of them, though not all of them stood in line. Many just sat alongside the road, often wearing nothing but rags for clothing.

At one spot, four smiling children chased each other around a pair of adults sitting in front of a dark-green tent. Unlike the children, both of the parents wore sullen expressions. The female adult, probably fifteen years older than Calum, met his gaze with sad brown eyes and a frown.

Calum broke eye contact with her and trotted up next to Lilly. "Why don't any of them have capes?"

She shook her head. "If you break a law in Aeropolis, one of the punishments is defrocking—the removal of one's cape. Some Windgales are born into families who don't have capes. Others can't find work in Aeropolis or nearby, and they end up selling their capes to make ends meet."

"What does it matter if they sell their capes? Can't they just find a new piece of fabric and use that?" Axel asked. His nose seemed to have stopped bleeding by now.

Calum raised an eyebrow. At least Axel was saying something.

"Not all fabric can be used for capes," Lilly said. "It needs to be made of Aerosilk, like mine, or at the very least a blended fabric that is mostly Aerosilk. The Sky Realm has suffered an Aerosilk shortage over the last decade, so the number of capes produced has dwindled, and they certainly don't last forever."

Calum glanced back at the Windgale woman. She no longer looked at him, but instead hung her head and stared at the ground. "Why don't Wisps like Condor need capes?"

"That—" Lilly hesitated. "—is a mystery to me. Only Wisps know, and only the premier or one of his officers can promote a Windgale, and they only do that when the Windgale is deemed ready."

Condor scoffed. "It's all about control."

Calum and Lilly turned to look at him.

"What do you know of it?" Axel sneered. "You're a traitor."

Condor's blue eyes narrowed. "I happened to be the Captain of the

Royal Guard, and one of fewer than a hundred Wisps throughout the entirety of Kanarah. I know the Sky Fortress's secrets. What do *you* know of it?"

Axel's jaw tensed.

"Like I was saying, it's all about control." Condor tilted his head and smirked at Lilly. As uncomfortable as it made Calum feel, it must've been ten times worse for Lilly.

She turned away from him and kept walking forward.

"The Premier is greedy. He's content to keep the poor in their caste and the wealthy in theirs," Condor continued. "Everyone in between works to satisfy the needs of the wealthy and the royal family. There's no room for advancement, no opportunity for anyone low-born to—"

"Then how do you account for yourself?" Lilly whirled around. "You have no right to make such accusations when you rose from nothing to the Captain of the Royal Guard as quickly as you did."

"I am an anomaly, to be sure." Condor showed off his white smile. "As are you."

Lilly extended her index finger toward his face. "Axel was right. You know nothing. You're as selfish as you claim the Premier to be."

"Am I? I could have revealed the Wisps' secrets to all of my men, but I didn't. And there are other secrets I could still reveal, but I haven't."

"That's because you wanted to have control over—" A realization widened Lilly's eyes, then she glared at Condor and turned back around and walked, her pace quicker than before.

Condor smirked again, and Calum wanted to backhand the expression right off his face.

As much as he'd been horrified at the cost Axel was willing to pay to kill Condor, Calum had to admit he understood Axel's rage. Every time he saw the bruise on Lilly's face, now somewhat faded, or a smug expression curling Condor's lips, he considered trying to teach the Wisp a lesson as well, but always he held back.

They continued to walk past multiple Windgales and their ramshackle homes. Some of them even looked semi-permanent.

Calum tilted his head. "Why don't we give the capes we confiscated from the Raven's Brood to some of these people?"

Lilly and Magnus stopped and turned back to face him.

"We have their leader," Calum said. "What do we need the capes for?"

Magnus nodded to Lilly. "It is an act of pure kindness. It will cost us nothing to do so, except time, but we may be waiting for awhile anyway. Perhaps you can proceed ahead and try to secure a way up?"

"I can do that. The Premier does really only care about Condor." Lilly's sullen expression melted into a guarded grin, which she directed at Calum. "You never cease to amaze me."

Calum returned her smile with one of his own. The compliment, especially coming from her, felt amazing. "I'm glad you, uh—you think so."

"Stay near Magnus and Condor. I'll fly up to the city and try to convince them to send the lift down." Lilly floated over to Condor and yanked the black-and-red raven pendant from his neck in one sharp jerk. "I suppose I'll need this to prove we actually have you, won't I?"

Condor chuckled at her. "It's a start, but I doubt you'll need it. I'm sure you can be very *persuasive* when you want to be."

Axel's boot lashed at Condor's shin from the side, and Condor toppled forward onto the ground. Axel followed the trip with a swift kick to Condor's ribs that left him gasping. "Do *not* talk to her like that."

"Axel—" Lilly started.

Just as Axel reeled his leg back for another blow, Calum stepped between them. "Enough, Axel. Enough."

Condor wheezed, then grunted. Calum tried to help him up to his feet, but Condor shook him away, hovered off the ground, and landed upright. He spat on the ground at Axel's feet.

"A day is coming when we will meet under different circumstances, Farm Boy," Condor said between ragged coughs. "And on that most glorious day, I will kill you."

Axel stepped forward, though not as close as he had last time. "I'm looking forward to it."

"I said that's *enough*." Calum pulled Axel away and started untying his bonds. He nodded to Lilly, who took off into the sky. "I'm untying you because I need your help handing these capes out. You and I will distribute them, and Magnus will watch Condor and Riley. If you try anything, Magnus will put you out again. Crystal?"

Axel's eyes narrowed at him. He didn't answer for a long moment as he searched Calum's gaze, then he finally replied, "Clear."

Calum let Axel's rope drop to the dirt, handed him the pack of capes, and tied Condor to Magnus before he untied himself. "Come on. Let's hand these out."

They left Magnus, Condor, and Riley behind and headed to the nearest capeless Windgale, a middle-aged man with a graying beard and brown rags for clothes.

Calum swallowed the lump in his throat and pulled a cape from the bag, which Axel held. Why did he feel embarrassed about this? He was about to do an awkward, somewhat foreign thing by giving these people a second chance at a life—at freedom.

In a lot of ways, it had been easier for Calum to agree to help Reginia, Stavian, and the people of Pike's Garrison by ridding them of the bandits plaguing their village than it was to step up to this haggard Windgale and offer him help. But Calum did it anyway.

"Excuse me, sir?" he said.

The Windgale man's weary eyes fixed on Calum. "Yeah?"

"I have something for you." Calum extended the cape to him.

The Windgale man glanced between Calum and the cape, then he looked back at Calum again. He scratched his scruffy neck. "This some sorta joke?"

Calum shook his head. "No joke. This belongs to you now. It's got Aerosilk in it."

After a moment of hesitation, the Windgale man snatched the cape from Calum's hand, slung it over his back, then fastened it to his ragged shirt.

"I don't know how long it's been since you last flew," Calum said. "But I imagine you may need some time to reacquaint yourself to—"

"Wahooooo!" The Windgale man rocketed into the air in a wild spiral toward the sun. He curved his trajectory into three large loops, all the while hooting and hollering as if he'd never flown before in his life, but flying like he'd never stopped.

Axel huffed. "Well, at least someone's happy."

The Windgales around them on the ground level pointed up at the Windgale man and began to murmur. Some even cast guarded glances at Calum and Axel.

"Come on," Calum said to Axel. "We're gonna get rid of these things and help some people."

Calum knifed his way through the muttering crowd of Windgales that had formed to watch the spectacle in the sky, and he began handing capes out to anyone who made eye contact with him. Soon enough the crowd's focus shifted to Axel and Calum, and they all began begging and reaching toward them.

Calum distributed capes freely until he got down to his final two capes. Rather than giving them away at random, he headed back the way they'd come.

"Why are we backtracking?" Axel called from behind him.

"There's someone I need to give a cape to. Someone I saw earlier."

Calum emerged from the edge of the crowd and saw the Windgale woman who'd stared at him when he'd walked past. Her head still hung down.

Calum approached her and touched her shoulder with his hand. "Excuse me?"

She looked up at him with those sad brown eyes. The crowd behind Calum stopped behind them and fell silent.

Calum held a cape out for her. "This is for you."

She blinked at him, then she stared at the cape in his hands. The kids who'd been chasing each other around her tent stopped when they saw Calum. Their mouths hung open when they saw the cape in his hands.

"Go on. Take it. Fly again." Calum smiled at her.

The woman glanced at the ground, then at the cape, then she reached out and took it. Her brown eyes filled with tears, and she looked up at Calum again. In a voice so quiet that Calum could barely hear it at all, she said, "Thank you."

Calum's heart ached for her. Did all rulers treat their subjects this way? Was the Premier just the Windgale version of the King?

"You're welcome." He nodded to her, then he pulled the last

remaining cape from the pouch in Axel's hands and extended it to the man who stood next to her. "Here. You can have this one."

The man shook his head and held up his hands. "I can't use it. I'm not a Windgale, but thank you anyway."

Calum tilted his head, and his gaze drifted between the kids and the woman, then back to the man. "Aren't you two—together?"

The man nodded. "Robynn is my wife, but I'm not a Windgale. I'm a human, like you two."

"And these are—your kids?" Axel asked.

The man smiled. "They are. Beautiful, aren't they?"

"Yes, very." Calum smiled. "So could one of them use the cape?"

"Children of Windgales and humans typically don't have flight ability," the man replied. "One is more than enough blessing for our family. You've given us our lives back. Give that last cape to another family and do the same for them. Thank you again."

Calum nodded and turned to face the crowd of Windgales waiting behind him and Axel.

"We've already given out almost thirty capes. There has to be at least a hundred more Windgales here, and we've only got one left." Axel tossed the bag aside and approached Calum. He lowered his voice. "You shoulda let me bring my sword. This could get ugly."

Calum smacked Axel's armored chest with the back of his hand. "Why do you always assume the worst about people? They're poor and hungry, just like I was. What if you had assumed the worst about me?"

Axel scoffed and folded his arms. "I'm beginning to think I should've."

Still, Axel had a point. With so great a need and only one cape left, how could Calum possibly choose just one person? He wanted to help them all.

Someday he would. Someday, after he freed Lumen, Calum would set things right. He didn't know how, but with Lumen on his side, there had to be a way.

He placed the cape in the hands of the Windgale nearest to him, then he backed up a step. Unlike what Axel had thought, the crowd did not rush forward and attack them, but unlike what Calum expected, they did not immediately disperse, either. Instead, they stood there, every set of eyes on Calum.

"What's your name, friend?" the man behind him asked.

Calum turned halfway back. "I'm Calum. This is Axel."

The man nodded. "Name's Bowman. You've already met Robynn, and these are our children, Rexane, Starrie, Luce, and Arquelle."

Calum smiled at them. "Pleasure. Now if you'll excuse me, I need to—"

"Let's hear it for Calum," Bowman called to the crowd. "Calum the Deliverer!"

The crowd crooned a loud whoop, all in unison, that reminded Calum of a type of bird he'd heard on warm mornings back at the quarry. He'd never learned that type of bird's name, but it had always reminded him that life wasn't always full of only bad things. Perhaps this was his chance to serve as such a reminder for many others.

When he looked at the crowd again, every single one of them had bowed their heads, but held their hands up against their chests. Their wrists crossed, their thumbs joined in the center and pointed up at their chins, and their fingers angled up and out toward their shoulders like the wings of a bird.

"I've seen that motion before," Calum said.

"Yeah." Axel folded his arms. "Condor did it when he introduced himself."

"It's a salute. Windgales salute those whom they owe respect, whether they be nobility, or royalty, or simply in a higher caste." Bowman smiled and motioned toward Calum and Axel with his hand. "Or emissaries of generosity, like yourselves. It is an act of submission."

Calum leaned closer to him. "Am I supposed to do it back?"

Bowman nodded. "Yes, but do not bow. Only bow if you initiate the salute."

Calum mimicked the salute with his hands on his chest but didn't bow, just as Bowman said. Axel just stood there, his arms still folded. Calum wanted to smack him for it.

Just when Calum wasn't sure if he should stop saluting or not,

Magnus's voice parted the crowd with an obvious tone of urgency. "Calum, Axel. Come quickly."

"What is it?" Calum asked.

Even from far away Calum could see Magnus towering over the Windgale crowd as he worked his way toward them. He no longer carried Riley in his arms, but he pulled Condor behind him in tow.

"I fear we may be too late," Magnus said. "Riley stopped breathing."

CHAPTER SIXTEEN

By the time Calum and Axel made it back to Riley, Lilly still hadn't returned. Just as Magnus had said, Riley no longer drew breath.

Calum caught his hands shaking. He still hadn't put his gauntlets back on after pressing his hands against Riley's bloody wound. Though he'd tried to wash them off at a stream along the way to Aeropolis, sticky bits of dried blood still clung to the creases on his knuckles, between his fingers, and under his fingernails.

"There's no time." Calum clasped his hands together to keep them from shaking and to calm himself enough to try to think rationally. Panicking on Riley's behalf wouldn't save him. "We need to get him to the lift."

"What if Lilly can't get it to lower?" Axel asked.

"We'll figure something out. We have to. Riley can't die."

"It may already be too late for that." Magnus's voice rang hollow.

"We have to try. Pick him up and follow me."

"Excuse me?" a voice behind Calum called.

Calum glanced back. It was Bowman.

"I'm sorry, Bowman. I don't have time to talk." Calum refocused on Magnus.

"Calum the Deliverer," Bowman said. "Let us help you."

Calum turned back around. "Help us how?"

Bowman pulled an older Windgale close, one to whom Calum had given a cape. "This is Kanton. He used to shepherd the royal flocks. He can help your friend."

Axel stepped forward, towering over both Bowman and Kanton. "How?"

Kanton tilted his graying head and rolled up his ragged sleeves. "In the thirty years I served the Premier, I saved the lives of countless livestock from wounds and illnesses of all kinds."

"Riley's a Wolf, not livestock." Axel folded his arms.

Calum wondered why Axel had decided to care about Riley now, all of a sudden. It grated on him, but to his credit, Axel was asking fair and helpful questions.

"Saved a few dozen of them too, if I recall. We're all more or less the same on the inside. It's knowing how to fix things that matters." His blue eyes centered on Calum. "You gave me a second shot at life when you gave me this cape. Perhaps I can return the favor for your friend, here. What do you say?"

"Do it." Calum pulled Axel aside and led Kanton over to Riley. About half the crowd of Windgales swarmed around them.

"Please step back and give me some room to work." Kanton waved them away.

Magnus stepped close to Calum. "He seems capable."

Calum glanced at Kanton, who hunched over Riley with his fingers in the fur on Riley's chest. "I hope so, for Riley's sake."

Axel's cold stare focused on something over Calum's shoulder, and Calum traced his gaze back to Condor. Still bound and tethered to Magnus, he sat on the ground with his legs crossed, leaning forward.

"He's breathing again," Kanton said.

Calum whirled around. Sure enough, Riley drew short, faint breaths, but his eyes remained closed. "How did you do that?"

"His heart stopped," Kanton explained. "I pumped his chest a few times to get it going again."

"That's what the man from Jake's crew did to Lilly and you," Calum said to Axel.

He nodded. "Yeah."

Calum turned to Kanton again. "Can you heal him?"

Kanton shook his head. "Not without proper tools. And medicine. We don't have much to work with here outside Aeropolis. Even then, I don't know. He's hurt pretty bad."

A soft double-thump sounded next to Calum, and Lilly stepped into his line of sight.

"I couldn't convince them to lower the lift," she said. "They won't do it, even though we have Condor."

Calum's gut seized. "Then Riley's gonna die."

"He doesn't have to die," Kanton said. "You just gave us capes. We can take him up there, and you too."

"You'd do that?" Calum asked.

Kanton smiled and faced the crowd. "What do you say, Windgales?"

The Windgales with capes stepped forward from the crowd. They saluted Kanton as they had to Calum only a few minutes before and let out the same whoop.

"You're really gonna carry us up there?" Axel raised an eyebrow, then eyed Magnus. "*All* of us?"

"If we have to, we'll make a separate trip for the mighty Saurian, but I don't think we'll need to." Kanton raised his arms and motioned toward Calum and his friends.

The Windgales with capes approached. Two of them hooked their arms under Calum's, and a third grabbed him around his waist. They lifted him off the ground and did the same thing to Axel.

It took nine Windgales to even get Magnus off the ground plus six more of them to get him airborne, partially because he refused to release Condor from his grip. Six more Windgales, including Kanton, lifted Riley with obvious care and began their ascent toward Aeropolis.

"You'd better not drop me," Axel grunted at the Windgales who lifted him.

The ground dropped away from Calum's feet, and he almost left the contents of his stomach behind as well, but at least he was going up this time instead of falling with Lilly's help—over a shark-infested lake.

When the Windgales ascended above the clouds and Calum got his first glimpse of Aeropolis, his lungs failed him.

Dozens of crystalline blue spires jutted into the sky, each of them shimmering in the sunlight. Some towered above others, some clustered together, and all of them encircled a palatial structure that consisted of at least eight spires, each of them tipped with gold points. It had to be the Sky Fortress.

Whether one spire or many, each structure extended from gleaming silver platforms atop the thick gray pillars Calum had seen from the ground.

As they approached, Calum noticed that none of the platforms connected to each other. No bridges stretched between them, nor any walkways. Each platform stood free, on its own. Windgales flitted between the spires and platforms like hornets darting between sparkling nests.

Why walk between platforms when you can fly? Calum mused.

He found his breath again and exhaled a sigh of wonderment as the three Windgales landed with him on the nearest silver platform. A thick, but solitary spire pricked the sky before him. Lilly landed beside him.

"You're from *here?*" Calum sucked in another deep breath, but it didn't satisfy his lungs like it should have, so he sucked in another.

She smiled and nodded. "Yes. Beautiful, isn't it?"

Calum granted himself another long survey and cleared his throat. He rubbed his arms. Even with his armor on, he could tell the temperature had dropped substantially the higher they'd ascended, despite the clarity of the sky and the burning sun that seemed nearer than it ever had before.

"That's an understatement," he replied.

"Alright, put me down. Put me *down.*" Axel's feet touched the platform just ahead of where Calum and Lilly had landed, and he shrugged out of the Windgales' grips. He shivered and exhaled a vaporous breath. "Finally."

"It's—it's harder to breathe up here for some reason." Calum inhaled another long unsatisfying breath.

"The air is thinner this high up. A lot thinner. Until you get used to it, you'll tire much faster, you might get headaches or nauseated, and you may even pass out." Lilly patted Calum's shoulder. "Just don't get into any fights while you're up here, and you should be fine."

Calum huffed, and it came out as a cloud of vapor, just like Axel's words had. "I'll try not to."

"If you start feeling lightheaded, there's a trick we teach to visitors that might help you." Lilly held her hand up to her mouth, fingers together, and pressed the side of her index finger against her lips. "Position your hand under your nose, like this, and inhale a breath through your mouth. It doubles the air pressure of your breath as you take it in. Sometimes it helps, and other times it doesn't do anything."

Calum squinted at her, but he tried it. His lungs definitely filled up faster, but he couldn't tell if it did much to help his breathing. "Thanks. I'll keep that in mind."

"These towers are all made of the same blue crystal." Lilly motioned to the spire in front of them. "Several millennia past, it used to be common on both sides of Kanarah, but when my people built Aeropolis, we used almost all of it. Now it's as rare as gold, and almost as valuable."

"Why did they choose crystal?" Axel asked. "I can see through most of it. There's no privacy."

"It's a tradeoff," Lilly said. "With less air up here, it's also much cooler."

"No kidding." Axel huffed another plume of vapor.

"By using crystal, we've created a means to trap the sun's warmth inside without letting it out as quickly," Lilly continued. "If someone wants privacy they have but to enter a spire's inner room. Those are usually made of opaque building materials."

Nearby, the fifteen Windgales who carried Magnus deposited him on the platform, and he set Condor down on his feet.

"Good to be home," Condor muttered.

Axel grabbed his rope and gave it a tug. "Not for long, I suspect."

"I wouldn't hold onto that too tightly." Condor smirked. "If I take off again and you're holding on—well, it's a long way down, Farm Boy, and you look like the type who would splatter instead of bounce."

Axel released the rope and glared at Condor.

135

Magnus opened his arms to receive Riley from the six Windgales who'd brought him up, then he focused on Kanton, who waved the rest of the Windgales away. "Which way do we go now?"

Kanton motioned toward the nearest spire. "Follow me."

The spire didn't have a door—just a large hole at its base. As they walked inside, Calum caught himself marveling at the inside of the spire just as much as he had on the outside.

The blue crystal glistened all the way to the top of the spire, which had to reach a hundred feet tall, if not more. Several hallways snaked off in different directions inside, and half of them had translucent walls.

About ten paces inside the entrance, a Windgale sat at an oak table. She wore a white cape and a matching robe with red accents and scribbled on a piece of parchment with a quill. A pair of spectacles, blue like the crystal all around her, perched so close to the end of her pointed nose that Calum didn't know how they even stayed on her face at all.

As they approached, she scanned Kanton from head to toe with one eyebrow raised. "May I help you?"

"With respect, Madame." Kanton showed her the Windgale salute and bowed low. "I humbly request that you provide us with aid. My friends have a wounded companion in need of serious medical attention."

The woman's head recoiled a few inches, not unlike a bird's head would bob backward. Though she was thin, the action created a double-chin effect on her neck. "What seems to be the problem?"

Kanton motioned toward Riley, whom Magnus still held. "This Wolf was stabbed in his side and is dying. He needs attention immediately."

"We will gladly help him." If she had intended to express any enthusiasm, her tone failed to indicate it.

She picked up a small crystal bell on her table and gave it four distinct jingles. Four Windgale men, also clad in white robes with red accents, emerged from one of the hallways with a white board.

"Take the Wolf into chamber sixteen and notify Lord Elmond that he is needed immediately," the woman said.

The four men nodded and approached Magnus, who carefully set Riley on the board. As quickly as they had arrived, they vanished into one of the hallways. When Calum started after them, the Windgale woman held up her hand.

"Staff only, I'm afraid. No visitors are allowed beyond this point without authorization."

Calum wanted to say something, but Kanton gave him a reassuring nod. Instead, he approached the table. "How much do we owe you for your help?"

The Windgale woman recoiled her head again, and her double chin reappeared. "*Owe* us? Sir, we offer complimentary aid. Anyone in need may partake in our healing works."

Calum cracked a smile. He never would have guessed that based on her attitude. "Thank you."

"I'm happy to stay here and wait for word on your friend." Kanton nodded toward Condor. "I'm sure you have somewhere you need to take him in the meantime."

Calum extended his hand to Kanton. "Thank you, Kanton. We're indebted to you for this."

Kanton shook his hand then gave him the Windgale salute again. "No. It is I who am still indebted to you. Now and forever, Calum the Deliverer. Go, take your prisoner before the Premier. I imagine he'll have nearly as many praises for you as I do."

Calum returned the salute, and then turned to Lilly. "The platforms aren't connected. How do we get across to the Sky Fortress?"

She showed him a smirk. "I'll take care of that."

"That's what you said about the lift, too," Axel muttered.

"This time I mean it," she countered. "We didn't have enough time before."

"Whatever the case, we need to get you back to your parents soon." Magnus tugged Condor close. "I imagine they will be delighted to see you returned safely."

"*Thrilled*, I'm sure," Condor said.

Lilly shot him a glare, then she refocused on Calum. "Give me a minute, and I'll be back."

She zipped out the spire's entrance and disappeared into the sky, leaving the guys alone with Condor.

"You know, it's not too late to set me free." Condor smirked at Calum.

"You shouldn't have attacked us," Calum said. "If you had let us pass, the Raven's Brood would still be at full strength, and you'd still be a free man."

"We would have overcome you had it not been for the Sobek," Condor said. "I'll admit I made a tactical error in attacking you with your big green friend here. He's the only reason the rest of you aren't all dead."

Axel huffed. "You're giving him too much credit, if you ask me."

"Except I *didn't* ask you." Condor's vivid blue eyes centered on Axel, and he displayed a polite grin.

Axel steeled his voice. "We did just fine without Magnus. I took out ten of your men with barely so much as a scratch on my armor."

Condor rolled his eyes. "As I said before, I look forward to the day when you and I get to cross blades again."

Axel's eyes narrowed. "Likewise."

Magnus stepped between them. "We will see what the Premier says. Until then, no blades will cross."

"Speaking of which, when are you gonna give me my sword back?" Axel asked.

It was a fair question, but Calum looked at Magnus.

"Not until Condor is in the Premier's custody," Magnus said.

Lilly drifted back inside the spire. "Come on out. Ride's waiting."

Calum followed Axel and Lilly outside with Magnus and Condor in the rear. There on the platform sat two large boxes, each big enough to hold a half-dozen people, and each adorned with gold edging and embellishments. Eight rods, two on each of its four sides, extended out from the boxes. Two teams of eight large Windgale men in vibrant purple armor with white capes stood nearby.

"What is this?" Axel asked.

"They're Aeropolis's shuttle service. They get visitors from place to place in these chariots," Lilly replied.

Axel closed his eyes and rubbed his forehead. "This is the only way over?"

"I fear I must agree with Axel's query in this case," Magnus said. "It took sixteen Windgales to carry me up here, but now eight of them can supposedly carry me to the other platforms in a box?"

"They can, and they will." Lilly nodded. "Don't worry about it. This is what they do, all day, every day."

Magnus's brow furrowed, but he relented. "If you insist."

A long sigh escaped Axel's mouth. "Fine. Let's go."

Calum and Axel took one of the chariots, and Magnus and Condor boarded the other. The trip to the fortress lasted only a few minutes, but it gave Calum another chance to absorb Aeropolis's splendor. Even in his wildest imagination, he never could've conceived of a place like this.

The Sky Fortress towered above all the other spires by at least a few hundred feet, and its silver platform would have more than filled the King's quarry back in Eastern Kanarah. Its spires' golden tips glinted with yellow sunlight, making it look more like a crown than a building.

More Windgales in bright purple armor zipped around the exterior of the Sky Fortress. Wisps, who always wore armor a much darker shade of purple and with no capes, flew past less frequently, but they were still more common here than anywhere else Calum had ever been.

More interesting still, not all of the soldiers were men. Calum noticed several Windgales with long, flowing hair and rose-colored armor among the purple shades.

The chariots landed on the front of the Sky Fortress platform, and the Windgales stepped aside. Though also made of crystal, the fortress's walls lacked both the translucent quality and the easy access of the other spires. Two guards in vivid orange armor with purple accents and capes stood on each side of a large double-door made of polished brass. Each of them held a long spear.

"What now? Do we just walk in?" Axel stepped out of the chariot.

"Follow me." Lilly started toward the brass doors, and the guys followed her. As she approached, the guards moved to the doors and opened them without so much as a word.

Calum looked at Axel, who shrugged, then he glanced at Condor. That same familiar smirk formed on his lips, and he raised a dark eyebrow.

It bothered Calum. Why wasn't he more nervous? If what Lilly had said about him was true, he should've been terrified of coming back here. So why wasn't he?

The interior of the Sky Fortress resembled that of the medical spire they'd just left, except more opulent. Crystal chandeliers hung from the lobby's lofted ceiling, and brass torches, all unlit, adorned the walls along with matching flower pots, each of them stuffed with colorful flora.

White marble floors stretched throughout the space, and one central staircase spiraled upward in the center, no doubt a convenience for non-flying visitors. Grand hallways lined with blue crystal, gold, silver, and marble emptied out of the lobby to the left and to the right.

While the Windgales outside the fortress darted around as if in a constant state of hurry, those inside the fortress floated through its halls at their leisure. About half of them wore armor and carried weapons of one sort or another, and the other half wore fine robes similar to those of the Windgale woman who had received Riley in the first spire.

Many of them regarded Calum and his friends with raised eyebrows and wide eyes as they walked through the fortress, but almost every person they passed stared at Lilly in total wonder.

Calum noticed, but he didn't know what that meant.

"Come on," Lilly said. "It's this way."

Lilly led them around the staircase toward another set of doors, these made out of a deep brown wood and set into a wall made of opaque blue crystal. Two guards in familiar orange armor and wielding spears squinted at her, then they quickly moved to open the doors. Their eyes widened, though, when they noticed Condor walking between Magnus, Calum, and Axel.

Something definitely wasn't right.

At first Calum had attributed the looks they'd been given to Condor, but it wasn't by his authority—or infamy—that the doors continued to open for them as they headed deeper and deeper within the fortress.

They walked through a final set of doors made of black steel, and guarded by two Wisps in dark-purple armor, into the largest room of them all so far. Instead of crystal walls, dark metal formed the room's perimeter. Two rows of marble pillars, white and colossal, outlined the main walkway and reached up at least two hundred feet to the ceiling.

In the center of the walkway at the far end of the room, two Wisps in dark purple armor flanked both sides of a throne made of the same blue crystal and adorned with gold. Another Wisp with long blond hair stood just to the throne's right. He wore dark gray armor the shade that Condor's had been.

And there, on the throne, sat the Premier of the Sky Realm.

A network of angular yellow crystals connected by blue threads adorned the top of his white robe. A crown, also made of yellow crystal, reached up in multiple symmetric points from atop the Premier's head. His white hair and beard betrayed his youthful face and bright blue eyes.

As they approached, the Wisp in the charcoal-colored armor grinned at Lilly like a handsome idiot, but her only response to him was a curt nod.

Then the Premier stood and fixed his eyes on Lilly. "You're late."

Calum glanced at her, then at Axel, whose face mirrored Calum's own befuddlement.

"I'm sorry." Lilly performed the Windgale salute then knelt down with her head bowed. "It's good to be home, Father."

CHAPTER SEVENTEEN

"*W*hat?" Axel's question split the silence and echoed throughout the throne room, but he didn't care. "You're the Premier's daughter?"

Lilly stood upright and stared at him. "Yes, I—"

"So this whole time you've been with us," Axel interrupted, "you've been lying to us?"

"I never once lied to you," Lilly replied. "I said I left my home and my parents in the Sky Realm."

"But not that you were the Premier's *daughter*." Axel squeezed his fists tight.

Why had she lied to him? This changed everything. When she was just a normal Windgale, he thought he might've had a shot at being with her, at least once he got Calum out of the way. Now, though…

"Not telling you I was the Premier's daughter is not the same as lying." Lilly glanced at Calum, who squinted at her, then she refocused on Axel. "Mostly. I didn't know for sure if I could trust you guys until we made it here and I knew I was safe."

Axel's eyes widened. "After everything we did for you, after all the times we saved you from danger, you *still* didn't trust us?"

"A young woman in my daughter's situation can never be too careful." The Premier stepped forward. "Had you and your friends been less honorable, any number of calamities might have befallen her. What if you had learned her identity and decided to ransom her?"

"We would *not* have done that." Calum stepped forward. "Lilly is our friend—a part of our family, even."

The Premier grinned at him. "My daughter has exercised great wisdom. There are few people in this world who are unquestionably trustworthy, and she was wise to recognize that the first three beings to take an interest in her might not belong to their ranks."

Axel followed the Premier's line of sight to Condor, all while bristling at his words. Who was he to assume Axel wasn't trustworthy or honorable?

"I know what it's like to endure betrayal, and it is an experience from which I'd like to spare my daughter." The Premier's eyes narrowed on Condor. "Bring him forward."

Two of the Wisps zipped forward and clamped their gloved hands on Condor's arms. They wrested him from Magnus's grip and darted back to the Premier before Axel or anyone could do anything about it.

Axel motioned toward Condor with his hand. "Hey, he—"

"He is in our custody now, along with my daughter," the Premier said. "For which you will be greatly rewarded."

Rewarded? Axel raised an eyebrow. A reward was just the start as far as Axel was concerned, especially given all he'd lost. Now that Lilly was back—and she was a feather-flyin' *princess*—he'd probably never see her again once they left Aeropolis. At the very least, he needed to leave here a rich man.

"We don't want your gold," Calum said. "Or anything else, except one thing."

Axel's head snapped toward him. "Wait, what?"

Calum gave him a slight nod and continued to address the Premier. "We want your help in finding the Arcanum."

The Premier's eyes narrowed at Calum, and he scowled.

"Calum, that's—" Axel faced the Premier. "—that's *not* what we want. We're more than happy to take your—to *accept* your gold, and whatever else you have to offer."

The Premier's scowl persisted. "You desire to free Lumen, the ancient warrior, the General of Light, do you?"

"Yes." Calum showed the Premier the Windgale salute and bent down on one knee. "I will free him, and he will save Kanarah from the King."

"And why do you presume you are the one to accomplish this?"

Calum looked up. "I've had dreams, Premier."

Axel rolled his eyes. Not the dream talk again. If anything was going to ruin their chances of walking—or being lowered—out of here with more coin than they could imagine, it was Calum's wacky dream-talk.

"Lilly, bring him forward," the Premier gently ordered.

Lilly touched Calum on his shoulder and escorted him up the marble steps toward the throne.

The Premier's hard visage didn't change as he stared into Calum's eyes. "What kind of dreams?"

"Lumen has appeared to me several times. He has called me to free him, and he's showing me how to find him," Calum said. "It started with him telling me to cross Trader's Pass and head to the Blood Mountains, and in my last dream, he told me to find the Arcanum, which I believe is at a specific spot in the Blood Mountains."

"Lumen means to rule Kanarah, you know. *All* of Kanarah, both the East and West. When you set him free, that's his goal." The Premier raised his chin and looked down his nose at Calum. "What makes him any better than the King?"

Calum's jaw hardened. "I only know one thing for sure. The King's men murdered my parents when I was a child, and then they took me to a quarry where I worked as a slave for the next eight years. Any King who treats his subjects like that doesn't deserve to be King."

Axel raised an eyebrow. This was not the same Calum he'd grown up with.

In his place stood a strong man, both in will and in body, determined to follow the path laid before him, no matter how crazy it seemed to anyone else. While Axel didn't put much stock in Calum's dreams, he realized now that he'd begun to trust Calum's resolve more with every step they took toward the Blood Mountains.

No, Axel still didn't believe they'd find anything there, but he believed that Calum believed they would, and for now, that was good enough.

The Premier's stony visage cracked with a smirk. "You've obviously endured more than your share of hardships."

"Respectfully," Calum said, "you don't know the half of it."

"My court scholars will immediately search our royal archives for information on the Arcanum. You've granted me the deepest desires of my heart—my daughter's safe return—" The Premier eyed Condor again. "—and the life of my greatest enemy. It's the least I can do."

"Premier?" Magnus nodded to him and executed the Windgale salute across his chest. "If it pleases you, we would appreciate shelter, food, and a few days to rest while your scholars perform their search."

The Premier stared at Magnus for a long time, then nodded. "You are welcome in the Sky Fortress as our guests for as long as you wish to stay. We will provide for all of your needs."

"Don't do anything special for us," Calum said.

"*Calum.*" Axel wanted to smack him upside his head.

Calum shot a glare back at him. "We'd rather you take care of the Windgales who live at the ground level and can't fly because they don't have capes."

Axel rolled his eyes. They'd finally gotten in front of someone who was not only willing to help them but who actually *owed* them, big time. And here Calum was trying to redirect their reward to a bunch of nobodies down on the ground.

They'd already handed out free capes. What more did they have to give up to help those people? Why couldn't they enjoy something for themselves for once?

The Premier eyed him. "Their plight is an unfortunate reality of our age."

Condor scoffed, and the blond Wisp in the gray armor backhanded him in the face. Condor took the blow, straightened up, and grinned at him. "Oh, Falcroné. You're gonna regret that, old friend."

"We are no longer friends," Falcroné said. "And you have no authority here anymore, *traitor.*"

"And you never had any to begin with," Condor countered, still grinning.

Falcroné drew his hand back for another strike, but the Premier spoke before Falcroné could deliver the blow. "Hold, Falcroné. His time will come soon enough."

Falcroné used his raised hand to brush his long golden hair behind his shoulders instead, and he donned a smirk of his own.

The Premier turned back to Calum. "As I was saying, those poor souls are either victims of circumstance, or they are criminals. I regret that we cannot help all of our citizens meet their needs."

"After we defeated the Raven's Brood and captured Condor, we distributed what few spare capes we could to those in need on the ground level, but the need is still great." Calum motioned toward Condor. "He seems to think you can do more. He suggested that was part of why he rebelled."

Axel noticed a slight grin on Lilly's face while Calum spoke, and her gaze remained fixed on him.

The Premier's scowl returned and he extended a finger toward Condor. "That man is a liar and a murderer. You would do well to disregard every single word from his wretched mouth."

Axel stepped forward. "We don't believe him. He tried to kill us, and he tried to kill Lilly as well. He's the one who put that bruise on her face."

Lilly's eyes widened, and she shot a scowl at Axel. "Father, it's almost healed. It wasn't even a bad—

The Premier held up his hand and motioned Lilly close to him. He examined her cheek. Without looking at Condor, he said, "Falcroné, you may strike the prisoner again."

"With pleasure, Premier." Falcroné reeled his arm back and delivered a hefty blow to Condor's left cheek.

Now it was Axel's turn to grin. He already knew he liked Falcroné, even if the only thing they had in common was wanting to beat on Condor.

Condor glared at Falcroné again, but this time a drizzle of red blood seeped from the corner of his mouth. "You never could hit very hard.

146

Why don't you summon General Balena? Perhaps he can show you how to throw an effective punch."

Falcroné drove his fist into Condor's gut, and he doubled over. A vicious uppercut from Falcroné jerked Condor's head back up, but the Wisps holding him didn't let go.

"Better?" Falcroné cracked his armored knuckles.

Condor spat a dollop of blood onto the floor at Falcroné's feet. "Easy to land a good blow when two men are holding your opponent in place. Untie me, and we'll see how things go then."

"I'd bring you down, just as I did when you rebelled."

Condor laughed. "You didn't bring me down. Not even close. I fled once I realized my men had turned against me. All you did was chase me for a few minutes until you gave up. You've never once defeated me in a fight, not in twenty years of sparring or otherwise.

"It's why, despite my caste, I made Captain of the Royal Guard and you didn't—at least not until I left the post vacant, anyway." Condor's condescending smile matched his tone. "I do worry for the Premier's safety now that I am gone, what with a lesser man filling the position. Tell me, Premier, how well do you sleep at night knowing you're protected by the second best?"

Falcroné raised his fist to strike Condor again.

"*Enough.* Falcroné, step back." Frustration lined the Premier's voice. "Condor will be dealt with according to our laws for treason, and not before then. Don't let him goad you into executing the law beyond your charge."

Falcroné bowed his head toward the Premier. "Yes, Premier. I apologize."

"You also can't think for yourself," Condor muttered. "Another reason why you didn't make Captain."

Falcroné whirled around and bashed Condor's face with his fist. "How's that for thinking for myself?"

Blood ran from Condor's nose onto his upper lip. He bared his teeth at first, but the corners of his lips turned up in a smile, and he laughed. "Barely felt that at all. Go ahead. Hit me again."

"*Falcroné.*" This time the Premier left his throne, actually grabbed him by the back collar of his armor, and jerked him away from Condor. "If you so much as lay another *finger* on him before his hearing, I'll try you for treason, too."

Falcroné's jaw tensed, but he nodded.

The Premier motioned toward the doors through which Axel and the group had entered. "Take him away. Lock him up until I have gathered the council."

The Wisps holding Condor yanked him down the main walkway. He protested the entire way to the doors, spouting off about the supposed injustices of the Sky Realm and the Premier's rule, but the sound of his voice ceased when the double doors shut.

The Premier refocused on Calum, his arms outstretched. "Forgive me for my rudeness. I have not properly introduced myself, and I do not know your names, either. I am Avian, Premier of the Sky Realm. Welcome to my fortress."

Axel frowned. Everyone always looked to Calum, always welcomed him as the group's leader.

At first it had been good for Calum. It had built his self-confidence, something which he'd been severely lacking.

Now it was just annoying. Axel had always been more decisive, more intelligent, more skilled, and thus more qualified to lead their little group, but he'd never gotten the chance to do it. Magnus had seen to that.

Someday that would change. Either he'd take control, probably when they reached the Blood Mountains and failed to find the mythological Lumen, or he'd leave. Then he'd truly be his own man, free to do whatever he wanted.

Avian waved his hand at another nearby Wisp, this one dressed in fine linen and adorned with silver jewelry instead of armed and wearing armor. "Ganosh will show you to your accommodations. Rest, relax, and recuperate in the safety of the skies."

Calum bowed again. "Thank you."

Let him make nice with the Premier. Why not? Axel needed to refocus on Lilly anyway. Even though Lilly hadn't so much as made eye contact with him for the past several minutes now, Axel was owed some answers, and he intended to get them.

Ganosh approached Axel and performed the Windgale salute. "Shall we?"

At least someone saw fit to acknowledge him. Axel cast another glance at Lilly and finally met her blue eyes. She showed him a half-smile then looked away.

Axel sighed and nodded to Ganosh. If nothing else, maybe he would get some rest. "Yeah. Let's go."

ALMOST A WEEK WENT by before Axel had an opportunity to talk with Lilly again. She had been busy re-acclimating herself to being home and to her role as princess, just as Axel, Calum, and Magnus had to adjust to life within the Sky Fortress and Aeropolis.

Tasks that Windgales would deem simple, such as moving from platform to platform, proved difficult, or at the very least inconvenient, and that made exploring the wondrous city challenging. For the most part, Axel had stuck with Calum and Magnus, though he'd also managed to get some light sparring in with some of the royal guards in a training facility.

Even so, the time to rest and recuperate had done Axel good. His aches from escaping the pirate ship and the Jyrak had all but deserted him by now, and the cut on his left cheek from Krogan's whip had healed into a scar he could be proud of for the rest of his life.

On top of that, he got to sleep in a bed again, the first time in months. It took a night to readjust to that level of comfort, but once he did, he slept as soundly as a freshly planted seed nestled in a soft bed of soil.

That day, Calum and Magnus had just left in one of the chariots to visit Riley, who had finally regained consciousness. Thanks to the combined efforts of Kanton and the elusive Lord Elmond, whom none of them had seen yet, Riley had started to recover from his wound.

Axel had elected to stay behind for this visit. He'd never been all that fond of Riley anyway, as he'd made more than evident after the battle with Condor and the Raven's Brood, so what was the point?

Still, some small part of him had to admit he'd acted irrationally, and he'd even considered offering Riley and the others an apology. Maybe he would, eventually. When he got around to it.

For now, he had just reclined in a feather-stuffed chair when a knock sounded on his door. Axel exhaled a loud breath, frustrated at the interruption and rubbed his eyes. "Come in."

At first, Axel didn't recognize the beautiful blonde woman who entered his room with Falcroné close behind, still clad in his charcoal armor. When he realized she was Lilly, he straightened then pushed himself up to his feet.

"Lilly, hi," he said, barely keeping himself from stammering.

Instead of her pink armor, Lilly wore a sky-blue robe with white accents. Her shimmering blue cape looked as if it had been replaced with a new version, this one a deep forest-green that matched the cuffs on her sleeves and the hem at the bottom of her robe. A silver tiara topped her blonde hair, which now coiled around her head in two braids instead of hanging down.

She looked incredible. Axel had appreciated the rough-hewn, armor clad warrior version, but the sight of her all cleaned up and wearing finer clothes than he'd ever seen on anyone, anywhere, set his heart quivering.

"Hello, Axel." She beamed at him then motioned toward her companion. "Have you met Falcroné yet?"

"I know who he is, but we haven't been introduced." Axel extended his hand.

Falcroné performed a casual Windgale salute and nodded but didn't reach to shake Axel's hand. "I owe you a debt of gratitude for saving my cousin."

Cousin? That explained their matching hair color. They could've been brother and sister, for all Axel knew.

"Does that surprise you?" The corner of Lilly's mouth curled upward.

Axel let his hand drop, clamped his mouth shut, and shrugged. "No, it makes sense."

"We're here to summon you and your friends to an audience with the Premier." Falcroné's sharp blue eyes flared wider for a moment, and then he grinned at Lilly, whose smile shrank slightly. "Now that Lilly has returned, we have some exciting news."

Axel squinted at him. "Which is…?"

"We'll save it for when we're in the Premier's presence," Lilly said before Falcroné could continue.

Axel looked to Falcroné for more, but the Wisp only showed off his pristine white smile, just like Lilly's. It made Axel self-conscious about his own teeth, and he made sure his lips stayed closed except when he had to talk.

"Well, Calum and Magnus just left to visit Riley," Axel said. "I don't know when they're coming back."

Lilly turned to Falcroné and put her hand on his armored chest. "Would you mind going over to fetch them? I'd like to speak with Axel alone, and we'll meet you in the throne room."

Axel's heart skipped at her suggestion. Finally, he had a chance to clear the air with her. Beautiful or not, she'd betrayed his trust, and he wanted—he *deserved* answers.

A spark of hope lit up his soul. Who knew where the conversation might go? Maybe once everything was sorted out, they could figure out what the future would look like. And maybe it might include the two of them—

"As you wish, Princess." Falcroné's voice yanked Axel out of his imagination. His pleasant demeanor faded and his eyes narrowed at Axel, but he nodded.

Once Falcroné floated out of the room, Axel raised an eyebrow and grinned at Lilly. "Thought I'd never get you alone."

Lilly showed him a half-smile. "I just wanted to thank you while I still have the chance."

Axel tilted his head. "What do you mean?"

"I—" Lilly bit her lip and stared at the floor. "I'm staying here. I'm not coming with you and Calum to free Lumen."

Axel raised his eyebrows. He'd expected as much, but her words implied he wasn't staying here, either. And that meant any hope of a future for the two of them was nonexistent.

Upon that realization, the spark in his soul fizzled to nothing.

When Axel didn't say anything, Lilly sighed and continued. "I'm home. I need to stay here now. I'm sorry, Axel."

He clenched his jaw to stifle the emotion rising in his chest. It felt foreign—and terrible—to him. He hated it, and he fought it with every ounce of his being. "It's not me you should apologize to. I have a feeling Calum is really gonna miss you."

Lilly took his hand in hers, and a shiver ratcheted through his bones. "You don't have to hide behind him. I know you're hurt, too."

Axel stared into her blue eyes, almost exactly the color of the crystal that formed the Sky Fortress's walls. The bitter emotion swelled in his chest, accompanied by an impulse—one he'd wanted to gratify ever since he first laid eyes on her in that golden field.

She was right there, in front of him, and they were alone.

That had to mean something, right? Something wonderful.

He pulled Lilly close to him, curled his arms around her, and pressed his lips against hers, but the kiss didn't last nearly as long as he had hoped it would. She planted her hands on his chest and pushed away.

"Axel, I—" Lilly's blue eyes focused on something over his shoulder, and her mouth hung open slightly.

Axel turned back.

There, in the doorway, stood Calum.

CHAPTER EIGHTEEN

Maybe he didn't see us? Axel's hope that Calum hadn't seen what he'd just done overwrote his dismay at Lilly's abrupt rejection. But the sight of Calum's rigid jaw and lowered eyebrows said otherwise.

"Hi, Calum." It was all Axel could think to say. He didn't even realize he was still holding Lilly until she twisted out of his grip and stepped back. Axel glanced at her then refocused on Calum. "Did you visit Riley already?"

"We have to meet with the Premier." Calum grabbed his sword from the inside of the door and hooked it to his belt. Unlike when they had arrived, neither Calum nor Axel wore any armor, but instead they had adopted the long robes customary for civilian life in Aeropolis. "Come on."

After Calum disappeared through the doorway, Lilly sighed and gave Axel a frown. "Are you coming?"

"Yeah." He found her eyes. "What just—"

"Don't, Axel." Lilly held up her hand. "Just don't."

He followed her shimmering green cape toward the door and grabbed his own sword on the way out. Calum had seen them kiss, and his reaction had confirmed Axel's long-held suspicion that Calum wanted Lilly for himself.

153

Well, too late, buddy.

Then again, it hadn't even lasted two seconds—glorious as they were.

But she had also seen Calum, so she understandably wouldn't want to engage Axel with him around.

But she was also staying here in the Sky Realm. Axel absorbed the sunlight that shone through the crystalline hallways and exhaled a pleasant breath.

He'd have to stay here, with her. He'd do it to make her life easier. He wasn't sure he was truly ready to give up the life of adventure he'd discovered over the last several months, but for a prize like Lilly, he'd give up anything.

Calum would just have to finish his quest alone—or at least without Axel.

He smiled. No more taking orders from Calum. No more bickering with and taking blows from Magnus. No more unending travel or sleeping on the hard ground only to wake up and have to fight off a bunch of bandits.

From now on, he'd live a life of luxury with Lilly at his side—or him at her side, anyway. *She* was the princess, after all.

"Hurry, will you?" Lilly's voice pulled him back to the present.

Axel smirked at her. "Anything for you."

She led him into the throne room again, a place to which he'd only been invited twice since their initial visit.

Premier Avian sat on his throne, still flanked by two Wisps on either side. He conversed with a female Wisp who wore attire similar to his, including a matching crown and a yellow crystal necklace that matched those draped over Avian's shoulders. Light-brown hair coiled around her head in a style similar to Lilly's. Axel figured she was Lilly's mother.

Calum stood before the throne already, his arms folded.

"So did you go to visit Riley, or not?" Axel whacked Calum's shoulder, probably harder than he should have.

Calum shot him a glare. "I realized I'd forgotten my sword in the room. I ran into Falcroné on the way back, and he told me to go to the throne room."

"Oh, I see." Axel smirked and watched Lilly float over to Avian and the woman he was speaking to. Lilly gave the woman a hug and they exchanged smiles. "I'm guessing you happened to—"

"If it's all the same to you, I'd rather not discuss it right now."

Axel bit his tongue. He wanted to flaunt his victory in front of Calum, but he restrained himself—mostly. "Alright. Whatever you say. We can always talk about Lilly and me later."

Calum exhaled a sharp breath through his nose but didn't say anything else.

Within moments, Magnus and Falcroné entered the throne room. They joined Axel and Calum, along with several dozen Windgales and Wisps. About half of them wore armor, and the rest wore regal robes in a variety of ethereal colors.

One Wisp stood out to Axel more than the others. Like Falcroné, his long hair hung down past his shoulders, but it was a mix of silver and black instead of blonde, and a thick beard of matching tones shrouded the lower half of his face.

His dark eyebrows perpetually arched down, and his hazel eyes constantly scanned the throne room. Black armor with golden accents covered his hulking body. He didn't look like he belonged with the rest of the Wisps and Windgales.

"Your attention, please." Avian raised his hands, and the assembled Windgales fell silent. "I have gathered you here today to make an announcement that will shape the future of the Sky Realm for generations to come."

Axel craned his head to get Lilly to make eye contact with him, but she didn't. Was she avoiding him on purpose?

"Lilly, come forward." Avian nodded toward her, and she hovered over to him. "My wife Zephyrra and I are eternally grateful to the humans Calum and Axel, the Saurian Magnus, and their Wolf friend Riley, who is recovering from a critical wound, for returning our daughter to us.

"We feared the worst when Lilly disappeared, but she is back, and she is safe. The four of you are to be commended for your service to the

Sky Realm." He extended his hand toward Axel and Calum. "Please come forward."

Axel glanced at Calum, but he didn't make eye contact, either. Instead, Calum stepped up to Avian and gave him the Windgale salute, complete with a deep bow.

Axel and Magnus mimicked Calum and stood behind him, almost shoulder-to-shoulder, and Axel couldn't help but think that he might actually be on better terms with Magnus than Calum for once.

Then Axel remembered how Magnus had knocked him unconscious and tied him up like a prisoner while they traveled to Aeropolis. He scowled.

"I'm still mad at you," Axel muttered.

"I still do not care," Magnus muttered back.

Avian nodded to Calum then motioned toward the big Wisp in the black armor, whom Calum turned to face. The Wisp took a medallion made of blue crystal and gold and fastened it to Calum's robe.

"Axel, come forward."

Axel approached Avian, whose gaze hardened until Axel performed the Windgale salute as Calum had. Better to do it properly now, seeing as though Avian might end up becoming a family member in upcoming years.

As with Calum, Avian directed him to the big Wisp, who pinned an identical medal onto Axel's robe. Avian called Magnus forward next, but since he hadn't taken off his breastplate to change into robes, the Wisp just handed it to him.

"These badges grant you the protection, authority, rights, and privileges afforded to all citizens of the Sky Realm, even though you are of different races," Avian said. "Whenever you visit our realm, you are always welcome guests, worthy of the highest consideration and treatment."

Axel looked at the medallion. A gold ring encircled two spread wings of stamped gold, set into a blue crystal background in the center—quite a display of craftsmanship and artistry, among the best Axel had ever seen.

"Behold your people." Avian outstretched his arms toward the crowd in the throne room, all of whom performed the Windgale salute and bowed to Axel, Calum, and Magnus, and then applauded them. After a long moment, Avian said, "Please stand aside, my friends. We have more to discuss."

Axel followed Calum and Magnus back down off the throne platform and waited by the nearest steel pillar among several Windgales and Wisps in the crowd. Axel caught Lilly looking at him, and he winked at her. She gave him a small, polite smile, then turned her gaze back to Avian.

Axel smirked. *Truly a princess.*

"Now that Lilly has returned and we are reunited as a family, Zephyrra and I are pleased to make one final announcement on our daughter's behalf." Avian clasped Zephyrra's hand in his. "Falcroné, please step forward."

Falcroné grinned and floated over between Lilly and Avian.

"You all know that Falcroné is both Captain of the Royal Guard— the second youngest in our illustrious history—and that he is Lilly's cousin—" Avian motioned toward the big Wisp in the black armor. "— the son of General Balena and his late wife, my beloved sister, Evangeline."

Axel glanced at Lilly, then he elbowed Calum. "Did you know that?"

His face still stoic, Calum shook his head. "No."

Avian listed Falcroné's numerous accomplishments and feats in battle and described his fighting prowess, intelligence, and speed, emphasizing how Falcroné had all but singlehandedly stopped Condor's insurrection.

None of it mattered to Axel. He leaned in to Calum again. "Come on. Don't be so bitter. Just 'cause Lilly wants me doesn't mean we can't still be friends."

"Just drop it, alright?" Calum hissed. "I don't want to talk about it. Especially not here while we're listening to the Premier."

"Alright, easy. It's not a big deal." Axel folded his arms and rolled his eyes.

"It *is* a big deal to me, which is why I don't want to talk about it here." Calum glared at him. "So stop."

"Fine." Axel had to get one more jab in, so he said, "Like I said before, we can talk about Lilly and me later."

Calum's jaw tensed, but he didn't say anything else.

"In light of Falcroné's many successes, his integrity, and his quality of character, I am pleased to announce the continuation of our royal blood line—" Avian clasped Lilly's and Falcroné's hands together within his own. "—through a holy union of marriage between Lilly and Falcroné."

Axel sucked in a sharp breath and stared at Lilly with wide eyes.

CHAPTER NINETEEN

"The wedding will commence in three weeks, and we will host an engagement party for the happy couple in two days' time, in the evening." Avian patted Falcroné on his shoulder. "I couldn't have asked for a better son-in-law or a better match for my only daughter. Together, you will rule the skies when Zephyrra and I are gone."

Axel's stomach sloshed with grief, almost to the point of vomiting. How could Lilly have done this to him? And after their kiss only minutes ago?

Or had Calum's entry into the room not been the reason she pushed away from him?

Falcroné bowed and saluted Avian. "We will make you proud, Premier."

Unbelievable.

Axel glared at Lilly, but she did not—or would not—make eye contact with him. Instead, she smiled at Falcroné—at her *fiancé*—and her father as if that kiss had never happened.

"The very day that Lilly returned home, we sent envoys to Solace, Reptilius, and to the Desert of the Forgotten with word of the good news that their courtship could now continue." Avian's smile widened.

"Perhaps you all didn't know this, but Falcroné has had his heart set on Lilly since they were children playing among the clouds."

A murmur of laughter swelled from the crowd around Axel. Falcroné had been after Lilly since they were children?

And they were *cousins?*

Creepy, to say the least—if not downright disgusting. The nausea in Axel's stomach returned, and he had to fight it from rising to his throat.

"Before Lilly's disappearance, Falcroné asked me for her hand in marriage. I hesitated to give him a response, and then she vanished from the safety of our realm." Avian shot a glance at Lilly. "But while she was gone, Falcroné organized dozens of search parties for her, and he stayed late into the night collecting information as to her whereabouts, all without neglecting his duties as Captain of my Royal Guard.

"It was then that I knew—though perhaps I've always known—that he was the perfect fit for my precious daughter. When she returned to us safe and sound, he asked me again, and I agreed immediately."

Axel couldn't believe what he was hearing. *Forming search parties? Collecting information?*

That was the standard for what passed as "love" in this backward place?

He'd fought for Lilly. Bled for her. Killed for her. He'd saved her, and she'd saved him. They'd battled monsters together, fended off bandits, and escaped from a pirate ship.

And Avian thought that *forming search parties* and *collecting information* somehow trumped that? Axel's insides shifted from nausea to boiling fury.

Avian draped his arms around both Lilly's and Falcroné's shoulders, and he grinned at Lilly. "You know it took my direct orders and three strong men, including General Balena, to keep Falcroné from flying in search of you when you disappeared?"

Axel's mouth hung open. If Falcroné had truly loved her, he would've gone after her *regardless* of Avian's orders and the three men trying to hold him back. *Nothing* would've stopped him.

Lilly smiled at Falcroné again, and he smiled back.

Unbelievable. Axel grunted.

"What's your problem?" Calum asked, his demeanor noticeably improved.

"Did you really just ask me that?" Axel wanted to knock the smug look off Calum's face, but he'd draw too much attention in such a public setting. He pointed toward the throne. Despite his rage, he managed to keep his voice low. "Lilly and I, we were—she—"

Calum patted Axel's shoulder and smirked. "Don't worry. It's like you said before—we can talk about Lilly and you later."

Axel clenched his teeth and his fingers curled into fists.

———

LATE THAT NIGHT, Calum sat on the edge of a balcony near the top of the Sky Fortress.

Above and all around him, white stars sparkled in the cloudless sky, much brighter than he'd ever seen before, even on the clearest night from on the ground. The half-moon cast silver light on him and illuminated the rest of the Sky Fortress sprawled out before him with an ethereal blue glow.

Absolutely beautiful.

He looked down at his boots dangling over the chasm of clouds below. What a rush it must be to fly—twisting, turning, looping, spiraling. It had to be incredible to leap off such a platform, to free-fall through the layer of white fluff that swirled below, all the way down to the ground with a quick upturn near the end to keep from slamming into the dirt.

"Calum?"

He turned and found Lilly hovering behind him just a few feet off the platform. She still wore the same evergreen-and-blue robes she'd worn to Avian's assembly in the throne room several hours earlier. Her boots touched down on the platform and she started toward him.

"Oh. Hi, Lilly." Calum knew his tone was too sullen, but he didn't care. He'd had his heart broken twice in the same day. That hadn't happened since his parents' murders.

"Do you mind if I join you?"

Calum considered telling her he wanted to be alone, but a huge part of him still longed to be near her. Perhaps he shouldn't have given in, but he patted the cool flat crystal next to him, and she sat down.

"I need to talk to you about what happened earlier today," she began. Unlike other conversations they'd shared in the past, this time her tone was decisive—formal, even. Though it was her voice, it didn't sound like *her*.

Calum huffed. "Which one?"

"Both of them."

"I'm listening."

"Falcroné and I were courting long before I was taken from my home. Like my father said, he's my cousin, so we've known each other our whole lives. With royal families and bloodlines being what they are, and with Falcroné and me being close enough in age, it was only natural that my father and my uncle, General Balena, would make such a match."

Calum sighed. As much as he didn't want to know any of this, he knew he had to hear it, if for no other reason than to turn the page on this part of his life.

"How old is he?"

"Falcroné is twenty-one," Lilly replied. "I'm seventeen, so we'll be married on my eighteenth birthday in three weeks."

A light breeze chilled Calum's face. "And this is what you want?"

Lilly stared out across Aeropolis and the cloudy night sky beyond. "I want what's best for my people. A marriage to Falcroné will ensure stability in the transition from my father's reign to ours, because Falcroné is my cousin. It couldn't have worked out any better."

Calum exhaled a long, vaporous breath through his nose and clenched his teeth. Even if that were true, it brought him no consolation. "If you say so."

She took his hand in hers. "Calum, look at me."

He didn't react at first, at least not outwardly. Her hand was warm and soft in his, and it sent familiar shudders down his arm and into his chest, quickening his heartbeat.

"You will always be important to me. You've saved my life more times than I can count. You're a great friend, but we aren't meant to be. I'm sorry."

"That's not the impression I got when we were traveling." Calum finally turned to look at her. "Call me crazy, but I was starting to think you liked me."

"I *do* like you."

"I guess you like Axel more." Calum looked out across the void again. Part of him wanted to scoot over the edge and be done with the pain of this conversation, the pain of this entire day, but he banished the thought as soon as it appeared in his head.

Lilly squeezed his hand. "Hey, are you going to let me explain that to you?"

"Didn't look like there was much to explain," he mumbled.

"He kissed me, and I pulled back."

"Because you saw me in the doorway."

"No. I pulled back because I didn't want him kissing me. I'm betrothed to Falcroné now, and I was then, too. He didn't know that, but I did, and I couldn't let him kiss me." Lilly showed Calum a half-smile.

Calum met her eyes and studied them, searching for the truth. "I want to believe you."

She nodded. "Whether you believe me or not, I *am* betrothed to Falcroné. I'm accountable to him and no other."

"Have you told him about it?"

"Not yet, but I will. Falcroné isn't the forgiving type. I'd hate to think of what he might've done to Axel if he'd seen it happen." Lilly chuckled. It might've been her way of trying to lighten the mood, but it wasn't working on Calum. "If I tell him after the fact, Axel has a better chance of surviving the—"

"Do you love him?" Calum blurted.

Lilly blinked at him. "Axel?"

"Falcroné."

She bit her lip. "Yes."

Calum shook his head. "You don't sound sure."

"Like I said, I've known him my entire life, and he's my cousin." Lilly sighed. "We grew up together. He's my best friend. Of course I love him."

Calum had to stop making eye contact again. It hurt too much to continue. "You don't seem happy about this arrangement."

"What gives you that impression?" Lilly leaned forward and tried to meet his eyes, but he wouldn't look at her. "Calum? Why won't you look at me?"

"It's your face," he blurted. "When you're around him, your face and your expressions don't match your words. And your body—" Calum searched for the right words. "—you're not affectionate with him at all."

Calum actually had observed those things about the two of them. He'd noticed even before Avian's announcement that night, but he hadn't thought anything of it at the time. Now, in hindsight, it made more sense.

"Hey." Lilly sat up straight again, took hold of Calum's chin and physically turned his head so he had to meet her eyes. "Let me make one thing perfectly clear. I *am* marrying Falcroné, and no one else. It is my duty to my parents, to him, and to my people."

Calum sighed. "Regardless of your feelings for him?"

Lilly pinched the bridge of her nose with her fingers. "I *just* told you that I love him."

"And I just told you I don't believe that." Perhaps Calum was saying too much, but at this point, what did he have to lose? "I believe you love him because you've known him all this time, but not romantically. And I believe you're only going through with this because you feel obligated to."

"Calum, this may come as a shock to you, but I don't *care* what you believe. If I say I love him, then I do." Lilly stood up. "I don't even know why I'm arguing this with you in the first place."

Calum looked up at her. He dared to press it further. "There must be something to it if you're getting so flustered."

Lilly stared down at him. "Can't you just be happy for me? What happened to the sweet, kind Calum I knew from not even a week ago? The Calum who gave thirty capes to my people in need at the base of the pillar? Where did he go?"

"You stabbed him in the chest when you let Axel kiss you." He stood up and matched her gaze, face-to-face. "And he died when your father announced your engagement."

Lilly shook her head. She looked as if she would burst into tears any moment, but instead she leaped into the sky. As she disappeared into the night air, Calum's chest exploded with grief, and he buried his head in his hands.

Had he imagined what he thought he'd seen? About her behavior with Falcroné? Or had he struck a nerve with her, and she just wasn't willing to admit it?

Either way, that was *not* how he'd intended that conversation to go, and now he couldn't shake the feeling that he'd made everything far worse for them both.

ON THE AFTERNOON of the engagement party, Ganosh swooped into Calum's room with a black robe in his hands. "Forgive the intrusion, sir. The Premier asked me to bring this to you at once."

"Another outfit?" Calum folded his arms and forced a smile that didn't match the ruins in his heart. "Don't you think you've given me enough already?"

"This is formal Windgale dress of the highest quality." Ganosh spread the garment on Calum's bed. "The Premier has spared no expense for you and your friends. Woven wool of the finest grain with a white Aerosilk undershirt."

Aerosilk? That fabric could've been used to make capes for the Windgales at the base of the pillars, yet the Premier had chosen to make a shirt for Calum instead, and presumably one for Axel as well. The fabric was soft and nice and shimmery and all that, but Calum couldn't fly, so it wouldn't have made a difference whether it was made of Aerosilk or burlap to him.

Ganosh leaned forward, and his long, brown ponytail slipped from behind his back and draped over his shoulder. "The Premier will be very disappointed if you don't wear this to the engagement party this evening. He specifically requested that I deliver this finery to you and that I ensure you wear it, according to our customs."

No sense fighting it. Calum held up his hand. "It's alright, Ganosh. I'll wear it."

Ganosh smiled and held out the Aerosilk shirt for Calum.

Almost fifteen minutes later Calum scratched the spot on his neck where the black wool touched his skin.

"Is it gonna itch like this all night?"

"If you are not used to this quality of dress, there will be a certain measure of adjustment required on your part." Ganosh folded his arms and examined Calum from head to toe. He hesitated, then he pointed at Calum's feet. "Don't you have anything other than those... *atrocities* on your feet?"

Calum stared at his boots, then looked up a Ganosh. "What's wrong with my boots?"

"First of all, they're brown and don't match the robe. Second, they're filthy and worn down. It's only a matter of time before your toes pop out the front of the leather." Ganosh rolled his eyes. "They simply will not do. Wait here. I'll be back with replacements for you."

"You really don't have to—" Calum stopped when Ganosh zipped out his door and disappeared. He sighed and scratched at his collar again.

Was all of this necessary? Especially in light of his conversation with Lilly? Had Riley been well enough to travel, he would've left the very night Avian announced Lilly's engagement to Falcroné. And maybe if he'd been lucky, he could've left Axel behind in the process.

Within another fifteen minutes, Ganosh returned with a pair of black boots shined so perfectly that Calum could see his face in them.

"These are much more appropriate." Ganosh set them at Calum's feet. Unlike his old boots, which would have flopped over on themselves, these stood upright like the Wisps who guarded Avian's throne room—and they looked about as unforgiving, too.

Calum sat on the bed and jammed his feet inside with Ganosh's help, then stood up.

Great. Itchy neck, and soon-to-be-sore feet. "I feel like I can't move."

Ganosh grinned at him. "But you *look* wonderful. I'm sure you don't yet understand how things work in our culture, but appearances are all that really matter at events like these."

"If you say so."

Ganosh scooped up Calum's old boots and started toward the door.

"Hey, where are you taking those?"

"I'm going to drop them off the edge of the platform."

Calum chuckled at first, but Ganosh's face showed no sign of amusement. "Wait, you're serious?"

"Of course I'm serious. That's what we do with unwanted items."

"I never said I didn't *want* them." Calum stepped forward—albeit awkwardly—and snatched the boots from Ganosh's hands. "Besides, it's probably not wise to just drop things from the sky. What if they had hit someone below?"

Ganosh shrugged. "The chances of that happening are infinitesimal."

Calum tilted his head. "They're what?"

Ganosh rolled his eyes again and sighed. "Small. Very, very small."

"Oh." Calum wondered why he hadn't just said that instead. "Even so, it can't be good for nature to just toss your trash over the edge."

"I have no time to debate civics with a foreigner." Ganosh jabbed his hips with his fists, elbows out. "*Especially* with a human. You have about a half-hour before the party starts. I suggest you walk around your room in those boots to break them in a bit before this evening, or your feet will rebel against you long before tomorrow morning."

No kidding. "Thanks, Ganosh."

Ganosh showed him the Windgale salute then darted out of the room.

Calum took Ganosh's advice and clomped around the floor for a half-hour, but by the time he finished, his feet felt far worse than when he'd started. If it persisted, he might have to sneak out of the party and change into his normal boots.

As a finishing touch, Calum pinned his Windgale medallion to the lapel of his robe.

Magnus ducked under the door arch and stepped into Calum's room. "Are you ready?"

Calum eyed him. "You're not wearing anything formal. How come you get to wear your breastplate and leather belt but I have to wear this stuff?"

"Have you ever seen a Saurian wearing clothes of any sort, aside from armor?"

"No, but I also haven't seen that many Saurians in the first place."

"We do not stand on ceremony for anyone with our attire. We wear what we wear, if anything at all, and the rest of Kanarah can deal with it."

"Alright, alright. I don't mean anything by it. I'm just making an observation." Calum scratched at his itchy neck again. "Where's Axel?"

"He was not in his room. I suspect he will meet us at the party when he is ready." Magnus clicked his talons on his breastplate. "I know he was displeased to hear the news of Lilly's engagement."

He wasn't the only one. "I guess we should go, then. No sense in being late."

———

LILLY PULLED ON HER BOOTS, then she stood and looked at her image in the mirror that hung from the crystal wall in her room. She pushed a stray lock of blonde hair behind her ear and admired her outfit again.

Gold embroidery accented her rose-colored gown in swirls and spirals that started at her strapless corset top and reached down to the hem of her dress. A gold Aerosilk cape hung from her neck.

She wished she didn't have to wear it, but she couldn't fly without it. She didn't yet know what it would take for her to become a Wisp, but she looked forward to the day when her father would honor her with that promotion.

A knock sounded on her door. "Come in."

The door swung open and Axel stepped inside. At first Lilly barely recognized him, clad in formal black Windgale robes with a burgundy Aerosilk shirt shimmering underneath.

Someone had even taken the time to comb his dark hair into something more presentable than the curled mess it usually was— probably Ganosh. The only thing that hadn't changed was his scruffy, unshaven neck and face, and the fact that he wore his sword at his belt.

Despite how she felt about him in light of what he'd tried earlier, Lilly had to admit he cleaned up really well. His dark blue eyes looked especially striking, and the scar on his left cheek added a sense of intrigue to his presence.

"We need to talk," he asserted in the way that only Axel could.

"You shouldn't be in here." Lilly faced him.

He wore his golden Windgale medallion on his robe, a reminder of what he'd done both for her and for the Sky Fortress. Even so, this conversation was *not* going to happen if she could help it, not after the one she'd had with Calum.

"And either way, we don't have time to talk," she continued. "The party has started by now, and I'm already late."

Axel's gaze started at her eyes, then he scanned her from top to bottom. He shut the door, positioned himself in front of it, and folded his arms. "I'm not giving you a choice. We need to talk. Now."

Lilly's vision darted to the marble vanity and the chair near her mirror, specifically in search of something—anything—she could use to defend herself from Axel if it came to that. Perhaps it was an irrational thought, but after what Roderick had put her through, she'd determined to never leave anything like this to chance again.

"I have nothing to say to you."

He stepped toward her with his hands still at his sides. "Why did you let me kiss you if you were courting Falcroné?"

Lilly bristled at his audacity, and she glanced at her vanity again. A hairbrush, a tin filled with crushed rose petals, a silver candle given to her by her late aunt Evangeline—all innocuous to the point that they wouldn't help her if Axel tried something.

"I didn't let you. I pushed you away as soon as you started kissing me."

"You could've pushed me away before that, when I got close to you, but you didn't."

"You're a big guy, Axel. Pushing you away isn't as easy as you make it sound."

The only other items within reach were two ivory hairpins that lay on her bed, both long with pointed ends. Lilly had elected not to use them in her hair tonight, but even so they wouldn't do much good against Axel's sword if he decided to use it.

Still, they were better than nothing.

"Had I known you would try to kiss me, I wouldn't have come at all," she countered. By the Overlord, she *really* didn't want to have this conversation.

"I don't believe that." Axel closed in on her. "I think you stopped because you saw Calum walk into the room."

What was with these boys not believing her? "Calum said the same thing, but I assured him that the reason I stopped kissing you wasn't because I saw him walk in. It's because I was about to announce my engagement to Falcroné."

"You don't love him."

"I don't need another person telling me what I do and don't feel. Calum already tried, and it didn't work then." Lilly glanced at the hairpins on the bed again, but this time Axel's dark-blue eyes followed. He'd noticed them, too.

"Really?" he scoffed and motioned toward them. "Is that what you think of me? That after everything I've done for you, I would try to hurt you?"

Perhaps she could dart around him and get to the door before he could try anything? Sure, she could get around him, but even if she did, she couldn't reach the door and get it open in time. And with so much extra fabric in her cape for him to grip as she tried to get past...

"Lilly." Axel's voice jarred her from her plotting. He stepped toward her again, this time with his arms outstretched to his sides. He must've known it would make it even harder for her to get past now. "I'm not gonna hurt you. I *love* you. I have since the moment I laid eyes on you."

"I know."

Axel huffed and took another step forward. "Of course you do. How could you not? It's not like I tried to hide it."

Lilly nodded and backed up a step, then she chastised herself for it mentally. She couldn't let him back her into a wall—it limited her

THE WAY OF ANCIENT POWER

options. One of General Balena's first lessons. "Yes, it has been obvious, alright."

"And that's how I know you didn't push away from me just because of your courtship with Falcroné. I've been so obvious, and you haven't tried to convince me otherwise, so—"

"*No*," Lilly interrupted. She couldn't let that line of thinking continue. "You're wrong. I like you just fine, but I'm *not* in love with you. I love Falcroné. Not you, not Calum. Falcroné. Crystal?"

Axel's jaw hardened and his gaze transformed into a glare. "No. *Not* crystal."

Speaking of Falcroné, where was he? She sure could use his help right now. "Axel, I'm leaving for the party. This conversation is over."

Axel's face hardened with anger. "It's not over 'til I say it's over."

He started toward her.

CHAPTER TWENTY

Lilly feigned a lunge for her hairpins, and Axel followed her trajectory toward the bed. Instead of going for them, Lilly reached back, grabbed her vanity chair, and slammed it against Axel's shoulder.

He let out a grunt, dropped onto the bed, then rolled onto the floor.

Lilly leaped over him and zipped toward the door. She flung it open, but fingers clamped around her ankle.

Axel looked up at her with rage in his eyes and gritted teeth. But amid those angry emotions, she also recognized deep, profound hurt.

Rage, hurt, love, or hate, Lilly was leaving. She spun around and whipped her other foot at Axel's face. Her boot connected hard with his jaw, and he let her go.

Now free, Lilly zipped out of her room. She rounded a corner and smacked into a broad purple chest embroidered with golden arcs. She pushed away, ready to fight him too, but she stopped when she realized it was Falcroné.

"Lilly?" He held up his hands, and the sleeves of his purple robe slid back on his muscular forearms. "Are you alright? Why are you breathing so heavily?"

Lilly stared into Falcroné's eyes and opened her mouth to speak, but hesitated.

———

"I WONDER WHERE AXEL IS." Calum craned his neck to peer at the small crowd of people not floating through the air around them. He figured Axel would be dressed more or less the same as him, but so were every other Windgale and Wisp in the room. "He should've been here by now."

Dozens of bronze lanterns hung from the throne room ceiling, each of them burning with flames that cast light through the multiple colors of glass that encased each one. The effect reminded Calum of a hundred tiny rainbows, captured and forced to enliven a dark space against their will.

Colorful ribbons stretched overhead between the pillars, each of them tied into bows on the pillars themselves. Servers clad in black robes with white sleeves darted through the air with trays in their hands, each of them loaded with drinks or food.

"Maybe he decided to stay in his room." Magnus waved down one of the Windgale servers and snagged a glass of bright-green liquid from the tray he carried. He downed the drink in one gulp and tried to place the glass back on the server's tray, but the server had already taken to the sky again. "Blasted Windgales. Too fast for their own good."

"That's not like Axel. He never passes up an opportunity for free food. Speaking of which…" Calum snatched a wooden skewer loaded with grilled vegetables, fruit, and meat from another server's tray as he hovered past. "…this looks delicious."

Just as Calum raised it to his mouth for a bite, a familiar voice stopped his motion. "What, not gonna share with your crippled friend?"

Calum turned his head and saw a gray-brown Wolf limp-walking toward him. White bandages covered the spot on his side where Condor had stabbed him, and Kanton walked alongside him.

Calum's mouth spread into a big smile. "Riley? I didn't think you were well enough to leave your room yet."

"He probably isn't." Kanton wore finery like Calum's, only he still wore the black-and-red Raven's Brood cape Calum had given him, just with the embroidered emblem plucked out. "But he insisted. And you're not crippled, just limping."

"Can't hide in my room. No shadows." Riley motioned over his right shoulder with his head. "It's nothing but clear blue crystal and sunlight streaming in from every angle. At night, they light a hundred lanterns to make sure I don't go anywhere. It's much darker in here, though. Feels better. Safer."

"He exaggerates." Kanton crouched down next to Riley and stroked the fur behind his ears. Riley snapped his jaws at Kanton's hand and he pulled back. "Was he this foul before the attack?"

"I'm not sure, to tell you the truth. I haven't known him for that long," Calum said. "But I know he's not a fan of people touching him or trying to pet him."

"I'm not some common dog that you can stroke my fur like a pet." Riley growled, then he carefully sat down on his hind legs with a wince. "I was serious about sharing your meat, you know. The stuff they gave me over there barely counts as real food."

"Now *that's* a statement I'm inclined to agree with." Kanton stood up and pushed his black-and-red cape behind him again. "Trust me—he's right about that. I get all of his leftovers."

Riley tilted his head and whimpered at Calum, his blue canine eyes fixed on the skewer.

Calum sighed, but crouched down in front of him and held it out. "Here. I can always get another one."

"Keep the plants for yourself." Riley's pink tongue curled up and licked his nose. "I only want the meat."

As Calum plucked the first chunk of seared mutton from the skewer, Avian's voice filled the throne room.

"Friends and family, your attention please." Avian drifted high above the crowd with his hands raised, flanked by two armed Wisps on each side, as usual.

The crowd sank to the ground, followed by Avian and his men. Zephyrra stood at Avian's side, wearing an elegant silver dress that shimmered under the colored lights.

"Thank you for joining us on this most excellent occasion. Partake in the wine, drinks, food, and desserts at your leisure, but first allow me to introduce our guests of honor—my daughter, Princess Lilliana, and her new fiancé Falcroné, Captain of the Royal Guard." Avian motioned toward the rear doors with his right arm.

As if on cue, the crowd parted, and Calum went along with them. The grand doors at the rear of the throne room opened, and a procession of armed Wisps in orange and purple armor filed inside with General Balena at the head.

Calum leaned nearer to Magnus. "That's an awful lot of soldiers for an engagement party, don't you think?"

He nodded, and his golden eyes flickered with colored light. "I am not well-versed in Windgale customs, but it is unusual, to say the least."

About a dozen Windgale soldiers led the way inside, and Falcroné and Lilly followed them. Six more soldiers, three on each side, marched between them and the crowd as if forming a sort of barrier. Another eight Wisps marched behind them, four in the same deep vibrant orange color worn by the Royal Guard, and four more in dark-purple armor.

The procession ended at the throne and spread into a formation in front of the platform with Lilly, Falcroné, and General Balena standing near Avian and Zephyrra.

Despite their tense conversation the night her engagement was announced, and despite his breaking heart, Calum could scarcely take his eyes off her. Just when he'd thought she could never be more beautiful, she showed up looking even better than ever.

But the longer Calum stared, the more the longing he felt for her stabbed at his aching heart.

As the happy couple waved, General Balena leaned over to Avian and whispered something into his ear, and Avian nodded.

"Behold the future of the Sky Realm." Avian raised his hands, and the crowd performed the Windgale salute to Lilly and Falcroné.

Calum did it too, but without the fervor of the Windgales around him. He wasn't going to lie to himself about what he felt.

Something nudged his leg, and Calum looked down. Riley whimpered at him again until Calum tore another chunk of meat off his skewer and fed it to him.

"For not being a 'common dog,' you're sure acting like one," Calum muttered.

"I got stabbed," Riley reminded him. "I'm entitled to behave in a questionable manner for one night."

"More like a 'desperate manner,'" Calum countered.

"Yet however wondrous an occasion their engagement may be..." Avian continued. "...one among us has cast a dark shadow over this night. His jealousy of our ways, our rituals, our culture, and most importantly of Lilly and Falcroné's engagement is the reason you see such a demonstration of the might of the Sky Realm arrayed before you."

Calum eyed Magnus, who shook his head slightly.

"He visited my daughter before this party and accosted her in her room, but she fended him off with great skill, no doubt thanks to her training from General Balena." Avian nodded to him, and he bowed. "Now the assailant is in custody. Bring him forth, and we will make an example of him as a warning to anyone who dares to stand against this union or the Realm."

The doors opened again and two Wisps dragged a man with dark, curly hair and clad in black clothes toward the throne. They thrust him to the floor, where he landed on his hands and knees. Then he slowly lifted his head.

It was Axel.

CHAPTER TWENTY-ONE

W ould the surprises ever cease? Calum groaned and shook his head.

"The fool." Magnus exhaled a long hiss and clacked his talons on his breastplate. "His reckless behavior is going to get us all killed."

Blood trickled from the corner of Axel's mouth, but other than a few scuffs on his borrowed robes, he looked unharmed.

"This man, whom we honored a mere two days ago for his role in saving my daughter's life, saw fit to attack her this evening after she told him she did not love him. She escaped through her own cunning and told Falcroné, who apprehended him and notified General Balena of the situation."

The two Wisps grabbed Axel, spun him around, and then forced him back down to his hands and knees before Avian, Lilly, and Falcroné.

"Should we go up there?" Calum asked.

Magnus shook his head. "Be still for now."

Be still? If Axel *had* attacked Lilly, Calum wanted a shot at him first.

But even with Axel's legendary temper and bad attitude, Calum still couldn't believe that Axel would do such a thing—especially after all he'd sacrificed and risked for her right alongside Calum.

"You are fortunate to have been made a citizen of our realm, Axel,"

Avian said. "Were you an outsider, your punishment would have been death. But as an honorary citizen, your action will be treated as treason instead."

Condor was charged with treason as well, Calum considered.

"You will be locked away until our Council of Wisps convenes to determine your fate."

"*No.*" Calum dropped his skewer, pushed his way through the crowd, and stormed toward the throne with Magnus close behind.

Perhaps it was rash, but either way, Axel was his friend. His oldest friend. Even though they'd dueled and fought each other along the way, especially in the last two days, Calum couldn't just let these people lock him up.

"You can't do that to him," Calum said.

The Wisps who guarded the throne platform leveled their spears at him and he stopped short of becoming the next piece of meat to be skewered. Behind them, Axel craned his head and looked back at Calum with confusion in his eyes.

Now up close, Calum could see a large bruise on Axel's jaw, plus he hunched over, something he never did. Lilly must have given him quite the beating—or perhaps Falcroné had done the honors.

Magnus's hand clamped onto Calum's shoulder. "Calum, do not—"

Calum shrugged free. "Premier, suppose Axel made this mistake. If he did, it was *one* mistake. He made a bad decision and he paid for it."

Avian stared down at him for a long moment. "What is your point, Calum?"

"Look, I'm unfamiliar with your laws, so I don't really know what I'm saying..." *Great start, Calum.* "But don't throw him in your dungeon, or wherever. We were all shocked to learn of Lilly's relationship to you at first, and—"

"This has *nothing* to do with Lilly's relationship to the Premier." Falcroné pointed a long finger at Axel. "It has to do with his profession of love for her and the subsequent attack."

"In Axel's defense—" Calum started.

Should he finish the sentence? Doing so could risk invoking the wrath of Falcroné and Avian as Axel already had. And what if Axel was guilty? Calum would find himself defending his friend's stupidity.

He decided he couldn't remain silent. "—Lilly is not hard to love. She's sweet and charming and beautiful and intelligent—all of which are testaments to her upbringing under two wonderful parents—"

"Spare me your flattery, Calum." Avian held up his hand. "Make your point."

"My point is that—" Calum's eyes locked on Lilly's for a moment, but she pursed her lips tight and looked away. It was probably a mistake, but Calum continued anyway. "My point is that I love Lilly, too. And if you're gonna lock Axel up for that, then you'd better lock me up too."

Falcroné's jaw tensed, and he glared at Calum. "But you didn't *attack* her. Your friend did. That warrants time rotting in a cell, if anything ever did."

"I don't disagree with you," Calum said. "But I'm asking you to show him mercy nonetheless. We've already been through so much. Think about how we helped bring her back here and how we—"

"I've heard enough." Avian held up his hand again. "This is supposed to be a festive occasion, not a hearing. Axel will be locked up, and Calum and the rest of his friends will remain free. But if any of you breaks even the smallest of our laws, you will soon join your friend. Crystal?"

Calum clenched his teeth. It wasn't the result he'd hoped for, but he'd tried.

He nodded. "Clear."

"Then go, enjoy the food and drink, and you may plead your friend's case tomorrow when the Council of Wisps convenes to decide his fate." Avian waved toward Axel, who gave Calum a slight nod. "Take him away."

The Wisps took flight with Axel in tow. They exited through the doors from which they'd entered, and the Wisps guarding the platform raised their spears again. Calum caught Lilly staring at him, then she turned her attention back to Falcroné, who stroked her face with his fingers and touched his forehead to hers.

Calum turned away. He'd seen enough.

He looked up at Magnus. "What'll happen at the council meeting tomorrow?"

Magnus shook his head. "I do not know. We will fight to save Axel using words instead of weapons, I suppose."

"I'm better with my sword."

"I disagree, Calum," Magnus challenged. "You are gifted in many areas, and that is one of them. Do not underestimate yourself."

"If you say so." Calum was pretty sure he'd just butchered his attempt to get Axel released, but he appreciated Magnus's encouragement all the same. "Come on. We'd better get back to Riley and Kanton."

AXEL SANK DEEPER and deeper into the abyss, along with the two Wisps that gripped his arms. Far below, a single torch burned in the darkness. As they neared the light, Axel made out the crisscrossed bars of a cage mounted to the sides of the vertical tube in which they descended.

The Wisps slowed their descent, landed on the cage, and set Axel on the bars.

One of them, the one clad in orange armor, leaned over to him, his face barely visible in the light of the solitary torch. "If you try to run, you'll fall to your death. If you try to fight or resist, we'll *make* you fall to your death. Crystal?"

Axel bit his tongue and nodded instead of saying anything.

The other Wisp, in dark-purple armor, unlocked the cage's hatch. "Hop in."

Axel peered through the bars. "That's a twenty-foot drop, at least. I'll break my legs if I just jump in."

"Then we'll lower you to ten feet and you'll have to manage from there."

"I don't—"

The orange Wisp shoved him toward the hatch. "Do it now, or you'll fall a lot farther than twenty feet."

Axel sighed but stepped toward the hatch.

A sharp blow to his back pitched him forward. He plunged into the

THE WAY OF ANCIENT POWER

cage headfirst, but he managed to curl his body so he landed on his left shoulder instead of on his face. The impact jarred his shoulder with a loud *pop*, and a familiar shock of pain shot down to his fingertips like lightning.

He groaned as the Wisps locked the cage door. A flurry of curses poured from Axel's mouth, but when he looked up, the Wisps were already gone. He tried to push himself up, but his left arm hurt so bad that he couldn't move it.

"Here, let me help you," said a voice from the darkness around him.

Axel's heart flipped in his chest. Who else was in here?

A set of arms curled around his waist and started to pull.

"Get off me!" Axel flailed his right arm, also sore from when Lilly had hit him with her chair, but he only managed to flop back down onto his chest. His mind ratcheted through an infinite number of possibilities of who could be in this cell with him—including someone like Yurgev. "Get away!"

"Easy."

The arms jerked Axel up in one quick motion, and he found his footing. He staggered across the cage and stood against the wall nearest the torch, which illuminated only about half of the entire cage.

His left shoulder burned with pain, and he couldn't move it. It was dislocated again, just like it had been after fighting the Gronyxes in the tunnel to Trader's Pass. How could he defend himself with only one functioning arm—"functioning," but also bruised and weakened?

"You don't have to be afraid. I'm not going to hurt you."

Axel squinted at the darkness. He'd stared at the torch for a moment too long on his way over to the cage wall, and the light had seared his vision, so he couldn't see properly. On top of that, the other man in his cell stood in the deep shadows on the far side of the cage.

"Who are you?" Axel demanded. "Step into the light so I can see you."

The man answered with laughter. There was something familiar about it, but Axel couldn't decipher what it was.

"After all the time we spent together on our way here, you have to ask who I am?" the man asked. "You know me so well already—*Farm Boy.*"

181

CHAPTER TWENTY-TWO

Axel's heartbeat multiplied, and he cursed again.

"I seem to remember you were looking forward to a day very much like this." Condor stepped out of the shadows with a cunning smile and sauntered toward him. The cuts on his face from Falcroné's beating had mostly healed, but that same old smirk remained.

"I remember agreeing with you at the time." Axel bit his lip and exhaled a sharp breath. Of all the people he could've gotten locked in a jail cell with, Condor might've been the worst. "You said you were gonna kill me. Looks like you finally get to try your luck."

Condor huffed and waved his hand, still bandaged with a blood-tinged cloth from when Riley had bitten him, in dismissal. "Please. You're in no condition to fight me. Or anyone else, for that matter."

Axel bristled at the comment, and he let his ego take over. "I could still take you down."

"Not with your shoulder dislocated, I imagine."

"Even with it dislocated, you wouldn't stand a chance."

Condor shook his head and smirked. "You don't need to keep up your tough-guy act down here, Farm Boy. The princess isn't here to admire your swelling ego, and you're not my type either."

Axel gritted his teeth and tried to rub his left shoulder, but it only felt worse. "You don't know what you're—"

"What did you do to earn yourself a holiday down here?" Condor leaned against the cage bars.

"That's none of your business."

"You don't have to tell me. I bet you made a move on the princess after you found out about Falcroné, didn't you? You probably couldn't help yourself." Condor chuckled. "And then he beat you like he beat me and had you tossed in here before your hearing."

"Falcroné barely laid a finger on me."

"Really? *That's* the only part of my guess you're denying?" Condor chuckled. "So you *did* make a pass at the princess. Was she the one who gave you that bruise?"

Axel touched his jaw with his right hand and winced at the pain in his arm.

"She *did*, didn't she? Oh, she always was a wily one. Unpredictable, even." Condor smiled, and his gaze wandered up into the tube's darkness. "Too bad you thought you had any chance with her in the first place."

"Whatever. Call me naïve, or stupid, or anything else you want. I don't care." Axel spat on the cage floor near Condor's boots. "And if you're gonna kill me, then get on with it already."

Condor stared at Axel's reddened spittle for a moment, then at him. "I'm not going to kill you when you have a dislocated shoulder and just got beat up by a girl half your size. Where's the fun in that? No, I'll wait until you're healed and feeling haughty before we settle our differences once and for all."

Axel rolled his eyes and sighed.

"Speaking of which, you should let me pop your shoulder back into place." Condor started toward him, but Axel shuffled away.

"Don't come near me, Condor. I mean it."

Condor held up his hands. "I'm going to help you. Be calm."

"I don't *want* your help."

"Whether you want it or not is irrelevant. You need it. Unless you can reset your shoulder on your own, you will endure profound pain for a long time. Unnecessarily so."

Reset his shoulder on his own? Axel didn't even know where to start. When Magnus had done it after the fight with the Gronyxes, Axel hadn't paid attention to how it had happened. He'd been too exhausted and beat-up from the battle.

Now he could barely see in the darkness of the cell, and the thought of even touching his shoulder made it hurt worse. But was the alternative of Condor fixing it for him any better?

In the end, he acquiesced. "Fine."

Condor nodded. He floated over and cupped Axel's left shoulder with one hand and his shoulder blade with the other. "This is going to hurt. A lot."

"Just do it, already."

"On the count of three. Ready?"

Axel nodded and clenched his teeth.

"One—"

Something popped, and a thousand arrowheads jammed into Axel's shoulder. He screamed and flailed at Condor with his right arm, but missed entirely. He had to fight to keep the tears pooling in his eyes from streaming down his cheeks.

Condor stood on the edge of the shadows with that same smirk on his face. "I told you it would hurt."

"It's been dislocated before. I knew it would hurt." Axel blinked away the remaining tears in his eyes and slowly rolled his left shoulder. "But you said you'd count to *three*."

"It's an old trick I learned from General Balena. He said that if you wait to count to three, the injured person will tense up and it's that much harder to pop the joint back into place. How does your shoulder feel?"

"Better," he admitted, though if it went anything like last time, the real soreness would come in a few hours.

"It appears you can move it now."

Axel rotated his arm slightly.

"In the meantime, at least you're right-handed." Condor chuckled

184

again. "You screamed so loud, I bet they heard you all the way up in Aeropolis."

"Just stop, alright?" Axel rubbed his left shoulder. "I'm not in any mood."

"Nothing you can do about it anyway. I could cackle all night and all day, and you couldn't stop me." Condor leaned against the cage wall again and smiled. "Fortunately for you, I'm not the gloating type."

Axel growled, then slumped down onto his rear-end. "Is there any way outta here?"

"Don't even think about it. You can't fly, remember?" Condor waved his arm in a half-circle over his head. "In my three years as Captain of the Royal Guard, I dropped more thieves, brigands, derelicts, defectors, and villains in this cell then I can remember. There's no way through the bars, and even if there were, you'd never get back up to the fortress.

"There isn't a rope or a chain in this world long enough to reach down here." Condor's annoying grin returned, full-force. "Best to just accept that you're stuck in here. But at least you have me for company. And..." Condor squinted at him. "Yes, it seems we even have matching scars."

Axel touched the scar under his right eye. He couldn't see Condor as well in the dim light, but he remembered Condor had a similar scar in almost the exact same spot on his face, too. Axel chalked it up as nothing more than a coincidence.

He scanned what he could see of the tube. "Where are we, anyway?"

"We're deep within the pillar that holds the Sky Fortress in the air. It's the perfect prison to put anyone who can't fly: out of sight, inaccessible, and dark. The bars are too thick for almost anyone in Kanarah to cut through, break, or bend, including your Sobek friend." Condor smiled. "Welcome to the Sky Fortress's version of living death."

Axel frowned. "So..."

"So you're stuck in here until they feel like letting you out."

Axel sighed. "They said we'll have a hearing tomorrow when the council gathers."

Condor nodded and ran his fingers through his black hair. "Yes. The Premier doesn't decide the fates of prisoners on his own. A council of eight high-ranking Wisps, including Falcroné and General Balena, assist in passing judgment. Avian serves as the ninth vote."

"So I can count on at least those three of the nine ruling against me?"

"That's a safe assumption. Given that your advance was on Princess Lilly, I'd be surprised if even two of the council members sided with you. Aside from Premieress Zephyrra, she is the most beloved citizen in the realm. At times, perhaps even more beloved."

Axel clenched his teeth. "And if they rule against me?"

"A unanimous vote is required for the death penalty. If you lose their favor in the hearing, a lifetime of slavery or servitude is a common punishment doled out to the worst offenders."

"And my crime classifies me as one of the worst?"

Condor sat in front of Axel. The light from the torch flickered in his sharp blue eyes. "It's all contextual. What you did pales in comparison to my crimes, for example. You'd better pray that the council calls me first so I get the bulk of their wrath and that little remains for you."

Axel stared at him. "Why did you help me with my shoulder?"

"I already told you why. If we're going to settle our conflict someday, you need to be healthy and confident." Condor reached out and patted him on his left shoulder, and the thousand arrowheads tried to carve their way out of Axel's arm a second time.

"Ow!" Axel tried to kick him, but Condor moved away too fast. "I *hate* you."

"Good." Condor grinned his perfect smile. "Never change, alright?"

Through clenched teeth, Axel said, "I won't."

"So you and your friends are searching for Lumen?" Condor folded his arms.

"I'm not searching for anyone anymore," Axel grumbled.

"Stop being so overdramatic." Condor tilted his head and smirked. "Looking for the Arcanum, are you?"

"What do you care?" Axel glared at him.

"It's not an easy place to find. The Premier's scholars might be able to point it out to you on a map, but it's hard to reach."

Axel raised an eyebrow. "And how would you know that?"

Condor shook his head and receded into the shadows, out of Axel's sight. "That's my secret, Farm Boy."

"And you said *I* was being overdramatic."

"I prefer to think of it as theatrics." Condor stepped forward again, back into the light. "What time was it when they brought you down here?"

"It's a few hours after sundown, and I'd like to get some sleep." Axel grunted, then closed his eyes. "Try not to kill me while I'm sleeping if you can help it."

"Likewise. And if you happen to find yourself inclined to get me in the night, just remember that you don't need any of your man-parts to fight. Come at me while I'm asleep, and I promise you won't have them when we finally do cross blades. Crystal?"

Axel rolled his eyes. "Whatever."

THE NEXT DAY, Calum watched as the council assembled behind a long oak table set up just in front of the throne platform. Eight Wisps of superior stature and reputation within the Sky Realm sat at the table, four on each side of Avian, who sat on the ninth chair in the middle.

Falcroné sat immediately to Avian's left and General Balena sat to his right, both clad in their dark armor, but Calum didn't recognize any of the other Wisps.

"This council will convene immediately." Avian raised his hand, and the room fell silent. "We will first hear the case of the human, Axel, to whom we have granted all the rights of a citizen of the Sky Realm. Bring him forward."

Two Wisps ushered Axel over to the table from behind a pillar on Calum's right and positioned him directly in front of Falcroné. Thin white ropes bound his hands in front of him. He still wore his dress clothes from last night, but wrinkles and grime tainted the fabric.

"Axel, you have the right to face your accuser and defend yourself," Avian said. "Princess Lilliana, come forth and profess your accusation."

Lilly drifted into view from the opposite side and stood near the far end of the table. Her eyes met Calum's for an instant, then she focused on Axel.

Calum had tried to meet Axel's eyes several times, hoping to reassure him, but he hadn't looked back.

Ganosh had explained the process to him: Lilly would accuse Axel of his crimes in detail as they happened from her point of view. Then Axel could refute the claims by telling his side of the story.

After that, witnesses from both sides of the conflict would come forward and testify to both the character of the accuser and the accused, as well as to their personal experiences with the supposed crime.

Once both sides presented their cases, the council would confer and then convey a ruling over the incident. That ruling could land Axel back in the dungeon for several months, if not forever, since he'd been accused of attacking the Princess of the Sky Realm.

Calum still didn't want to believe that it had happened, but Axel's temperament had fractured more and more the longer they traveled together. What's more, he knew how Axel felt—used, betrayed, and then forgotten.

It's not that Lilly had deserved the attack—not in the least. Such a thing could never be justified, but Calum could at least appreciate the source of Axel's frustrations and the emotions that might have led him to behave so rashly.

Lilly stared at Axel for a long time, but he refused to look back at her.

Finally, she exhaled a long sigh. "I withdraw my claim."

CHAPTER TWENTY-THREE

Falcroné pushed up and away from the table so fast that the back of his chair smacked against the marble floor. *"What?"*

Axel's eyebrows went up, and he turned toward Lilly. Why was she saying this? He had, in fact, been the aggressor, but now she wanted to withdraw her claim?

"You said he *attacked* you." Avian's blue eyes fixed on Lilly's. "Are you suggesting something to the contrary?"

"Axel came to my room and we had an argument," she began. "He told me he loved me, and I told him I loved Falcroné. I tried to leave, and he blocked my way because he wanted to keep talking, but I overreacted and hit him with my chair, then I kicked him while he was down." Lilly lowered her head. "Then I went out and told Falcroné that Axel had attacked me."

A subtle smirk formed on Axel's lips, and the heavy weight of the situation lifted from his shoulders. He couldn't believe it.

Maybe she *did* love him after all.

Falcroné hovered over the table and landed next to her. He took her hands in his and looked into her eyes. "The shock and fear you conveyed when you told me what had happened—those emotions are not easy to falsify."

"I was shocked and afraid of what *I* had done, and you heard my story with ears attuned to my well-being rather than the truth of the situation." Lilly shook her head and broke eye contact with him. "I lied to get myself out of trouble at Axel's expense. It is I who deserve punishment."

"You are aware that if you withdraw your accusation now, you may not ever bring the same accusation before the council again?" Falcroné said more than asked.

"Yes, I know. I choose to withdraw my claim, and I will face the consequences of my actions."

"You will not be charged with any crimes, Lilly," Avian said.

General Balena cleared his throat and stood. "I apologize for what I am about to say, but, Premier, the princess is bound to the laws of the realm just as you or I or anyone else would be. Her punishment is no longer a matter that you may excuse since it has been brought before this council."

Avian gave General Balena a glare that could have split a mountain in half. "I will *not* subject my daughter to a hearing."

"You will, or by law you must assume her place as the accused." General Balena's deep voice shook Axel's insides. "That is, if Axel chooses to make an accusation of the princess's guilt in this matter."

Avian's gaze whiplashed over to Axel.

Axel swallowed the lump in his throat and stared at Lilly, who met his gaze with eyes full of remorse. He could serve her up before this council's judgment with one sentence if he wanted to. He could make her pay for her lies, her duplicity. She had been right when she said she deserved punishment.

But he couldn't do it.

"No," he said. "I'm not gonna accuse her of anything."

"You do not need to fear repercussions for accusing the princess of wrongdoing." General Balena's dark eyes glanced between both Avian and Falcroné. "You are protected under our laws, the same as she or any other citizen of the realm."

Axel eyed Avian again then rotated his sore shoulders. "I'd rather just get outta here and never return, if that's alright with all of you."

General Balena motioned to the two Wisps who had escorted Axel into the throne room. "Free him at once."

One of the Wisps unsheathed a curved dagger from his belt and sliced through the ropes that bound Axel's hands.

"You may rejoin your friends." General Balena extended his open hand, palm up, toward Calum and Magnus.

Axel shook the bonds from his hands and nodded at General Balena, then he cast a lingering gaze at Lilly before he headed back to Calum and Magnus. She'd done the right thing in the end by following her heart, and he'd been right about her all along.

She gave him a solemn nod and then looked away.

Axel chuckled to himself. *Still playing aloof.*

The stares of dozens of Windgales who had gathered in the throne room for his hearing weighed on him, but he walked toward Calum and Magnus unashamed and confident.

"I don't believe it." Calum held his arms out at his sides. "You're free."

"I guess so." Axel admitted, "I wasn't expecting that."

"Why? Because you actually did accost her?" Magnus asked.

Axel frowned at him. "That's none of your business, Scales."

"I have my answer, nonetheless." Magnus folded his arms across his chest and scowled at him.

Axel started to say something, but Avian's voice filled the throne room again.

"The council's next and final hearing is that of Condor, the disgraced former Captain of the Royal Guard and leader of the rebel faction known as the Raven's Brood." Avian motioned toward the pillar to the right of the throne, and four Wisps, all of them clad in dark-purple armor and wielding swords, escorted Condor into view.

Where the Wisps had only secured Axel's hands with ropes, a thick chain bound Condor's wrists behind his back, and a matching strand stretched between his ankles. One of the Wisps gripped another chain attached to a steel collar around Condor's neck.

To top it all off, no one had bothered to change out the bandage on Condor's hand. The same ragged, frayed, and bloody cloth that they'd wrapped around his wounded hand after catching him still covered his hand.

Axel rubbed his sore left shoulder and recalled Condor's words from last night in the prison. *You'd better pray that the council calls me first so I get the bulk of their wrath and there isn't much leftover for you.*

Too bad exactly the opposite of that had transpired. Axel and Condor might not get their day of battle after all.

"Good luck," Axel muttered. His shoulder had already started to feel better.

WHEN CONDOR'S piercing blue eyes met hers, Lilly's heart beat faster.

At first she disregarded the uneasiness in her stomach as the result of him trying to take her hostage, but the longer he stared, the more she realized the source of her anxiety wasn't their history—it came from him.

Just him.

Lilly had to look away.

"Since the accusations against you are innumerable, this council has elected to reduce the number of claims to the following list." Avian held up a scroll. "Insurrection, rebellion, treason, attempted extortion of the Premier for personal gain, theft, and the battery and murder of multiple Sky Realm citizens."

"I object." Condor's voice indicated very little, if any emotion whatsoever. He stood tall, stoic, and stared right at Lilly's father.

Avian shook his head. "You cannot object. These are the summations of the countless accusations we received from citizens regarding your—"

"I object because I do not recognize this council's authority."

"Regardless of your objection, this council stands in authority over you."

"You have me in chains, in shackles. You've kept me in a jail cell for the last week, or however long it has been. But you do not have any authority over me. Why are there only Wisps on this council and not mere Windgales as well?"

"Please do not play coy with us," Avian said. "You know full well that Windgales are not appointed to the council because—"

"Without representation from the lower caste, this council is a farce," Condor interrupted, shaking his head. "Everyone knows that *you* make the final decision on every issue. Everyone knows that the only man bold enough to side against you consistently is General Balena, and even he—"

"Condor, enough." General Balena held up his hand. "Your beliefs are not the subject of this hearing. Do you deny any of the Premier's accusations?"

"I deny all of them."

Grunts and murmurs swelled throughout the crowd. The Wisps who guarded Condor exchanged subtle glances, but Lilly noticed.

"So you deny that you instigated a rebellion?" General Balena leaned forward.

"No."

"You just said you denied all of the accusations."

"I deny that it was a rebellion. The people took a stand against corruption."

"It was a rebellion, regardless of what you call it." Avian rubbed his forehead. "And you admitted to leading it."

"It is the people's right to—"

"We're not talking about the people's rights. We're talking about your actions. Yours alone." Avian pointed at Condor. "More than one hundred people—*our* people—died as a result of your 'uprising.' How do you account for that?"

Condor scoffed. "*Your* soldiers killed them."

"What few members of the Royal Guard who followed you died at the hands of General Balena's soldiers, as well as some of the soldiers themselves, before you fled from the Realm," Avian said. "All of their deaths rest solely on *your* shoulders."

"And how many poor Windgales have died on the ground below Aeropolis because you refuse to provide them with aid? Because your excesses have diminished their resources, and thus their chances of survival? Because of your secrets?"

Condor stepped forward, but the Wisp who held his chain pulled him back. He winced, but otherwise it didn't prevent him from speaking.

"Those hundred fighters died because you refuse to divulge the truth, a truth that would make every Windgale free for the rest of their lives. If I bear the weight of a hundred deaths on my shoulders, you and your oligarchy bear the weight of *thousands* on yours."

Lilly glanced at her father, but he remained focused on the accused. *What is Condor talking about?*

"Your hypocrisy is boundless." Avian stood and smacked his palms flat on the table. "You could have revealed that secret to the dozens of Windgales in your brood, but you didn't. You maintained it for the same reasons that we do."

"Even if I had revealed it, it would've changed nothing for the Windgales who followed me, and you know exactly why that's the case." Condor's impassioned tone persisted. "You keep it secret solely because you need to maintain control."

"We need to maintain *order*."

Secrets? What are they talking about? What mysteries of Lilly's people had her father not yet revealed to her?

Condor shot back, "You're manipulating our people to enhance your luxurious lifestyle."

"When you were Captain of the Royal Guard, you partook in them as well, yet now you hang the blame on me? More hypocrisy," Avian countered.

"Except that unlike you, my excess ceased when I chose to try to level the terms. I gave up everything to reconcile our misdeeds to the people."

"*Enough*." Avian held up his hands. "My reign is not the subject of this hearing. *Your* decisions landed you before this council, and this council will now rule on your fate. Whether you recognize our authority or not, those chains that bind you belong to us, and thus, so do you."

General Balena leaned nearer to Avian. "Premier—"

Condor sneered. "You may own these chains, but you'll *never* own me."

"Premier?" General Balena touched Avian's forearm, but Avian brushed his hand away.

Avian shouted, "Your fate is all but sealed! I'll see you *executed* for your crimes."

"*Avian.*" General Balena clamped his armored hand around Avian's wrist and pulled him away from the table so their backs faced Condor and the crowd. General Balena outweighed Lilly's father by at least fifty pounds, and he had no trouble physically moving Avian.

Lilly wished she could hear what General Balena whispered to her father. Instead, Condor's eyes met hers again, and her stomach leaped. Something about his eyes swirled her emotions.

She didn't feel this way when she looked at Falcroné, or Axel, or even Calum. His allure transcended any of theirs, but it was also accompanied by a sense of danger. Maybe that's why she found him so intriguing in the first place.

When Condor winked at her, Lilly had to look away again. *Dangerous, indeed.*

General Balena turned around first, then Avian, who said, "We will hear no more discussion on your crimes, Condor, as I have decreed."

Condor craned his neck to address the crowd. "Like I said, all the final decisions are made by one man instead of by the people."

General Balena pointed his index finger at Condor. "If he utters so much as another word without us asking him a direct question, cut out his tongue."

As far as Lilly knew, General Balena had never made a joke in his life, nor had he even laughed at one. His command regarding Condor was no exception.

The Wisp produced a small knife from his belt and held it near Condor's lips, but Condor's indignation persisted in the form of a rebellious smirk.

General Balena sat in his chair, but Avian remained standing.

"Condor, disgraced former Captain of the Royal Guard and leader of the defunct rebel faction called the Raven's Brood," Avian said, "on the charges brought against you for your crimes against the Sky Realm, we, the council will now rule on your case."

Down the line, from the Wisp closest to Lilly on the left side of the table down to the Wisp farthest from her on the opposite end, the council members repeated the word, "Guilty." As was their custom, the Premier's vote came last. Like all the rest, her father said, "Guilty."

"According to our laws, with a unanimous vote of guilt, we are obliged to call for a second vote to determine whether or not you deserve the death penalty." Avian motioned toward Lilly's end of the table. "By law, that vote—yea for the death penalty and nay to stay the sword of justice—must also be unanimous. Do you have anything to say in your defense before we decide your fate?"

The Wisp pulled the knife away from Condor's mouth, and Condor straightened his posture. "I'd rather die as a traitor than live as a servant of corruption."

"Very well." Avian's frown deepened, and he looked down the line. "Votes?"

"Yea," said the first council member.

Twice. Three times. Falcroné added a fourth without any hesitation, and then the vote fell to General Balena, who remained silent for a long moment. Finally, he looked at Condor with steel in his eyes and said, "Yea."

Condor bowed his head. He must have known, as Lilly did, that the three remaining council members would also vote for his death, and they did.

But neither of them expected Avian to say "Nay."

CHAPTER TWENTY-FOUR

C ondor's head popped up and he stared at Avian with his mouth open slightly. Lilly, Falcroné, General Balena, and everyone else in the room did likewise.

"Death is too convenient for you, Condor. You expected an easy way out, a swift end to your miserable life in exchange for the harm you inflicted on your people." Avian shook his head. "I will not grant it.

"Executing you would make you a martyr to those in the Sky Realm who believe the lies you espouse, but martyrs cannot earn that title with the blood of others. No, you will live the remainder of your life as a slave. Not to me, nor to anyone in this Realm, but to harsher masters than any known to Kanarah."

Lilly covered her hand with her mouth. She already knew where her father meant to send Condor for his crimes.

"I sentence you to one hundred years of hard labor in the Blood Chasm."

The crowd rumbled with mutters and gasps until General Balena held up his hand. "Premier, decisions like these must be made by majority vote of the council. To send Condor to that place without—"

"Then we'll vote." Avian's gaze met those of each of the Wisps on the council. "What say you, Lord Elmond? Yea or nay to Condor's punishment?"

The Wisp nearest to Lilly shook his head. "Nay. That place ought to be shut down for good. No living creature deserves a fate like what you're suggesting."

"Very well. Lady Sandaria?"

"Yea."

Avian nodded to her, then focused on the next Wisp. "Lord Jansson?"

"Nay."

"Yea," Falcroné said before Avian could call his name. "He deserves the worst. I say we give it to him."

Having been captured by slave traders, the idea of anyone being enslaved grated against her judgment. Worse yet, having encountered two Gronyxes in the tunnels under Trader's Pass, she knew all too well what Condor might have to face in Western Kanarah's subterranean realm.

Lilly's eyes locked with Falcroné's, and she set her jaw. Falcroné had given his answer out of spite more than from a desire for justice. They'd once been friends while training to become officers, even as close as brothers, despite Condor's ascension from the lower caste.

Apparently, Condor's betrayal had destroyed whatever friendship they'd shared, but even so, Lilly couldn't help the disdain she felt for his behavior.

Avian smirked at Condor then turned to General Balena. "General?"

"I have seen the Blood Chasm and witnessed the evil that dwells there firsthand," he began. "I've watched the slaves fight for their lives against them, only to die slow, torturous deaths. I will not vote to subject even the worst offender to such a fate.

"Furthermore, the Blood Chasm should be abandoned indefinitely for the good of all Kanarah, not perpetuated by sending another soul to his demise there." General Balena folded his arms and stared at Avian. "I vote 'nay.'"

Avian's smirk dissipated while General Balena spoke, and it devolved into a scowl by the time he finished. He looked at the next council member. "Lady Katalina?"

"Nay. I agree with General Balena, Lord Jansson, and Lord Elmond. The punishment is too severe for one of our own."

Lilly raised her eyebrows. One more vote, and Condor would avoid the Blood Chasm.

Avian's scowl hardened. Through clenched teeth, he asked, "And what do you think, Lady Gremia?"

"Yea. Send him to the pit, and may he die the slow, miserable death General Balena described." Lady Gremia frowned and narrowed her dark eyes at Condor. "My eldest son is gone because of him. If I cannot ensure him the death penalty, I must do what I can to ease the pain and suffering he has caused my household and that of the other families whose sons died in his rebellion."

"Lord Namuel, the vote is yours."

For as hard as Lilly's heart pounded in her chest, she couldn't imagine what Condor's was doing in his. She knew nothing about Lord Namuel. Had he, too, lost someone in the rebellion? Did he tend toward mercy?

Lord Namuel rubbed his bare chin with thick fingers. "May he live to die a hundred deaths, one for each year of his sentence, one for each citizen who perished because of him. Yea."

The crowd erupted in a mix of cheers and droning boos. All but one of the Wisps who stood guard around Condor faced the crowd with their swords at the ready. The crowd did not advance toward the council, but their ruckus continued nonetheless.

Lilly watched as her father, General Balena, and Falcroné all ascended into the air from their seats. Avian extended his arms in front of him, palms down, and boomed over the crowd, "Condor, disgraced former Captain of the Royal Guard and leader of the Raven's Brood rebel faction, I hereby sentence you to one hundred years of slavery in the Blood Chasm."

Condor's stoic face did not crumble with emotion. He simply bowed his head again and closed his eyes.

Avian motioned toward the throne room doors. "Take him away."

The Wisps who guarded Condor shoved him toward the crowd, their swords still unsheathed and ready for action should it find them.

The Wisp who held the chain connected to Condor's neck led the way, and the other three Wisps formed a diamond around Condor.

As they walked through the crowd, objects soared through the air at them. Shoes, rotten fruits and vegetables, and even stones whipped toward Condor from the crowd. The Wisps hurried him forward, but the crowd sealed off their exit before they could get out.

Lilly swiveled her head toward Falcroné, but he and General Balena had already darted toward the doors. They landed between Condor's guards and the crowd and barked orders in ferocious tones.

The crowd parted just long enough for Condor and the Wisps to get through, and General Balena followed them out. Falcroné took to the air and returned to Avian's side.

Lilly would never see Condor's piercing blue eyes again. Perhaps it was for the best.

"This hearing is dismissed," Falcroné bellowed. "Return to the day's labors at once. Stragglers will be considered a threat to the realm's safety and will be jailed immediately."

As the crowd dissipated, Lilly couldn't help but wonder if justice had been served in any capacity that day. She had lied to cover for Axel's transgression, and her father had damned Condor to a terrible fate, one arguably worse than death. And Condor had accused her father of multiple wrongdoings as well.

Secrets. Rebellions. Threats. Injustice. Death. Where was the truth in all of it? Why was the Sky Realm so broken, so confused? Or the rest of Kanarah, for that matter?

Lilly clenched her fists. *Someone ought to do something about it all.*

RILEY WHIMPERED, careful not to be loud enough to wake Calum. He lay still, taking short shallow breaths, concealed in the shadows to the left of Calum's bed.

He should've been safe there in the dark, but his brutal memories always managed to find him no matter where he went.

Silver flashed in his mind's eye, and pain flared in his side. Condor's blade pierced him again and again, every night in his memories and in his dreams. Nights like this one.

Hiding was about all he could do anymore. The wound may not have killed him, but he could no longer run, much less leap or jump or pounce.

He'd never amounted to much of a fighter anyway—he preferred to rely on his speed and his stealth to gain the advantage. When those failed, Riley could resort to the vicious, crazy part of him that he didn't let out except in the very worst of times.

But his speed was gone now, taken away with one vicious stab from Condor's blade, maybe permanently.

Perhaps he should have unleashed that vicious part of himself when he'd fought Condor. But even that vicious part had limits. Physical limits, more so now than ever.

Where Riley had always provided for himself, Condor's sword had reduced him to little more than a beggar who could *maybe* rob other beggars. He would have to depend on Calum and his friends for food since he couldn't hunt without pain.

Who was he kidding? He could barely *breathe* without pain.

Riley whimpered again and lay his head down on the floor. He was useless. A drag. He might as well stay here in the Sky Fortress as the Premier's hound, like the common dog he'd insisted he wasn't. He could eat scraps from the Premier's dinner table and gnaw the meat off the bones leftover in the kitchen.

In time, perhaps he would even learn some tricks. He could already roll over, already play dead. Condor had taught him that one.

A long sigh escaped his mouth until it hurt to exhale any more. He closed his eyes in the darkness and wondered what misery he'd have to endure tomorrow.

———

WHEN AVIAN SUMMONED CALUM, Axel, Magnus, and Riley for a private audience, Calum knew what it had to mean. He'd dreamed of Lumen in all his glory again last night, and they'd stayed at the Sky Fortress for far longer than he'd intended already. Aside from Axel's sore arms and Riley's ongoing recovery from his wound, they were healthy and ready to go.

Lilly stood at her father's side in the throne room. Her golden hair seemed to sparkle under the sunlight that poured through the crystal-covered shafts in the throne room's ceiling.

Falcroné stood next to her, and his hair shimmered just as much, if not more.

Calum suppressed a disheartened chuckle as he approached them. Falcroné was almost as "pretty" as Lilly was.

Zephyrra sat next to the Premier in a chair smaller than the throne with a pleasant smile on her face.

"My friends, welcome." Avian lifted his arms, but did not stand. "Come forward."

Calum performed the Windgale salute first and snuck a peek back to make sure Magnus and Axel did as well. Riley just bowed slightly and licked his nose.

"We have news for you. In poring through our expansive archives, my court historians have discovered a map that may lead you to the Arcanum."

Calum glanced at Magnus, who nodded. "May we see it?"

"You may *have* it." Avian grinned. "No one in the Sky Realm desires to use it, so it is yours for the taking. Kanton?"

From behind the pillars on the right side of the throne room, Kanton floated into view. He held a rolled-up, yellow-brown piece of parchment in his left hand. He landed in front of them and extended the parchment to Calum.

"You're a court historian now?" Calum asked.

"No. Not in the least. I can't read a single word on this map, much less an entire book."

Calum glanced at Avian, then back at Kanton. "Then what are you doing here?"

Kanton smiled then turned back to the Premier. "Do you want to tell him, or can I?"

Avian grinned again and waved his hand toward them, palm up.

"I'm going with you." Kanton winked at Calum.

"What? Really?" Calum couldn't help but smile too. "Are you serious?"

"Serious as any man ever was." Kanton nodded toward Avian. "The Premier was kind enough to grant me this grand favor in light of my small role in helping Princess Lilly get home—that is, helping her rescuers up to Aeropolis in a time of need. When I asked to join your group, he gave me his blessing immediately. That is, if you'll have me."

Calum eyed Lilly over Kanton's shoulder, but she looked down at the floor instead of at him. She really wasn't coming along, just like she had said. Kanton was supposed to be her replacement, in a way. It was a nice gesture, but the thought of her not traveling with them ripped the hole in Calum's heart all over again.

"You already know I'm good with my hands—from a healing perspective, that is—but I'm also not too bad with a staff or a spear. Had plenty of years protecting the Premier's sheep on the ground level by fending off his kind—" Kanton nodded at Riley. "—and wild beasts of other sorts too.

"Even killed a sabertooth cat once. Got a nice pair of fangs from him, but had to sell them when my third cape wore out. Wish I'd kept them, though. Would've been worth a fortune in Aeropolis nowadays."

Calum and Axel eyed each other.

"Anyway, you don't mind if I come along, do you? I know I'll come in handy more than once." Kanton's blue eyes glistened with delightful expectation. "What so you say?"

Calum looked back at Magnus, who nodded and said, "We could use someone like him."

"Yeah, any time Calum gets himself injured, he'll have a healer to patch him up," Axel said.

"You're the one with sore arms and a bruise on your chin. I feel fine."

Axel glanced at Lilly, then he refocused on Calum. "Come over here, and we'll see how fine you feel after thirty seconds of me thrashing you."

Calum ignored Axel. "The answer is yes, Kanton. We'd love to have you join us."

Kanton let out a whoop, launched into the air, and executed a backward loop. He landed almost exactly where he'd been standing and nodded to Calum. "Sorry for the excitement, but I thought you'd say I was too old for an adventure."

"You think *you're* old?" Axel huffed. "Magnus here is two hundred sixty-something."

"Two hundred and *three* years old," Magnus said. "Not two hundred sixty-something."

Axel held up his hands. "My mistake. Didn't realize you were so sensitive about it."

"I am not sensitive about it. I just care that my age is represented accur—"

"Friends, friends," Avian interjected. "Let's not get sideswiped with meaningless chatter. You have your map. You have Kanton. You are free to go. The lift awaits your arrival for immediate descent. May the Overlord bless your journey."

Calum and Axel made eye contact again. They'd both taken the meaning of Avian's words.

Axel stepped forward and squinted at Avian. "What do you mean, 'immediate descent?' Are you throwing us out?"

Avian tilted his head and gave Axel a manufactured smile. "Of course not. You are welcome to stay as long as you please. I just wanted you to know you are free to go whenever you so desire."

Axel gave an incredulous nod. "Because it really sounded like—"

"We understand," Calum interrupted before Axel managed to get them tossed off one of the platforms. "Thank you for your generosity and hospitality so far. We'll head out this evening."

"It's too bad you'll have to miss the wedding." Falcroné's lips curled up in a sly grin, and he pulled Lilly close to him. "It will be an occasion like none in recent history."

Calum's jaw set, but he forced a smile and nodded. "We wish you all the best. Come on, guys. Let's go pack our things."

"Wait," Lilly said.

Calum's eyes found hers. What was it this time?

"Father." She looked at Avian. "I'm going with them."

CHAPTER TWENTY-FIVE

S ilence overtook the throne room, and part of Lilly couldn't even believe she'd said it.

Avian raised his eyebrows at her.

"No, you're not." Somehow, Falcroné managed to say the words even before her father had the chance.

Lilly looked into his blue eyes and, her voice firm, said, "Yes, I am."

"No, you're *not*." That time her father said it. "Absolutely not. You just returned to us. If it were up to me, I'd never let you outside of the fortress walls again."

Of course he'd say something like that. Most fathers would, wouldn't they?

But he didn't understand what she'd experienced out there in the rest of Kanarah. He didn't comprehend the state of things with the King in power—the corruption, the suffering. He couldn't even acknowledge the struggles of his own people, so how could he possibly have any sense of what the land as a whole was dealing with?

Lilly renewed her resolve. "I'm going with them, Father. I want to help them free Lumen."

"No." Avian waved his hand laterally in front of him as if dividing the room in half. "Not in a millennium."

Mother stepped forward. "You have duties here. Obligations to fulfill."

"You're getting married in less than a month," Avian said. "That alone is reason enough for you not to go with them, and I have hundreds more besides."

"I don't care what I'm supposed to do or what your reasons are for wanting me to stay." Lilly's stern tone shocked even her, but she'd stated her plans and refused to back down now. "You tried to force me into a life I didn't want months ago, and look what happened: I got kidnapped by slave traders when I left here. You're not going to dictate my life to me anymore. I'm going with them, and that's final."

"Nothing is final until *I say* it is final, Lilliana!" Avian thundered. He leaned in close to her, his voice calmer as he said, "When you left, my heart broke. I will not allow it to happen again."

"Then *hear* me, Father," Lilly pleaded. "I left because you gave me no choice. I've agreed to your terms regarding my marriage, but with this delay. That's all. Can't you grant me leeway in this?"

Avian's eyes narrowed. "No. You are staying here, and you are marrying Falcroné on the eve of your eighteenth birthday. That is not negotiable."

"I'll marry him, but I'll do it when we return from freeing Lumen." Lilly glanced at Falcroné, whose sullen expression had softened at her most recent comment. She might have won him over, but how could she convince her father? "Kanarah is in a state of confusion and disarray. Lumen will—"

"You don't know what you're saying. Lumen will overthrow the King, and he intends to reign over all Kanarah. *All* of it. That includes *our* realm, Lilly." Avian's hot breath hit her face when he spoke. "Why would you free someone who intends to overthrow your own father?"

Lilly hadn't thought about it that way before. "He's... he's not going to overthrow anyone. Calum said he's going to bring order and peace to Kanarah by defeating the King."

"And you believe what *Calum* says? Why?" Falcroné asked.

"He's dreamt of Lumen multiple times. He's seen him, spoken to him, followed his instructions—and now I'm back home, safe because of

THE WAY OF ANCIENT POWER

what Calum has seen in his sleep." Lilly unclenched her fists. She didn't remember clenching them in the first place. "I *know* Calum is going to set Lumen free. I can feel it inside of me. I want to be there when it happens."

Falcroné huffed and folded his arms. "*If* it happens."

"Oh, it'll happen alright, Sunshine." Axel muttered.

"What did you just say?" Falcroné stepped off the platform toward Axel until they stood face-to-face.

"All that hair must make it hard to hear." Undeterred, Axel's eyes narrowed. "I said, 'oh, it'll happen, al—"

"Enough, both of you," Avian said. "Falcroné, come back up here."

Falcroné obeyed, but he snarled at Axel as he hovered back to the platform.

"Lilly, we don't know what Lumen is going to do if—or *when* he gets freed." Her mother frowned. "There's just no telling what's going to be affected by his return."

"Then who better to put right near the action than your own daughter? I can make sure we're in his good graces when the time comes to—"

"You are the *worst* person to have near the action," Avian said. "You are my only heir, who together with Falcroné must produce the next in our lineage to rule after you. What if you're stuck down or wounded, and are unable to have children? What will happen to our house then?"

Finally, a question Lilly had practiced answering in advance. "Falcroné can rule in my stead. He's my cousin, after all, and shares my ancestry."

"No, I can't." Falcroné reached for her hand and intertwined his fingers with hers. "Because if you go, I'm going with you."

"*What?*" Avian yelled. "No! She's not going, and neither are you."

"I think she may have a point, Premier," Falcroné said. "The prophecy regarding Lumen is clear—he will be freed 1,000 years from the day he was banished. Wouldn't it be better to help free him and side with him in his rebellion than to try to remain neutral in a conflict that will engulf the whole of Kanarah?"

"The prophecy says nothing about whether or not he will *defeat* the King, just that he will be released from his prison." Avian rubbed his forehead with his index finger and his thumb. "You want to go to your deaths, both of you. What did I do to make you wish to die far away from your home? Name your deepest desire and I will grant it, but not this. Anything but this."

"Father." Lilly let go of Falcroné's hand and took Avian's hands in hers. She stared into his eyes. "This is what I want. *This* is my deepest desire. I promise that when Kanarah sees justice, Falcroné and I will be wed, and in doing so, we will ensure the future of not only our line but also of the entire Sky Realm."

"I will see it done, Premier." Falcroné stepped forward, next to Lilly. "I will not allow any harm to come to her. I let her go once, and it is not a mistake I intend to repeat."

Falcroné really wanted to come along? Lilly hadn't figured on that. Not in a millennium.

Zephyrra touched Avian's arm and nodded, then Avian exhaled a long sigh. "Who will lead the Royal Guard in your place?"

"Promote Helion. He is a remarkable warrior of great strength and wisdom for his age," Falcroné said.

Avian's scowl deepened. "The boy is fifteen years old, Falcroné."

"All the same, he is as fit to succeed me as anyone. General Balena can provide him with extra insight as he did for me. Helion will excel if given more responsibility."

"He'll also beat Condor's record for youngest Captain of the Royal Guard by three years." Avian squinted at him. "Does that factor into your suggestion?"

Falcroné shrugged but donned a wry grin. "It couldn't hurt to wipe Condor from the realm's memory entirely."

"Please, Father?" Lilly employed her sad-eyes-pouty-lip face. It was a cheap ploy, but it almost always worked on him.

Avian frowned at her. "Lilly, I don't want anything to happen to you. I *just* got you back, and now you want to leave on a journey far more dangerous than the one which brought you home."

It *almost* always worked. "Father, Falcroné will protect me. Plus, I'll be traveling with Calum, Axel, Magnus, Riley, and Kanton, the former of which have already proven that they can keep me safe."

"None of them give me half as much comfort as knowing Falcroné would be with you. Even so, I would send a contingent of soldiers with you for extra protec—"

"No, Father," Lilly shook her head. "We'll draw too much attention that way. Better to keep a low profile."

"She's right, you know." A deep, almost melancholy voice sounded from behind Calum. He stepped aside, and Riley tilted his head.

"Excuse me—she's right, you know, *Premier.*" Riley gave a modest bow. "I know a little something about stealth, and I can tell you it's much easier with fewer people to go unnoticed. The more men you send with us, the more of us won't make it back, in my opinion. Group's already too big for my taste *without* the happy couple."

Avian narrowed his eyes at Riley.

"That's—that's just what I think." Riley's voice quivered at the end of his sentence. Then he slunk behind Calum and murmured, "I'm gonna shut up now."

"Avian, let them go." Zephyrra touched his shoulder. "You can't protect her forever. She needs to discover the world and find her place in it. If you deny her this, you may lose her again for good, and our line will be lost with her."

Avian sighed and rubbed his forehead. "Even you are convinced now?"

Zephyrra nodded.

"I had hoped she would've 'found her place in our world' in the last few months she was gone, but now she wants to leave again." Avian shook his head and let out another sigh. He leveled his gaze at Lilly. "Promise me you'll come back unscathed."

Lilly didn't fight the smile that cracked her lips. "I promise."

Avian grabbed the sides of Falcroné's breastplate and yanked him close. "And *you*, boy. Promise me you'll bring her back unscathed, or so help me, your fate will be even worse than Condor's."

Falcroné nodded. "I swear on my mother's grave."

Avian released him. "Then you both may go."

CALUM WASN'T SURPRISED that Avian's attitude toward them didn't change all that much after he agreed to let Lilly go with them, but his approach certainly did. Specifically, he did everything possible to ensure they were well prepared and well stocked for their journey.

He ordered Ganosh to take Axel, Kanton, and Calum to the Royal Armory to update their armor and weaponry. By the time they left, Calum and Axel wore new lightweight armor—navy blue for Axel, in addition to Magnus's old light-blue Blood Ore leg and arm plating, deep forest-green for Kanton, and crimson red for Calum.

They'd tried to get Calum to replace his old boots for new ones, but he refused. Instead, they compromised at repairing and resoling his old ones. They also dyed the leather black at his request. He hadn't minded the brown, but Lilly had said black would look better with his new armor, so he'd gone for it.

The armorist even outfitted Riley's right foreleg with a steel cast of sorts that started just above his paw, covered his shoulder, and reached almost back to his hind leg along his torso. It more than covered the wound he'd take from Condor's blade, but the armorist warned that a blow to his right side would likely still hurt because of the original wound's severity.

Riley growled a bit and grumbled something about his stealth and speed abilities suffering as a result, but he kept the armor on nonetheless and nodded to the armorist in thanks.

Next, they visited the Sky Fortress's quartermaster, who took their old swords and exchanged them for lighter-weight blades.

Axel protested at first, saying that the lighter weight would mean less heft behind his swings, but the quartermaster assured him the blade's sharpness and speed would more than account for its lower weight. Both of them also received a curved dagger, which they strapped to their belts.

Calum gladly traded Tyburon's red blade for a new one. After so many battles, its once sharp edge had both dulled and sustained a variety of gashes and nicks that reduced its effectiveness in fights. A part of him regretted letting it go, but when he received his new weapon, he forgot all about it.

The quartermaster handed him a sword very similar in shape to the one Calum had given up, only it weighed two-thirds what Tyburon's did. Its blade gleamed silver with golden engravings of swirls and wispy designs befitting the Sky Realm.

Kanton received a short sword and a steel spear that had a hollow shaft. A broad-headed spearhead topped it off. The quartermaster pointed out a slight curve on the bottom of one of the spearhead's edges near the shaft and told Kanton he could use it to lock his opponents' weapons in place or even disarm them entirely.

The only one of their group who did not accept anything new was Magnus. He insisted that his Blood Ore breastplate and broadsword were more than sufficient, despite both the quartermaster and the armorist arguing otherwise.

He did, however, accept a new vial of veromine from the royal apothecary when Kanton requested a variety of medical supplies to bring along. Over time, he could've extracted some from his own blood, he'd explained, but the process was long and tedious, and not an ideal undertaking for a journey through the wilds.

By the time they made it back into the throne room, the sun had just begun to set. As before, Lilly stood next to her father, only this time she wore the same light pink armor she'd worn before they arrived.

Avian beckoned them forward, and as Calum approached, he noticed that Lilly's armor was indeed the same, only the various nicks and gashes had been repaired and retouched with pink lacquer the same color as the rest of the armor. When Calum got closer, he noticed the chips in the armor's faint white engravings of eagles and hawks had also been retouched.

Her new bow, a long white recurve with silver designs etched into its sides, hung with its string across her chest. A quiver full of arrows with silver shafts and white fletching hung from her hip.

The short sword she'd used before their arrival was gone, replaced by a curved blade with a white hilt that hung from her belt in its sheath. It looked like the same style as the daggers Calum and Axel had received.

She looked every bit as beautiful as she had the first time Calum saw her, only she now exuded a renewed sense of strength and confidence as well.

"What a transformation," Avian said. "Were you in orange or purple armor instead, you could have passed for General Balena's soldiers or Royal Guards."

Calum performed the Windgale salute and bowed low. "We appreciate your generosity, Premier. We're far better equipped than we've ever been."

"This is only the beginning, Calum." Avian smiled and leaned back in his throne. "You haven't seen the provisions I've had Ganosh and the kitchen prepare for your journey."

"We are very grateful."

Falcroné soared in from behind them and landed next to Lilly. He still wore his charcoal armor, only now he carried a spear like Kanton's in addition to the sword strapped to his belt. "Everything is ready. Are we heading out tonight or tomorrow morning?"

"Tonight," Axel said.

"Tomorrow morning." Avian's eyes narrowed at Axel. "Get a good night's rest here before you head out."

"Father." Lilly clasped Avian's hands in hers. "You have to let us go at some point."

"I definitely prefer to travel at night," Riley said. When Avian glared at him, Riley added, "But that's just me. We can leave whenever."

Avian cupped Lilly's cheek with his hand. "Are you so eager to leave me behind that you won't even stay one more night?"

Lilly chuckled. "It's not that. I just don't think you'll ever actually let us go."

"You can't fault me for wanting you around. You're my one and only daughter, and I love you."

"I love you too, Father." Lilly pulled away from him. "But we need to leave tonight."

Avian sighed, but nodded. "If that's what you desire, then so be it."

"Nice." Riley smirked. When Avian glowered at him again, he started to back into the shadow of one of the pillars. "You know what? Just ignore me. I'm not even here."

"Ganosh will provide you with the rest of your supplies," Avian said.

Lilly hugged Avian and smiled. "Thank you."

After their hug, Avian grabbed Falcroné by the sides of his breast-plate as he had earlier that day. "Protect her. If she's not with you when you return, don't bother returning at all."

Falcroné nodded. "I understand."

"Go." Avian waved them away. "Before I change my decision, go. And don't forget to say goodbye to your mother, Lilly."

She smiled again. "I won't."

Calum saluted Avian again and bowed. "Thank you, Premier. We'll bring her back safely."

Axel, Magnus, Kanton, and Riley followed Calum toward the doors, and Lilly and Falcroné landed next to him and walked alongside him.

Then the throne room doors swung open before them, stopping the group in their tracks as a cluster of large dark-green figures stepped inside. Not Saurians—Sobeks, like Magnus. Six of them.

A pristine golden breastplate decorated the chest of the lead Sobek, who towered over the rest of the Sobeks by at least six inches. He had to be nearly eight feet tall—even larger than Magnus.

Four of the others wore black breastplates, and the last Sobek, shorter and stockier than the others yet still over seven feet tall, wore a scratched-up brown breastplate. His scarred face was stuck somewhere between a snarl and a perpetual sneer.

Calum couldn't help but stare as he passed them. They didn't give him a second look, but the lead Sobek eyed Magnus for a moment before refocusing on Avian.

"That's Vandorian in the lead," Falcroné whispered to Calum. "He's the nephew of Kahn, the Dragon King of Reptilius."

"He's *huge*. And I thought Magnus was big." Calum glanced over his shoulder. "Do you know him, Magnus?"

But Magnus wasn't walking behind them anymore.

Instead, he followed the group of Sobeks—and his hand was clamped around the hilt of his broadsword.

CHAPTER TWENTY-SIX

The *shing* of Magnus's broadsword leaving its sheath sent shivers ratcheting through Riley's body. There wasn't supposed to be a fight here, now, but Magnus was starting one anyway.

One by one, the Sobeks turned back to face Magnus as he charged toward them with a room-rattling roar.

The first Sobek took the worst blow—a deadening shot to his scaled snout from Magnus's left fist. Magnus passed by the Sobek with the brown armor, who stepped well clear of Magnus's path and didn't even try to intervene. Then Magnus drove his shoulder into another of the Sobeks in black.

The final two Sobeks in black drew their own swords and positioned themselves between Magnus and the tall Sobek in gold, who finally turned back to assess the commotion behind him. Magnus ducked under the first Sobek's swing, parried the second Sobek's blow, and broke through to the lead Sobek with ease.

With another roar, he leaped at the Sobek in gold with his sword raised.

The lead Sobek showed no sign of fear, concern, or any emotion. Instead, he lunged forward as Magnus began to swing his blade and delivered a colossal blow to Magnus's breastplate with his fist.

The punch reversed Magnus's trajectory and knocked him back several feet. He skidded along the marble floor, and as his back smacked against one of the pillars, his broadsword clattered out of reach.

Three of the four Sobeks in black swarmed Magnus with their swords ready.

Riley had seen enough. Anyone who could hit Magnus hard enough to make him drop his sword was someone Riley had no intention of tangling with.

Amid the shouts of Calum, Falcroné, and Avian, Riley darted away from the group and took refuge in the shadow of one of the pillars. Fighting now was a terrible idea. Definitely not against six Sobeks.

Falcroné took to the air and zipped toward the Premier, whose four guards formed a barrier between him and the Sobeks' scuffle.

Calum drew his sword and hurried to join Magnus, and Lilly, Kanton, and Axel followed him, but the Sobek in brown, still upright, positioned himself between them and Magnus. He hissed at them and drew a ragged-looking curved sword.

"*Enough*," a thunderous voice boomed, shaking Riley to his core.

The lead Sobek still hadn't drawn his sword, but the entire room ceased to move at his command. He stood in place, his face as calm as when he had leveled Magnus, and all eyes watched him.

"Get him up," he ordered. "Hold him."

The three Sobeks pulled Magnus to his feet. He strained against them, but they anchored him in place.

The lead Sobek tilted his head. "Bring him to me."

They dragged Magnus over to within ten feet of him, and Magnus roared, but he still couldn't get free.

"Be *silent*." The lead Sobek narrowed his eyes. "I know you, do I not?"

Magnus hissed at him, long and low. Riley had scarcely ever heard a more threatening sound, and it sent chills spiraling through his body.

"Please, Magnus." The lead Sobek shook his head. "That is no way to treat your brother, is it?"

Riley's eyes widened.

THE TENSION in Calum's body went slack. Vandorian and Magnus were brothers? But that meant—

"Calum!" Axel shouted.

Calum barely got his sword into position in time to absorb the blow from the Sobek in brown, and Axel joined him. But the force of his swing sent both Calum and Axel sliding across the marble floor until they smacked into one of the pillars, just as Magnus had.

"*Hold*, Oren." Vandorian's voice filled the whole throne room once again.

"No one 'oo raises arms 'gainst my lord or me gets off wiffout *punishment.*" Oren almost spat the words.

"You have made your point. Hold."

"What is the meaning of this?" Avian asked from behind his Royal Guard.

"Patience, Premier." Vandorian gave a slight bow and held his right fist against his gilded chest. When he spoke, his voice carried an air of distinction and superiority to it. "All will be revealed soon."

Calum pushed himself up first, then helped Axel to his feet. Kanton and Lilly darted over to them, their weapons ready should Oren attack again, but instead he sheathed his weathered old curved sword and scowled at them.

"I hardly recognized you—until you chose to attack me." A smirk formed on Vandorian's lips. "But now you stand before me, wearing our father's old Blood Ore breastplate, and wielding his old broadsword. When last I saw you, you were a tiny lizard. Now you're a Sobek, just like me. You have certainly grown, brother."

Little? To Calum, Magnus had never been *little*.

"You ceased to be my brother the day our father died," Magnus uttered.

"That was a tragic day, indeed. I am surprised you survived, to tell you the truth." Vandorian clacked his talons on his breastplate, just like Magnus often did. "We thought you were dead."

Avian motioned for Falcroné to come near. He whispered something to him, and Falcroné darted through one of the throne room's side doors.

"It takes more than the likes of you and your seditious warriors to kill me."

With every word, Magnus's mysterious past further unraveled before Calum's eyes.

"Clearly." Vandorian stepped closer to Magnus. "Tell me, brother, where you came by a Dragon Emerald?"

"That is none of your concern," Magnus growled.

"It *is* my concern. There are no more Dragon Emeralds in Reptilius, or anywhere, that we know of." Vandorian eyed the leather pouch that hung from Magnus's belt.

"Take your query to our uncle instead."

Vandorian snorted. "Or I can take yours."

Magnus jerked and thrashed against the Sobeks who held him, but he couldn't get free.

Vandorian reached for the pouch.

"Stop this at once, Vandorian." Avian's voice split the commotion. He hovered behind his guards with steel in his eyes. "I did not receive you into my realm that you might steal from my guests."

Vandorian retracted his hand. He glanced at Calum and faced Avian. "No, Premier, but your 'guests' have attacked my warriors and me."

"Then we will deal with them under our laws. They are not subject to your command, nor is any of their property."

"This Saurian is a wanted fugitive, partially responsible for the death of our father, the mighty Dragon King Praetorius."

"That's a lie!" Magnus shouted.

Calum's mouth dropped open. It all made sense now.

"He fled the Crimson Keep five years ago, unbeknownst to us. We thought he was killed the same day of his rebellion." Vandorian's head swiveled and he stared at Magnus. "I am taking him back with me for judgment."

"No, you are not."

Vandorian turned back and he glared at Avian. His voice lowered and sharpened, losing most of its regal tone. "What did you just say to me?"

"I said you're not taking them with you." Avian returned Vandorian's glare with one of his own. "Magnus has attained citizenship here and is partly responsible for my daughter's safe return. He is now under my authority, and thus he is mine to protect."

"I am taking him, and that is final," Vandorian insisted. His voice low and threatening again, he added, "And you cannot stop me."

Avian floated toward him, beyond the safety of his men, until they were eye to eye. "If you remove him or any of his property from this fortress—even from this *room*—I will treat it as an act of war."

Calum glanced at Lilly, but she just gave him a slight shrug. An act of war? Over Magnus? What had gotten into Avian all of a sudden?

Vandorian's jaw hardened, and he exhaled a long hiss through his nose. "You would not dare. We would annihilate your people and destroy your fortress within less than one day. We have Kahn, a direct descendant of the original Saurians first created by the Overlord, the only dragon known to Kanarah. You tiny birds are no match for his might."

A loud slam sounded from the back of the room. All heads turned for a look as General Balena stormed into the throne room, followed by dozens of armored Wisps and Windgale soldiers who filled the air. They surrounded Vandorian and his Sobeks with weapons brandished and blocked the exits.

"Sheathe your weapons immediately," General Balena bellowed, "or we will view your noncompliance as a threat to the Premier's security, and we will be forced to attack."

At the word "attack," every Windgale soldier in the room pointed the tips of their weapons at the Sobeks. Calum froze in place until Axel and Kanton pointed their weapons at Oren, then Calum did as well. Like Avian had said—they were *not* taking Magnus.

Oren drew his old curved sword again and beckoned them forward with his long green fingers. "C'mere, li'l babies. Let's see 'ow you fare."

"Easy, Oren." Vandorian chuckled, at first, then he shook his head. "Premier, I came here as a gesture of goodwill to honor your daughter for her engagement, and you receive me with a third of your army?"

"The engagement party was several days ago, and this isn't even close to a third of our army." Avian's voice didn't waver. "Now do as

General Balena commands, and tell your warriors to sheathe their swords, or we will take action against you. We may be 'tiny birds,' but with enough of us, we can yet peck you to death. There is no need for you to die today."

After a long pause, Vandorian nodded to his Sobeks. "Do as he says."

All of them except Oren complied. Instead, he leaned toward Calum, Axel, and Kanton and bared his jagged teeth in what almost passed for a smile. "I ain't afraid of any o' you bugs. Come at me, an' you'll learn the true meanin' of sufferin'. Make your move, li'l babies."

"*Oren.*" Vandorian's voice cut through the tension. "Sheathe your sword, or I'll use your hide to reupholster my throne."

Oren grunted but straightened his spine and sheathed his old sword. "Next time, babies. Next time."

"Release Magnus," Avian said.

Vandorian straightened to his full height. "By Saurian law, we are within our rights to—"

"Look around you, Vandorian," Avian cut in. "You're not in Reptilius. These walls are blue crystal, not red granite. The floors are white marble, not black obsidian. In the Sky Realm, you will obey Sky Realm laws. Those who do not will be punished."

"And what will happen to Magnus for his attack on me?" Vandorian tilted his head. "What justice will you dole out, oh great and powerful Premier?"

"The punishment will fit the crime, but it is no concern of yours. We will deal with him in our own way, as we would any citizen of our realm."

"How can I be assured—"

"You *can't*," Avian snapped. "But as I said, it is not your concern. You will leave him to us for judgment, and then you will leave."

"We traveled a great distance to pay homage to your daughter and her fiancé. You would send us away?"

"My daughter is in this very room, hovering near your anxious friend in the brown breastplate." Avian nodded toward Lilly. "You'll know her by her blonde hair, her pink armor, and her overly ambitious personality. You may honor her this very moment."

Vandorian's head turned, and he found Lilly. He started toward her with a cunning grin on his face that made Calum want to put himself between the two of them, but Avian's voice stopped Vandorian's progress first.

"That's far enough, Vandorian. You can wish her well from that distance."

"Had I wanted to do that, I would not have journeyed so far to do it in person."

"Even so, you'll do it now all the same."

Vandorian grunted, then he donned a malicious smile. "All the best, Princess, to both of you in your forthcoming nuptials. I had a gift for the both of you, but in light of all this chaos, I seemed to have—*misplaced* it. Do forgive my thoughtlessness. I'll just have to bring you something extra on your wedding day."

Lilly lowered her bow and arrow and faked a smile of her own. "Thank you for your kind words, Lord Vandorian. I trust our peoples can continue to live in peace, despite this small, isolated incident. You are always welcome in my court as an honored guest—any time after today, at least."

Vandorian clacked the talons of his right hand against his golden breastplate, then he closed his fingers into a fist and pressed it against his chest. "May the Overlord bless your union and give you peace, long life, and many children."

"Again, thank you." Lilly nodded.

"There. You've given your regards to my daughter," Avian said. "Now release Magnus and go in peace."

"In almost four hundred years of life, I have never experienced such rudeness and disregard from *anyone*, let alone the ruler of an entire realm." Vandorian shook his head and faced Avian. "Your hospitality has atrophied of late, Premier."

"Enough words, enough games. Release Magnus, or we will take him from you by force, whatever the cost." Avian's hands balled into fists. "*Now.*"

Vandorian stepped near Magnus and leaned his head close. He half-whispered, "It is too bad you failed to kill me, brother. Now I know you yet live. We will meet again, and I will finish what I started the day our father died."

Magnus didn't say a word. He just continued glowering at his older brother.

"*Now*, Vandorian," Avian nearly shouted.

Vandorian sighed and stepped back. "Release him."

The Sobeks shoved Magnus to the floor and backed away. He immediately pushed himself to his feet and stood face-to-face with Vandorian.

"I look forward to that day." Then Magnus left Vandorian behind, bent down and picked up his broadsword, sheathed it, and stood next to Avian with his huge arms folded.

Vandorian knocked his fist against his breastplate again and gave Avian a slight bow. "By your leave, then."

The Sobeks helped their injured friend—the first one Magnus hit—to his feet, and started toward the main throne room doors. All around them, the Windgale soldiers parted so as not to impede their progress, but neither did they lower their weapons.

They walked out the doors with Oren at the rear of the group. He turned back one last time, shot Calum a wink, gave a flourishing gesture with his hand, and then he disappeared around a corner.

Two Windgale soldiers shut the doors behind them, and immediately every weapon in the room reset to a relaxed position, including Calum's. He started toward Magnus.

"Thank you, Premier," Magnus said. "I owe you my life."

"You are Praetorius's heir. Why didn't you reveal this to me when first we met?" Avian asked.

"As you said the day we returned Lilly to you, 'there are few people in this world who are unquestionably trustworthy.' This is a secret I have kept from everyone, not just you." Magnus eyed Calum, who now stood next to him. "My companions did not even know the truth of my identity."

Axel scoffed and folded his arms. "You can say that again."

"Like my daughter, you are wise to have withheld this information." Avian nodded to General Balena, who motioned toward the doors. The soldiers began to form lines and file out of the throne room.

"But I am not my father's heir." Magnus hung his head. "Vandorian is."

"Vandorian is also a co-conspirator in your father's death."

Magnus looked up at him. "You know this? How?"

"The whole of Kanarah knows by now. It has been almost five years since Praetorius's untimely death. Everyone thought you perished along with the rest of his children. Besides, when Kahn and Vandorian arose from the ashes to take power, the rest wasn't hard to fill in."

Calum couldn't believe it. In less than two weeks, he'd learned that two of his traveling companions weren't just a Windgale and a Saurian, but the princess of the entire Sky Realm and the long-lost heir of Reptilius.

What next? That Axel was a distant relative of the King?

"Suffice it to say that Vandorian gave up his right to the throne when he helped Kahn rise to power. That makes you, the sole surviving child of Praetorius, his sole heir as far as the Sky Realm is concerned." Avian smiled and patted Magnus's forearm. "You have our support."

Magnus nodded. "Thank you."

"Frankly, dealing with you would be much more pleasant than dealing with either Vandorian or your uncle."

"I had hoped to remain anonymous for longer, but when I recognized Vandorian, I knew I would never get him alone with only five guards ever again. I beg your forgiveness, but I had to take the chance." Magnus sighed. "Now Vandorian will tell my uncle that I yet live, and they will both be on their guard. I have squandered whatever element of surprise I would have had."

"I understand what you mean. However," Avian stared at Magnus, "for the time being, I am beholden to Vandorian's demands concerning your attack."

Magnus's reptilian brow arched down. "What do you mean?"

Avian frowned. "I mean that since you're a citizen of our realm now, I still have to punish you for attacking him."

CHAPTER TWENTY-SEVEN

"What kind of glass-backward place is this?" Axel stepped forward with his arms extended out to his sides. "He was totally justified in attacking. You can't punish him for that!"

Calum shook his head. Leave it to Axel to side with Magnus after all this time, after everything that had happened, just because he found out Magnus was royalty.

Magnus eyed him. "You do not even like me. I punched you in the head, humiliated you, and took your sword away. Why defend me now?"

"You're the same as I am, Scales. I didn't see it before, but I do now. You got handed a foul deal in life, just like Calum and me." Axel pointed at the throne room doors. "Plus, Vandorian and his friend Oren were a couple of arrogant harpies."

"That doesn't negate the fact that you broke our laws when you attacked Vandorian and his men. Typically, a crime of this caliber would be addressed through a hearing like those we held for Condor—" Avian shot a long glare at Axel. "—and your friend, here, but in this case, I believe I can make an exception since the other council members are indisposed."

Lilly hovered toward him. "Father, take into account Magnus's—"

Avian held up his hand. "I'll hear no testaments to his character, nor to his innocence or his guilt, Lilliana. He will be punished according to our laws, and my decision will be binding. Otherwise, I can summon Vandorian and his men back, if you prefer their brand of 'justice?'"

"No." Lilly bowed her head.

"Very well, then." Avian floated up to Magnus's eye level. "Magnus, I hereby banish you from the Sky Realm until you find and free Lumen, the General of Light. Not a moment longer, nor a moment shorter. You are banished for exactly as long as the journey is meant to last."

Calum grinned, and so did Axel, Magnus, and Lilly.

"Should you return for any reason before your quest is complete, you will be given three *full* days to vacate the realm once again, or you will face the penalty of death." Avian pulled Lilly close and positioned her between Magnus and himself. "And while you are banished, I implore you—I *command* you to safeguard that which is most important to me. Do you understand your punishment?"

Magnus smirked and gave a modest bow. "I do."

"Good. Then get out of my sight, and watch out for those Sobeks. I imagine there is an entire encampment of Saurians somewhere nearby, and they're headed in the same direction as you. Best to go now before they realize what I've done for you."

Calum performed the Windgale salute again. "Thank you again, Premier."

A yelp turned their heads.

From behind one of the pillars, a Windgale soldier in purple armor pulled a mass of brown-gray fur out of the shadows by the scruff of its neck. "I found this dog hiding. Don't know how it got in here, Premier. What should I do with it?"

"I'm not a dog, you moron." Riley snapped at the Windgale's hand and he let go, but then he leveled his spear. Riley hobble-darted back around the pillar into its shadow again, and the soldier followed.

"Oh, no you don't. Not getting away that easily, pup."

"He's with us, soldier," Falcroné said. "Leave him be."

Calum made it over to Riley first, then Lilly. She crouched next to him and asked, "Are you alright, Riley?"

"Fine. Why wouldn't I be?"

Axel came up behind them. "Were you hiding that whole time?"

Riley didn't answer him. He just growled from within the shadows.

"What happened to those razor sharp fangs of yours?" Axel scoffed and folded his arms. "Condor didn't stab you in the mouth, did he?"

"Cut it out, Axel," Calum warned.

"Yeah, leave him alone." Lilly scratched behind Riley's ears—she was still the only one he allowed to do that. "Come on. We need to get our supplies from Ganosh, and I need to say goodbye to my mother."

NIGHT FELL within a matter of hours after Axel and the team left the Sky Fortress. When he'd first left his farm behind to accompany Calum and Magnus, he'd never expected anyone else would travel with them, but now their number had grown to seven in total.

Axel didn't know whether to be impressed that they'd become so popular or annoyed because of all the extra people around to bother him. He supposed it would be better to have greater numbers when it came to fighting, especially since battles kept finding them wherever they went.

Speaking of battles, they located a large encampment near the base of the northernmost support pillar, just as Avian had suggested. Falcroné took to the sky to scout for patrols, then Magnus led them around the encampment where he supposed the Saurians would not be. Sure enough, they didn't encounter anyone.

Hardly anyone said much of anything for the first hour after they passed the Saurians' encampment, but that suited Axel just fine. It gave him time to think through everything that had happened at the Sky Fortress.

He still hadn't talked to Lilly about why she'd lied about the attack. She'd told him she loved Falcroné—another obvious lie. Her actions before the Council of Wisps suggested otherwise. They *strongly* suggested otherwise.

Yet even that didn't hold Axel's attention as much Magnus's revelation of his royal heritage. Despite their previous contentions, Magnus's plight had placed him securely in Axel's "He's alright" category. Still, Axel couldn't help but wonder who else might be hiding something from him.

He and Riley walked near the back of the group. The thought reoccurred to Axel that he should probably apologize to Riley for how everything that had transpired when Condor had stabbed him, but Riley hadn't brought it up, so Axel decided to keep ignoring the impulse.

Axel nudged Riley's left shoulder—the one on his uninjured side. "Hey, Riley."

"What?"

"*Shhh*," Axel hissed. "For someone who's supposed to be stealthy, you sure talk loud sometimes."

Riley sighed and rolled his eyes, but he lowered his voice. "What do you want, Axel?"

"You're not secret royalty too, are you?"

Riley barked a laugh. "Me? You gotta be kidding."

Calum turned his head back from the middle of the group about ten paces ahead of them. "Hey, don't lag behind, guys. Magnus and Falcroné said we've got another hour of walking before we camp for the night."

Axel gave him a slight wave, then he refocused on Riley once Calum faced forward again. "What's so funny about it?"

"Wolves don't operate like humans, Windgales, or even Saurians. Your hierarchies are all based on lineage and bloodlines, but we don't do things that way."

"How do Wolves do it, then?"

"Our structure is based on strength, not family lines. The strongest of us rules the tribe, the pack. If you think you can lead the tribe better, you challenge the Alpha. If you beat him, you become the new leader." Riley's ears lowered. "But if you lose, he kills you."

"Where's your tribe?" Axel asked.

Riley stifled another pitiful laugh. "Don't have one. Why else do you think you found me wandering the woods alone?"

"Why not?"

"Seriously? Look at me, Axel. For a Wolf, I'm tiny. Weak. Not a good fighter, and apparently not a very good thief either since you, Calum and Magnus managed to catch me in the act." Riley shook his head. "No one wants me in their tribe."

"Yeah, I can see that."

Riley shot him a glare.

"What? Would you rather I lie to you?"

"Forget it." Riley rolled his eyes again and trotted forward until he walked between Calum and Lilly.

Axel squinted at the two of them and rotated his sore shoulders. They weren't nearly as bad as they had been, and in only a few more days, he should be pain-free.

As far as Lilly was concerned, Axel had Falcroné to worry about, of course, but did Calum still think he had a chance with her, too?

She'd told Calum the same lie about loving Falcroné. If he also didn't believe her, then would he keep pursuing her as well? Or would he stand aside?

Time would tell, but no matter what happened, Axel had no intention of losing the contest. After all, he could beat Calum in pretty much every other category already. Adding one more to the list wouldn't be hard.

LILLY SAT ON A STONE, admiring the starry sky above while Calum and Magnus stacked wood next to the fledgling campfire Axel had just ignited.

Something nudged her shoulder, and she found Falcroné at her side. She scooted over to make room for him, grateful for his company on a cool night.

As he sat down next her, he asked, "So you didn't want to marry me?"

Lilly tensed. She'd known this conversation had to happen eventually, but she hadn't wanted to have it with him tonight. "Do you really want to talk about this here and now?"

"You said it aloud to your father in front of them. I assume you don't mind further discussing it in their midst."

Annoyed and frustrated, Lilly stood and pulled Falcroné to his feet. "Come with me."

They took to the sky together, and she led him deeper into the woods until several trees separated them from the group. She glanced around to make sure no one had followed them—Axel in particular.

She'd given a lot of thought to how this conversation needed to go, and it always circled back to one essential statement, so she led with that. "Fal, I'm sorry."

He shrugged—not the reaction she'd been expecting. "What for? You spoke your mind."

Nor were those the words she'd expected. She shook her head. "That doesn't mean it didn't hurt you."

"Lilly, I'm not worried. I know now why you left. I don't want to make a big issue of it. I just want to make sure this... *us*... is actually what you want."

At least he was making it easy on her. For that, she was very grateful.

She wrapped her arms around Falcroné's midsection, pressed her cheek against the cool armor covering his chest, and smiled. "It is."

I think.

He hugged her back. "Good. Me too."

She released him. "Come on. Let's get back to camp."

RILEY CROUCHED in the darkness beyond the perimeter of the camp they had set up, watching. Even from so far away, he could still hear every word they said, every piece of wood snapping, every footfall of every creature skittering through the trees around them.

Benefits of being a Wolf—even if he couldn't run and couldn't fight, he could still hide and hear and see better in the dark than any of the rest of them.

"If Vandorian and his Sobeks find us, we run." Magnus stoked the modest campfire with a long stick and ashes billowed into the air. "There is no way we could overcome even three of them, much less six.

Taking on an entire encampment would be suicide. At best we could handle two of them, and that assumes one of them is not Vandorian."

"You took down four of them on your own," Axel said. "And you almost got Vandorian, too."

Magnus shook his head and reclined against a boulder he'd dragged into place near his spot. "I got lucky. Had those warriors been expecting trouble, I would not have made it past the first two before they surrounded me and struck me down."

Axel shrugged. "Looked like you were doing fine—up until the end, at least."

"My point is, if they come for us, we are in for a world of trouble," Magnus said. "If we can get away, fine, but if not, I will try to fend them off so the rest of you can escape. Vandorian likely wants me alive, anyway."

"We're not gonna leave you, Magnus." Calum extended his legs while seated and stretched out his hamstrings. "After all we've been through, we can't let them get you. We won't. We'll stay and fight."

"That cannot happen," Magnus said. "I wish it were that simple, but I cannot allow it. Falcroné, Lilly, and Kanton could all escape if things escalated too quickly, but the rest of us would be stuck on the ground, outnumbered and overmatched. It is an impossible situation."

"I don't know." Axel eyed Falcroné and Lilly, who sat shoulder-to-shoulder near the flames. "I think we could take 'em. Especially with Sunshine over there on our side."

Riley smirked. Axel despised Falcroné. Riley could smell it in his sweat whenever Axel and Falcroné stood too near each other—and even more so when Falcroné got close to Lilly like he was now.

Of course, Riley didn't like Axel, either. How anyone did, he couldn't fathom. He was a top-tier idiot, rude, and cruel.

Riley had suspected as much when they first met, but when Axel tried to kill Condor instead of getting Riley help for his near-fatal wound, it sealed Riley's opinion of him forever.

"I'd appreciate if you didn't refer to me by any monikers other than my name. Or 'Captain.'" Falcroné's gaze hardened.

Axel squinted at him, but gave him a slight nod. "Whatever you say, 'Croné."

"It's *Falcroné*."

"Don't encourage him, Fal." Lilly patted Falcroné's knee with her hand. "He's just trying to jab you to get a reaction."

"If he jabs me again, I might have to *jab* him back." Falcroné tapped the pommel of his sword, which hung from his belt in its sheath.

The pheromones in Axel's sweat had intensified when Lilly patted Falcroné's knee, but the next swell hit Riley's nose like a flood.

Axel stood up. "You go right ahead, *Fal*. Skin that steel and find out what happens."

"Enough." Calum hopped up to his feet and stepped between Axel and Falcroné. His eyes locked on Axel. "You're not gonna do this again. Falcroné is on our side, and you won't alienate him from us."

"He's a pompous—"

"I said *enough*," Calum snapped. "If you keep causing division in our group, we'll leave you behind. I'm serious. There is no longer any place for that kind of talk here, so either fall in line, or we're done with you."

Axel scowled. Now both their pheromones wafted in Riley's direction—similar, but unique. Both very potent.

"I know how you feel, Axel," Calum said, his voice low so only he and Axel—and Riley—could hear. "Believe me, I do. But you're not gonna solve anything by fighting him."

"Is Axel always like this?" Falcroné leaned close to Lilly and asked, his whispered words overlapping the end of Calum's sentence.

"Somewhat, yes," she whispered back. "It takes some getting used to."

"I still don't understand why you covered for him at the council," Falcroné muttered. "We both know what really happened and what punishment he deserved."

Riley glanced at Axel.

"You don't know anything about what's going on between Lilly and me. We have a future together, and you don't, and it bothers you." Axel tapped his index finger on Calum's crimson breastplate. "You'd do anything to keep us apart so you can have her for yourself. She kissed *me*, not you."

Riley raised an eyebrow. Did Falcroné know about that? He turned back to their conversation.

Lilly shook her head. "After all we went through, I couldn't let the council jail him for something so trivial."

"*Trivial?*" Falcroné clamped his hand on Lilly's arm. "Lilly, he *attacked* you. That's not trivial."

Hmmm. Riley must have missed a few things while he was recovering.

"I'm done with this conversation, Axel." Calum turned away and sat down, his eyes fixed on the fire.

"Yeah, we're done alright." Axel sat down in his spot and folded his arms. He glared at Falcroné, but Falcroné didn't look at him.

"Just leave it alone, Falcroné," Lilly whispered and lay her head against his shoulder. "It's not worth getting worked up about."

Falcroné frowned at her. "Regardless, I don't trust him. I'm not letting you out of my sight if I can help it."

Lilly smiled and looked up at him. "I'll have to go to the bathroom at some point, you know."

"Then I'll watch *him* while you're gone."

Kanton floated over between Calum and Axel, and he glanced between them both. "So, who's taking the first watch shift tonight?"

Riley smirked. He preferred the night, the shadows. If he had things his way, he'd stay up all night and take the whole watch, but then someone would have to carry him during the daytime since he couldn't just sleep in the same spot, and *that* wasn't going to happen.

He lay his head down and listened to Kanton and Calum talk about the shifts, with Magnus interjecting every now and then, and his smirk stretched into a smile. Good to finally have friends, even if they didn't all like each other, and even if he didn't like Axel.

"Which route are we taking to the Blood Mountains?" Falcroné asked. "Do you intend to cross the Desert of the Forgotten?"

Riley's ears perked up at that. They weren't seriously considering going through that horrible place, were they?

"That is the most direct route." Magnus nodded to Calum. "Let me see the map."

Calum pulled it from his pack and handed it to Magnus, who studied it for a moment.

Falcroné hovered over to him and stared at it over Magnus's shoulder. "The only other route is through the Green Highlands to the east and then up the main road that connects farther south near Trader's Pass."

Magnus shook his head. "That path is circuitous and would take almost twice as long. We have enough supplies and water to take the desert path. That's what we'll do."

"*No*," Riley barked from the darkness.

CHAPTER TWENTY-EIGHT

A ll eyes looked toward Riley, but he knew they couldn't see him.
"Riley? Where are you?" Calum stood and looked out over the fire.

Riley sighed, and he reluctantly emerged from the shadows and stood next to Axel. Then he thought better of it and took a few steps farther away from him. "Here."

"Why don't you want us to go through the desert?" Magnus asked.

"It's—" Riley growled. He really didn't want to have to explain everything that had happened between him and Rhaza. "—not safe. That's where my kind live."

"What's a few Wolves?" Axel waved his hand in dismissal. "If they're all like you, we should be fine."

Riley leaped at Axel with his front paws extended and pushed him down onto his back. The impact sent pain shooting through his torso, but it was worth it to pin a wide-eyed, unarmed Axel to the ground and snarl in his face. "They're worse than me, Axel. They're faster, stronger, and a whole lot meaner than I am."

"Get off me!" Axel shoved him to the side, and Riley couldn't help but collapse. "What do you think you're doing?"

Riley stifled a whimper as he pushed himself back onto all fours and growled again. "Making a point."

Axel brushed himself off and stood up. "Well, don't make it anymore."

"Wolves are merciless. We hunt to kill. If we're gonna rob you, we'll tear you apart, too, if the numbers are in our favor." Riley eyed Axel. "And the numbers are *always* in our favor. We make sure of it. We're pack creatures, and our highest concentration is in that desert. No one passes through without us knowing."

"How do the Saurians get across, then?" Calum reached for the map, and Magnus handed it back to him.

"They travel in large groups, and Wolves typically don't attack Saurians to kill them anyway. Too difficult, usually, and not worth the effort." Riley sat down and nodded to Magnus. "Especially when they're Sobeks like Magnus. Our teeth can't usually penetrate their scales. Instead, we just rob them in the night while they sleep. They're slower, so it's not hard."

Magnus grunted and folded his arms.

Riley shrugged. "No offense. You actually move pretty well."

"For a Saurian?" Magnus asked.

"In general, actually. The only more adept Saurian I've seen is Vandorian."

Magnus grunted again.

"Anyway, we need to avoid the desert. With this group, we don't stand a chance against a pack of seventeen Wolves and nine Were-wolves, or whatever assortment may come up against us out there."

"I'm inclined to agree with him," Falcroné said. "Windgales can fly, so we don't have to worry about the Wolves when we cross, but with more than half our party on foot, the risk of attack is heightened."

"No, no. Don't look at it as a risk. It's not." Riley stared at Falcroné. "It's a certainty. If we go to the Desert of the Forgotten, we'll be ambushed, attacked, scattered, and hunted down until we're all killed, with the possible exception of the Windgales who could fly away."

"What's more, based on what Riley is saying, Vandorian and his entourage will probably take that route as well," Lilly said. "If we go that way but can't make it through, and we need to go back, we could run into them. Then we'd be caught between Wolves and Saurians with no way to escape."

"Exactly," Riley said. "It's a losing scenario, and frankly, I don't want to die. Tried it once. Didn't take, but it wasn't any fun. So we need to take the long way."

Magnus turned to Calum, who looked back at him, then they both turned to Falcroné. Axel rolled his eyes, Lilly held Falcroné's hand in hers, and Kanton shrugged.

"Then we'll take the long way, starting tomorrow," Calum said.

THE GREEN HIGHLANDS were unlike any place Axel had ever seen, though it vaguely reminded him of the quarry, but with infinitely more grass and vegetation. He liked it for what it was, but he couldn't see how anyone would want to live there—not if they meant to do any farming, anyway.

They'd been traveling for three weeks, with Calum leading the group along one of the many paths that cut between the tall green hills and mounds that the Green Highlands were named for. Along the way, they'd encountered a mixture of rocky terrain, lush valleys, sparse forests, and the occasional jagged ravine with a shallow river flowing through.

Falcroné soared above the group in wide arcs and scouted ahead while Kanton hovered at the rear of the group to make sure no one crept up behind them.

Magnus, Riley, and Lilly filled in the center of the group, and Axel brought up the rear at Calum's order. Well, Calum had phrased it as a request, but it felt more like an order to Axel.

Either way, it meant Axel had no one to talk to except for Kanton, and half the time he just babbled on and on about how he used to shepherd the Premier's flocks, and how he'd saved the life of an albino saber-tooth cat once, and how he'd lost his first cape. The other half of the time he had to ascend higher into the air to check their surroundings.

Axel preferred the half when Kanton wasn't around.

As he walked, he noticed a crystalline pebble on the path, and he scooped it into his hands. Not worth anything, but maybe…

He tossed it at Lilly and it plunked off the back of her left calf armor. She turned back and glared at him, then she faced forward again and resumed her conversation with Riley. Axel found and chucked another pebble at her, but this time she didn't even turn around.

"Lilly," he half-hissed, half-whispered.

She still didn't turn back.

"Lilly." This time he called for her with his regular voice, firmly. Maybe too firmly, in hindsight.

She looked back at him with the same glare.

"Mind if I talk to you for a moment?"

Lilly glanced at Riley, who nodded without looking at Axel, and then she stopped so he could catch up. "Yes?"

"Hi." Axel smiled at her.

Lilly rolled her eyes and accelerated her walk to catch up with Riley again, but Axel caught her by her arm. She gave him a look that could melt mountains, and he let go and held up his hands in surrender.

"Sorry." He'd learned his lesson the first time—no question there.

"Do you have something to say or not?"

"I wanted to apologize for what happened back at the Sky Fortress. I was out of line, I admit, and I acted foolishly. I'm sorry." Axel stared at her, but she continued to face forward as they walked. "And I wanted to thank you for doing what you did before the council. It's more than I deserved. Far more. So, thank you."

Lilly exhaled a sigh through her nose—her cute little nose. "I don't think I want to talk about this with you."

"Come on, Lilly," Axel said. "I'm trying to make amends here. Give me a chance."

"It's going to take more than an apology for you to make amends."

"What did you have in mind?" Axel leaned close her and whispered, "Another kiss?"

Her livid blue eyes locked on his. "You're hopeless."

That wasn't a no. "Lilly, I—"

She started to pull ahead again, so Axel grabbed the end of her cape and tugged her backward. Lilly whirled around and smacked his jaw with her fist, then kicked his chest. He dropped to the dirt on his back and glared up at her.

"Don't touch me anymore, Axel." She turned and kept walking.

Kanton dropped out of the sky and landed beside him with his hand extended. "You alright, son?"

"I'm fine." Axel scrambled to his feet without Kanton's help, only to find Magnus and Riley staring back at him. "What are you lookin' at?"

They, too, faced forward and began walking once Lilly had caught up.

"Saw what happened." Kanton patted Axel's shoulder. "Don't worry, son. Plenty of girls in this world will break both your heart and your bones. She's one of them. I remember one time there was this girl named Calraia. She—"

"Thanks." Axel shrugged Kanton's hand away. "Shouldn't you be scouting?"

Kanton pursed his lips and squinted at him. His voice flat, he said, "Yeah. Suppose I should."

Axel rubbed his jaw as Kanton took to the sky again. Somehow Lilly had managed to hit almost the exact spot where she'd kicked him about three weeks earlier. The original bruise had long since healed, but the familiar pain had returned with Lilly's punch.

He found another pebble as he walked, took aim, and lobbed it at Lilly's head. It bounced off the back of her head and skittered to a stop on the ground, and she turned back to face him again with rage on her face. "What?"

"I wasn't done talking to you," Axel said.

"Too bad. I'm done talking to you."

"I learned my lesson—again. Please, just two more minutes?" Axel didn't want to sound like he was begging, but he figured a little groveling might get her to come back. "Please?"

Lilly sighed, but she waited for him to catch up.

"Thanks." Axel grunted. "You didn't have to hit me, you know. You definitely didn't have to kick me, either."

"See, that's what you don't understand, Axel. I *did* have to do those things. Both of them, because you don't understand what I've been telling you." Lilly stared at him. "We're never going to happen, Axel. I'm marrying Falcroné, and that's the end of it. You don't have a chance."

Axel clenched his teeth, ignoring the arrows she'd just shot into his heart and his gut. "I don't believe that."

"Well, you'd better start."

"Lilly, I love you."

She faced him and opened her mouth to say something, but stopped. Her eyes fixed on something in the hills above them, and she stopped walking entirely.

Axel stopped too and followed her line of sight. "What is it?"

"I thought I saw something."

"Like what?"

"Movement." Lilly shielded the sun from her eyes with her hand. "I don't know."

"What kind of movement?"

"I said *I don't know.*" Lilly's tone hardened. "I'm going to go take a look."

Before Axel could say anything else, Lilly burst into the sky toward the hill. Convenient excuse to get out of the conversation. He'd mention that when she returned.

High above, Lilly looped around the hill with her bow in hand and an arrow nocked, but not drawn back. Good for show, but Axel wasn't fooled.

Until she pulled the drawstring back and launched an arrow downward. From behind the hill, a green form reared up and writhed, then it hurled a boulder at Lilly. She barrel-rolled out of its trajectory and nocked another arrow.

A roar reverberated through the valley, and the group stopped.

"Weapons!" Magnus called. "Form up!"

Calum fell back to the rest of the group, and Axel charged toward his spot in their formation, his eyes on Lilly the whole time. He drew his sword and watched her shoot another arrow at the thing. A thick tail lashed through the air and a loud hiss sounded.

It was a Saurian.

Falcroné and Kanton landed among the group, which formed a loose circle, until Falcroné noticed Lilly engaging the Saurian. He shot away from the ground and drew his sword.

"Falcroné!" Calum tried to call after him, but Falcroné kept flying.

He executed a loop and zoomed down toward the Saurian, who now faced Lilly. In one brutal blow Falcroné jammed his blade through the back of the Saurian's head, and it fell behind the hillcrest out of Axel's sight.

Falcroné and Lilly darted back down to the group and took their places in the formation as reptilian silhouettes materialized around them at the tops of the highlands and then started down toward them. Saurians, all of them armored, except for one Sobek who wore only a leather breastplate and gripped a large double-bladed battle-axe in his hands. Their leader.

Hissing and growling, they constricted around the group like a noose on a condemned man's neck. They likely weren't part of Vandorian's group; that much became clear as Axel noticed their mismatched and weatherworn armor. They were the Saurian version of bandits, apparently.

Then again, Vandorian still might have sent them or alerted them to the group's approach. Axel didn't know for sure.

Either way, this wouldn't make for an easy fight. Axel counted ten of them, including the Sobek.

The Sobek stepped to within fifteen feet of Magnus and displayed his jagged smile. "Well, well. If it ain't seven stragglers just waitin' to be snapped up. The lot of ya will make a nice haul for sure. Now lay down your weapons, an' we won't gotta cut nothin' off ya while we tie ya up."

The Sobek's odd manner of speech reminded Axel of the way Oren had talked. Perhaps they knew each other, or they'd come from the same town in the Blood Mountains.

"The only hauling you can expect to do if you refuse to let us pass is hauling your own carcasses out of this valley." Magnus straightened to his full height, at least six inches taller than the enemy Sobek. "Now stand aside."

"Can't do it, bub." The Sobek's tail swished back and forth in the gravel on the path. "Livelihood's at stake, an' all. You'll be slaves 'fore the week's out."

"Forget your livelihood, Saurian," Falcroné warned. "You forfeit your life if you so much as lay a hand on any of us. We've already killed one of your number, and we'll do it again if we must."

Axel raised an eyebrow. Regardless of what he thought of the pretty Wisp captain, Axel couldn't deny that Falcroné could back up his haughty talk—so far, anyway.

"Talk all ya want. We'll see 'oo's standin' an' 'oo ain't by the end o' this." The Sobek motioned toward them with his arm, and the Saurians advanced forward.

CHAPTER TWENTY-NINE

Scaly green monsters surrounded Riley. Green monsters that he'd have to fight if he wanted to survive. Green monsters with swords, spears, and axes.

The wound he'd taken from Condor in his side had healed substantially in the three weeks since they'd left the Sky Fortress, but the damage remained nonetheless—both to his body and to his mind.

Ten against seven. Ten Saurians, all but impossible to kill with his teeth, much less his claws. Bigger than humans, far more difficult to knock down. And even if he could knock them down, he couldn't get to their throats easily thanks to their armor, makeshift though it may be.

They would catch him. Stop him from biting them. Then they'd take their swords and run him through, just as Condor had.

Only this time it wouldn't just happen once, but twice. Three times. Four. Five.

They might never stop.

Pain flared in Riley's side, then spread throughout his body. He knew most of it was artificial, contrived, imagined, but it still hurt anyway.

He had to run, had to escape. Had to find shadows and hide.

He wouldn't let them get him. He had to run.

––––––––

PEBBLES SPRAYED into the air and clinked against the armor plates on the side of Calum's left leg. He stole a look and saw Riley bounding away from the fight, away from the Saurians and toward a gorge up ahead.

"Riley?" he called, but Riley kept running. "Where are you going?"

Two of the Saurians reached for him as he ran past, but he eluded them and darted down the path until he disappeared entirely behind some rocks in the gorge.

"Stay in formation," Magnus growled. "Tighten up and take his place. He can no longer help us."

"What do we do?" Calum asked, only loud enough for Magnus and Falcroné to hear.

"We fight." Falcroné nudged Calum with his elbow. "We kill as many of them as we have to until they leave us alone."

"You got that right," Axel said.

Well, at least they agreed on something.

"No. We run. Make for that gorge where Riley disappeared. Not everyone can fly away when they encounter trouble, so we need to adjust our strategy." Magnus nodded. "Falcroné, Kanton, and I will clear a path. Calum and Axel, run for the gorge. We will fight them there, where we can use the terrain to our advantage. Lilly, cover them with your bow. Ready?"

Calum nodded. "Ready."

The Sobek lunged forward and flailed his battle-ax at Magnus, who parried the attack with his sword then jammed his fist into the Sobek's armored gut. The blow stunned him for a second, and Magnus whirled around and whacked the Sobek's shoulder with his tail, sending the Sobek skidding along the gravel away from them.

"Go!" Magnus roared.

Falcroné, Kanton, and Lilly took to the sky, and Calum and Axel charged behind Magnus. Calum ran hard until one of the Saurians lurched toward him and lashed his sword. Calum ducked under the blow, but lost his footing and tripped. He slid to a stop in the gravel on his side, and when he looked up, the Saurian towered over him, sword raised.

An arrow plunged into the base of the Saurian's neck, and he twitched. He roared and ripped the arrow out of his neck, then he hissed up at Lilly, who stuck him with another one, this time in his throat just under his chin.

The Saurian dropped his sword and clutched his throat with wide reptilian eyes.

Calum pushed himself up and swung his sword at the Saurian, but he blocked the blow with his armored forearm. The Saurian spun around and battered Calum to the ground with his tail.

The impact might've snapped Calum in half were he still as scrawny as he'd been back at the quarry. Even so, he wondered if he'd ever be able to walk or even stand again. His lower half ached, and he cursed himself for his weakness again.

He'd grown enough to handle human bandits and pirates and soldiers, but trying to fight Saurians made him feel just as frail as the day he'd fled his life as a slave. He had to get stronger, fight better, or he wouldn't survive long enough to reach the Arcanum to free Lumen.

Despite the arrow in his throat, the Saurian just wouldn't go down. Worse yet, the other nine Saurians had closed in and started toward Calum.

Another arrow plunged into the Saurian, this time in the back of his neck. He roared again and reared back, alternating between groping at his throat and the nape of his neck with his free hand.

The next thing Calum knew, two sets of arms scooped him into the air and carried him away from the Saurians. Kanton and Falcroné.

"Thanks, guys," he said.

"Their skin is thick, and with all that armor on, it's hard to deliver a killing blow unless it's to their necks," Falcroné said. "If you don't kill them quickly, they heal."

Calum nodded. *Just like Magnus healed from the arrow he took back on the rooftops in Kanarah City.*

His feet touched down in the gorge about a hundred feet ahead of the nearest Saurian, and he met up with the rest of the group. Magnus had been right—the Saurians would be forced into a bottleneck here. That gave the six of them more of a level field.

The Sobek bellowed a command to halt that stopped the Saurians before they could enter the gorge. He tapped four of them on their shoulders and motioned toward the walls that formed the gorge. The Saurians nodded, split into two groups of two, and walked along the tops of the walls. Then he and the rest of the Saurians advanced into the gorge.

They were still trying to surround them.

"Deeper. We must venture deeper into the gorge," Magnus said. "We cannot let those four Saurians cut us off, or we will not make it."

"I can slow them down." Lilly nocked another arrow. "Kanton and I will take one side, and Falcroné can take the other side."

"Do it," Calum said.

Falcroné nodded, then he took to the sky toward one pair of Saurians, and Lilly and Kanton launched toward the other pair.

"Attack!" The Sobek yelled, and the Saurians lumbered forward, two at a time.

"Axel, Calum," Magnus said. "Retreat. I can handle two at a time."

Calum glanced at Axel, then looked at Magnus again, whose gaze remained fixed on the approaching Saurians. "Are you sure?"

Magnus shot him a glare. "*Go.*"

Calum didn't hesitate. He and Axel ran deeper into the gorge. Above them, Lilly fired arrows at the two Saurians on her side of the gorge while Kanton executed quick diving attacks on them with his spear.

Across the gorge, the opposite wall became more of a steep hill. Falcroné zipped back and forth between the Saurians who ran across the top. Every time he passed them, a new spurt of dark blood flung down into the gorge.

The Saurians jerked with each of Falcroné's slices and tried to swing back at him, but he moved far too fast for them. Still, they kept moving forward, until Falcroné's next blow knocked one of them down into the gorge.

The Saurian smacked against a half-dozen boulders on his way down and rolled to a stop in front of Calum and Axel, who skidded to a halt. Behind the Saurian, his sword clanged down the wall's slope, accompanied by a miniature rockslide.

Before Calum and Axel could get around him, the Saurian pushed himself up to his feet and snatched up his sword. He snarled and stalked toward them, hunched over. Dark gray armor covered his chest and back, his arms, and his legs, but he'd lost his helmet on the way down into the gorge. Lacerations lined his face and neck.

Axel rapped his knuckles against Calum's arm and shifted to the right. Calum caught his intention and shifted left. If they could divide the Saurian's focus, they stood a better chance of bringing him down.

The Saurian slashed his blade at Calum but he leaped back in time to avoid the swipe. Axel darted forward and hacked at the Saurian's left arm, but its tail swept Axel's feet from under him before his blow could connect. He landed face-first in the dirt.

On his return swing, the Saurian brought his sword down at Axel, who rolled away just in time. Calum saw an opening and lunged, and his sword plunged into the Saurian's right thigh between two of his armor plates.

Before Calum could pull his sword back, the Saurian roared and backhanded him in the face. Calum's vision ceased in a white flash, then it reset to the blurry gray of the gorge around him as he hit the ground. Warmth trickled from his nose down to his lips, and the metallic tang of blood stung his tongue.

When Calum looked up, the blurred form of the Saurian blotted out the setting sun. He raised his sword.

A navy-blue mass slammed into the Saurian from the right and knocked him off-balance.

Axel.

The Saurian adjusted and swung his sword at Axel instead, but Axel ducked under the blow and sliced his blade straight up at the Saurian's wrist. The blade severed the Saurian's right hand from his arm, and it dropped to the ground next to Calum's shoulder, along with his sword.

The Saurian roared and clutched his bleeding wrist with his other hand. Calum's sword remained in the Saurian's thigh, so he rolled to the side, snatched up the Saurian's sword, and hacked at its leg. The dull blade lodged about halfway through its knee, and the Saurian crumpled to the ground.

Axel jammed his sword through its throat so far that it stuck into the ground. The Saurian convulsed once, then it stopped moving. Calum scrambled to his feet and wrested his sword from the Saurian's leg.

"Thanks," he said.

Axel planted his boot on the Saurian's snout and jerked his sword free of its throat. "No time to chatter now. We gotta keep running. Magnus was right. We can't fight all of them like that."

Calum nodded and looked up at the three Saurians who still ran across the top of the gorge. Far behind Axel and him, Magnus battled two Saurians at a time in the bottleneck, and another lay at his side, motionless and slicked with red. He'd already killed one of them?

A hiss sounded to Calum's left, but not from one of the Saurians. Small rocks and pebbles tumbled down the side of the gorge wall toward them. Far above, a network of gray boulders oozed rocks into the gorge. It looked like it could give way any—

That's it. Realization hit Calum harder than the Saurian's backhand. He knew how they could even the odds.

Axel's hand clamped onto Calum's wrist. "*Come on.* We gotta keep running."

"No, wait!" Calum shook free and pointed to the rocks above. "We can trap them in a rockslide."

"What?" Axel glanced at the boulders then back at Calum. "You're losing your mind. Let's go."

"No. Go help Magnus. He needs you." Calum motioned toward the sky. "Let them back you up, and Falcroné and I will loose the rocks. When you hear me yelling, run for it. The boulders will do the rest."

"But—"

"Just *do it*, Axel." Calum turned and bolted down the gorge. He couldn't waste time arguing—not if this was going to work. He called for Falcroné as he ran, and Falcroné met him in the gorge.

"What is it?" Dark blood streaked across Falcroné's face and charcoal armor, but Calum knew none of it was his own.

"Can you get me up to those boulders?" He nodded toward them.

Falcroné glanced at them. "Why?"

"I'm gonna create a rockslide to—"

"Say no more." Falcroné held up his hand. "I'm with you. How much do you weigh?"

"Uhh…"

"Stay here. I'll be back with Kanton." Falcroné burst into the air.

"Bring Lilly back with you," Calum shouted. He hoped Falcroné had heard him.

Behind him, Axel had joined Magnus in the fray. As they backed up, the Saurians approached. Soon they weren't fighting just two Saurians at once, they had to fight three. They would need help—Lilly and Kanton's help—if this was going to work.

Lilly, Kanton, and Falcroné landed next to Calum.

"Lilly, go shoot the Saurians who are fighting Axel and Magnus. Kanton and Falcroné—"

"We've got you, Calum." Kanton hooked his arm under Calum's, and Falcroné did the same. As Lilly sped toward Magnus and Axel, Calum ascended toward the boulders.

MAGNUS PARRIED two blows from two of the Saurians then slammed his sword down on one of them who'd left himself exposed. The hack cut through the Saurian's armor and severed his left arm at the shoulder. He roared. Magnus's follow-up lateral lopped off the Saurian's head, silencing him.

Two down. Four to go, including the Sobek.

As they backed deeper into the gorge, it widened, and the Saurians spread out. No way he and Axel could contend with four of them alone. Had they been humans, or even Windgales, Magnus could have taken them on his own, but not Saurians. They were too hard to kill.

The Sobek launched forward and battered Magnus's sword with his battle-ax. Magnus threw three quick counterattacks then absorbed another thunderous blow from the Sobek that vibrated through his arms.

The Sobek showed him an insidious grin, and his golden eyes flickered with malice.

Magnus readied another counterattack, but one of the Saurians whipped his blade at Magnus, so he had to parry instead.

Next to him, Axel dodged a blow from the second Saurian and blocked another from the third that almost knocked him off his feet in the process.

For being only a human, Axel was handling himself admirably against these Saurians, at least up until that moment. The second Saurian would've finished Axel off right then and there had it not been for the arrow that hit him in his neck. The Saurian recoiled a step, and Axel recovered his footing.

Lilly swooped into view behind them and shot two more arrows in succession, one that plunged into the shoulder of one of the Saurians, and another that skidded off the Sobek's head. The Sobek just shook his head and sneered at Magnus. He knew, as Magnus did, that arrows wouldn't do much beyond annoying and distracting these Saurians.

The Sobek started toward Magnus again, his battle-axe ready.

Whatever Calum had planned, he'd better do it quickly.

KANTON AND FALCRONÉ set Calum down near the top of the boulders.

"Kanton, go help the others in the gorge. When I yell to move, get outta the way."

He nodded then zipped away.

"Falcroné, I need you to hover on the other side of the rocks and tell me when they're gonna give out. And tell me when the Saurians are in place, too. Crystal?"

"Clear." Falcroné took his position and waited.

From Calum's vantage point, it seemed as if one of the boulders at the top could trigger the whole slide. He placed his foot on it and pushed, but it didn't budge.

It shouldn't have surprised him—the boulder looked about the size of a small cow and had to weigh over a thousand pounds. He stomped on the boulder again, but still no movement.

"Where are we at, Falcroné?"

"You've got about thirty seconds."

That was it? No time. He needed to loose these boulders *now*. He planted his right foot on the boulder and stepped onto it with his left. From so high up he could see into the gorge, and Falcroné had been right: Magnus, Axel, Lilly, and now Kanton were almost even with the stack of boulders.

Calum jumped, and landed hard on the boulder. It was a small jump, more of a test than anything. The boulder still didn't budge. Calum jumped again, this time higher, and he landed harder too. Still nothing.

He cursed. What if this didn't work? Had he just doomed his friends?

He jumped and stomped on the boulder a half dozen more times, but to no avail. Magnus and the others were even with the boulders now. If he didn't loose them soon, he'd miss his chance.

Why couldn't he just be stronger?

"Do you see any sign of them moving?" Calum called to Falcroné.

"No."

Calum grunted and jumped again. *Come on.*

The Saurians overlapped with the boulders' assumed trajectory.

"*Come on.*" Calum jumped again and stomped, then jump-stomped once more.

On the third jump-stomp, the boulder budged.

The next thing he knew, Calum was tumbling down into the gorge, surrounded by boulders the size of livestock.

He'd become part of the rockslide.

CHAPTER THIRTY

A hand clamped onto Calum's wrist, and the rockslide dropped out from under him. Falcroné pulled him up and glided with him across the gorge down toward Magnus, Axel, Lilly, and Kanton.

Calum noticed right away that although Falcroné still couldn't fully fly with Calum's weight added on, they didn't drop nearly as fast as he had when Lilly had glided with him back over the lake water. Falcroné was definitely stronger.

As they coasted toward a landing about thirty feet behind the rest of their group, Calum yelled, *"Run!"*

When Magnus heard Calum's voice, he parried a blow from the Sobek then drove his shoulder into the Sobek's chest. With the Sobek off-balance, Magnus turned back and charged away. As he ran, Magnus bent down and hooked Axel around his waist, hefted him over his shoulder, and carried him away from the incoming rocks.

Twenty long strides later, he watched as dozens of huge boulders tumbled into the gorge and smashed into the Saurians. At first, Magnus thought he'd pushed the Sobek back too far, but a boulder three or four times his size smacked into his chest, and he disappeared under the pile of rubble that consumed the other three Saurians.

"Hey!" Axel whacked Magnus's back. "Put me down, already."

Magnus obliged him, and Lilly and Kanton landed next to them. Together they watched as the final boulder settled on top of the pile. "I must admit, that worked a lot better than I expected it would."

"Yeah. No kidding," Axel said.

"Over here!" Calum called from behind them.

Magnus whirled around and saw the three remaining Saurians approaching Calum and Falcroné. He ran toward them along with Axel, and Lilly and Kanton zoomed overhead.

The six of them lined up together and faced the three Saurians, who stepped back. Several arrows protruded from the hides of two of the Saurians, and dark cuts streaked the other's face.

"Go now," Magnus hissed. "Or we will kill you, too."

The Saurians glanced at each other for a moment then refocused on Magnus.

"That way." Magnus pointed toward the pile of rubble. "And do not stop until you reach Trader's Pass. I do not want to so much as see you again."

The Saurians hissed at him through their noses but nodded. They passed by the group and kept going until they disappeared from the gorge entirely.

Magnus motioned to the others with his sword, and the rest of the group sheathed their weapons. He walked over to the pile with his sword still in hand and studied it until a faint hiss reached his ears.

He bent down and moved a couple of smaller rocks out of the way. There, pinned beneath a gigantic boulder, lay the Sobek, covered in gray dust.

He coughed and then hissed at Magnus.

"Next time Vandorian wants to capture me, he had better do it himself."

The Sobek chuckled, and dark blood trickled from the corners of his mouth. "Vandorian ain't sent us."

Magnus squinted at him and crouched down. He held his sword out for the Sobek to see. "Tell me who did, and I will accelerate your passing."

"'Oo else?" The Sobek coughed, and more blood oozed from his mouth. "There's only one slave lord in Western Kanarah. It's 'im 'oo sent us."

Magnus scowled at him. "Oren?"

The Sobek smiled. "Oren. My master. He'll bind you in chains an' send you to the Blood Chasm f'this."

"And why should he care about a mound of refuse like you?"

"My name's Troden. He's my brother. He'll make you suffa' *centuries* of agony for my death." The Sobek bared his reddened teeth.

Magnus raised his sword, tip down. "I will share your final remarks with him when next I see him."

Wide-eyed, Troden slung a string of curses, and Magnus drove the point of his sword through his head and into the gravel below. He retracted his sword, cleaned off its blade, and sheathed it as he stepped down off the mound of rubble toward the rest of the group.

"What did he say?" Calum asked.

"He was Oren's brother."

Axel shrugged. "So?"

Calum nudged him. "The Sobek in the brown from the Sky Fortress. Remember?"

Axel shrugged again. "So?"

"He is unlikely to forgive the death of his brother, even if his brother instigated the fight." Magnus exhaled a long hiss through his nose. "Plus, he heads of all of West Kanarah's slave trade."

LILLY'S EYES WIDENED. What was Magnus talking about? "What do you mean he's the head of West Kanarah's slave trade? Outside of the prisoners banished to the Blood Chasm, West Kanarah doesn't have any slave trade. It's the humans who deal in slaves."

Magnus shook his head. "I fear that is not the case, Lilly. The slave trade here has been in operation since even before my father was murdered. I had never encountered Oren before our meeting in your father's throne room, so I had no idea who he was. But apparently, Oren is the slave trade's prime operator, and perhaps its architect as well."

"This can't be true." Lilly stared at her boots. Had she been blind to this reality before she'd left the Sky Realm the first time? Had it taken her own capture and enslavement to reveal to her the bitter truth of it? Or had she been willfully ignorant all along? "How could anyone allow this to happen? Those slaves are *people*."

"Oren reports directly to Vandorian. That much is evident. That explains why Oren accompanied him to the Sky Fortress." Magnus clacked his talons on his breastplate. "And it is not a stretch to assume that Vandorian receives a tribute every month to look the other way when it comes to Oren's dealings, even though slavery violates Saurian law."

Axel huffed. "It's against human law too, but that doesn't stop the King from enslaving whoever he wants—for entire lifetimes."

"Yes, but when we free Lumen, that will change," Calum said.

"Slavery violates Windgale law as well." Lilly focused her attention on Falcroné. Did he know anything about this? "You're the Captain of the Royal Guard. Why doesn't my father do something about this?"

Falcroné's mouth hung open for a moment, probably to Axel's delight. "Lilly, I merely follow orders and relay them to my men in order to protect the Premier. I'm not privy to—"

"Don't lie to me, Fal." Lilly pressed her index finger into his armored chest. "You're in the same room with him almost every waking hour of the day. I know you've heard things that normal Windgales don't hear."

"I—" Falcroné gulped. "I am not at liberty to divulge the content of the Premier's dealings with anyone unauth—"

"I'm his *daughter*, to whom you're engaged." Lilly hovered up higher so she could look him in the eye. "I'm going to *rule* the Sky Realm some-day. If you think you can convince me that this isn't my business, you're wrong. Tell me what you know, Fal."

"Even if I could tell you what discussions he has, I wouldn't say anything with *them* around." Falcroné motioned toward their other companions.

Lilly didn't back down. She continued to stare into his blue eyes, unrelenting. He knew something, and she was going to drag it out of him.

"Either you tell me now, or this engagement ends immediately."

She could scarcely believe the words had just come out of her mouth, but they had. Lilly didn't dare look, but she imagined Axel was just short of all-out celebrating the potential death of her relationship with Falcroné, and Calum probably was, too, albeit less overtly.

But she didn't care. Right now, the issue at hand was far more important.

"That's unfair, Lilly." Falcroné glanced around. His voice had taken on a calm but firm tone. "And inappropriate, too, considering those around us."

"You don't have to worry about them," Lilly asserted. "You have to worry about me. When all of this is said and done, they'll go back to their homes, and you and I will go back to the Sky Realm. Whether you and I are still together when that happens is up to you, right here and right now. So tell me what I want to know, or we're done."

"*Please*, Lilly." Falcroné leaned in close to her with his voice lowered and tinged with desperation. "You are asking me to betray my oath to your father, and you're doing it in front of these people."

"Relationships are built on trust, Fal," she countered, not bothering to lower her voice as he had. "If I can't trust you, then there is no relationship. Do you understand?"

"If they could just grant us some privacy, or if we could go off somewhere to have this conversation instead, I—"

"Anything you tell me, they will hear from my lips afterward anyway, so you might as well spill it all, here and now." Lilly waited as the wheels in Falcroné's mind turned.

Finally, he sighed. "Your father is, more or less, unopposed to the slave trade."

Kanton shook his head, and Calum and Axel muttered between themselves.

Lilly ignored them all. Her voice hardened. "What do you mean by 'more or less?'"

"It means that he lacks the resources and manpower to fully shut the slave trade down—" Falcroné paused. "—but also that he participates in it from time to time."

Falcroné's admission hit Lilly like blow to her gut, and she felt physically sick upon hearing it.

"But it's not what you think," Falcroné quickly added. "He only sends criminals, derelicts—people like that—which you already know. That's exactly what they're going to do with Condor."

Falcroné was right. She'd been right there in the throne room when her father sentenced Condor to life at the Blood Chasm, but...

"Does he accept remuneration for the people he sends?" she asked.

Falcroné's jaw tensed, and he slowly nodded.

Lilly closed her eyes and shook her head. Her own father, a willing participant in Kanarah's slave trade? Even if it was only on occasion, it was still heinous. At the thought, Lilly wanted to vomit.

Roderick had captured her and sold her into slavery, and she'd barely escaped with her life. She would have never seen her home or her family again. Now she'd learned her father had supported people just like Roderick and his men.

It was wrong. All of it.

"In my opinion, there is only one thing for us to do now," Magnus said. "We must to venture to Oren's fortress near the Blood Chasm and put a stop to his enterprise once and for all."

Axel scoffed. "Talk about a waste of time."

Lilly redirected all of her anger at him with a single glare. "A waste of *time?*"

"Easy." Axel held up his hand. "I mean we're better off going to free Lumen. Won't he just take care of this sort of thing anyway?"

"And in doing so, do we forsake the people currently enslaved?" Calum asked. "I'm with Lilly and Magnus, here."

"I call that acceptable losses." Axel cracked his neck. "Think about how many we're gonna save once we free Lumen."

"Going to free Lumen instead of helping those people means we're giving up on them. Is that what Lumen would do?" Calum stepped toward Axel.

"Beats me." Axel shrugged and folded his arms. "You're the authority on ancient warriors. You tell me."

"He's coming back to liberate *all* of Kanarah," Calum replied. "He's made that perfectly clear."

"Then that's your answer," Axel concluded. "He'll take care of it."

"Practically speaking, it is wise for us to destroy Oren before he can rally a response to the death of his brother," Magnus said. "If we leave now, we can still catch him by surprise. If we cut off the head of the serpent, the body will wither and die."

Axel kept shaking his head. "If we just head straight to Lumen—"

"You still don't even believe Lumen exists," Calum cut in. "So why are you insisting on this now?"

"Consider me swayed toward believing," Axel replied. He still stood in the same position: legs spread apart with his arms folded across his chest.

"Why?" Calum pressed. "What swayed you?"

Axel began numbering his responses with his fingers. "The Premier certainly seemed to believe Lumen is real. Then he gave us a map that supposedly leads right to the Arcanarium, or whatever it's called. Lilly wanted to come along, so she obviously believes there's something to it.

"Lastly, you won't shut up about these dreams you keep having, so I'm starting to think he might be real." Axel held up four fingers. He considered telling them about how Condor had hinted at knowing something about the Arcanum as well, but he held that one back. "There. Four reasons. Good enough for you?"

"I'm glad you're finally on board with us," Calum said. "And now that you've caught up to that point, catch up to this next one: Lilly wants to free the slaves at Oren's fortress, so that's what we're doing."

Axel rolled his eyes again and folded his arms again. "Whatever."

When Calum looked at Lilly, she had to consciously stifle her smile.

"This is what you want, right?" he asked.

She nodded. "Yes. We have to help those people. Magnus and I know what it's like, and so do you, Calum. Better than anyone."

"Yeah. That's probably true." Calum rubbed the back of his neck. "Magnus, how far is it out of the way?"

"According to the map, once we reach the Blood Mountains, it is only a day's journey in the opposite direction from the Arcanum, near where the edge of the mountains meets a forest. We can reach it there in about a week."

"It's settled. We're going," Calum declared. "And we can raid the place for supplies while we're there, too. It makes sense to go. Right?"

Aside from Axel, who rolled his eyes again, everyone in the group nodded, some more enthusiastically than others. Falcroné's head barely moved.

Lilly frowned, and he frowned back at her.

"You alright with this, Falcroné?" Calum must've noticed it, too.

"I am charged with keeping Lilly safe above all else. If she goes, I'll go as well." He reached out and placed a gloved hand on her shoulders, but she shrunk away from him.

She wasn't ready to receive anything from him other than space and perhaps more answers, at least for the time being. Falcroné wouldn't like it, but he'd just have to deal with it.

"Good. Let's go." Calum faced north and took a few steps.

"What about Riley?" Kanton asked.

Calum stopped and turned back. "I don't know where he went. I hope he's alright. Where should we start looking for him?"

"Leave him. He ran away when we needed him." Axel waved his hand in dismissal. "If he doesn't need us, then we don't need him either."

Lilly wanted to smack Axel upside his head.

"Don't talk like that, Axel," Calum said.

Magnus started toward Axel. "What if someday we decided we did not need you?"

"Hey, *I* didn't run from the fight like a scared little puppy. *He* did." Axel met Magnus until they stood face-to-breastplate, with Magnus looking down at him. "Don't pick on me for it."

"Spread out in groups and start looking for him," Magnus said. "Call out his name. Wolves have excellent hearing. If he is nearby, he will hear us and will hopefully return. If we do not find him within the next hour, we will leave, and he can catch up to us later if he so wishes."

Calum gave Magnus a reluctant nod. Then he looked straight at Lilly and said, "Come on. Let's start looking."

RILEY? Rileeeeeeeey? Where are you, Riley?

Friendly voices filled Riley's mind first, and then his ears. He hid under a rocky overhang in a space totally shielded from the sun.

Upon discovering the space, he'd chased a rock wallaby out of it and claimed it for his own. It was beautifully dark inside. The Saurians would never find him in there... if they even bothered looking.

"Riley?"

"Riley, helloooooo?"

The voices solidified, now more real than imagined. He recognized them, distantly, as friends, but his mind refused to identify specifically whom they belonged to.

In general, since the attack, his mind had refused to do a lot of things that it used to do just fine. Something in his head had severed along with Condor's stab, and he couldn't put it back the way it was.

Nor could Riley go back out to them—his friends. Not after he'd fled and left them to fend for themselves. How many of them had died because he wasn't there to help?

How many of them died anyway, regardless of whether or not you'd been there? His thoughts countered.

"Riley? Can you hear us?"

"The fight's over Riley. You're safe now."

Safe. But for how long? They'd fight again.

That's all that ever seemed to happen to this group—fights.

Fights with monsters in tunnels.

Fights with pirates—at least he'd missed those.

Fights with Windgale rebels that ended with him skewered like a stuck pig.

Fights, fights, fights.

He was better off hiding in here and waiting for them to pass him by.

They were better off, too. If they couldn't count on him for help, he might as well not weigh their group down.

"Riley?"

"Are you in there?"

Calum and Kanton. His mind finally ascribed names to the voices—voices which were much closer now.

Aside from Lilly, those two were his favorites. Calum had spared his life back in Eastern Kanarah, and Kanton had saved it after Condor ran him through.

Still, he couldn't go out to them. Even if they welcomed him back, he couldn't face the shame of deserting his friends. His only friends.

His only friends *ever*.

"It's dark in there." Kanton's legs came into view as he landed near the opening of the overhang. He bent down and peered into the hole right at where Riley hid in the darkness. "I don't see too well these days. Maybe you'd better have a look?"

Calum's crimson armor showed up next, all scratched and chipped, probably from the fight. It certainly hadn't been beforehand. If he'd taken that kind of damage just to his armor, how bad had the rest of the group gotten it?

Calum got down on all fours and peered into the shadows. "It's definitely Riley's type of hiding spot. I can't make out what's in there, if anything. If he was in there, he'd have heard us by now, anyway."

"He would have heard us a long while ago," Kanton said. "If he's around, you don't think he'd be too timid to come out, do you?"

Calum shook his head and pushed himself back up to his feet. "He knows we're looking for him. He knows we don't want to leave him behind, but he's gotta make the call on whether or not he's coming with us, if he hasn't already."

Leaving? They were leaving? They were going to leave Riley behind?

How could they do such a thing? After all, they were friends… weren't they?

"Come on," Calum said. "We've got a lot more ground to cover and only ten minutes before we said we'd leave."

"Alright. I'll fly some more reconnaissance." Kanton's legs sprang into the air, and Calum's walked off to the side.

They'd left him.

They'd been right there, and they'd left him behind.

But it wasn't because they wanted to leave him. They'd made that clear.

It was because *he* hadn't spoken up. He hadn't made a sound. He'd hidden himself well—too well.

At least he was still good at something.

Riley raised his head. He was still good at *something*. And if they were still looking for him, even after he ran away, then they must still want him around.

And, he realized, he wanted to be around them, too, shame or otherwise.

Good enough.

He stood to his feet and padded his way out of the overhang.

CHAPTER THIRTY-ONE

A week later, they reached Oren's fortress.

Lilly hadn't known what to expect before she saw the Blood Chasm. Its name conjured nightmarish images in her mind of a river of blood flowing through a fissure, but when she flew overhead for a look, the reality of what she saw dwarfed her imagination in both scale and terror.

Instead of a red river in a crevice, Lilly found a half-mile-wide bottomless pit in the crimson rock around it. Networks of rope bridges with wooden planks stretched between anchors mounted to the Blood Chasm's perimeter, and more rope bridges extended from those in every direction out over the chasm itself.

A ramshackle staircase, also made of wood and rope, spiraled deep into the chasm and ended in the first of many tunnels carved into its sides. Narrow walkways carved from the stone lined the outer edges of the chasm farther down.

Inside the chasm, slaves of every race milled about. Some of them pushed carts of red rocks to the edge of the chasm and dumped them into the abyss. Others hefted bulging bags of usable materials like iron and Blood Ore up the spiral steps or across the rope bridges.

How many of them had fallen into that Chasm while trying to carry their loads to the surface? How many had given their precious lives for a few pounds of raw metal?

Lilly's eyes narrowed. They would stop Oren tonight, and then they'd free these slaves. Every one of them.

At sundown, a pair of armored Saurians pulled about fifty or sixty slaves from the chasm. The third member of their group, a man in dark armor, tallied their number on a piece of parchment. One Saurian anchored the slaves to each other, and the other collected all of their various tools into a big cart.

Lilly couldn't make out what they were saying from so high in the air, but she caught enough to realize that the tally-man's hand signal—four fingers up—meant they had lost four slaves that day to the Blood Chasm.

She shook her head and scowled. Had they managed to get there only a few hours sooner, perhaps those four slaves would have lived. She was too late to help them now, but she took comfort in knowing that no more slaves would die after tonight.

As a unit, the Saurians marched the slaves toward the fortress, a two-story wooden structure made of vertical logs with their tops sharpened to points. The doors to the fortress swung open and swallowed the slaves, the Saurians, and the tool cart whole, then it shut again behind the tally-man, who entered last.

Night fell, and several torches within the fortress ignited. A few armored men stood watch on the fortress's flat roof, but mostly they gambled with dice for whatever small coins or trinkets they had with them. Probably property they'd taken from new slaves when they arrived.

Lilly completed her round of scouting then nodded to Falcroné, who had completed his own scouting flight, and together they flew back to the rest of the group hidden in the trees at the edge of the Blood Mountains.

"Well?" Calum asked.

"I saw two Saurians and one man, plus three more men on the roof," Lilly said. "And about fifty-five slaves."

Falcroné nodded. "I can confirm all of that, but I saw another Saurian inside in addition to the two that Lilly saw."

"That makes eight of them, including Oren." Magnus crouched down. "This is definitely doable, if we can be surreptitious. Those three Saurians and Oren himself concern me the most. Vandorian would never have granted him such a position of authority if he were not worthy of the job. He will not be an easy foe to defeat."

"What do you want to do?" Calum asked.

"I anticipate I will need help in defeating Oren. I want Axel and Falcroné with me on that. The rest of you must release the slaves and find a way to overcome the guards."

Lilly nodded. The plan was sound enough, and it left a little room for improvising if need be. Together with Kanton and Calum—and maybe Riley, if he could keep from running off again—Lilly believed they could get the job done.

"If we can reach the slaves, I imagine they'll help us fight," Kanton said. "I know I would."

"They pushed a cart of mining tools into the fortress behind the slaves." Lilly motioned toward the fortress with her head. "We can arm them with those."

"Perfect." Magnus smirked. "Even a simple pickax can be effective in the right hands."

Axel matched Magnus's smirk, and Calum nodded.

"The only question that remains is our approach. Riley, you are the stealth expert. What do you suggest?"

Before Riley could say anything, Axel held up his hand. "Whoa, wait a minute. He's not coming with, is he? He'll just run away again as soon as it gets too hot in there."

Riley growled, and Lilly considered joining him.

"We've been through this already, Axel," Calum said. "And we're not going through it again. Riley is still useful to this group, and if he wants to, he's coming along. Crystal?"

Axel scowled at him and sighed. "Yeah, clear. He's not gonna be in my group anyway, so he can't get me killed by not watching my back."

Calum ignored him and turned back to Riley. "How do you want to do this?"

"Thank you." Riley glared at Axel for a long moment, then faced the fortress. "It's exposed, right out in the open. That'll make the approach a pain. Did you see any other entrances besides the main door?"

"Entrances, no," Falcroné said. "Other than some windows and a hatch on the roof for the guards to get in and out, no."

"Alright. We've got enough manpower—and the right kinds of manpower—to get in there all but unnoticed, even though the place is exposed."

"What does that mean?" Axel asked.

Riley turned his head toward him. "It means *shut up*, and I'll tell you. Lilly and Falcroné need to take out the guards on the roof first. Once they're down, we can creep over to the fortress easily enough. You don't even have to be good at stealth to pull that off." He stared at Axel again. "And that's a huge advantage since some of us don't know the meaning of the word."

Lilly didn't bother to conceal her smirk. Riley's sarcasm was her favorite thing about him.

Axel folded his arms and leaned forward. "At least I don't run from fights."

"Stop it, both of you." Calum looked at Riley. "Continue, please."

"From there it's just a matter of sneaking inside without them hearing. The roof access seems like a natural place, but it'll be too hard to get all of us up there. I don't think the three Windgales combined could get Magnus up there, for example.

"Climbing isn't a quiet option, either, but if the three of you can get at least Calum and me onto the roof, then we can go in from the top. Then we'll meet you at the main entrance and let you inside."

"No problem." Falcroné grinned. "We'll get you up there, easy."

"From there, just try to take the guards by surprise if you can, and bring them down quietly. If even one of them hollers, we're all in trouble." Riley sat up straight and tilted his head. "Any questions?"

Calum smiled. "Let's go free some slaves."

CALUM WISHED he'd been close enough to see how they did it, but even from far away, he got the gist of what happened in the five seconds it took Lilly and Falcroné to deal with the guards on the roof. Two of Lilly's arrows had combined with two quick slashes from Falcroné's blade to silence the three of them for good.

Then Falcroné picked up one of the torches from the roof and darted through the air a few times to signal Calum and the others to head for the fortress.

Within minutes, Riley, Kanton, Lilly, and Calum all stood on the roof while Magnus, Axel, and Falcroné headed for the main doors.

A rope ladder lay on the roof next to the hatch door, and Calum pushed it away, but as he reached to open the hatch, he hesitated. When Lilly hovered directly over it with an arrow nocked in her bow, Calum subdued his nerves and quietly opened the hatch.

Riley poked his head down into the hatch for a moment, then he came back up. "Clear."

Calum nodded. "Can you get down there?"

Riley shook his head. "Not quietly. The drop is too far for me to land without making too much noise, especially with this shoulder armor on. Falling from this height wouldn't feel great, either. You'll have to use the rope ladder to get down there, and these two will have to lower me down since I don't have opposable thumbs."

"Let's do it," Calum said. "I'll go last."

Riley put his forepaws on Kanton's shoulders, and Lilly held him around his waist, and they squeezed together, making a Riley sandwich, and lowered down through the hatch. Once they gave Calum the all clear, he lowered the rope ladder and climbed down as quietly as he could.

From that platform they descended down to the floor. A pair of torches illuminated the room, empty aside from the rope ladder and two beds stacked on top of each other. The door on the south end of the room was shut.

"Walk softly, Calum," Riley whispered. "The Windgales can hover. You can't, and your boots are noisy. Watch your step."

"Got it," Calum replied.

The floor creaked on his very first step, and Riley glared at him. Calum shrugged and kept going. He couldn't know where the floor would and wouldn't creak.

They made it through the door and into an open walkway that led in two opposite directions. Two wooden staircases, one on each end of the walkway, led down to the first floor where the main entrance fed into the lobby.

Riley nodded to Lilly, who hovered over the rail that lined the edge of the walkway. She checked below to make sure no one was around and then dropped down. Calum and Kanton peered over the edge of the rail and watched her unbolt the doors. Magnus, Axel, and Falcroné filtered inside in total silence.

Riley trotted past each of the rooms to Calum's right, then nodded to him, and Calum followed, stealing a glance in each one. They were empty, too. He crept down the staircase behind Riley and met up with the others on the first floor.

"Maybe they're eating dinner or something?" Calum murmured.

"Makes sense. It *is* just after sundown." Kanton's hushed tone matched Calum's.

"Or there's a lower level," Riley whispered. "There isn't anywhere to hide the prisoners up on the second floor."

Something stirred behind them, and they whirled around. Lilly nocked an arrow in her bow, and Calum's hand went to the hilt of his sword.

Toward the back of the lobby, a large cage with black iron bars extended up to the ceiling, but Calum couldn't see anyone inside the deep shadows within. If anyone was in there, they'd get whoever it was out once they freed the slaves on the lower level.

"There is a staircase toward the back of this room." Magnus motioned to an opening in the floor next to the cage. "If you find Oren, stay down there, and we will confront him together. I suspect he is in the room to the right of that cage with several of his guards, though."

On the opposite side of the lobby, a wall of vertical logs partitioned almost a third of the first floor into a separate room. The tool cart, loaded full of mining equipment, sat in the corner immediately to the right of the main doors.

Though the setting differed from his life at the quarry, the heavy oppression of the place still felt all too familiar to Calum. But he could deal with his memories later.

First, he and his friends had to walk past that room to get downstairs. At least the door was closed; as long as they stayed quiet, it shouldn't be a problem.

"Go ahead," Falcroné urged. "We won't make our move until you get downstairs."

Riley started forward before Calum could respond, so Calum kept quiet and just followed. They descended down the stairs, Riley leading, into the dark basement under the fortress.

Several torches lined the walls of the lower level, which amounted to nothing more than a dungeon. Some of the original slaves had probably carved the lower level out of the red rock specifically for that reason.

A row of iron cages lined the basement's square perimeter. Even in the low light, Calum could see dozens of people inside—people of every race and type. Eager to get to work freeing them, he started toward the nearest cage.

"Calum, wait!" Riley hissed.

A dark figure emerged from the shadows and swung his blade at Calum's head.

CHAPTER THIRTY-TWO

A xel bristled. Together with Falcroné and Magnus, he stood ready to kick open a door to a room that held three Saurians, one man, and one Sobek—at least according to Lilly and Falcroné's scouting report. Who knew what they would actually face once they made it inside?

Too late now.

Magnus held up two fingers, then three, and then he threw his entire weight against the door.

Wood snapped, and the meager door all but shattered. Falcroné darted inside first and slit the throat of one of the two Saurians in the room. Axel charged in behind Magnus and jammed his blade into the chest of a man who came at him with a sword.

Magnus parried the second Saurian's sword then lashed his blade straight down, cleaving into the Saurian's skull. He dropped to the floor, dead.

Axel smirked. They were doing better than he'd expected.

Then a green-and-brown mass slammed into Magnus.

The impact sent him careening into the wall next to the door, and his body snapped through it as if the logs were little more than dried sticks. He landed on the dirt floor about where Axel had stood before they broke through the door.

Oren stood in the center of the room and drew a curved sword, but it wasn't the ragged-looking one he'd drawn back at the Sky Fortress.

This one was bright blue, just like Magnus's armor.

MAGNUS PUSHED himself up to his feet and stepped back into the room through the hole in the wall. The pain in his chest from Oren's blow had already begun to fade.

"You're gonna pay for this, bugs." Oren hissed at Magnus, then eyed Falcroné and Axel. "All three o' ya."

Magnus noted Oren's blue blade. Even without a Blood Ore sword, Oren made a formidable foe, but with a weapon equal to Magnus's, Oren could very well win the fight.

Even so, Magnus remained undeterred. "Your slave trade ends tonight, Oren."

Oren tilted his head and gave an expression caught somewhere between a sneer and a snarl. It was hard to tell for all the scars on his face. "Ohhh, I recognize you now. You're Vandorian's kid brother. Speaking o' brothers, you done killed mine, ain't you?"

"Your brother and his Saurians attacked us. We gave him plenty of opportunities to let us pass, but he refused."

The Saurian whose throat Falcroné had cut crawled across the floor and groped at Oren's legs.

"Izzat right?" Oren shook his head and looked down at the Saurian. "That's not what I 'eard from Jerome, 'ere. But now you've cut 'is froat, so we can't ask him again, can we, my babies?"

Falcroné smirked. "You can blame that one on me."

"I saw you do it, an' I *do* blame you." Instead of helping Jerome, Oren kicked him down and ran him through. Once Jerome stopped convulsing and lay still, Oren pulled his sword out of his chest and glared at Magnus. "Now we really can't ask 'im. So I gets to believe

whatever I wanna believe, an' we'll just 'ave to come to some sort of…
agreement."

Magnus growled at him.

"As for Vandorian, he'll pay me a hefty sum if I bring you to 'im—or
if I lock you up 'ere 'til the next time he arrives."

Magnus stared at the dead Saurian at Oren's feet. He'd just finished
off one of his own soldiers instead of trying to help him. What kind of
sick person did that?

"What're you gawkin' at, li'l brother?" Oren smirked at Magnus. "I
know you've seen a murder before, 'ey? Namely, your father?"

Magnus shifted his grip on his sword. Oren was trying to get inside
his head. "Enough idle chatter. Will you fight, or will you continue to
stall?"

Oren waved him away with his free hand, but he didn't lower his
sword. Instead, he turned toward Axel.

"An' what're *you* lookin' at, ya bug?" Oren hissed.

"Nothing." Axel smirked just like Oren had a moment earlier. "I'm
just really looking forward to making a new pair of boots outta your
ugly hide after you're dead."

Oren's eyes narrowed, and instead of facing Magnus, he stormed
toward Axel with a roar.

***

LILLY'S ARROW knocked the Saurian off-balance, but his sword still
crashed down on Calum's left arm with incredible force. Had he not
been wearing armor, the blow would've severed his arm. As it was, pain
ratcheted through his bones from his shoulder down to his fingertips,
and he hit the ground hard.

The Saurian's foot landed next to Calum's head. When he looked up,
the Saurian had raised his blade for another swing. Despite his injured
arm, Calum twisted around and held his own sword up in time to block.
Even so, the strike sent jarring vibrations through his left arm, nearly as
bad as the first hit.

The Saurian kept pushing his sword down, closer and closer to

Calum's chest, and Calum couldn't push it away. As usual, he was too weak to do much of anything, and his weakened arm wasn't helping at all.

Kanton's spearhead zipped into view and hooked the Saurian's sword, which began to rise thanks to Kanton's help. Mostly thanks to his right arm, Calum gave the sword one last shove and then rolled away from the Saurian, and his sword clanged against the stone floor.

The Saurian flailed his free arm and sent Kanton flying across the room. Kanton smacked into the bars on one of the cages and dropped to the floor, either stunned or unconscious—Calum couldn't tell.

As soon as the Saurian turned around, he caught an arrow in his throat from Lilly, then another to his exposed chest. He roared, ripped the arrows out, and leaped toward her, but she darted away from his grasp. More enraged than ever, the Saurian returned his attention to Calum.

Calum recovered his footing and waited for the Saurian to come at him instead of pursuing him. Once the Saurian closed to within striking distance of Calum, he swung his sword in a wide arc. Unwilling to parry, given his left arm's condition, Calum backed away from the swipe and the one that followed.

The Saurian hefted his sword over his head again, and Lilly shot another arrow. It lodged in the left side of his stomach just above his belt, and the Saurian winced and abandoned his strike. When the Saurian reached for it, Calum lurched forward and drove his sword into the Saurian's gut.

The Saurian dropped his sword, but he also clamped his hand on Calum's wrist, anchoring him in place. Then he grabbed Calum's throat with his other hand and lifted him into the air.

The Saurian began to squeeze.

Calum tried to pull his sword free, and he tried to pry the Saurian's thick fingers away from his neck, but neither tactic worked. Calum felt as if his head was about to pop off his neck.

Kanton zoomed into view, spear-first. As its tip knifed into the Saurian's side, he released his grip on Calum. The Saurian swatted Kanton away again, but the spear remained lodged in his flank. Then

Lilly drew her sword from its sheath and jammed it into the Saurian's flesh at the base of his neck.

He roared and convulsed wildly, but he didn't stop trying to fight them. No matter what they did, the Saurian wouldn't go down.

HAD FALCRONÉ not tackled Axel out of the way, Oren would have crushed him. They landed on the floor in a tangled heap of armored limbs and exchanged quick glares, but Axel gave Falcroné a nod nonetheless.

They could have a stare-down some other time. Right now, they had a bigger problem to deal with.

As the two of them pushed to their feet, Magnus traded blows with Oren, who moved faster than Axel knew a Saurian could. He efficiently parried Magnus's blows then threw several counterattacks in quick succession. Magnus fielded most of them, but one of them clanged against the scales on his left arm, and he recoiled.

"In some trouble, are ya, Magnus?" Oren scoffed. "This blade's Blood Ore, jus' like yours. It's sharp enough to rend even your fine scales."

"You talk far too much." Magnus rubbed the spot where Oren had hit him, then he advanced again.

Falcroné swooped around the room and came up behind Oren with his blade out. Still flying fast, he jabbed it at the back of Oren's head, but Oren ducked and Falcroné crashed into Magnus instead. The impact all but leveled Falcroné, but it only knocked Magnus off-balance.

Oren took advantage of the situation and shoved Magnus back through the same hole in the wall which he'd broken through, and he kicked Falcroné to the side. That left Axel alone to face him.

Oren chuckled. "You babies make me laugh, thinkin' you can best me. You're all gonna die—if you're lucky. Otherwise, it's the chasm f'you. All o' you."

But despite Oren's words, he didn't advance. Either he was toying with them, or he was buying time. Given the way he'd fought so far,

Axel worried it was the former. And if Oren was really that good, they might not make it out of this alive.

Falcroné got up next and shifted several long locks of blond hair from his face. He readied his sword again, glaring at Oren. Finally, Magnus stood to his feet, reentered the room, and raised his sword for battle.

"We attack him together, as a unit," Magnus said. "That is how we will bring him down."

"Ha!" Oren shook his head. "You fink you're in a dream world, but I'll bring you back to real life. Then I'll put you in a real cage, just to drive 'ome the point."

"Ready?" Magnus asked.

Axel nodded and raised his sword, and so did Falcroné.

———

AMID THE STRUGGLE FOR CONTROL, Calum managed to get ahold of his sword, which still protruded from the Saurian's gut, and he ripped it out.

The Saurian jerked to his left and wrenched Kanton's spear from his side. He feigned an attack that got Calum to raise his sword, then he kicked Calum square in his chest, launching him back into the bars. His head took the worst of it, and a white light flashed past his eyes upon impact.

He dropped to the ground, stunned. His vision fogged over and spiraled all at the same time, and he tried to stand but couldn't.

Lilly had her bow out again and shot another arrow, this time into the Saurian's head. It lodged just behind the Saurian's eye, and he whirled around and hurled the spear at her with a roar.

She ducked under it, but the spear pierced her cape and plunged into the wall. She yanked on it, but couldn't get it free.

Calum wanted to get up and help her, but his body refused to comply with what his brain tried to tell it. All he could do was stumble as he tried to get up. He couldn't even cry out to her to warn her.

All he could do was watch.

Oozing blood and rage, the Saurian picked up his sword and limped toward Lilly.

RILEY COWERED in the shadows as the Saurian thrashed his friends. The Saurian had taken multiple arrows, been stabbed three times in vital areas, and he *still* hadn't fallen. At this point, Riley didn't blame himself for not joining in the fray.

Except now that the Saurian had pinned Lilly to the wall, Riley knew he should intervene somehow. He should do *something*.

Everything in him yearned to emerge from his hiding spot and clamp his jaws down on that Saurian's ankle and shred his tendons, but his body refused to obey his commands.

But it was *Lilly* hanging there, all but helpless. Had it been Axel, he could have stayed hidden forever, but this was Lilly, his favorite of his friends. She'd always been the kindest to him.

He had to do something. He *wanted* to do something.

But he couldn't. The fear coursing through his muscles froze him in place.

Like Calum, still trying to stagger to his feet, all Riley could do was watch.

LILLY'S SCREAM snapped Axel's focus on Oren. He glanced back and almost caved to his urge to run to help her.

Falcroné's response nearly matched Axel's, except that his mouth hung open for a moment first. Then he turned and darted toward the door, but Magnus caught him by his arm.

"I need you *here*, Falcroné." Magnus's eyes narrowed. "I cannot defeat him without you."

"And I swore to protect Lilly above all else." Falcroné twisted out of Magnus's grasp and zipped out the door, even as Magnus called for him to come back.

Axel refocused on Oren. He wanted to go play the hero, too, especially for Lilly's sake, but someone had to make sure the ugly Sobek didn't try something in the interim.

Oren stretched his arms into the air and rotated his head on his neck in a cacophony of cracks. "Don't worry, li'l babies. I ain't goin' nowhere."

CALUM'S LEGS FOUND PURCHASE, and his hazy mind began to clear. He had to stop the Saurian, but a messy flow of thoughts interfered with his progress.

Where's Riley? Did he run off again? They sure could've used him right now.

Calum marshaled all his strength and focus, but he only managed a pitiful lunge. Without even turning around, the Saurian whacked him aside with his tail, and Calum skidded into a different set of bars, albeit not as hard.

He looked around. Maybe Kanton had recovered and could help.

Lilly yanked on the cape. The fabric tore, but not enough—she was still stuck.

But Calum couldn't see Kanton from where he lay. All he could see was the Saurian cocking his sword for a final swing. *"Lilly!"*

A gold-and-gray blur shot collided with the Saurian with such force that it knocked him into the nearby cages. It scrambled up to its feet immediately.

Falcroné tore the spear from the wall, freeing Lilly, and tossed it to Kanton, who was still on his hands and knees trying to get up. Lilly zipped behind Falcroné and drew an arrow from her quiver.

The Saurian roared and charged forward.

OREN'S TAIL crashed into Axel's breastplate and sent him flying out of the room through the hole Magnus had made. He skidded to a stop

275

BEN WOLF

against the cage in the lobby and sucked in short, shallow breaths to steady his cognition.

Through that opening, as Axel tried to get back up to his feet, he watched as Magnus deftly engaged Oren on his own—at least at first.

They exchanged several blows with their swords, legs, and fists before Oren leveled Magnus with a stunning blow from his tail. He raised his curved blade and whipped it down at Magnus hard enough to split a boulder, but Magnus blocked it with his own sword and an unimaginable amount of strength and control.

Oren snickered, then he kicked Magnus in his left side twice. Magnus winced and grunted each time, but on Oren's third attempt, Magnus caught his foot with his left arm, jerked it forward, and swept his lower half at Oren's other leg. Oren dropped to the floor as well.

As Axel made it up to his knees, a voice hissed from the darkness behind him.

"*Hey.*"

Axel sprang the rest of the way up to his feet and recoiled from the voice with his sword ready. "Who said that?"

"In here." The whispered voice came from the cage, still drenched in shadows. "Let me out, and I'll help you kill Oren."

Metal clattered behind him, and Axel glanced back. Magnus's and Oren's swords tumbled across the floor toward Axel, and they grappled with each other in a myriad of roars, grunts, and hisses.

Axel eyed the lock that hung from the latch on the door. "I don't have a key."

The prisoner chuckled. "That wouldn't stop an industrious Farm Boy like yourself, now, would it?"

Axel's eyes widened.

CHAPTER THIRTY-THREE

"*C*ondor?"

"We really must stop meeting like this."

Axel couldn't believe his ears... or his eyes.

The prisoner stepped out of the shadows so his face was visible. Even in the meager torch light Axel made out his piercing blue eyes, the pronounced scar that ran from the outer edge of his left eyebrow to the top of his cheek, and his black hair.

"Let me out, Farm Boy, and I'll help you." Condor nodded to Magnus's sword. "Your friend's blade could certainly cut through the lock, if you give it enough heft."

Magnus twisted Oren around onto his stomach and shoved his snout against the dirty floor with his left hand, then he wrenched Oren's right arm behind his back with the other.

But Oren jerked his body forward and Magnus toppled over his head, losing his hold. They scrambled, but this time Oren mounted Magnus. He drove his fist into Magnus's snout twice before Magnus managed to get a block up.

Axel shook his head. He couldn't justify releasing Condor.

Instead, he abandoned the cage and charged Oren with his sword raised, even as Condor called him to come back.

Axel lashed his blade down on Oren's right forearm, but it just clanged harmlessly off of Oren's scales. Oren's tail smacked into Axel's knees, and he dropped, but he rolled away in time to avoid Oren's fist, which slammed into the floor where Axel's head had just been.

The instant Axel made it back up to his feet, Oren's other fist hit him square in his chest, and he careened across the room until his back hit the wall of logs.

A torch dropped from its mount on and rolled toward the wall, and some of the pitch slathered between the logs at the base began to sizzle and burn.

Axel wheezed and sucked in more air to try to catch his breath. Oren's last blow not only knocked the wind out of him but also sent a bolt of pain ratcheting through his entire body. And it had left a sizable fist-shaped dent in his new breastplate.

"Farm Boy," Condor hissed again. "*Axel.* Free me, or Oren will kill you both."

Axel looked back at Magnus and Oren, who again rolled around on the floor, trading vicious punches and elbow strikes.

If Axel grabbed Magnus's sword and tried to use it on Oren, he might be able to end the fight. But if he failed, or if Oren saw him coming, there was no way could Axel take another blow like Oren's punch to his chest. No sense in getting himself killed while trying to help.

When Oren got back on top of Magnus again and fastened his hands around Magnus's throat, Axel knew what he had to do. He rushed over and picked up Magnus's sword, and instead of trying to hit Oren with it, he hauled it back to Condor's cage. As he hefted it over his head, he realized it wasn't as heavy as he'd expected.

A wretched gurgling noise sounded from Magnus's throat as he strained against Oren's grip.

Axel slammed Magnus's sword down on the lock, and it snapped off in one strike.

The door to Condor's cage swung open.

CALUM AND FALCRONÉ took turns swinging at the Saurian, Kanton jabbed at it with his spear, and Lilly circled him and pumped arrows into his hide.

Having Falcroné there to help more than made up their disadvantage, but Calum had no idea how Axel and Magnus were faring with Oren upstairs. He hoped Falcroné abandoning the plan hadn't ruined everything for them.

"Lilly, aim for his belt," Falcroné called.

Calum wondered why Falcroné wanted her to aim there, but Lilly nodded, nocked an arrow, and let it fly.

When the arrow hit his hip, the Saurian whirled around and swung his sword at Lilly, but she dropped out of the air under the blow and shot another one at him. This time it knifed through the leather strap around his waist and plunged into the side of his underbelly.

The belt dropped to the floor.

And so did the attached key ring.

Now it made sense to Calum. He called out, "Kanton, can you—"

"On it." Kanton's spearhead hooked the keys and slid them away as the Saurian bent down to reach for them.

While the Saurian was still bent over, Falcroné whipped his sword at the Saurian's face. The blade severed through the Saurian's lower jaw, and dark blood streamed out from the grotesque wound.

In blind rage, the Saurian roared and whipped his sword in a wide arc. Falcroné tried to block it, but the force hurled him into the bars behind them. Falcroné dropped to the ground, motionless.

"Fal!" Lilly hollered. She nocked another arrow and fired it into the Saurian's back.

"Unlock the cells, Kanton!" Calum yelled, and Kanton inserted a key into the nearest lock.

The Saurian charged Calum, who stood near one of the corners.

He didn't have anywhere to go. He couldn't get anywhere in time. He readied his sword, and braced himself for his one opportunity to run the Saurian through before it pulverized him.

A rush of bodies intercepted the Saurian as he approached and stopped his progress. Freed slaves sprang from the two cells that

Kanton had unlocked and swarmed the Saurian, who thrashed at them but couldn't break free.

"Over here," called a gravelly voice from the cell behind Calum.

He turned back and saw another Saurian, one at least as big as the lizard they were fighting, gripping the bars of his cell.

The Saurian prisoner grunted at Calum. "Free me, and I'll finish him for you."

"Kanton, over here!" Calum shouted above the fracas. Kanton swooped over and eyed Calum for a moment, but he unlocked the cell and set the Saurian free.

With a roar, the Saurian slave launched into the fight. The other slaves parted, exposing the Saurian guard, and the Saurian slave took him down in one stunning punch.

The Saurian slave got on top of the Saurian guard and clamped his hands around his head. With one vicious jerk, a loud crack sounded, ending the fight.

DARKNESS ENCROACHED on the edges of Magnus's vision as Oren squeezed his throat tighter and tighter. Magnus pushed against Oren's wrists to try to pry his hands away and bucked with his hips to force Oren off of him, but Oren was stronger. Much stronger.

The tip of Magnus's snout tingled, as did his lips as less and less blood reached his brain. Just when Magnus lost feeling in his fingers, a loud metallic *pong* sounded above, and splinters of wood rained down on him. A shovelhead clanged on Magnus's shoulder then came to a stop on the ground next to him.

Oren's grip released, and fresh air flooded Magnus's lungs. The tingling in his extremities stopped, and his mind began to right itself.

Above him, Oren wobbled and clutched his head with his right hand. Magnus jerked up and decked Oren with a hardy blow under his chin, and Oren toppled onto his side on the ground.

Magnus wasted no time—he mounted Oren and threw punch after ferocious punch at Oren's scarred face. He only stopped when he realized Oren was no longer fighting back, even though he still drew breath.

When Magnus looked up, none other than Condor stood before him, clad in a white linen shirt streaked with red and holding a wooden staff in his hand.

One end of it was broken off.

AXEL GAWKED AT THE SITE. Condor had moved faster than anything he'd ever seen, including Falcroné. Now Oren lay underneath Magnus, unconscious, and the fight was over.

Behind Axel, the wall had caught fire from the torch, and dozens of people streamed from the basement staircase—mostly humans and Windgales—but also a gigantic Saurian. Axel wearily readied his sword, but Calum popped into view behind him and waved him off.

The slaves plodded through the main hall and out the main doors, to which the fire had not yet spread. Last of all, Lilly and Kanton helped Falcroné up the stairs. A moment later, Riley's perky Wolf ears and head peeked up from the basement as well, and then he bounded up the stairs last.

Axel clenched his jaw and glared at him. From the look of Riley, he hadn't fought again. What good was that special shoulder armor he wore if he refused to fight?

"Axel, bring me the chains from my cage." Condor tossed his broken shovel shaft aside.

Free for less than two minutes, and already Condor dared to give orders? Perhaps Axel had been too quick to free him after all. Even so, it was too late now, and he went ahead and retrieved the chains from the cell.

The fire on the wall spread up to the ceiling, eagerly lapping at timber that made up the second floor.

"Condor?" Lilly gawked at him.

Falcroné's head lifted, and whatever strength he'd lacked to make it up the stairs instantly returned to his body. "*You.*"

THE MOMENT RILEY heard Condor's name, his fur prickled, and he froze in place with wide eyes, only able to turn his head to look. Sure enough, Condor stood near Magnus and Oren, the latter of whom lay unconscious on the floor.

Condor had a sword in his hand before Falcroné could make a move, and he shook his head. "I advise that you don't come near me, Falcroné. I'd hate to have to cut you down so soon after we've been reunited."

"You have no authority to give me orders, *traitor*." Falcroné drew his own sword and shrugged Lilly and Kanton away.

Instinct cranked Riley's bones into action. He darted to the nearest shadow, which happened to be inside the cage at the back of the room, and shrank into it.

This couldn't be happening. Condor was alive, and he was here, and someone had freed him.

Given the sentence Avian had passed over Condor at the council, it made sense that he'd be here, but Riley hadn't even given it a second thought. Even when the suggestion to find Oren and stop him at this exact place came up, Riley didn't put it together that Condor might be here.

Memories from that fateful day flashed through Riley's mind, and his side ached from phantom pain. Now that Condor was free, it was going to happen all over again.

Lilly grabbed Falcroné's arm. "Fal, you're in no condition to—"

"Let me go." Falcroné jerked his arm away. "I'm going to do what Avian and the Council of Wisps should have done on the day of your hearing."

Yes, kill him. A low growl rumbled from Riley's throat. If Condor died, then perhaps Riley would finally find some semblance of peace. *Kill. Him.*

"Hold, Falcroné." Magnus stepped between them, holding his Blood Ore sword once again. "Condor saved my life and helped me defeat Oren—in your absence, no less. You must not harm him."

What? Magnus was siding with Condor? He'd tried to murder Riley, and now Magnus was defending him?

"He's a convicted criminal," Falcroné said. "And he's dangerous to Lilly. He already attacked her once. I will *not* allow that to happen again."

Condor pointed to Axel, who dropped two pairs of heavy shackles at Condor's feet. "He attacked Lilly, too, but you don't seem all that worried about him."

Axel glared at Condor.

"No offense, Farm Boy. Just making a point."

"I *am* worried about him." Falcroné scowled at Condor, then at Axel.

Several flaming logs collapsed onto the floor between the others and Riley's hiding place, and Calum jumped. "Uh… do you guys think we can take this conversation outside? I don't think this fort is gonna last much longer."

Magnus eyed the ceiling. "Calum is right. We must go."

Condor zipped out the doors first, followed by Axel and Magnus, who carried Oren out with him. Kanton left next, then Lilly and Falcroné. Calum hung back and stared right at Riley's hiding spot.

"Are you coming?"

Riley growled again. Perhaps he should just die here, in the flames, rather than face the possibility of Condor stabbing him again. He would become a pile of ash, the same as everything around him, and then Condor could never hurt him again.

"Come on, Riley." Calum extended his hand. "I won't let him hurt you."

Another large chunk of the ceiling fell to Calum's right, and he jumped out of the way.

"Last chance. Come with me."

Riley closed his eyes and exhaled a long breath. When he inhaled, the smell of smoke and burning wood intensified. Did he want to stay put and add the putrid smell his own burning flesh next?

"Please, Riley?"

Above Calum's head, the ceiling crackled with flames, and he looked up.

Riley's heart clenched. *No.*

He bolted out of the cage as the ceiling collapsed and sprang at Calum with his forepaws extended. Riley's momentum knocked Calum away from the falling ceiling's wrath, and they tumbled against the wall adjacent to the doors. Both of them quickly jumped to their feet and rushed outside as the rest of fortress caved in on itself.

"I could've been in there." Riley stared at the dancing flames as the reality set in.

Calum crouched down next to him. "We *were* in there, but you saved us."

"I'm sorry I can't fight anymore, Calum. I just—" Riley bowed his head. He didn't want to admit it, but he had to. "I'm scared. I don't want to get stabbed again. And now that Condor's back, it's only gonna get worse."

"Maybe." Calum placed his hand on Riley's back and stroked his fur. Were Calum anyone other than himself or Lilly, Riley would have nipped at his hand. "But maybe this is a chance for you to face your fear once and for all, and in doing so, to overcome it."

Riley sighed, and the phantom pain in his side returned. "That almost sounds worse than getting stabbed again."

Calum patted Riley's shoulders. "It may be, but it's the only way to free yourself from your fear. The next time something like this happens, I may not be around to save you from a burning building. Either you face this, or it'll eventually get you killed, and that'll be the end of it. I really hope it doesn't come to that."

"Me neither." Even as Riley said it, he still wasn't convinced that he meant it.

"Hey." Kanton landed in front of them with his back to the flaming fortress. "Are you two alright?"

Calum smiled and stood. "We're a little singed and scraped up, but nothing too bad."

"Oh. Alright, then. I'm going to tend to some of the slaves. A few of them are in pretty bad shape, but I might be able to help them out." Kanton leaned close to Calum. "You'd better get back to the group. They're going to need a voice of reason right about now."

Kanton zipped away, and Calum looked down at Riley. "You coming?"

Riley steeled himself and nodded. "Yeah. I'm coming."

———

AXEL VOICED MORE than his fair share of arguments on both of the issues at hand: what should they do with Oren, and what should they do with Condor? Unfortunately, with so many extreme opinions and so much discord, his thoughts didn't seem to register with anyone.

Then Calum showed up, and everyone started listening to him.

Of course.

Within five minutes, everyone had their say: Magnus insisted they keep Oren alive so that a ruler like Lilly's father could pass judgment on him for his crimes, but Lilly pointed out that her father's involvement in the slave trade had compromised his integrity. Therefore, they should just throw Oren in the Blood Chasm where so many of his slaves had died over the years.

Falcroné agreed with her but didn't agree that they should dole out capital punishment. He thought they should send Oren back to Avian anyway and grant him the chance to bring Oren before the Council of Wisps. When Axel finally got his chance to speak, he shrugged.

"I didn't come all this way and risk my life to bring down Western Kanarah's slave trade only to allow for the chance that it might start back up again. If we let him live, that's a real risk." He pointed to Oren, who knelt before them with his wrists and ankles bound by the heavy shackles Axel had retrieved from Condor's cage. "I say we finish him off right now."

Axel glanced at Condor, who stood motionless at the fringe of their group, watching everything and being watched by Falcroné virtually nonstop.

"You couldn't even land a blow on me, baby boy, an' now you wanna kill me?" Oren chuckled amid the blood dripping from his snout. "You're a funny one, you are."

"He is our prisoner. We cannot just kill him. It is unjust," Magnus said.

"*Unjust?*" Lilly stared at Magnus. "He's responsible for hundreds if not thousands of deaths over the years. I could even argue that he's ultimately responsible for Roderick taking you and me into captivity."

"Oh, it's been more'an that, I'd wager." Oren's jagged smile oozed arrogance—and blood. "We 'ad a logbook in the ol' fortress. I could've given you an exact number if you 'adn't burned 'er down."

"Shut up." Axel glared at him. "Your life hangs in the balance. You wanna live? Start acting like it."

"You don't scare me. Not even a li'l." Oren sneered at Axel. "If you was gonna kill me, you'd 'ave done it by now."

Axel pointed at him. "I said—"

"I 'eard what you said. You say a lot o' things, baby boy, but you don't take no action. You're jus' a scared li'l bug, an' I'm gonna squash you." Oren bared his jagged smile again.

Axel started toward him, but Magnus held him back.

"He needs to face judgment from a ruler, not from people like us," Magnus insisted.

"You and I *are* rulers, Magnus," Lilly said. "Or at least we will be. A few years from now, we'll be making exactly this sort of decision for criminals like him."

Oren laughed. "No one's like me, ya bugs. Not a one. Nobody could 'ave run this enterprise like I done. Nobody could 'ave built it up from nuffin' into an empire that spanned Kanarah like I done. Nobody could 'ave—"

The metallic ring of steel leaving a sheath filled the air, and the next thing Axel knew, Oren knelt before them with the hilt of a dagger protruding from his left eye. He convulsed once, toppled onto his side and convulsed once more, and then he stopped moving entirely as blood oozed from the grisly wound.

Condor stood next to him and admired his handiwork, his face fixed in a contented smirk.

CHAPTER THIRTY-FOUR

"What have you done?" Falcroné roared. He sprang forward, his hand on the hilt of his sword, but Condor met him halfway and held another sword to Falcroné's throat before he could even draw his.

Axel gawked at the exchange. Condor had moved impossibly fast. And where was he getting all these weapons from?

"You always were too slow, Falcroné. It's why your own father promoted me to Captain of the Royal Guard instead of you." Condor locked his eyes on Falcroné's. "On your knees."

"Don't, Condor!" Lilly held up her hand. "Please, don't."

"I have no desire to kill Falcroné or any of you," Condor said.

He stared at Falcroné until he finally knelt down, then he turned his attention to Oren's body. His usually cheerful voice began to quiver.

"That *thing* beat me and abused me from the day I first arrived. Day after day, he and his soldiers chastised me until my back was raw from his whip, yet some of you wanted to grant him the mercy of bringing him before *Avian?* The very man who sent me to this abominable place?"

Axel glanced at Magnus, whose hand gripped the hilt of his broadsword, still in its sheath. No way he'd get the blade out in time.

Condor could kill Falcroné and take to the sky before any of them could so much as think about intervening.

Condor's voice solidified again, and his optimistic timbre began to return. "Oren got what he deserved. That's my judgment. And anyway, it's done now, so if you're willing to move on, I say we ought to do just that."

Falcroné swallowed noticeably, but he didn't move otherwise.

"I'll even go one step further, if it puts you all at ease. Falcroné, my old brother-in-arms, if you want to kill me, then do it." Condor pulled his sword away from Falcroné's throat and tossed it aside. "I won't resist, and I can die with pleasure knowing that brigand is dead."

Falcroné's sword flashed in the moonlight, and he pinned Condor to the ground. Beyond them, the fortress continued to burn like a gigantic torch under the night sky.

"You attacked Lilly," Falcroné growled.

"*Enough*, Falcroné." The hard tone in Lilly's voice surprised Axel. "He just said he wouldn't hurt any of us."

"And you *believe* him?" Falcroné scoffed, still refusing to take his eyes off his prey. "Forgive me, Princess, but your youthful naivety is hardly enough to prop up this traitor's word."

"I know where the Arcanum is," Condor said.

No one made a sound until Calum asked, "How do you know where it is?"

Condor glanced at Axel, wearing that same cunning smirk as always. Condor had alluded to this piece of information when they were locked in the cell under the Sky Fortress together, but Axel couldn't convince him to elaborate.

"I've been there. A secret reconnaissance mission from before I earned my promotion to Captain." His piercing blue eyes showed no sign of deception. "I can take you there, too."

"He's lying," Falcroné said. "Everything he says is a lie. There's not an ounce of good in him anymore, if there ever was to begin with."

"How's your shoulder, Farm Boy?" Condor raised his chin and grinned at Axel.

"It feels fine." Axel rubbed it. "It came out of its socket again when the Wisps dropped me into the cell under the Sky Fortress. He popped it back in for me."

"He helped you?" Lilly asked. "And... you *let* him? You wanted to kill him after you learned he'd struck me."

Axel couldn't deny that. Even thinking about it now made him want to tear into Condor along with Falcroné, but he had to consider the rest of his experience with Condor as well.

"He was wrong to harm you. No question there," Axel said. "But when we were in that cell, he fixed my shoulder, didn't kill me even though he could've, and he also hinted that he knew about the Arcanum."

"You're sure?" Lilly eyed them both. "What did he say?"

"He said that your father's scholars might be able to point it out to you on a map, but it's hard to reach. When I asked him how he knew that, he just told me it was his secret and nothing more."

Lilly's eyes narrowed, and she turned to Falcroné. "Let him go."

"He's a murderer. He'll kill us in our sleep, starting with you," Falcroné said.

"I said *let him go.*"

"Lilly, you don't understand how dangerous he—" Falcroné stopped talking when Lilly started toward him. "What are you doing?"

"If you won't let him go, I will free him from your grasp with my own hands. He knows exactly where to find the Arcanum, which means he is the key to freeing Lumen and liberating all of Kanarah," Lilly said. "If you think I'm going to let you kill our greatest hope for saving the entire realm, you're dead wrong."

Calum stepped toward her with his hands up. "Lilly, we still have the map. Are you sure you—"

"Stay out of it, Calum," Lilly snapped. "This is between Falcroné and me. A map is only good to a point. We need to free Lumen now, and Condor can to take us right to him." She faced Falcroné again. "Last chance. Let him go."

"I'm here to *protect* you," Falcroné said through clenched teeth. "Not to follow your every command, especially when you don't know what you're talking about."

"Nonetheless, you'd better follow this one." She reached toward Falcroné, but he swatted her hands away without removing his sword from Condor's throat.

To his credit, Condor didn't move a muscle.

Lilly reached for Falcroné again, and again he pushed her arms aside. "Lilly, *stop*. Your behavior is abhorrent. We're engaged to be married."

"I can find another husband," she countered, her voice cold as ice.

Condor smirked at that, and Axel's eyebrows rose. He glanced at Calum, whose mouth also hung open.

Falcroné glared at Lilly for a long moment, but he withdrew his sword from Condor's neck and stood.

Lilly didn't move. "Help him up."

"You can't be seri—"

"I said *help him up*."

Falcroné grumbled something Axel couldn't understand and extended his hand to Condor, who took it and stood to his feet. He nodded to Lilly, who only then relaxed her posture.

She floated over to Condor and hovered off the ground a few inches so she looked him directly in his eyes. "Condor, I'm offering you a chance to join us. Do you pledge your life to the successful completion of our quest and to protect the Sky Realm and its rulers, including me?"

Condor grinned at her. "I'd be honored to serve you, Princess."

Falcroné fumed at Lilly with wide, angry eyes, but didn't say anything.

"Your first duty will be to lead us to the Arcanum."

"It would be my pleasure."

"Then kneel." Lilly drew her sword from its sheath and tapped Condor's shoulders with the flat of the blade. "I reinstate you as Captain of the Royal Guard, answerable only to me."

"You—you can't do that!" Falcroné pushed between her and Condor. "*I'm* the Captain of the Royal Guard, not *him*."

"Easy, Fal." Lilly urged Falcroné back with the tip of her sword at his chest. "You will remain Captain alongside Condor. You are *both* my Captains of the Royal Guard, and you will *both* protect me with your lives. Crystal?"

Condor smirked and nodded. "Clear as the purest skies, Princess."

"No. Not clear. Not remotely." Falcroné waved his hand laterally in front of his chest as if cutting a person in half with it. "This man tried to kill you and your friends. He stabbed Riley, and he's responsible for a rebellion that almost resulted in your father's death and *did* result in the deaths of more than a hundred people... yet you're giving him his title back?"

"Yes, Fal. That's right." Lilly stared at Condor. "I'd rather earn him as a friend with my trust than have to kill him as my enemy."

Condor's eyebrow rose at that remark, but his smirk remained nonetheless.

"I don't believe this." Falcroné shook his head. "I don't agree with it. Your father will never approve."

"My father approved of Kanarah's slave trade by sending people like Condor into it for their crimes—the same slave trade that saw me captured and sold to the highest bidder. I'm not interested in his approval right now." Lilly stared into Falcroné eyes. "You will either accept this development or fly home and await my return. What's it going to be?"

Falcroné's jaw tensed.

As LILLY WATCHED the remains of Oren's fortress burning in the distance, she and the others made camp under the trees of the nearby forest.

The freed slaves had elected to move on as a group toward Aeropolis, led by Chorian, the big Saurian who had intervened to stop the Saurian guard in the fortress basement. They all wanted to get as far away from that place as possible, and many had families and loved ones to return to, so they left after Kanton finished tending to them.

When Condor pulled his shirt off for Kanton to tend to him next, Lilly's stomach dropped, partly at his physique, but also at the sight of the lattice of red slashes on his back. Some of them had scabbed over, but many looked fresh, as if Oren had whipped him only minutes before they'd arrived at the fortress.

Kanton applied some ointments and some salves and patched the worst of them. Condor put his shirt back on, and Lilly's racing heartbeat slowed.

The fortress continued to smolder late into the night. To no one's surprise, Falcroné offered to take the first watch, and he made it clear that it was because he didn't trust Condor.

What's more, Riley hadn't said a word or even made eye contact with Lilly since she'd welcomed Condor into their group. She didn't blame him for it, but she knew she had to do something to make it right.

After everyone else had fallen asleep, aside from Falcroné, of course, Lilly hovered across the camp to where Riley resided in the shadows. He lay there, perfectly still and totally awake.

The instant her feet touched the ground, Riley's ears perked up, and he raised his head. The waning light from the campfire reflected in the pair of blue eyes that stared at her from the darkness.

"Hey," she whispered and sat in front of him. "I wanted to talk about Condor."

Riley lowered his head.

"I know he stabbed you, and that it happened while you were trying to save me." Lilly held her breath. "I mean, you *did* save me."

Riley still didn't move.

"It sounds ridiculous now that I'm saying it out loud," she admitted. "I know I just recruited a man who attacked us both, but I did it because I see something in him that gives me courage and hope for the future."

Riley blinked slowly. He really wasn't giving Lilly much to work with. All she could do was press on.

"I don't expect you to understand, but I hope you do someday," she said. "I know Condor can help us, and I believe him when he says he knows where to find the Arcanum. More than that, I think he needs someone to believe in him so he can get his life back on track."

Still nothing from Riley. He just stared back at her with emotionless blue eyes.

"I also want you to know that I'm not doing this to attack you or anything like that. I really like you and don't want anything bad to happen to you, but at the same time, Condor needs our help." Lilly bit her lip. This wasn't going as well as she had hoped. "Aren't you going to say something?"

Riley broke eye contact with her for the first time since she'd come over and looked at the ground. "No."

Lilly exhaled a quiet sigh. "I understand. You know I'm still your friend, right?"

He muttered, "Yeah."

When she reached to scratch Riley's ears, she hesitated, but Riley still allowed her to do it. She smiled. "If there's anything I can do to help allay your concerns, will you let me know?"

"Yeah," he repeated, just as enthusiastically as the first time.

What more could Lilly do? Probably not much, if she were honest. She'd tried to make amends, and she wasn't going to change her mind. She just hoped she'd done enough to restore Riley's faith in her.

"Well, good night," she said.

"Night."

With another sigh, Lilly floated to her place near the campfire. Within minutes, exhaustion claimed her, and she drifted off to sleep.

———

TRY AS HE MIGHT, Axel couldn't sleep that night. The crickets chirped too loudly. The campfire crackled too loudly. Even Axel's own breathing was too loud.

He wanted to blame it only on the ruckus of sounds all around him, but he couldn't. Not if he wanted to be honest with himself—honest about the conflict churning in his heart.

For once, it wasn't about Lilly. Rather, the fight with Oren had shown him something about himself. Something he hadn't wanted to face. He'd wanted to ignore it, to push it aside, to pretend it had never happened, but it had.

Axel couldn't do it any longer.

So he got up, careful not to wake anyone, and headed over to Riley's spot, where he lay crouched among the trees and underbrush, mostly hidden.

Even as Axel walked over there, the conflict raged within his chest. His pride reminded him that he'd been doing the right thing in trying to avenge Lilly after Condor had hit her. At the same time, his conscience reminded him that doing so had almost gotten Riley killed.

His pride fired back that Riley was weak and frail. He'd run away instead of joining his friends in battle. He'd abandoned them in their time of need.

Axel's conscience reminded him that he'd abandoned Riley in *his* time of need. He'd run away from fights and hid because of Axel's reaction to Condor. He was weak and frail because he didn't get the proper help soon enough, thanks to the frivolous delay that Axel had caused.

Axel groaned. It was all too much.

But despite the myriad of thoughts clunking back and forth in his mind, his legs continued to carry him toward Riley's position.

When he reached the edge of the trees, he stopped and searched for Riley's form amid the dark leaves and bushy branches, but he saw nothing.

A voice nearly scared him out of his armor. "If you're gonna urinate, do it somewhere else."

"What?" Axel squinted at the area where the voice had come from and spotted a vaguely wolflike shape among the plants. "No. I'm here to talk to you."

"I think I would've preferred the urine."

Axel bristled at the comment, not because he'd found it especially clever or biting, but because Riley had said it with absolute sincerity. He'd *meant* it.

"Well, say whatever stupid thing you came to say. Get it over with," Riley said.

His tone tempted Axel to lay into him like he usually did, but his conscience made him resist that urge. Instead, he forced himself to say the two words he'd been avoiding ever since the incident had happened.

"I'm sorry."

By the Overlord... Riley had been right. Axel had sounded stupid—

THE WAY OF ANCIENT POWER

exceptionally stupid—in saying that. Why had he even bothered to say it at all?

Riley didn't move. Didn't speak. Didn't respond in any noticeable way at all.

Then his Wolf ears perked up, and he raised his head. He sniffed the air several times and stood up, his body rigid.

At first, Axel wondered how any of that could possibly relate to his apology. He quickly realized it was a heightened wariness on Riley's part instead.

"What is it?" he asked, his voice low.

"Quiet," Riley whispered so softly that Axel almost couldn't make out what he'd said. His lupine head swiveled, and his light-blue eyes widened.

Axel tried to follow his line of sight, erratic as it was, into the trees around them, but he saw nothing.

A howl split the night, but it hadn't come from the woods around them. It came from Riley.

"What in the Overlord's name are you doing?" Axel hissed. "Everyone's asleep!"

"We need to wake them up. Now." He howled again, and Falcroné jerked upright, his sword in hand.

"What's going on?" he slurred.

Calum popped up next, then Magnus, Condor, and Kanton. Along with Lilly, they surrounded Riley and Axel in seconds, all with questions on their lips.

Riley shushed them. "Listen."

From the woods all around them, a cacophony of howls and yips sounded in varying tones and volumes.

"What is that?" Axel unsheathed his sword as he scanned the woods.

"Wolves," Riley replied. "Thirty of them or more, and at least one Werewolf. We're already surrounded."

CHAPTER THIRTY-FIVE

"What do we do?" Kanton asked.

Riley's fur bristled. Thirty-plus Wolves against the eight of them. At night. And they had a Werewolf as their Alpha. What *could* they do?

"If you try to run, they'll ambush you and kill you," he said. "Stay together. Make them come to you. The nearer you are to the campfire, the less effectively they can hide in the shadows."

Several weapons unsheathed around Riley, which only made his skin tingle more.

He glared at Condor. "And try not to kill me by accident. We all look similar in low light to the untrained eye."

"That won't be hard. You're wearing that shoulder armor," Axel said.

"No, I'm not." Riley craned his head back toward the armor and bit the leather strap that held it on his body. In one yank, the whole apparatus loosened, and he pawed it over his head and off.

Now more than ever, they needed his stealth and his speed. If he wore the armor, he could employ neither.

Axel cursed. "Then how will we know it's you?"

"I'll be the only Wolf not attacking you," Riley snapped. Axel reminded him of a walking brick sometimes. "Speaking of which, don't chase any of the Wolves back into the woods. Stay near the fire, like I said. They'll ambush you in the dark and rip you apart. Crystal?"

"Clear," Calum said.

"Stay near me," Magnus said. "Their teeth and claws won't penetrate my scales."

"The Werewolf's can. Even so, watch your throat, Magnus. All of you, watch your throats. We learn at a young age that if we can get our prey by the throat, we're all but guaranteed a kill." Riley nodded toward the fire. "Come on. Get near the flames."

A snarl sounded behind them as they took their first steps toward the fire. A blurred mass of fur and teeth launched at them out of the darkness, but Condor felled the Wolf from the air in one brutal swing of his sword. The Wolf landed next to a tree, dead.

Riley glared at him.

"What?" Condor shrugged. "At least it wasn't you this time."

"That's not funny," Lilly said.

"Look out!" Calum yelled.

A trio of Wolves dashed out of the woods and knocked Kanton off his feet. His spear clanged on the ground as the Wolves' teeth and claws scraped against his armor. One of the Wolves latched onto his gauntleted right hand, and he screamed.

Riley sprang forward and clamped his jaws around the ankle of one of the Wolves and yanked him away from Kanton, and Falcroné killed the one gnawing on Kanton's right hand while Magnus batted the other away.

The Wolf whirled its head around and snapped at Riley, but Riley kept pulling back so it couldn't reach him. Then a swift blow from Axel's sword downed the Wolf.

Riley's eyes met Axel's, and they exchanged nods. For now, given his abrupt apology only moments earlier, that was good enough.

"I'm going out there," Riley told the group. "I can run interference while they try to attack."

"Wait! Don't you think—" Calum's voice trailed off as Riley bounded into the woods, but it was too late.

Riley had committed to this, and he'd see it through.

LILLY GRIPPED her bow and drew back an arrow, but between the darkness and the Wolves' speed, she had yet to fire even a single shot. No sense in wasting the arrows if she couldn't hit anything. Thanks to the Wolves' hit-and-run tactics, she couldn't see her targets well enough.

Meanwhile, Condor helped Kanton to his feet. Blood dripped from his right hand—his dominant hand—and instead of holding his spear he wielded his short sword in his left hand.

"Are you alright?" Lilly floated down next to him.

Kanton shook his head. "I can't use my right hand. It's bad."

"Condor, stay with Kanton. Keep him safe."

The campfire's reflection flickered in Condor's piercing blue eyes, and he nodded. "I've got him."

"Lilly, watch out!" Falcroné's voice cut through Wolves' barking and howling.

She whirled around in time to see a mass of gray fur charging toward her with Falcroné chasing it through the air. Lilly drew her arrow back, but the Wolf had already leaped at her. No chance of bringing it down in time.

Instead, Condor's sword leveled the Wolf in one swift blow, and he darted back to Kanton's side before Lilly fully comprehended what had happened.

"Looks like I've got you, too." Condor gave her a wink then continued to scan the woods around them.

"I would've had him," Falcroné hissed as he drifted to a stop near them.

Enough of this. Lilly slung her bow over her back, dropped the arrow into her quiver, and drew her sword instead. If these Wolves wouldn't give her a decent shot, she'd bring the fight to them.

"Stay together, like Riley said." Calum shouted from the other side of Magnus, who occupied the spot just to Lilly's right. Falcroné covered her left side and stood next to Condor, who still guarded Kanton. Axel rounded out the circle between Kanton and Calum. "We'll wear them down, one by one."

The moment after he said it, at least a dozen sets of eyes appeared in the woods around them, illuminated by the campfire.

Lilly wished she'd kept her bow out after all.

THE FIRST WOLF padded right past Riley's hiding spot, then two more. Just hours earlier, he'd hid so as to avoid the fight, but now he was hiding with the hope of accelerating it to its end.

As the fourth Wolf trotted past, Riley lunged out of the underbrush at him and used his full body weight to slam the Wolf into a thick tree. The impact roused a dull pain in Riley's old wound, but a loud crack sounded from the Wolf's body and he yelped.

The Wolf slumped to the ground, and Riley latched onto his throat and finished him off in silence.

As Riley released his grasp on the Wolf's throat, a new scent reached his nose. It was similar to something he'd smelled before, but not since he'd been around Rhaza and the rest of the desert Wolves. He turned around in time to see a massive brown hand swinging at him.

The blow sent him careening through the underbrush where he'd just hidden, and he landed on his injured side, facing away from his assailant. The old wound throbbed with fresh pain. Riley pushed himself up to his feet and scanned the woods for his attacker, but he was nowhere in sight.

Another swipe hurled Riley across the ground, and his body smacked against a tree. The throbbing in his wound accelerated and intensified. He couldn't take much more of this.

This time, instead of just standing up and searching, he darted away from the tree and zigzagged through the woods, weaving around trees.

Even though he hadn't gotten a good look at his attacker, it had to be the Alpha. And if Riley could find a way to kill the Alpha before the rest of the Wolves closed in on his friends, then he could save them.

But killing an Alpha wasn't an easy thing. The more Riley thought about it, the more he regretted ever having run off to face the Alpha alone.

It was too late now, though. And no one else would ever be able to find it. Either Riley succeeded, or they'd all die. There were far too many Wolves in the pack to overcome.

Riley couldn't let that happen. He was their only chance. As long as he still drew breath, he wouldn't let any more harm come to his friends.

And that even included Axel.

As Riley ran, claws slashed his face, but Riley recoiled a step. When he opened his eyes, the Alpha Werewolf stood before him at its full height and snarled.

The next slash came before Riley could get out of the way, this time to the other side of his face. Pain streaked across his snout, and he couldn't stifle the whimper that squeezed out of his lungs as he staggered away from the Werewolf's hulking bipedal form.

The pain reminded him of the futility of what he'd set out to do. He couldn't outrun the Werewolf. Couldn't hide from it, either. As good as Riley's hearing, sight, and sense of smell were, even in the dark, the Werewolf's were better.

What options did he even have?

Only one, he realized.

And if he failed, it would absolutely cost him his life.

TEN WOLVES HIT the group in quick succession. Calum swung at the first of four Wolves who charged him, but it eluded his sword and nipped at his legs. Alone, their nips proved harmless, but as soon as Calum hacked at the Wolf at his legs, another leaped at his head.

The Wolf's claws scratched Calum's left cheek, and his arm absorbed most of the Wolf's mass, but the impact knocked him to his back nonetheless. The Wolf weighed close to a hundred pounds, and before Calum could try to push it away, the three other Wolves swarmed him. They chomped at his limbs as he covered his face and flailed his sword, but they didn't stop.

A sharp yip sounded above him, and one of the Wolves was gone, followed by the other three. He glanced up.

Magnus stepped over Calum and rumbled toward the four Wolves, who ran off. Magnus followed them a few strides away from the circle.

Calum started to call for him when a set of hands yanked him to his feet.

"Back at it, Calum." Axel smacked his armored shoulder.

"Thanks." He refocused on Magnus, who now stood separate from the circle and hissed at the woods around them. Calum cupped his hand on the side of his mouth. "Magnus, come back over here!"

"No." Magnus shook his head. "We must end this now. Let them come."

The howling intensified from among the trees, and the remaining Wolves who had engaged in the attack disappeared into the darkness again. Only ten of them had attacked the first time, and the group had managed to kill three of them.

Except for the campfire, silence reigned in and around the campsite

Then dozens of Wolves poured out of the shadows and flooded toward them.

Calum tightened his grip on his sword.

RILEY DODGED the next attack before it ever came. It was a risk, but a calculated one.

He'd endured enough blows from the Werewolf by now to figure out a pattern, and he knew that unless he dodged early and timed things just right, the Werewolf would hit him again.

When Riley dodged, the Werewolf's slash missed.

And when the Werewolf missed, it left him exposed.

Too fast for his own good.

Riley sprang at the Werewolf from the side and aimed his jaws for the Werewolf's neck. To his great surprise, they connected. He dug his teeth into the Werewolf's throat with what little strength remained in his body after the thrashing he'd suffered to learn the correct timing.

The Werewolf howled, but Riley clamped his teeth tighter around its neck and pushed against the Werewolf's chest with his paws. He was

301

trying to use his body weight to tear the Werewolf's throat out of its neck or at least drag him to the ground, but the Werewolf refused to go down.

Instead, it grabbed Riley by his sides and dug his claws into Riley's fur, then into his skin.

Then through his skin.

Pain pierced into Riley's body, just like when Condor had stabbed him, only much, much worse.

Riley just bit down harder. Regardless of whatever happened to him, he had to hold on. He had to kill this thing, or the Wolves would overwhelm his friends.

THE WOLVES SWARMED THE GROUP. Everywhere Axel turned, he found another Wolf to fight, to kick, to slay. He'd cut down at least four of them so far—or maybe three—but they just kept coming.

Definitely more than thirty. Possibly even more than fifty.

Around him, Condor and Falcroné zipped through the air and dodged most of the Wolves' attacks, but their faces showed signs of strain with each new swing. Lilly hung just above the fracas and again launched arrows at the Wolves, but nothing stopped them from attacking.

Something heavy collided with the back of Axel's left knee. It hadn't hurt much, but he still went down.

Another Wolf barreled into him from the side and knocked him to the ground. Three sets of canine eyes darted toward him accompanied by three sets of teeth.

He lashed his sword at them and felled one, but the other two pounced on top of him. They started biting and scratching at his face, then at his arms when he tried to shield himself from them. Had it not been for his armor they would have shredded his forearms.

Axel should've figured something like this would happen. He'd just apologized to Riley, and now three of his distant relatives were trying to rip him apart.

"Magnus?" he yelled. "Calum—*anyone*, help!"

One of the Wolves toppled off him with a yip. An arrow lodged in its side. Axel grabbed the other by its left ear and wrenched it downward, then he bashed its head with the pommel of his sword. A quick follow-up stab killed the Wolf.

Axel tried to make eye contact with Lilly to thank her, but she had already nocked another arrow and focused her attention on the incoming Wolves.

With a half scowl, Axel did likewise.

ALMOST A DOZEN WOLVES CONVERGED on Magnus. Upon seeing them, Calum wondered how long it would take Magnus to fling them off.

But when Calum saw them take Magnus down instead, his jaw hung open. If they lost Magnus, they lost a third of their strength, if not more.

Axel went down next, overwhelmed by six wolves. When the Windgales zipped over to help Magnus and him, the Wolves pulled them out of the air, all except Condor, who looped around the fight and executed surgical strikes on the Wolves, but he could only do so much against so many—

A force knocked Calum to the ground, and a snarling mouth clamped down on his armored right wrist.

Calum gritted his teeth and swung his left fist at the Wolf, but the punch barely fazed it. Another Wolf went for his neck, but Calum jerked his body to the side and shoved its snout away with his free hand.

Two more Wolves replaced that one. One of them went for his ankle while the other aimed for his throat. He wouldn't last long with so many of them on him, and he wasn't strong enough to free himself. With his sword hand otherwise occupied, he couldn't even fight back.

Another Wolf latched onto his right wrist, and Calum's sword slipped from his fingers. Yet another mounted his chest and exhaled hot breath onto his face. It leaned in toward Calum's neck with its teeth bared.

RILEY COULD FEEL his life fading away, even as his jaws squeezed tighter around the Alpha's throat. Hot blood trickled down his sides, leaving him weak and dizzy.

The Werewolf's knees hit the ground, and Riley's back paws touched the earth. If he'd been stronger, he would've used the forest floor to help him jerk back and tear out the Werewolf's throat, but he barely had energy left to keep his jaws tight, so he just hung there, limp everywhere except for his merciless jaws.

The Alpha had abandoned its attempts to gut him, and instead, its bloody hands now groped at Riley's throat. They latched onto his neck and began to tighten, and its talons threatened to pierce into him once again.

One of its hands released its grip on Riley and braced against the ground.

All Riley could do was hold on. He would die here, but in doing so, he would save his friends, just like they'd saved him time and time again.

He closed his eyes, and with the last of his strength, he bit down on the Werewolf's throat even harder.

CHAPTER THIRTY-SIX

A howl split the night air and silenced the Wolves' snarls and growls. The Wolf chomping toward Calum's neck looked up, and the Wolves gnawing on his limbs released their grips and did the same. Between their legs, Calum saw a glowing form emerge from the woods.

Another Wolf, covered in blood.

A thin red light outlined the Wolf's lupine form as it approached. It walked on all fours at first, but three steps into the clearing it stopped, reared up on its hind legs, and started walking upright, just like Captain Brink had.

Its front paws elongated into clawed fingers, and its forelimbs shifted up and back with a loud snap, becoming arms. The muscles in the Wolf's forelimbs enlarged until they resembled shapes similar to those of a human's, only covered with fur.

The Wolf's leg muscles swelled like those in its arms. It hunched over at first, but it spread its hulking arms wide and straightened its back and neck in a chorus of loud pops and cracks.

A series of gouges and lacerations covered its torso and face. But as the creature stood there, the wounds sealed up as if the beast had never sustained them in the first place, leaving behind only the blood that streaked and matted its fur.

From its throat, another howl reverberated off the trees, this one deeper and more haunting. The glowing red outline around it faded. It was no longer a Wolf, but a Werewolf.

Its head rotated, and it looked at Calum and the others with a pair of familiar light-blue eyes.

Calum's voice rasped against his throat. "Riley?"

The Werewolf barked, and the Wolves rallied around him away from Calum and the rest of his group. He leveled his gaze at Calum and smirked. "Who else?"

Ten feet from Calum's spot on the ground, Axel sat up, gawking. "What in the name of the Overlord happened to you? Why aren't the Wolves attacking anymore?"

"I told you our hierarchies aren't based on bloodlines or lineages but on strength. Whoever's the strongest, whoever dominates the group, leads." Riley tilted his head and curled his new fingers. "I killed the Alpha Werewolf, so now *I'm* the Alpha Werewolf."

"But—how?" Axel asked.

"Wolves can transform by defeating a Werewolf in battle. I killed the Alpha who led this pack—and managed not to die in the process—and now I lead them." Riley grinned. "In other words, they're with us now."

Calum and Axel stared at each other.

Lilly swooped over to him. "Are you hurt? You're covered in blood."

Riley shook his head. "The transformation process is like a rebirth. All my old wounds and injuries were healed, wiped out as if I had never sustained them in the first place.

"It was the same when I became a Sobek." Magnus stepped toward Riley and his Wolves, many of which growled at him. He nodded to Riley, who now stood only a foot and a half shorter than him, which meant Riley had surpassed both Calum and Axel in height as well.

Calum got up next and went over to him. A sense of pride filled his chest on behalf of his friend, who no longer had anything to fear from anyone. "You did it, Riley. You saved us all."

Riley's light-blue eyes fixed on Condor. "I know."

As the first ray of morning sunlight filtered through the forest, Axel stood near Magnus and Calum, watching as they tended to Kanton's wounds.

"I don't know what I'd do if I lost my right hand." Axel leaned over to stare at the bloody mess attached to Kanton's wrist, and he cringed. He'd seen worse—and done worse—to enemies, but for some reason, Kanton's wound unnerved him. "I'd be so unsure of myself in battle."

"He didn't lose it," Calum said. "A Wolf bit it."

"Chomped it, mangled it, more like." Kanton sucked in a sharp breath as Magnus fastened a bandage around his hand. He'd already applied a liberal portion of his new vial of Veromine to it, along with some other medicines from Kanton's pack. "In any case, for the time being, it's as good as lost."

"See?" Axel pointed at Kanton with his thumb.

Magnus snorted. "You are both overreacting. Your gauntlet sustained far more damage than your hand. These punctures are deep, but with the aid of the Veromine, you should regain full function of your hand in time."

Kanton sighed. "If you say so, Magnus. I've seen many a wound in my day, and I don't share your confidence."

Axel scoffed. "At least we felled the mangy beast that bit you."

A chorus of growls rose from the Wolves lounging behind Riley.

Axel turned and glared at them. "What? *You* attacked *us*."

Riley cleared his throat. "You're not helping, Axel."

"You're the one in charge." Axel gave him a dismissive wave. "So calm them down."

"Or I could sic them on you." As Riley said it, the thirty-plus Wolves that remained rose to their feet and snarled, primed to leap at Axel.

His eyes widened and his mouth hung open for a moment, then his expression hardened into a snarl of his own. This was the kind of treatment he got after apologizing? "That's not a good idea."

"That's what I thought." Riley barked, and the Wolves reverted back to their relaxed positions.

Axel sneered at him. "Whatever."

As much as he hated to admit it, the battle with the Wolves had shown him how ineffective he actually was when it came to fighting multiple quick opponents. But at least now that they were all on the same side, he'd have plenty of opportunities to practice fighting them.

"What happened to trying to keep a low profile when it came to traveling?" Axel muttered.

Riley must've heard him, because he replied, "The benefits of traveling with this pack far outweigh the drawbacks."

Of course Riley had heard him. It had been bad enough before, but now, as a Werewolf, Riley's senses had heightened even further. The only thing Riley couldn't hear was Axel's thoughts, and he wasn't even sure they were safe anymore.

"There." Magnus released Kanton's hand and stood to his full height. "Allow it time to rest and recover, and you will be healed in short order."

Kanton tried to grip his spear in his right hand. He winced and switched it to his left. "Guess that'll have to do for now. Afraid I may not be much good beyond what I can manage left-handed."

"We'll watch your back," Calum said, "and you can watch ours, too. And we can still rely on you if we get hurt."

Axel whacked Kanton's back. "Yeah. Like always."

Kanton grunted. "Thanks."

"I hate to interrupt," Condor said from behind them, "but the Arcanum is still weeks away. Now that Oren's dead, I suspect reinforcements aren't far behind. The lack of Blood Ore flowing from that Chasm won't be ignored for long."

"I agree. Condor's assessment does not even factor in the possibility of Vandorian following us. Now that day is upon us, we must go." Magnus picked up his pack and started walking.

THROUGHOUT THE COURSE of the next few weeks, Axel had never felt safer while traveling. With nearly three-dozen Wolves stalking their footsteps, plus a Werewolf, a Sobek, and two Wisps, he'd also never felt more obsolete.

Magnus had been all but invincible since he'd transformed into a

Sobek, with the exceptions of when he'd fought other Sobeks. Falcroné and Condor were both trained soldiers—*leaders* of trained soldiers—which meant they ranked among the best the Sky Realm had to offer with regard to their fighting prowess and speed.

Even Riley, the scared "puppy" who had run away and hidden from the last handful of battles, had grown into a Werewolf bigger than Axel. Plus, he also led a pack of Wolves who would do anything he commanded them to do, including dying for him.

Besides being fast, Lilly could fly and shoot her arrows with phenomenal accuracy. Even Kanton, despite being an old man with an injured sword hand, still had the advantages of flight and speed over Axel, plus he knew some of the healing arts.

At this point, the only member of their party who didn't have anything amazing about him was Calum, yet somehow he still led the group and received dreams from Lumen, the ancient and mythical General of Light.

Axel exhaled a long sigh and unslung his pack as he walked at the back of the group. The morning sun shone above, and the forest had long since given way to rocky red terrain. Crimson peaks capped with snow loomed all around them, and according to Calum's map and Condor's direction, they should be reaching the Arcanum any time now.

He dug inside his pack and removed a piece of dried venison wrapped in a cloth, but before he could bite into it, a trio of Wolves rushed to his feet and whimpered.

"Noooo, no. Not a chance." He held it above his head so they couldn't reach it. "You all attacked me. This meat is mine."

"Come on, human," said a black Wolf with green eyes. "We're hungry, too."

"Yeah." A she-Wolf with yellow eyes and a silver coat pushed in front of the male that had just spoken. "You can spare a little bit for us, can't you?"

"I said *no*." Axel had thought Riley was annoying, but these three were pushing the very boundaries of the word. "Now get lost."

The Wolves who had spoken shot glares at him, then they bounded over a rocky crest, where they disappeared. Once Axel confirmed they had gone, he lowered the venison and took a bite.

A black blur darted in front of him and yanked the rest of the meat from his hands with its jaws.

"Hey!" Axel started to chase the Wolf, but another cut in front of him. He tumbled over its torso and hit the ground on his chest, but when he looked back, the Wolf who had tripped him was already gone. He slung a slew of curses at them and pushed himself up to his feet. "Bring that back!"

Lilly turned back with a grin on her face and shook her head. The sight of her pretty face both further frustrated Axel and brought him a much-needed distraction.

"What are you smiling at?" he grunted.

"Nothing. I'm just amused." She waited for him to catch up so she could walk next to him.

"They stole my snack."

Lilly shrugged. "They're natural thieves, Axel. It's what they do."

"That was my *last* piece of venison. Now it's gone."

"Is it really so life-altering?"

Axel rolled his eyes. He'd already resigned himself to knowing Lilly would never side with him again in anything less than a life-or-death situation, so he abandoned his complaint. "How far are we from the Arcanum?"

"Last I talked to Condor, he seemed to think we only had a few hours left of traveling, if not less. That was about an hour ago."

Ahead of them, Condor landed near Calum, and the whole party stopped once they caught up. Six of the Wolves formed a loose perimeter around Riley, and several more did the same thing around the group as a whole. Axel scoffed. Useful as they were, they were still dirty thieves, just like Riley had been before Calum spared his life back in Eastern Kanarah.

"It's just beyond that ridge," Condor said. "I didn't recognize it at first, but I'm almost certain that's the place. We're only five minutes away from the Arcanum, Calum."

A smile split Calum's lips, and he nodded. "Show me."

Axel raised an eyebrow and folded his arms. The moment of truth was near. Either they'd find out Calum had been right the whole time, or they'd realize it was all just a silly myth from Calum's loony brain and perpetuated by misinformation from everyone else who wanted to believe.

Whatever happened, Axel would be there to see it firsthand.

ANTICIPATION SWIRLED from Calum's stomach up into his chest as he approached the crest of the ridge. If Condor was right, then... well, he really didn't know what it meant, aside from being vindicated. It would prove his dreams really had come from Lumen and that he wasn't crazy after all.

When he reached the top of the ridge, all he saw was another ridge. Nothing struck him as out of the ordinary or unique about the landscape, and he didn't see anything that resembled the mouth of a cave anywhere ahead.

He turned to Condor. "Where is it?"

"I recognize that rock formation over there." He pointed to a weathered section of a rock that curved upward from its base. "One of my old mentors, General Regelle, showed it to me before he died. He swore me to secrecy and said I should never reveal its location except to the ruler of the Sky Realm. I figure Lilly's close enough."

Calum pulled the map from his pack and unfolded it. "I don't think this is where the map has it located."

"General Regelle said the maps were wrong," Condor explained. "Upon our return, he actually saw to it that they were never corrected so the Arcanum's true location would remain secret."

Calum frowned. He'd chosen to trust Condor, but this string of last-minute revelations unsettled him.

Condor held up his hands. "Hey, don't look at me. I'm just repeating what I was told. If it helps any, General Regelle was the most honorable person I've ever known. He wouldn't lie to me."

Lilly landed next to them, followed by Falcroné. "Is this the right spot?"

Calum shook his head and replaced the map in his pack. "I don't know."

"You said Lumen showed it to you in your dreams. What did it look like there?"

In his mind's eye, Calum recalled the image as Lumen had presented it in his dream.

Tall red mountains, some with snowy caps, sharpened under Kanarah's golden sun. The image panned down to the base of the mountains, swooped over several red snowcapped peaks, and lowered down into a valley set between two ridges. The picture ended at a wall of red rock. A concealed door set into the wall opened like the giant mouth of a crimson beast.

Calum opened his eyes and looked around. Despite the discrepancy between the map and General Regelle's account, he nodded. "This may be the place."

As he descended into the valley between the ridges, his heart rate quickened. After such a long journey, he may have finally reached the Arcanum. Now he just had to find out how to get inside.

The closer he got to it, the more the wall of red resembled the one in his dreams, and the more excitement flooded his veins. He took a few steps to his right, then he stopped. Backed up a step.

He pointed his hand toward the stone. It matched his memory perfectly. "There."

Condor, Falcroné, and Lilly landed next to him, and Magnus, Axel, Riley, Kanton, and the Wolves followed.

"Uh... you sure?" Axel asked from behind him. "I hate to break it to you, buddy, but that's a solid wall of rock."

It didn't matter what Axel said anymore. Calum had found the exact spot from in his dreams. Now he just had to prove it.

"This is it," he insisted. "I know it is."

"Mm. If you say so."

Axel's skeptical tone didn't deaden Calum's certainty.

"My only concern is how to open it," Calum said. "In my dream, it sort of just... did."

"And you are certain this is the exact spot?" Magnus stepped next to him.

"This is where General Regelle said it would be," Condor said. "The map was drawn to General Regelle's specifications, and only he and I knew the truth about it. Even Avian didn't know the map was wrong."

"Why wasn't he told?" Lilly asked, her eyebrows arched down.

Condor shrugged. "General Regelle trusted him about as much as I do."

Calum stepped toward the rock, his body centered in front of the spot from his dream. He waved his hand in front of it, but nothing happened.

"That's your plan? Just waving your hand in front of it?" Axel scoffed. "Good luck with that. I doubt it's gonna—"

CRACK.

A fissure split a section of the rock into two even sections. Red dust billowed from the rift, and hung in the air in front of the wall. The sound of heavy rocks scraping and grinding against each other echoed throughout the valley until the last of the red dust settled to the ground and the rocks fully separated.

A dark rectangle-shaped opening beckoned Calum to enter.

He turned back and stared at Axel with a grin and one eyebrow raised.

"Whatever." Axel folded his arms and rolled his eyes.

After almost an entire year of traveling, fighting, struggling, starving, and more fighting, they had made it.

They had found the Arcanum.

CHAPTER THIRTY-SEVEN

Calum had always envisioned himself taking that first step into the Arcanum, regardless of who was with him at the time. This had been his quest, his journey. That monumental step was his to take before anyone else.

But even though Calum wanted to enter first, he yielded to Magnus's suggestion that Riley take the lead since he could see so well in the dark. That way, Magnus had reasoned, Riley could identify any booby traps or other perils potentially concealed within the cave's deep shadows. It made good sense, so Calum had agreed to it.

Magnus followed Riley in next, and then Calum went in third. Condor, Lilly, and Falcroné came next, and Axel brought up the rear while Kanton and the Wolves guarded the entrance. Riley had instructed them to obey to Kanton's orders should any trouble arise, and he also told them to behave themselves around the supplies the rest of the party had left behind.

The Arcanum plunged them into perfect darkness within a matter of a few sharp turns, so much so that Calum resorted to holding near the tip of Magnus's spiked tail as a guide while they walked. With each step they descended deeper into the mountain, farther into subterranean depths of unending dark.

The whole scenario reminded him of their time in the tunnels under Trader's Pass, of the Gronyxes they had defeated there, and of Nicolai, who had saved Calum once and then given his life to save them all.

Calum hadn't known Nicolai for long, and Nicolai had certainly done some terrible things before Calum added him to the group, but in the end he'd chosen a better path, one that ensured Calum and his friends could move on. With Lumen freed, his sacrifice—and those of everyone else in the group—would no longer be in vain.

"Stop." Riley's whisper bounced off the walls a half-dozen times.

Calum released his grip on Magnus's tail and felt his way up to Riley. "What is it?"

"The tunnel ends here," he replied. "We're about to walk into a cavern. I can't see how big it is, but it's huge and too dark, even for me to see. The darkness here is... different. Thicker, somehow. I can't explain why, but I won't be able to tell if there's danger ahead unless it's right in front of me."

"Strange that the 'General of Light' would have anything to do with a place this dark," Axel muttered from behind Calum.

"I'll go in first," Calum said, ignoring him. "I'm the one with the dreams that led us to this place. I'll go."

Magnus's heavy hand found Calum's shoulder before he could step forward. "Better not."

Calum turned to face Magnus, even though he couldn't see him. "We didn't come this far for me to get killed while on the cusp of learning how to set Lumen free. I have to do this."

Magnus sighed. "Do as you will. We're with you."

Calum exhaled a long breath and brushed his fingertips against the pommel of his sword as a reminder that it was there if he needed it. He calmed his bristling nerves and stepped past Riley into the darkness.

The sounds of his footsteps and his deep breathing accompanied his progress, but he neither heard nor saw anything else around him. His dreams with Lumen ended just after entering the Arcanum, so he had no idea what he was supposed to do now that he'd made it inside.

Nothing tugged at his chest, no instincts directed his movements, no ethereal light guided his steps. Instead, he wore a shroud of uncertainty.

Was he doing something wrong? Was he supposed to have brought something along with him? All Lumen had said was to go to the Arcanum. Did Calum need to sleep to have another dream?

Something twinkled above him, then it disappeared into the darkness. He stopped and stared up, but after a moment, he wasn't even sure he'd locked on to the right spot anymore. Maybe he'd imagined it in the first place.

Another light flickered, this time lower, and off to his left. He'd only caught it in the corner of his eye, but it looked as if a small tongue of fire had ignited then extinguished the next instant. Instead of the traditional yellow-orange color of fire, it had burned a vibrant blue. It returned a third time, off to his right, then it vanished again.

He stood there, motionless for a long time, just waiting to see what would happen, but nothing did. He still wasn't fully convinced that he'd actually seen the lights. Had any of the rest of his group seen them? He glanced back but saw only darkness.

With no better options, Calum took another step forward.

A column of blue fire burst from the floor in front of him and swirled upward. Calum staggered back and dropped to his rear-end as a dozen more fiery columns erupted all around him in a circle. Above him, the columns spiraled together into a single massive firestorm of blue flames.

Only then did Calum realize he was trapped in a cage made of blue fire.

The churning conflagration above him began to change shape. Parts of it separated, leaving black holes where the fire had once been. Other areas of the flames became shallower and more transparent, and the color of the fire paled to white, but the flames remained, nonetheless.

It didn't take Calum long to recognize the image of two eyes and a white armored mask that covered the face's mouth and nose.

It was an image of Lumen.

"Rise, Calum, son of Wilhelm," Lumen's voice boomed all around Calum, "you have proven yourself worthy, brave warrior. The location of my prison, the Hidden Abyss, is now made plain to you."

Calum pushed himself up to his feet and stared up at Lumen's face, his eyes wide and mouth open, but he didn't dare say a word. The blue fire around him continued to blaze, but it didn't cause him any harm.

"Behold the Tri-Lakes." The fire seemed to pulse with each syllable of Lumen's words. His face disappeared into the flames but gave way to an image of the Valley of the Tri-Lakes. The image closed in on the Central Lake then sharpened even more on the point where the lake bent at an angle and curved toward the north.

Calum knew that bend. He'd seen it on maps of the lake before.

"Deep within the waters you will find a submerged cavern."

The image plunged into the lake water adjacent to the bend. It dove down to an opening in the rocks that formed the lake's underwater perimeter, but the view did not venture inside the opening.

"The Hidden Abyss resides within that cavern. Access it and release me so that I may liberate Kanarah once and for all. One soul from each of Kanarah's four people groups must unite with that of yours; a Saurian, a Wolf, and a Windgale must accompany you in order to release me."

Lumen's face resurfaced in the flames.

"The portal ahead will take you to Trader's Pass, and then this place will close to the world forever. Time is short. Go, and know that I am with you, brave warrior."

Calum started to ask a question, but Lumen's face and the firestorm dissipated into nothing, and the columns of blue fire receded into the floor, all within a matter of seconds. The cavern plunged into darkness again as if it had never been illuminated in the first place, and silence enveloped the space.

A clawed hand gripped Calum's shoulder, and Riley's voice broke the quiet darkness. "You alright, Calum?"

"I—I'm fine." He turned back but still couldn't see Riley. "Did you see it?"

"I saw nothing except you falling backward. I came after you to make sure you were alright. What did you see?"

They hadn't seen it? They hadn't seen the towering blue flames or Lumen's face coming down and speaking to him? They hadn't heard Lumen's loud voice? How could they have missed it?

It didn't matter whether they'd seen it or not. Calum had, and he knew what they needed to do. "Not now. We need to—"

A shaft of golden light pierced through the shadows, and an opening across the cavern spread wide. The portal?

When Calum looked back, he saw Riley's lupine face aglow with golden light. "Tell me you see that, at least?"

Riley nodded. "That, I see."

"That's where we're going." Calum pointed at it. "Get your pack and everyone else. And hurry. We're going now."

PILLARS OF BLUE FLAMES? A firestorm that spoke and gave Calum instructions on how to free Lumen? A prison in a secret cave under one of the Tri-Lakes? A "portal?"

To Axel, it all sounded like vivid hallucinations. Had the Arcanum not opened on its own, and had that shaft of light at the far end of the cavern not started shining out of nowhere, Axel wouldn't have believed a single word out of Calum's mouth.

Even so, when the group reached the portal, Axel waved his hand. "There's no way I'm walking into that thing."

In place of an opening in the rocks, a glowing wall stretched ten feet high and half as wide. Shaped like a circle, it wavered as if wind rippled its surface, sort of like fire, but also like water.

Whatever it was, Axel wanted nothing to do with it.

Calum began, "Lumen said it would—"

"I don't care what Lumen said," Axel interrupted. "I said I'm not walking into that thing, and I meant it."

"Then get used to dark places with no food or water." Riley emerged from the shadows behind them, and Axel still had to marvel at his size increase since the fight with the Wolves. "After Kanton and the last of my Wolves entered the Arcanum, it shut on itself again. If this portal isn't the way out, we gotta find another one, because we can't get out that way."

"How many different ways do I have to say it?" Axel glared at Riley.

"I'm. Not. Walking. Into. That. Thing."

"Good. Maybe we'll finally get rid of you." Riley folded his arms, but he didn't conceal the faint smirk curling the edge of his mouth.

Axel scoffed. "You're lucky to have me around, and you know it."

"Yes, Farm Boy," Condor said. "You're quite useful when it comes to obnoxious commentary."

"I'm going," Calum cut in before the conversation could devolve further. "Lumen said it will take us directly to Trader's Pass."

"How is that possible?" Lilly asked. "We're a month's travel away, at least."

"It is not possible," Magnus said. "But neither is solid rock supposed to open and close on its own, nor do shimmering portals appear out of nowhere. Calum has led us this far. I will not give up on him now."

"Maybe we should throw something into it. Test it out first?" Falcroné shrugged.

"Yeah," Axel said, "let's throw the Wolves who stole my last piece of venison in it. See what happens to them."

"No one's testing anything. Lumen said to go through it, so I'm going through it." Calum eyed Axel and Falcroné. "You don't want to go through it, then don't. Stay here if you like. Lumen said we need one Saurian, one Wolf, one Windgale, and one human to set him free. As long as we have who we need to free him, I'm satisfied."

Calum walked toward the wavering wall and stopped only inches away. He sucked in a deep breath, then he stepped into the golden light.

The portal warped as his body entered it, sending dramatic ripples throughout as if he were walking into a suspended pool of illuminated water. Calum's face and chest disappeared first, then his arms, shoulders, and finally the rest of his body.

Wherever he was, he wasn't inside the Arcanum anymore. The portal had at least succeeded in that, if nothing else. But Axel had no way of knowing that Calum wasn't dead, perhaps shredded into a million tiny pieces or segmented into seven big bloody chunks on the other end of that portal. It just wasn't worth the risk.

Without so much as another word, Magnus stepped into the portal after Calum. The last Axel saw of him was his tail, which snaked into the portal after him.

"I'm going too." Lilly started forward, but Falcroné grabbed her by her wrist.

"Princess—"

She pulled free from his grasp. "Don't you *dare* try to stop me, Fal. I thought I made it clear that—"

"*Lilly.*" Falcroné clamped his hands on her shoulders. "I was going to say you should let me go first. If I make it, I can ensure the area is safe for you in advance."

Lilly's frown and arched eyebrows relaxed, and a smile curled the corners of her mouth. She nodded. "By all means."

Falcroné stepped toward the portal, but Lilly clamped her hand on his wrist.

"Wait."

"Yes?"

She leaned forward and kissed his cheek. "I love you. Be safe."

The gesture twisted Axel's stomach, and he hoped all the more that Falcroné wouldn't make it on the other end.

Falcroné grinned at her. "I will. See you soon, one way or another."

He vanished into the portal, and Condor stepped up to Lilly next.

"Do I get a kiss, too?" He winked at her, then he darted into the portal before Lilly could respond, but she stood there with her mouth hanging open and a look of disdain on her face.

Axel grinned and started to say something, but she held up her hand.

"Don't even think about it." Lilly turned and entered the portal as well, followed by Kanton.

Only Axel, Riley, and the Wolves remained. "You wanna go first? It's gonna take awhile to get my whole pack through there."

Axel scowled at him and rolled his eyes.

Riley motioned toward the way they'd come in with a nod of his head. "I saw the entrance seal up with my own eyes, but if you want, I can leave a pair of Wolves with you to help you try to find a way out."

"No. Not interested." Axel waved his hand and shook his head.

Riley's generous offer had surprised him, but the idea of wandering around in the dark with two hungry Wolves didn't sit well with him. If, in fact, they were trapped inside, they'd soon be fighting each other over who would get eaten first.

"So you're going through, then?"

Axel sighed. He didn't want to, but... "Whatever."

He charged forward into the glowing waves.

Axel's body spiraled and rotated end-over-end in a tunnel made of rippling, waving water-fire, but the experience ended as quickly as it had begun. The next thing he knew he found himself skidding across a patch gray dirt on his chest. When he finally came to a stop, that same gray dirt caked the surface of his tongue and his teeth.

He dug a dollop of dirt out of his mouth and expelled the rest in half a dozen sputters, regretting that he'd kept his mouth open while jumping through.

Then his stomach lurched, and his sputtering became vomiting, and suddenly he no longer minded that the Wolves had stolen his last chomp of dried venison.

Two pairs of strong hands helped him to his feet once the last of his lunch cleared his stomach.

"Rough ride, Farm Boy?" Condor asked.

Axel moaned and wiped his mouth with the back of his left gauntlet. "I'm never doing that again."

Falcroné patted him on the back. "I doubt you'll have a chance. Look around."

The morning sun shone through the crystal blue skies above. In the distance, a large body of water shimmered against the dead gray terrain surrounding it.

Axel recognized his surroundings immediately—they were on Trader's Pass near where they had decided to head toward the lake to go fishing.

It was right where Calum had claimed the portal led. Axel couldn't deny it.

"Yeah. I guess you're right." Axel brushed the dirt from his chin and his breastplate and shot a glare at Calum. He'd been right, but so what? Axel had thrown up because of his stupid portal.

A howl sounded behind him, and Riley emerged out of nowhere—literally—followed by Wolf, after Wolf, after Wolf, until his entire pack appeared on Trader's Pack. They nipped at each other amid growls and snarls, but all of them fell silent with one sharp bark from Riley.

"See?" Axel pointed at the Wolves. "I'm not the only one who didn't like it."

"They're not reacting to the trip through the portal," Riley said. "They smell Dactyls. So do I. Probably only a few miles away, and getting closer."

"We need to get to Sharkville right away," Magnus said. "I do not care how many of us there are now. We still cannot risk running into them."

"Then let's go." Calum started north, toward the Central Lake.

To Calum's relief, they reached Sharkville in little more than half a day. The same dinky wooden sign, still stuck in the arid ground in front of the town, bore its name, and the dismal gray buildings still stood like weathered gravestones.

The Central Lake glimmered in the afternoon sun. The dock where they had boarded their chartered ship looked exactly the same, only this time each of its slots had a ship floating in it. Perhaps fishing season had hit the town, or perhaps it had recently come to an end. Either way, the lack of people in the empty streets indicated otherwise.

Calum smiled. People in the streets or not, they were there to free Lumen. Maybe even today, depending on how long it took them to reach the bend in the lake. All they had to do was find and charter a vessel to get them there.

A familiar weatherworn sign hanging from an equally familiar building caught Calum's eye. The sign bore the word "Fishig," which was scrawled next to an image of a fish caught in a net. Gill's place.

Calum started toward the door with Magnus and the others right behind him, but he stopped short when the door under the "Fishig" sign shattered. The body of a large man skidded to a halt about ten feet from Calum, followed by a double-sided battle-ax.

It was Gill.

Inside the door to Gill's place, a tall form materialized, and a pair of dark-green reptilian feet stepped out. As the form ducked under the doorframe and walked forward, its thick green fingers curled around the hilt of the sword that hung from a sheath on its belt, and sunlight glinted off its gold breastplate.

Vandorian.

CHAPTER THIRTY-EIGHT

When Vandorian stepped out of Gill's place, Lilly's heart began to hammer in her chest. How had he found them? And how had he made it there before them?

Calum and Axel rushed over to Gill and helped him to his feet, battle-axe and all. He groaned, but they helped him get clear of Vandorian's path.

They leaned him up against the nearest building then dashed to Magnus's side with their swords drawn, and Kanton floated over to tend to the bloody gash in Gill's forehead.

"Magnusss." Vandorian elongated his pronunciation of Magnus's name with a long hiss. "Fancy meeting you here, of all places."

Magnus urged Calum aside and positioned himself between Vandorian and the rest of the group. "This is impossible. You should be at the Crimson Keep."

Vandorian tilted his head and smirked. "That would make sense, would it not? Unfortunately, your detour to murder Oren and burn down my fortress at the Blood Chasm cost you precious time—time that enabled me to get here first."

"You could not have known where we were headed," Magnus growled.

Vandorian dismissed Magnus's objection with a wave. "It was not difficult to ascertain your destination after a few short conversations with the Sky Realm's Premier. He hesitated to disclose much at first, but in the end he proved quite helpful after a bit of—" Vandorian's golden eyes fixed on Lilly. "—*persuasion.*"

"What have you done?" Like lightning, Lilly drew an arrow, nocked it in her bow, and took aim at Vandorian's left eye, but she didn't release. If he had hurt her father, she would finish him off just like Condor had killed Oren, and she would regret it even less.

"You have nothing to fear, Princess. Your father still draws breath, and the Sky Fortress still stands—for now." Vandorian bared his pointed teeth at her. "Though I cannot guarantee their state of being will remain so for long."

She drew the arrow and her bowstring back and homed in on Vandorian's face. The shot was difficult enough because of the relatively small size of his eyes. Worse yet, if he moved his head even an inch, she could miss him entirely. Still, it was worth—

Magnus's big hand blocked her line of sight. "Do not attack him. He is my adversary, and you would only be wasting your arrows anyway."

Lilly fumed, but she nodded and relaxed the tension in her bowstring. She still kept the arrow nocked, though, just in case.

"That still does not explain how you knew to come *here* instead of the Arcanum," Magnus said.

"Right you are, brother." Vandorian sauntered toward him. "But consider the reason you went to the Arcanum in the first place. You needed to find the location of the Hidden Abyss. Do you really believe that in all of Kanarah, *no one* would know where it was without first finding the Arcanum?"

Magnus's mouth hung open as a revelation dawned in his golden eyes. "Father told you before he died."

"Aside from the King and his generals, he was the only other soul old enough to have witnessed Lumen's defeat and his descent into the Hidden Abyss. Father divulged that final secret just before Kahn crushed his head."

A violent yet brief shudder racked Magnus's huge body. Throughout all their time together, in spite of all the perils they'd encountered, Lilly had never seen him do anything of the sort. The sight made her want to shudder as well.

"The moment Avian told me of your plans, I headed straight here." Vandorian smiled again. "And now here I am, ready to finish what I began so many years ago."

Magnus drew his broadsword from its sheath. "Then come forward. My blade will taste your flesh this day, brother."

Vandorian grinned, then he cocked his head back and unleashed a roar that seemed to shake the ground itself.

Behind him, the wall that housed the doorframe to Gill's place burst into pieces, and four Sobeks in black armor stormed out. Across the street, the same thing happened from within another building, and then more Sobeks broke through the walls of a third not far from that one.

The Sobeks lined up around Vandorian, twelve in all, not including him. When they stalked forward, accompanied by an air of absolute confidence, Magnus backed up, and so did the rest of the group.

At the sight of Magnus's recoil, Vandorian laughed. "Do not tell me that the mighty Magnus is afraid? Surely you did not expect us to engage in this battle on equal footing?"

"If you had any honor, you would face me yourself in single combat," Magnus countered.

"It is not a question of honor, but of power. We have it all, and you have none," Vandorian replied. "Where power reigns, honor dies."

Vandorian and the Sobeks' approach continued, slow and methodical.

"We cannot withstand them," Magnus said aloud as he stepped back, his sword still ready. "Had it just been Vandorian and a few others, I would have said to fight, but against so many, we stand no chance."

"We're already here." Calum raised his sword higher. "We wouldn't have made it this far if we weren't supposed to free Lumen."

"No, Calum. Now is not the time. We need to flee." Magnus shot a glare at him.

"Though I hate to walk away from a battle, Magnus is right," Axel grumbled. "We'll all die if we fight these lizards. You weren't around when we had to fight Oren, and he was just *one* Sobek. Even with Riley's Wolves, thirteen is a death sentence."

"I know it seems like that," Calum said. "But there has to be a solution. We didn't come this far just to die on the verge of freeing Lumen."

A solution. Lilly's mind raced through the possibilities. There was a solution indeed—a risky one, but a solution nonetheless.

Lilly tucked her arrow back into her quiver, slung her bow over her back, and smacked the shoulders of Condor and Falcroné. "Come with me."

"What? Where are you going?" Axel's eyes widened.

"Just hold them off for a few minutes." She sprang into the sky amid protests from Axel and Calum, with even more coming from Falcroné as she soared in the opposite direction they had traveled, back south toward Trader's Pass.

Falcroné caught up to her in the air as she zipped along. "What are we doing? They need our help back there."

"You'll see. Just get ready to fly with all the speed you can muster when the time comes." Lilly pushed ahead of him, only to watch Condor cruise past her with a smirk and a wink.

Oh, how she loved to hate him.

Perhaps Lilly had a plan that could actually help them. Whether or not that was the case, Magnus resolved to give her as much time as he could.

"Riley, tell your Wolves to spread out and encircle the Sobeks." Magnus motioned to him with his free hand. "But urge them to use caution. These are the twelve members of Vandorian's personal guard, and all are formidable foes."

"Done." Riley howled, and the thirty Wolves darted away from the main group. They formed a perimeter around the Sobeks, who hissed at them and turned to face them.

"I see Father's tactical training still serves you well, brother." Vandorian smirked. "But thirty Wolves plus the few friends who have not yet deserted you cannot hope to overcome us."

Magnus squinted at him. Even if he had no other weaknesses, Vandorian was overconfident. Perhaps Magnus could somehow exploit that to his benefit.

"But I will offer you a bargain." Vandorian pointed his sword, its blade also blue Blood Ore like Magnus's, at Magnus's chest. "If you surrender now, I will spare your friends. I will not even deign to harm them. I will allow them to go free, and I will grant them a whole day to flee my presence."

Magnus glanced down at Calum. For the sake of his friends, he couldn't pass up that kind of deal. "You need to go, now. Take Axel and the others with you. This fate is mine, not yours."

Calum shook his head. "Not a chance. We're friends. If you die, I die, too. There's no way around that. And we need you to help us free Lumen anyway."

"Frankly, I'm sick of taking orders from both of you," Axel piped in. "At this point I'd rather die than continue to deal with your rudeness and constant disregard for my ideas. I'm not going anywhere."

Magnus snorted. Of course he wasn't.

Kanton left Gill leaning against the side of a building, retrieved his spear, and aimed its tip at the approaching Sobeks. His right hand had healed enough that he could use it again, just as Magnus had promised. "I'm with you, too."

Magnus looked at Riley, who shrugged.

"Hey, I *just* became a Werewolf," he said. "Supposedly my teeth and claws can penetrate Sobek scales. I'm dying to try them out, see what I can do. Well, hopefully *not* dying, but you know what I mean. Either way, I'm in, and my pack's in, too."

Magnus sighed. "Try not to fight them one-on-one, any of you, and especially avoid Vandorian. He is by far the most dangerous, and—"

"And you wanna kill him yourself." Axel rolled his eyes. "Yeah. We know, Scales."

Magnus couldn't help but smirk. "Exactly. Let's go."

This time, instead of backing up farther, they held their ground as the Sobeks approached.

AT FIRST, Lilly didn't know if she'd seen a bird flying through the air ahead of them or something else, but the nearer she drew to it, the more its image sharpened, and the fouler the air smelled around her. It noticed her and started toward them, along with two others just like it.

They each had expansive wings like a bird's, though they more resembled a bat's, plus four spindly limbs and bodies not unlike a Windgale's, all covered in pale-green skin. Huge charcoal-gray beaks protruded in place of their mouths, and talons tipped each of their three toes, their three long fingers, and thumbs on each hand, with one more on the tip of each of their tails.

Dactyls.

They screeched dissonance and swirled toward Lilly, Condor, and Falcroné.

Their beaks and talons can pierce Saurian skin and most armor. Only dragon scales and exceptionally rare types of metal can withstand their attacks, Magnus had said. *Their blood gives off a pheromone that attracts other Dactyls.*

Time to attract some Dactyls.

Lilly drew her sword. The lead Dactyl lurched toward her, and she severed its head from its body. Glowing purple blood sprayed into the sky from its neck, and the monster's wretched stench intensified.

Next to her, Condor jammed his sword into the second Dactyl's chest, and Falcroné cleaved the third clean in half with one vicious hack. Purple blood spattered all over his face, arms, and breastplate, and he sputtered.

"This is disgusting." Falcroné wiped the blood from his eyes. "You brought us out here to kill three of these things? How is that supposed to help the rest of the group?"

Lilly scanned the horizon to the south for a moment. "Dactyls can smell their dead from miles away. These three functioned like scouts. I figured that we could try to—"

She stopped at the sight of a solitary winged form rising from the horizon. It started toward them. Then another followed. Then another.

Soon dozens of them ascended into the sky, until hundreds of dark forms swarmed toward them.

Falcroné's eyebrows raised. "Oh."

"Brilliant." Condor gave Lilly a smile that accelerated her heartbeat. Or perhaps it was the army of Dactyls she'd summoned instead.

The Dactyls were approaching fast. Really fast.

"We have to lead them back to Sharkville," Lilly said. "Fal, they'll come after you first since you're covered with their blood. Be careful."

Without another word, she zoomed north with her captains right behind her and the Dactyls right behind them.

CALUM ROLLED under the Sobek's swing and hacked at its leg, but his sword just clanged off its ankle. The Sobek's other foot slammed into Calum's chest, and he soared across the street into the wall near where Kanton had tended to Gill.

The impact almost knocked him senseless. When his vision finally righted itself, Calum refocused on the fight in front of him.

If his sword couldn't even penetrate the Sobeks' skin, how was he supposed to kill any of them? Had Lilly not taken Condor and Falcroné with her, perhaps they could've found a way to sever the straps that held the Sobeks' armor in place and thus expose their vulnerable underbellies, but she'd gone. What chance did they have now?

The Sobek who'd kicked Calum whirled around and felled one of the Wolves with his sword while another Wolf gnawed on the same ankle Calum had just struck.

Beyond them, Riley wove between several of the Sobeks and slashed them with his claws. He even managed to clamp his teeth onto one of the Sobeks' throats, but he caught a stunning punch to his ribs that dislodged him before he could finish the Sobek off.

Axel and Magnus worked in tandem, a far better team than either of them would ever admit, and Kanton darted over to Calum.

"Are you alright?" He extended his left hand.

Calum nodded. He had to find a way to win against these guys. And on top of that, Magnus had to survive the battle. Lumen's release depended on unifying one soul from each of the four races to set him free. Without Magnus, it wouldn't work.

Calum grabbed Kanton's hand and pulled himself up to his feet.

Kanton blinked at him, then stared over his shoulder. "Where's Gill?"

Calum stole a quick glance at the wall he'd just been leaning against. "I have no idea. Didn't you leave him right there?"

Kanton nodded. "He looked really out of it when I left him."

A loud slam sounded down the street, but no one still in the battle turned to look amid the cacophony of swordplay, roars, and barks. Calum craned his head in time to see Gill storm out of another gray building, his battle-axe in hand.

At his side, a wiry young man about Calum's age led a small army of humans and Windgales armed with spears, harpoons, and swords toward the fracas. Calum blinked.

It was Jake, the fisherman. Puolo's son.

So much for Sharkville being deserted.

Gill, Jake, and dozens of fishermen charged into the fight, and Calum did likewise. Maybe they had a chance after all.

───────

LILLY FLEW AS FAST as she could, but somehow the Dactyls had caught up with her. It hardly seemed possible, even with Condor and Falcroné flying at her side, but they'd done it.

One of them clamped its long fingers around her ankle—its fourth attempt after three near-misses—and tried to pull her back, but a quick lash from her sword split its head wide open, and it dropped from the sky. Three more Dactyls took its place.

Lilly couldn't hope to fight them all, even with Condor and Falcroné's prowess at her disposal. Out-maneuvering them was her only hope.

She twisted and spun through the air, changing her altitude at unpredictable moments to throw the Dactyls off. Normally she enjoyed this kind of tense chase, but the pervading hunger and evil emanated by the Dactyls erased any semblance of joy from her evasions.

"This was not—" Falcroné looped underneath her then reappeared on her opposite side. "—a good idea."

Condor felled two Dactyls from the air and then joined them. "What are you complaining about? At least you still have armor to wear."

"You'd still have your armor if you hadn't—"

"Rebelled?" Condor finished for him. "Far too late for that now."

"I see Sharkville." Lilly pointed at a smattering of gray buildings in the distance. They looked more like tiny children's toys from so high up. "Come on."

They spiraled down toward it with the Dactyls still in close pursuit.

MAGNUS PARRIED Vandorian's first several blows with ease, but he could tell his brother wasn't engaging him with the full extent of his ability. He threw a ferocious counterattack that could have felled a Gronyx, but Vandorian deflected it as if Magnus were only a child swinging a stick.

"You never ranked among the stronger of our siblings." Vandorian shoved Magnus backward. "It baffles me that you survived when all of them perished that day."

Magnus ducked under the next swipe and lashed his broadsword at Vandorian's chest. His blade connected with Vandorian's breastplate and clanged off, but the impact forced Vandorian back a step to maintain his footing.

He smirked at Magnus. "Perhaps I was wrong. Even so, not even Blood Ore can penetrate this breastplate. If you wish to kill me, you will have to cut off my head."

From the side, one of the other Sobeks whipped his blade at Magnus's head as if Vandorian's taunt had commanded it.

In response, Magnus batted the blade away and slammed his tail into the Sobek's knees.

Vandorian raised his sword for another swing, capitalizing on

Magnus's distraction and the newfound opening his Sobek guard had created.

But Magnus wasn't distracted.

As the Sobek pitched to the side, off-balance, Magnus adjusted his angle and drove his shoulder into the Sobek. He careened toward Vandorian, who had already initiated his attack. His sword cleaved deep into the Sobek's torso, and he fell under Vandorian's blade, dead.

Now it was Magnus's turn to smirk while Vandorian's countenance darkened.

WHEN AXEL SAW GILL, Jake, and almost a hundred men storm into the battle, he had to grin.

Gill might not have been able to draw or spell the word "fishing" on his sign, but he sure knew how to use his battle-axe. He plowed into the nearest Sobek with his full weight and swung his battle-axe with abandon, shouting something about the Saurians owing him coin for trashing the perfectly good wall of his shanty.

When Axel saw Lilly, Falcroné, and Condor dropping out of the sky at them with a few hundred Dactyls behind them, his grin evaporated, and his heart stuttered in his chest. *That* was her idea of helping?

May the Overlord have mercy on us all.

CHAPTER THIRTY-NINE

Calum had just threaded through the skirmish to Jake when dozens of pale-green bodies pelted them from the sky. When Calum finally looked up, a dark gray beak set under a pair of glowing white eyes rushed toward his face.

He reacted and sliced at the thing with his sword, which clanged against its beak. A follow-up hack spilled the Dactyl's intestines from its belly, and it dropped to the ground, screeching and writhing.

What in the—

A man screamed next to him.

Jake.

In two slices, Calum cut down the two Dactyls on top of Jake and pulled him to his feet. Both of them were covered in glowing purple blood that reeked of death and refuse.

"Thanks." Jake shifted his harpoon in his hand. "Where in the depths did they come from?"

In the distance behind Jake, Lilly fired off arrow after arrow while Condor and Falcroné covered her. Calum exhaled a sharp breath. "I think I know where, but that's not important right now. What are you doing here?"

"Gill told us you guys were gettin' ambushed, so my men and I came to help."

"*Your* men?"

He nodded. "Like I said when we parted ways a few months ago, I headed to Kanarah City, met up with my dad's friends, and got a few ships out here. Turns out he had a lot of friends."

"Apparently." Calum smiled. "Jake, we need a favor."

Jake shoved Calum aside and skewered another Dactyl with his harpoon. Calum's sword severed its head from its body. Jake nodded. "Anythin'. Name it."

"We need you to take us to the bend in the Central Lake right away."

"You got it. I'll have my crew ready a ship for departure."

Calum chopped the wing off a Dactyl as it flew by them, and it spiraled into one of the Sobeks and smacked into the street. The Sobek turned back and stomped its head to goo.

"Thanks," Calum said. "We'll meet you over there soon."

A SURPRISE KICK from Vandorian knocked Magnus onto his back. Vandorian would have finished Magnus off were it not for the flurry of pale-green flesh that smacked into him and knocked him off-balance. Magnus looked up.

Dactyls. Hundreds of the winged monsters cascaded toward them.

If this was Lilly's idea of saving everyone—well, Magnus appreciated the thought, but she'd definitely underestimated the consequences of this decision.

A pair of Dactyls dropped down onto Magnus and dug their talons into the scales on his legs. Pain spiked through his thighs, and he cut both Dactyls in half with one furious swing of his sword.

He scrambled to his feet in time to see Vandorian's sword tear through another Dactyl, then it reset and crashed down toward Magnus next. He barely got his sword up in time to fend off the strike, which rattled his sword and stung his right hand. Vandorian's follow-up swing glanced off Magnus's breastplate and carved a long scratch in its wake.

Amid the chaos of hundreds of carnivorous monsters descending on Sharkville, Magnus righted his sword and stared into Vandorian's eyes, but something behind him stole Magnus's attention.

One of the Sobeks fell to the ground, covered with Dactyls. They jammed their gray beaks into his flesh and tore at him with their talons as he flailed, but he couldn't shake them. Eventually he just stopped moving, and the Dactyls craked his bones open to get at the marrow inside.

That would *not* happen to Magnus.

Vandorian flung himself forward and slashed at Magnus, and the brothers traded vicious blows once again.

IT DIDN'T TAKE LONG for the Dactyls to overwhelm the battle. Soon enough, Axel and his friends, the fishermen, and the Wolves no longer fought the Sobeks but instead focused on killing the invading Dactyls.

The Sobeks' focus also shifted. The remaining seven of Vandorian's original twelve guards rallied together in a tight circle and fended off Dactyls by the dozen, whereas the Wolves and Windgale fishermen darted throughout Sharkville's otherwise bland streets and airspace while engaging the rest.

Glowing purple blood streaked the buildings, the streets, and the town's occupants who'd taken up arms against their enemies, but Axel could hardly call it an improvement. The purple certainly added color to the gray town, but the horrible stink accompanying it threatened to overpower every other one of Axel's senses.

Axel and Kanton had joined up with Lilly, Condor, and Falcroné, all of whom fought as a team against the Dactyl swarm. Where Condor seemed to almost enjoy the back-and-forth with the Dactyls, Falcroné's face showed nothing but sheer determination and fury.

Lilly fired arrows when she could, relying on the rest of the group to protect her from stray Dactyls. Axel happily obliged, but he didn't enjoy having to fight next to Kanton. With his right hand healed but hardly fully restored, what little fighting prowess Kanton possessed had dwindled to almost nothing.

So far, by Axel's count, Kanton hadn't killed any Dactyls. He'd only managed to wound a few before another of the group finished them off. What's more, he'd been attacked and overwhelmed almost a half dozen times until Axel or Falcroné, who occupied the spot on the other side of Kanton, saved him.

Every time they came at him, Kanton ended up with more cuts on his face and more scratches on his armor. If they didn't find a way out of this mess soon, Axel had to assume Kanton wouldn't make it. And if Kanton went down, who would guard Axel's left side?

RILEY'S CLAWS dripped with a foul mixture of dark red and glowing purple blood.

His ears prickled with the sounds of battle—swords severing Dactyl limbs, shouts and screams, blood spattering on the ground, talons scraping against armor—but the smells were worse. Dactyl blood smelled even more wretched than their skin, and with so much of both scents so close nearby, Riley wanted to tear his own nose off.

The fishermen stank of fish, and the Wolves reeked of their own unique scents, but the Sobeks cast a very different scent, one surprisingly cleaner than he'd expected. In a brawl of this size, he could pick out the rare clean scents even easier amid the onslaught of grotesque smells.

Yet despite the mass assault on his nose, Riley couldn't deny how well the Dactyls' presence had worked in his favor. The Sobeks were so distracted by battling the Dactyls that they didn't see him coming. Then again, as a Werewolf now, he could move so fast that it didn't really matter anyway.

He leaped at the one farthest from the group and tackled him to the ground. He could have fastened his teeth around the Sobek's exposed neck or cut his scaled face into ribbons with his claws, but he didn't. Instead, he recovered his footing and darted away in time to avoid the half dozen Dactyls that landed on the Sobek and did the rest of the work for him.

He smiled, then he ducked between two low-swooping Dactyls. Ahead, a trio of human fishermen grappled with four Dactyls, and they weren't faring well. Not now, at least. He charged toward them and—

Something tripped him. Riley dropped to the ground face-first, and dirt caked on his snout and the fur under his chin. A dark green tail snaked out of his periphery, and he rolled over to find a Sobek towering over him. It bore teeth marks on his throat—Riley had tried to kill him at the beginning of the fight.

"Finally caught up to you, you filthy *dog*," the Sobek snarled.

He raised his sword to deliver the killing blow, but a blood-streaked blur zipped by, and a deep gash opened on the Sobek's neck, right between Riley's bite marks. Were Riley not a Werewolf now, his vision might not have been able to discern what had happened.

The Sobek convulsed once then dropped to the ground on his side, his eyes wide with shock and surprise. He clutched his bleeding throat and trembled.

Riley sprang to his feet and glared at Condor, his savior.

"Can we be friends now?" Condor asked.

Riley touched the spot on his side where Condor had stabbed him. The injury was long gone, totally erased during the process of becoming a Werewolf, but Riley remembered the pain all too well.

He wasn't ready to forgive Condor just yet. "Maybe next time."

"Fair enough." Condor raised an eyebrow at him then shot into the sky, leaving Riley alone with the dead Sobek.

Riley spun around and hurled himself at the Dactyls attacking the fishermen.

ABOARD HIS SHIP, Jake thrust his harpoon into the air and waved it around his head in a large arc.

Calum saw its blade glistening in the sunlight. He turned back toward the fracas, located Axel, Lilly, and the others, and then charged toward them with abandon. Jake was going to get them all out of there and get them to Lumen, but Calum had to round everyone up, first.

By now, more than half of the Dactyls littered the ground, most of them in pieces, but many still haunted the skies around Sharkville and dove down at their prey with their talons bared and beaks spread wide. If Calum and his companions didn't get out of there soon, there was no telling what might happen.

He whacked a Dactyl from the sky with the flat of his blade as he ran, then he ducked under another one but barely cleared it. Its talons scraped against the armor on his back, and Calum resolved to duck a little lower next time.

By the time he reached his companions, half of them had already noticed him.

"Come with me!" He pointed toward Jake's ship. "We can get away from here and free Lumen!"

No one hesitated. The Windgales all took to the sky and wove through the encroaching Dactyls with ease while Calum and Axel bounded over the corpses of Dactyls, Wolves, fishermen, and the occasional Sobek toward Jake's ship.

He still needed Magnus and Riley. Calum scanned the battle. To his right, a tall Wolf-shaped form thrashed four Dactyls that were attacking some humans.

To his left, in the distance, Magnus and Vandorian still clashed blades. Pulling Magnus away from that confrontation would be all but impossible.

———

MAGNUS PARRIED EVERY ATTACK, but Vandorian moved too quickly and was too strong. Every time Magnus thought he'd found a way to exploit one of Vandorian's mistakes, his efforts backfired, and Vandorian punished him for it.

Even so, he'd held his own against his older brother this long. Perhaps if he could endure a few minutes longer—

Vandorian's elbow smacked into the side of Magnus's snout, and the impact twisted Magnus's whole body. The blow itself hurt, but worse than that, Magnus knew he was exposed, and he couldn't do anything about it.

Fire seared through his right forearm from the surface, through his flesh and bone, and then out the other side again. The weight of his sword dropped away, and he staggered back a few steps.

When Magnus recovered his composure, he stared down at his sword. How would he retrieve it with Vandorian now standing over it?

A growing pool of red under the hilt seized his attention.

His hand still gripped the sword, but it was no longer attached to his arm.

CHAPTER FORTY

Calum saw it happen, but he didn't believe his eyes. In one horrifying instant, Vandorian had severed Magnus's hand from his forearm. The fight was over.

He whirled around and hollered for Riley, who sped toward him at an incredible rate then ran past with a howl when he noticed Calum's finger extended toward Magnus. Not far behind, the remaining ten or so Wolves who had survived thus far bounded after him.

"Get to the ship," Riley called back at him. "I'll get Magnus."

Calum wrenched his anchored feet from the ground and bolted toward the ship.

A ROAR SWELLED in Magnus's chest and erupted from his throat as he clutched the bleeding stump where his right hand had been.

"I have to *hand* it to you, Magnus," Vandorian said between disdainful chuckles. "You fought well—mostly."

Magnus stood there stunned until Vandorian leveled him with his tail.

"You were always a disgrace." Vandorian stood over him, sneering.

BEN WOLF

"Always the weakest of my siblings, never an especially talented fighter. Intelligent, but ill-equipped to do anything with your breadth of knowledge. Twenty-first in line for our father's throne. It amuses me that you, of all my siblings, would survive so long, only to die here in the middle of nowhere."

Somehow Magnus mustered the clarity and fortitude to speak. "Kill me if you wish, Vandorian. If you do not, I will never stop coming for you. Ever."

Vandorian smirked, and his golden eyes fixed on the pouch that hung from Magnus's belt. "That reminds me. You have something very precious in your possession. Something I need if I am to succeed our uncle as ruler of Reptilius someday. I suppose I owe you for finding it and using it to become a Sobek. Had you not, it would have been useless to me."

All Magnus could do was watch as Vandorian reached for the pouch and pulled the Dragon Emerald from it. Pain ravaged his right arm.

"Such a small thing, but so powerful, so important." Vandorian rotated the dark-green stone in his hand and grinned. "And now it is all mine."

About a hundred feet above Vandorian's head, four Dactyls spiraled down toward them. Magnus diverted his gaze from them the instant Vandorian's focus returned to him.

"I will give your regards to our uncle." Vandorian bared his sharp teeth in a smile.

The Dactyls dropped toward them, and Magnus shifted his tail so it lay between Vandorian's feet.

Vandorian raised his sword in his right hand, still holding the Dragon Emerald in his left. "Goodbye, little brother."

The Dactyls smacked into Vandorian from above and clawed at him, and one clamped onto his left shoulder.

A howl split the air, then several more.

Magnus's tail hooked Vandorian's left ankle and yanked, and Vandorian toppled down onto his back.

A mass of dark fur appeared in Vandorian's place. It reached down and grabbed Magnus by his good arm and hauled him to his feet.

Riley.

Vandorian roared and thrashed at the Dactyls, but their attacks persisted. Amid the confusion, one of the Wolves leaped and clamped his jaws around the Dragon Emerald, then the Wolf wrenched it from Vandorian's hand.

"Come on," Riley said. "We've got a ship. We're going to Lumen."

"Until next time, brother. Do not forget to give my regards to Uncle Kahn." Magnus bent down, scooped up his broadsword with his left hand, and followed Riley away from Vandorian.

"That's everyone," Calum said to Jake as the last of the surviving Wolves scampered aboard the ship. Somehow the core of their group had all made it. Good. "Cast off before the Dactyls realize we're abandoning the fight."

Jake gave the order, and the ship eased away from the dock thanks to the two-dozen men diligently rowing from the lower deck.

Magnus moaned and growled and slumped down against a large barrel on the ship's deck. Calum had never seen Magnus in such a state, and he wished he could do more for his friend, but Magnus hardly wanted anyone near him.

When Kanton hovered over to him with a clean white cloth in his hands, Magnus held up his left hand. "Do not bind it with anything. Whatever you do, never bind this sort of wound on a Saurian."

Kanton blinked. "You'll bleed out. He's severed major arteries in your arm, and—"

"Do *not* bind it, Kanton. Do not even touch it." Magnus stared steel at him, and Kanton backed away.

Calum started toward him. "Magnus, you're gonna—"

"I will be fine. Just leave me in peace." He clutched his bleeding stump of an arm with his fingers and growled again. "Where is my Dragon Emerald? One of the Wolves picked it up."

"Dallahan, turn it over," Riley said.

A light-gray Wolf with white accents in his fur and blue eyes a shade darker than Riley's trotted forward and dropped the Dragon Emerald on Magnus's lap with a whimper.

"Thank you." Magnus exhaled a contented breath and tucked the Dragon Emerald back into the pouch at his belt. "I am indebted to you, friend."

Dallahan squinted at him and growled. "You're not kidding. That thing's gotta be worth a fortune."

Axel huffed. "That's what *I* said."

"How long until we reach the bend in the lake?" Lilly asked. Streaks of purple blood on her face and armor gave off a light glow, but sitting next to Falcroné, she looked clean by comparison.

"We're a day away, at least, and that's if the men row the whole time. I'd count on a day and a half before we make it there." Jake, also streaked with Dactyl blood, grinned at them. "Take a rest, why don't you? Heal up. There's plenty of room aboard the ship for you to stretch your legs, get a little shut-eye, perhaps. We'll let you know when we're getting' close."

Calum stretched his sore limbs. Enough fighting, already. At this point, he just wanted to free Lumen and be done with it. He stared back at Sharkville, over which a few dozen Dactyls still swarmed, then he closed his eyes.

They were almost there.

VANDORIAN BATTED three of the Dactyls away with his sword. The fourth gnawed on his shoulder until he dropped his sword, took hold of the monster, ripped it in half with his bare hands, and hurled it to the ground. Even then, its beak still stuck in Vandorian's flesh, so he yanked that off too and tossed it aside.

He retrieved his sword and felled six more of them, then he reunited with the five Sobeks who's survived the fracas. The rest of the fishermen had scattered. The Windgales among them had taken to the sky, and the others had boarded the rest of the ships and set off onto the lake after the lead ship, the one his brother had boarded, free from Vandorian's grasp.

Free for now, anyway.

With only a few dozen Dactyls left, most of them had either found carcasses to feed on or still circled high above the town. They likely wouldn't attack anymore, not with so few of them left and so much meat on the ground just waiting to be consumed.

"You." Vandorian tapped the shoulder of one of the remaining Sobeks, the one with the fewest number of scratches and claw marks on his head. "Swim after the nearest ship. Kill all who are on board and bring the ship back to shore."

The Sobek blinked, then he glanced at the other Sobeks. "But... Prince Vandorian... I—"

Vandorian grabbed the Sobek by his throat and threw him to the ground. "Go, or I will kill you right here."

The Sobek scrambled to his feet, lumbered down to the docks, and jumped into the water with his black breastplate still secured to his chest.

"What do we do now, my prince?" another Sobek asked.

"We wait." Vandorian watched the Sobek swim after the ship. "If our comrade succeeds in bringing back that ship, we go after my brother and his friends."

A huge black mass broke the surface of the water and slammed down on the Sobek teeth-first. He thrashed for a moment then disappeared under a swell of red that tainted the water.

Vandorian hissed. It was as he'd suspected, but he couldn't have left this place behind until he was certain he had no other options.

"We will return to the Reptilius," he declared. "Kahn must know of what has transpired here. I suspect he will demand a reckoning for the wrongs committed against our people this day. Gather what supplies you can for the journey home. We leave in ten minutes."

"Yes, my prince." The Sobeks smacked their breastplates with their knuckles and dispersed.

Vandorian stared at the lead ship, now far in the distance. *You were right, Magnus. This is far from over.*

AFTER SEARCHING ALMOST the entire ship—twice—Lilly finally found Falcroné in the crow's nest, of all places. She landed and shifted a coil of thick rope aside so she could sit beside him.

Like him, she let her legs hang off the edge of the platform and stared out across the lake. Stars glimmered in the night sky, and their reflections danced along the water's surface.

"What are you doing up here?" she asked.

Falcroné shrugged and didn't make eye contact with her. Instead, he stared into the starry night sky. "Just watching. After you returned home and told me of the Jyrak, I've been uneasy about venturing out onto this lake."

"It was horrible. Axel and I both almost died. He would have for sure had I not—"

"I know, Lilly. You told me already."

She bit her lip. Was he actually upset with her about having saved Axel? "What's wrong, Fal?"

"Nothing."

"Then why won't you look at me?"

He turned his head and stared right into her eyes, but it wasn't out of love. Instead, he'd donned fearless eyes, the kind only hardened soldiers knew how to employ. "Better?"

She squinted at him and exhaled a silent sigh. "No. It's not."

Falcroné looked away again. "Then I don't know what you want from me."

Lilly cupped his jaw with her hand and turned his face back toward her. "I want *you*."

His soldier's glare softened. "Sometimes I wonder."

"Fal, how could you ever doubt my feelings toward you?" Even as Lilly asked him, she asked herself the same question.

"You let Condor join us. You refused to accuse Axel of a crime that we both know he committed against you." Falcroné numbered her offenses with his fingers. "And it seems like every time you look at Calum, you're about to start drooling over him."

Lilly's eyebrows rose. His accusations stung straight to her heart, but his characterization of her reactions concerning Calum filled her with rage. "That is *absurd*. I do *not* look at him that way."

"You don't see what I see. You're attracted to him. I know you are. Every time he's near you, you change. Your mannerisms adjust, you phrase things differently, and your eyes..." Falcroné sighed.

A pang of guilt stabbed Lilly's heart. She'd denied Falcroné's allegation because he'd framed it so rudely, but a part of her knew what he said was true. Calum was so—refreshing compared to everyone else she knew. His passion, his faith, his resolve.

He had sacrificed so much for what he believed, and now it was finally paying off. How could Lilly not be attracted to that?

"That's the look. You're doing it right now." Falcroné pointed at her face. "Those longing eyes, that slight frown. You look like you want something you can't have."

"I want *you*, Falcroné, and that's all you need to be concerned about."

Falcroné shook his head and gazed up at the stars. "I don't believe you."

"You have no idea what Calum means to me, or even Axel for that matter. They both saved my life countless times. They rescued me from—"

"They rescued you from Roderick, the slave trader. You've told me."

"It's more than that. So much more." Lilly took her turn staring at the stars.

"Then tell me."

"Why?" Lilly frowned. She could see where this was going. "You'll just use it against me."

"No, I really want to understand." He clasped his hands around hers. "What do you mean?"

Lilly's jaw tightened, and she sucked in a sharp breath as she stared into his eyes. She wanted to tell him the truth. Really and truly, she did. "I—"

Falcroné raised an eyebrow.

But if she told him the truth, everything between them would crash to an end.

"I can't." She bowed her head. "I'm sorry."

A long pause lingered between them. Lilly tried to use the time to formulate some sort of acceptable response, but everything that came to mind sounded successively worse than the previous idea.

"I release you from our engagement." Falcroné said it so softly that Lilly wondered if she had imagined it.

She squeezed his hands, her heart pulsing with anxiety. "No, Fal. That's not what I want. I—"

"You don't know what you want." Falcroné stroked her face with his fingers. It felt soothing, even as it grated against her nerves. "Don't try to tell me you do. You're young, and you have lots of time to figure it out. If it's me, then I can wait. And if not, then—"

"I want *you*. I'm telling you I want you." She grabbed him by the collar of his breastplate, resisting the urge to shed tears at this loss. Why wasn't he listening? "Don't you hear me?"

"I hear what you're saying, but your actions tell me something altogether different." Falcroné shook his head. "I can't continue to live a lie, and neither should you. I certainly won't be a part of it."

She released her grip on his breastplate, then she leaned back against the mast and rubbed her forehead with the heels of her hands. Part of her wanted to cry, and part of her wanted to fly away, but another part wanted to inhale her first breath of the freedom Falcroné had just granted her.

"Like I said, I'll be around when you make your decision. If it's me, I promise I'll do everything I can to make you happy." Falcroné's tone faded as he stood up. "And if it's not me, I'll try my best to be happy for you."

He faced the stars and bent at his knees to spring into the air, but she caught him by the wrist. She had to try one last time. "Don't do this, Fal. I love you."

Falcroné pursed his lips and nodded. "I know. I love you too, but I have to do it."

He pulled free from her grasp and plunged over the edge of the crow's nest, then he looped up into the starry sky and out of sight, leaving Lilly alone.

The first of what would be many tears that night streamed down her face.

LONG AFTER THE others fell asleep, and several hours after Magnus had managed to stanch the bleeding from his arm, soothing warmth spread throughout his wound, and the pain began to dissipate.

The veromine in his blood had begun its work.

LUMEN'S bright form burned Calum's eyes as it had so many times before. "You are near. I can feel your presence."

Calum shielded his face with his hands, but Lumen's light penetrated Calum's very being, deep into his soul.

"You will succeed, Calum. You will free me, and together we will liberate Kanarah."

Lumen's image spiraled into darkness with a loud pop.

SHOUTS, screams, and the nearby snapping of wood jerked Calum from his sleep. Exhausted from the battle, he'd fallen asleep on the ship's main deck well before yesterday's sun had set.

He groped for his sword and found it lying next to him in its sheath. He stood and strapped it to his belt in a hurry.

"What's going—" The words caught in his throat as his eyes fixed on the ship's central mast, which snapped in half and toppled off the side of the ship into the water. Splintered wood burst into the air and rained down on the deck, including on him. Lake water washed onto the deck up to Calum's feet, then receded.

What in the world could have—

A loud roar droned behind him, one all too familiar to his ears. He

349

whirled to face the other side of the ship and his eyes panned up the tall, dark form that towered above them.

A long neck suspended a monstrous reptilian head in the air. A dark red tongue snaked from between its bronze teeth. Spikes adorned its head, and two large horns jutted out from just behind its blank glowing yellow eyes. Black talons tipped each of the four webbed fingers on its hands.

The Jyrak.

CHAPTER FORTY-ONE

"What in the Overlord's name is *that?*" Condor's piercing blue eyes widened. It was the first time Lilly had ever seen actual fear register on his face.

"It's a Jyrak. Probably the same one we encountered last time we braved these waters." Jake motioned toward one of his crew. "We've got no sails left. Get the men rowin' immediately, or we're all dead."

"How far are we from the bend?" Calum asked.

"It's right there." Jake pointed at the Jyrak. "Behind *him.*"

A chill bristled Lilly's skin. They had to get *around* the Jyrak to reach Lumen's prison?

The Jyrak loosed another droning roar and turned its attention to another of Jake's ships, which it capsized in one ferocious blow with its enormous hand. Lilly could hear the screams of a dozen or so men before their bodies crashed into the surf.

"What do we do?" she asked, her attention fixed solely on Calum.

It wasn't just her, though. Axel stood at her side and stared at Calum with a look of terror on his face. Magnus gripped his wounded arm, which seemed to have sealed over during the night, and set his eyes on Calum.

Condor, Falcroné, and Kanton landed near Lilly and gave Calum their attention as well, and Riley and the remainder of his Wolf pack rounded out the circle. Even Jake, who didn't even know Calum that well, wouldn't look away from him.

This was what Lilly couldn't explain to Falcroné. Moments like these, when everything was at stake, she would turn to Calum, and Calum would make a way.

It was an irresistible force. An inevitable attraction.

It made Calum unique compared to everyone else she'd ever met.

"We need to work together." Calum peered across the water and squinted. "Jake, I need your other ships to head in one direction around the Jyrak, and we'll head the other."

Jake nodded. "Got it."

"Riley, take your Wolves to the ship's stern. If there's trouble, they can jump off before the Jyrak destroys the ship. Maybe they can swim to safety." Calum held up his hand. "But you stay with me. I need you to help me free Lumen."

Riley nodded too, then he shooed the Wolves away.

"Axel and Kanton, help out on this ship. Work together. Secure sails, tie knots—whatever Jake tells you to do, do it. Then find something heavy that will help us sink nice and fast so we don't drown on our way down to the Hidden Abyss."

They nodded and darted after Jake.

Calum pointed to Magnus and his voice hardened. "And you—don't you dare leave my sight. You're the only Saurian for miles. If we lose you, we can't free Lumen."

Magnus nodded.

"Lilly, take Condor and Falcroné. You three have the most dangerous job, but only you three can do it. Do whatever you can to distract that thing. Buy us time to work around it so the other ships don't have to sacrifice themselves to get us to Lumen." Calum's eyes locked on hers, and a flood of emotion filled her chest and stomach. "Whatever you do, don't get yourself killed."

She gave him a half smile then took to the sky, leaving him behind. He had never let her down before, and she wasn't about to let him down now.

Falcroné and Condor soared alongside her toward the Jyrak, which thrashed at the remnants of the ship it had just destroyed. As they approached, Lilly unsheathed her sword. What she planned to do with it, she wasn't sure, but she would try nonetheless.

The ring of two more swords leaving their sheaths sounded behind her. At least she had two of the best fighters in all of the Sky Realm with her. Together they would find a way to give Calum the time he needed.

———

CALUM STOOD at the edge of the deck, his fingers clamped on the rail, and watched Lilly fly toward the Jyrak. She had better make it out of this. If she didn't, he'd never forgive himself.

"We're pickin' up speed." Jake cranked the ship's wheel to the right and the ship curled away from the Jyrak. "I gotta take 'er wide at first to make sure we clear its tail, or it could tip us without even tryin'."

"Do what you must, Jake," Calum said.

Magnus's left hand gripped the rail on Calum's right, and Riley's did the same on his left.

"Wish I could do more," Riley said, his voice much softer than what it could've been given the situation. "But I just don't do boats. Or swimming. Or gigantic monsters."

"You'll have your chance soon enough. You're coming with me to free Lumen."

"You heard me say I don't like swimming, right? Because I just said it like five seconds ago."

Calum eyed him and motioned toward the Jyrak with his head. "I bet you'll like it more than you'll like *dying*."

Riley raised a furry eyebrow, then he nodded. "Tried it twice already. Not my favorite. So I guess you're right."

"You know I will have to dive down and find the entrance to the Abyss, right?"

Calum clenched his teeth. He hadn't considered that, but Magnus *was* the only one with a large enough lung capacity to survey the area without drowning. Still, if they lost their only Sobek... "If you get caught by a shark or some other—"

"No one else can stay down long enough to verify its location. Besides, the sharks swam away when the Jyrak showed up last time. Either way, you must let me do this, Calum."

"I know. I know I do." Calum sighed and focused on Magnus's right arm, which had scabbed over. "You sure you're up to it?"

"I will be fine. My arm is regenerating. I have never lost a limb like this before, but I have seen what happens if the veromine in our blood is allowed to do its work. I expect to have a new hand in a matter of days."

So unfair. Calum had to wear armor and do everything he could to defend himself, whereas Magnus, whose scales were nearly invulnerable in the first place, could just regrow lost limbs if he happened to lose one in battle.

"I trust you, but take your sword in case you run into any lake creatures that want to eat you."

As if on cue, the Jyrak roared again. Three dark forms zipped around its head, each of them wielding a gleaming metal blade that flickered under the afternoon sunlight.

Calum raised an eyebrow. "Like that one."

———

THEY HIT the Jyrak's left eye first. Lilly whipped past the glowing yellow orb and chopped at it with her sword, and Falcroné and Condor did the same thing. The Jyrak released a roar that shook her to her bones and clenched its eye shut. A trickle of glowing orange blood oozed out onto its scaly cheek.

Lilly wanted to celebrate, but the Jyrak's hand swung at her before she could so much as smile. She managed to barrel roll out of its path in time, and when she looked back, both Condor and Falcroné had avoided it as well.

They exchanged furtive glances and nods then curled back toward the Jyrak's head, leaving Lilly alone in the sky above. At first, Lilly was angry that they'd decided to go in for another attack without her, but watching them fly in tandem filled her with awe.

They wove between the Jyrak's flailing limbs and arced up toward its open mouth. Their swords lashed orange streaks across its extended tongue several times before it could retract it into its mouth. When the Jyrak tried to chomp at them with its bronze teeth, they split apart, circled around both sides of the its head, and slashed at its eyes again.

It reared its head back and roared as it clutched its eye with its enormous hands, but that just opened it up to more attacks on its tongue and gums from Condor and Falcroné.

Even amid the mayhem, Lilly had to snicker. For as much as they despised each other, Condor and Falcroné made the perfect fighting duo. They anticipated each other's actions and synchronized their attacks to inflict maximum damage on the Jyrak without endangering themselves.

Enough watching. Lilly propelled herself down toward the Jyrak, ready to fling herself into the fray once again.

———

FOR ALL HIS concern for Lilly, Calum had to admit she and the two Wisps were handling themselves just fine. The longer he watched, the more at ease he began to feel.

"We're clear of the Jyrak's tail!" Jake shouted. He cranked the wheel hard to his left. "Gimme five minutes, and I'll have you right at the bend."

Axel and Kanton came up behind Calum, Magnus, and Riley, and Calum glanced back at them. "Everything set? Did you find something we can use to help us sink?"

Axel nodded. "We'll use the ship's anchors. They're the obvious choice."

"Are they on this side of the ship?" Calum asked.

Axel's brow furrowed. "Yeah, why?"

"We need them on the opposite side. When Jake turns the ship, the side opposite of the Jyrak is the one we're jumping off." Calum scanned the deck. "Where are they?"

"I'll show you." Kanton darted toward the ship's stern and pointed to a pair of gigantic black anchors with ropes fastened to their ends, and Calum and the others followed.

"Cut them loose, and then we gotta carry them across the ship." Calum glanced over his shoulder at the Jyrak, which had just begun to turn toward them. "Hurry. We don't have much time."

DESPITE THEIR COMBINED EFFORTS, Lilly, Condor, and Falcroné hadn't managed to keep the Jyrak from noticing Jake's ship sneaking around behind it. When it began to turn toward the ship, Lilly knew she had to do something.

She knifed under the Jyrak's chin, looped up to its open mouth, then jammed her sword into its gums right between its two center teeth. Orange goo spurted onto the front of her armor and on her face.

The droning roar that erupted from the Jyrak's throat deafened her until she clamped her hands over her ears. She didn't see its tongue lash out of its mouth until it was too late.

The Jyrak's tongue plowed into her with the full force of a charging Sobek and sent her spinning through the air. Her senses dulled, and she tried to right herself, but she couldn't find her bearings.

Her body smacked against something solid and her momentum stopped. She rolled over and her fingers brushed against the smooth stones paving the surface below her.

Paved? How could she have landed on a street?

When her vision regained some focus, she saw three tall thick forms rising toward her, and she gasped at her realization.

The stones paving the street weren't stones at all.

They were scales.

Lilly had landed in the center of the Jyrak's open hand.

CONDOR SAW the Jyrak's tongue ram into Lilly, and in the worst example of bad luck he'd ever encountered, she careened straight into its waiting hand.

He immediately hurtled down toward her. He had to save her, and he would.

Condor swooped at her as the Jyrak's fingers closed and extended—

A heavy blow knocked him off course, and he missed the Jyrak's hand entirely. His sword slipped from his grasp and fell toward the churning waters below. Condor realized he would never get it back in time as he realized what had happened.

The Jyrak's other hand had swept in from the side and batted him away in the second worst manifestation of bad luck he'd ever encountered.

Now too far away, he righted himself and watched, helpless, as the Jyrak's fingers closed on Lilly.

A blur of blond hair and charcoal armor zoomed in, jammed a sword into the underside of the Jyrak's middle finger, and braced himself against its palm.

Falcroné.

Condor zipped toward them again.

STILL DAZED, Lilly couldn't believe her eyes.

Somehow, Falcroné had wedged himself between her and the Jyrak's middle finger with his sword, and he'd kept it from crushing her. Then Condor appeared next to Falcroné and also pushed against the Jyrak's finger with his hands.

Though both Wisps strained against the monster's might, the finger continued to lower, threatening to crush them all. Lilly tried to move, tried to fly away, but she couldn't.

"Get her out of here!" Falcroné yelled at him.

"Not without you!" Condor shouted back.

"*Do it*, Condor," Falcroné almost pleaded. "Take care of her."

Condor's mouth opened slightly. His eyes fixed on Falcroné's wobbling legs for an instant, then he scooped Lilly into his arms and sprang away from the Jyrak's hand while Falcroné bellowed a war cry that Lilly would never forget. She reached back for him, helpless to do anything else.

The Jyrak's middle finger slammed down on Falcroné, and his sword plunged into the churning waters below.

CHAPTER FORTY-TWO

L illy tried to scream, but nothing came out. When it finally did, it
sounded distant, faint. She inhaled a sharp breath and screamed
again, and this time her lungs delivered their full payload.

She begged Condor to take her back, to help Falcroné—anything,
but he just kept repeating, "It's over. He's gone."

The Jyrak raised its hand and thrust Falcroné's rag-doll form into its
gaping mouth, and Lilly's heart shattered.

CALUM and the others had just managed to get the second anchor across
the deck when Jake crowed from the captain's wheel.

"We're there!" He stomped on the deck three times, and the men who
rowed from their spots on the inside of the ship's hull raised their oars.

His ship had lined up with a large gray rock formation that jutted
about a hundred feet above the surface of the lake and formed part of its
perimeter for about a half-mile. Because of the way the surf thrashed
and the proximity of the rocks, Jake couldn't have docked the ship even
if he'd wanted to.

"Without anchors, I can't keep us steady for long. Go, now!"

Magnus leaped off the side of the ship nearest to the bend and dove into the water while Calum watched. If he didn't survive, if something happened to him down there, they were all as good as dead.

The double-thump of a Windgale landing sounded behind him, and he turned around. Condor stood there with Lilly in his arms, both of them coated in glowing orange blood. Lilly clung to Condor's neck, her body heaving with sobs.

Calum's mouth hung open. He searched the skies and looked up at the Jyrak, but he saw no one else. There were only two of them.

He swallowed the lump in his throat and managed to choke out one word. "Falcroné?"

Condor stared at him with the same stoic look in his blue eyes as the day the Premier had banished him to the Blood Chasm, and he shook his head.

Sickness twisted Calum's gut. So many had died for this cause already, and danger still loomed above them and swirled all around them. Would freeing Lumen be worth it all?

"Uh, Calum?" Jake motioned toward the Jyrak. "Your friend had better hurry. We're in trouble."

The Jyrak had turned toward them again. One step and it would come within reach of the ship.

"Get the anchors as close to the edge as you can. We need to be ready to go the moment Magnus resurfaces." Calum turned his attention back to the waters below, and muttered, "Come on, Magnus. Come on."

"Lilly, it's over. We still need you here."

Condor's velvet voice coaxed her to open her eyes, but when she saw his face, all she could think of was Falcroné's horrible death, and she burst into tears again.

"Shhh, it's alright," he crooned.

It wouldn't be alright. She *had* loved Falcroné, even if her emotions had been mixed. He was her oldest and closest friend, and now he was gone. Dead. Killed by that abomination.

"Put me down," she whispered. "Please."

Condor complied, but he gripped her shoulders in his hands. "He loved you, Lilly. That's why he did what he did."

She nodded and wiped the tears from her eyes. It came as little consolation now that he was gone. "I know."

"We're not done yet. We have to go find Lumen now."

Lilly stared at him. Ever since he'd joined their group, she had barely heard so much as a peep from him about Lumen's existence aside from sharing the location of the Arcanum.

Behind Condor, the Jyrak stepped closer to the ship.

"I'll protect you, Lilly. I promise I will." Condor gave her a faint smile. "Even if it means doing for you what Fal did."

"He did it for you, too, you know," Lilly said.

Was she trying to console him from her own hurt?

No. Her words were truth—truth that needed to be spoken.

"He always admired you. Always respected you. Even after—"

"I know, Lilly." Condor closed his eyes and gave a sullen nod. "I know."

"I don't need anyone else dying for me, so you stay alive. Crystal?"

He raised his head and met her eyes. "Clear."

Something about the way he said it chilled her from the inside out. She didn't have time to investigate the sensation before Calum's voice snatched her back into the real world.

"Over here!" Calum yelled. "Magnus is back up!"

Lilly and Condor zipped over to the edge of the ship. Sure enough, Magnus's dark-green head bobbed at the water's surface.

"I found it. It is quite far down, but I think we can—"

"*Look out!*" Jake's voice split the air.

Lilly turned around in time to see the Jyrak's hand descending toward the ship.

THE JYRAK'S hand hit so hard and so fast that Calum didn't even have time to jump off the ship. When he finally resurfaced, he realized that the Jyrak's blow had flung him and everyone else aboard the ship into the water, along with the anchors.

The anchors. Their only way of getting down.

If they were both lost—

"Calum!"

He turned his head in time to see Magnus's head disappear under the water along with the end of something black and curved.

One of the anchors.

"Quickly, over here!" Calum yelled.

Riley, Axel, Condor, and Lilly joined him while Kanton, the surviving Wolves, Jake, and what remained of his crew clung to shards of the ship's wood.

"Down, now!"

Calum sucked the deepest breath he'd ever taken into his lungs and let his armor weight pull him under.

Below him, Magnus was still in view, struggling to slow the anchor's descent, but Calum could see he wouldn't last much longer. If they didn't get ahold of that anchor in time, they would drown before they ever reached the cavern that led to the Hidden Abyss.

Calum kicked and clawed at the water with all his might. He had almost reached Magnus's outstretched arm when a current pushed him away. Magnus reacted and lashed his tail through the water at Calum, who grabbed ahold of it. As his descent accelerated, something clamped onto his ankle.

It was Riley. In turn, Axel held onto him, Condor held Axel, and Lilly held Condor. They descended to the lake's depths as a unit, together.

The air in Calum's lungs had already begun to stale, but the anchor sank them deeper and deeper into the lake.

He stole a glance up at the surface. They'd descended far enough now that there was no hope of turning back. Calum would either find the Hidden Abyss and free Lumen, or he would die in these waters. He hoped he hadn't been imagining everything Lumen had told him up until this point.

All at once, Magnus released his grip on the anchor and it dropped into the darker waters below. He motioned toward the wall then swam toward a large, black opening. Calum released his tail and followed him into the hole, and the rest of the group followed him as well.

With each stroke of his arms and legs, Calum exhaled more air until he had no more breath in his lungs to expel. His chest burned from deprivation, but he swam forward through the darkness nonetheless, flailing, kicking, scraping his way through the murky water without knowing where he was going.

No air. No salvation. No Lumen.

He realized he was going to die in that underwater tunnel. He'd die with his friends. With Magnus, with Axel, Riley, Condor—if he could consider Condor a friend, anyway—and with Lilly.

Lilly, with whom he'd shared so much, but not even half as much as he would've liked.

Calum's vision darkened. His mouth opened and water cascaded into his lungs, and everything went black.

THE NEXT THING HE KNEW, Calum lay on his side, coughing that very same water onto an uneven stone floor. He sucked in a deep breath of musty air. Ancient air.

He was alive.

And they had made it.

"Are you alright, Calum?" Magnus's deep voice reverberated off the jagged walls inside the small cavern.

Calum rolled onto his back and looked up. Instead of total darkness, a faint white light from somewhere illuminated Magnus's green face. Calum coughed again and nodded. "Yeah. I'm alright."

Two sets of hands pulled him to his feet—Condor and Riley. Lilly and Axel stood on either side of Magnus wearing relieved expressions.

Calum was just as glad to see them, but he didn't dare tarry any longer. He took a few tentative steps forward and surveyed the cavern.

The space didn't compare to that of the Arcanum by any measure. The ceiling hung no more than twenty feet above their heads at its highest point, and stalactites jutted down at random. Overall, the entire cavern couldn't have been larger than a forty-by-sixty-foot area, and a solid ten-by-ten pillar of solid rock occupied the middle of the cavern.

Yet it was that ten-by-ten section that gave off the faint light.

Upon closer inspection, Calum realized the pillar amounted to little more than several large stalactites that had stretched so low that they eventually melded with the cavern floor. Over time, the mineral deposits had spread and widened the stalactites into one massive pillar that looked as if it supported the entire cavern's ceiling.

But Calum realized exactly what it was.

Faint light glimmered through dozens of tiny crystals embedded within the stone, no doubt refracted from the prisoner trapped inside. A round platform made of four sections of white marble encircled the pillar, identical except for the worn carvings in the center of each one: a Wolf, a Saurian, a Windgale, and a human.

"What are we supposed to do now?" Axel asked.

Calum eyed him. "So do you believe me yet?"

"Don't get smart." He glowered at Calum. "I almost died like a hundred times today."

"Some of us did die." Lilly's voice barely registered above a whisper, but the cavern amplified her words.

Axel's jaw tensed, and he didn't say anything else.

"At this point, there's only one thing to do." Calum motioned toward the marble platform. "Magnus, take your place."

Magnus nodded, then he stepped onto the section of marble designated for a Saurian.

"Riley, you next." After Riley complied, Calum looked at Condor and Lilly. "Which of you wants to do it?"

"I will." This time Lilly's voice rang clear. She looked up at Condor, who stood by her. "As long as you don't mind."

Condor grinned. "Not in the least. Fal would have wanted it this way."

Lilly showed him a shallow smile and took her place on the platform.

Calum turned and faced Axel. He motioned toward the platform. "Go ahead."

"What?" Axel's mouth hung open. "You're joking, right?"

"No." Calum shook his head. "I want you to be the one who sets Lumen free."

"Not a chance. I'm still not convinced this'll even work." Axel folded his arms and winked at Calum. "Besides, this moment, if it ends up being real, is for you. I can't take it from you."

Calum smiled at him. Axel had proven more of a burden than he'd had ever imagined when they first left his farm. Even so, Calum never would've made it this far without him. His first friend. His best friend.

"Go on, already." Axel nodded toward the pillar. "It's too cold in here for us to keep standing around like a bunch of idiots."

Calum chuckled, and he started toward the platform. He stopped just in front of it, exhaled a long breath, and placed his right foot on the marble, then his left.

The instant his left foot touched the platform, it lowered into the rock by three inches. Unsure what to do, Calum backed off, as did Lilly, Riley, and Magnus.

The platform sections jerked toward the pillar one at a time and slammed into it, sending long fissures up its sides. Rocks and dust trickled from the fissures as the last platform struck the pillar, and then all fell silent.

The faint light from within the pillar intensified and pierced through the fissures into the cavern. Each fissure branched into a hundred smaller cracks that spread around the pillar until the stone began to crumble away altogether, leaving only blinding white light in its place.

Light. So pure that it penetrated Calum to his very soul.

He tried to shield his eyes with his hands, but it burned through him.

Now, at long last, his friends knew what he'd experienced in his dreams, and he was finally experiencing it in real life. It saturated him with sheer joy, and he wanted to whoop and shout in delight.

An ethereal voice groaned in the ancient air around them, and the light faded enough that Calum could look upon Kanarah's savior with his real eyes for the first time. He stepped free of his prison and his presence filled the entire cavern with radiance.

There before them stood Lumen, the General of Light.

EPILOGUE

EPILOGUE

Inside his throne room, the King turned his head to the west. The words of the nobleman addressing him faded to nothing as a new awareness engaged his mind.

"Summon Matthios."

The nobleman silenced, and he stared at the King with wide eyes. "Your Majesty?"

The King fixed his eyes on the nobleman. "Summon Matthios *now.*"

With a low bow, the nobleman retreated to do the King's bidding.

Not two minutes later, a muscular man in bronze armor, stood before the King. He, too, bowed low. "What is your bidding, Majesty?"

"Muster your army. Head to the Golden Plains outside of Kanarah City."

Matthios raised his head and stared at the King with eyes like molten bronze. "Has the time come, my King?"

"Yes, Matthios. Lumen has been released." The King stood from his throne and handed Matthios the bronze staff he'd used to banish Lumen a thousand years earlier. "You once forged this weapon that I might use it to battle our enemy. It is yours to wield from now on. May it keep you safe as you face our enemies."

Matthios accepted the weapon and bowed. Then he turned back and headed for the throne room door.

SHAMELESS COMMERCIAL

Lilly handed *The Ghost Mine* back to Magnus. "You weren't kidding. That was a wild ride. Especially that scene in the gravity lift shaft with the androids…"

"Ben Wolf is a legendary author," Magnus agreed. "His work should be celebrated in every culture and translated into every language."

"Have you finished the second one yet?" Lilly asked. "I'm kind of dying to get my hands on it."

"Yes, I finished it the other night." Magnus dug *The Ghost Pact* out of his pack and handed it to her. He also held up *The Ghost Plague*. "After the way the second book ended, I started reading the third one the next morning. I could not wait."

"Riley and I have really been enjoying the Blood Mercenaries series as well." Calum gave Riley a nudge. "Helps that you've got opposable thumbs now. You can read on your own."

"Trust me when I say that nobody is happier about that than me," Riley muttered, and he shot a glare at Condor.

"Don't look at me." Condor held up his hands. "I've already read all of those books. I've written reviews and posted them. Even shared them with my friends."

Axel scoffed. "You don't *have* any friends."

"Your words strike like a fiery arrow plunging into my very soul, Farm Boy," Condor fake-lamented. "I shall never recover from such a grievous wound."

Axel rolled his eyes. "This is *why* you don't have any friends."

"Nonsense," Condor said. "*You* are my friend, Farm Boy. My truest, noblest, most long-suffering friend. I am honored to have such a staunch and valued confidant at my side."

"I'm not 'at your side.' If anything you're at *my* side."

"Aha! See? I *knew* we were friends," Condor exclaimed. "Come over here and give me a gigantic hug of friendship, Farm Boy!"

"Don't you—hey! Stop!" Axel recoiled as Condor flew toward him. "Get away from me, you flying freak!"

As the two of them scrambled and sparred with each other, Riley melted into some nearby shadows.

"Hey, you," he whispered, motioning with his paws—now hands with opposable thumbs. "Come here. Yes, you—the person reading this book. I have a secret to tell you. Come closer."

Even in the darkness, Riley's blue eyes remained visible.

"I need your help with something. You liked this book, right? Liked reading about our adventures and exploits? Good. I need you to do me a favor. I need you to write a review of the book on Amazon.

"It's easy—just find the book's product page and write a review. Doesn't have to be long. Just give others an idea of what you liked about it (or didn't). Come on. I'm asking nicely. Please? After all, I almost died like eighteen times in this book.

"And don't forget to read the next book to find out how our story ends. I don't even know what's gonna happen, but I know it'll be good. Alright... I gotta go."

With that, Riley evaporated into the shadows and disappeared entirely.

———

THE ADVENTURE CONTINUES IN *THE RISE OF ANCIENT FURY*
BOOK THREE OF THE CALL OF ANCIENT LIGHT SERIES

Need more books? Check out www.benwolf.com
or email me directly at ben@benwolf.com to place your orders.

If you enjoyed this book, please leave a review on Amazon.com!

ACKNOWLEDGMENTS

I first started this series twelve years ago (in Feb. of 2009) because of a map I saw in a dream, much like Calum did in this story. At the time, I was working in Brooks Brothers as a sales guy, and jotting this story helped me pass the time in an otherwise mindless and miserable job.

Like Calum, I felt I was meant for something more, but I didn't know how to get out of my daily rut. Seven months later, I attended the first writers conference of my life—one that changed my life forever.

Now this book has not only been published, but someone—you—chose to pick it up and read it. So thank YOU for reading.

Thank you to Jesus Christ for changing my life forever.

Second, thanks to my parents for believing in me from an early age and for helping to support my dreams and my growth. I love you both.

Thanks to my all-star beta readers, Daniel Kuhnley, Luke Messa, and Paige Guido, for your excellent feedback and encouragement.

Thank you to Andrew Winch and Davis Bunn, who both critiqued early horrible versions of this book. Your input helped me out so much.

Hannah Sternjakob, you are a genius. The cover is exactly what I'd envisioned (only better). Thank you for your long-suffering patience!

Thanks to all of my readers! Without you, I wouldn't be doing this.

Lastly, thank you especially to my intelligent, beautiful, and ultra-supportive wife, Charis Crowe. Your flexibility with my weird writing schedule makes all the difference in getting my writing done. I love you.

ABOUT BEN WOLF

In 7th grade, I saw the movie *Congo*. Then I wrote a parody of it set in Australia that featured killer kangaroos. So began my writing career.

I've spoken at 50+ writers conferences and comic cons nationwide. When not writing, I occasionally choke people in jiu jitsu. I live in the Midwest with my gorgeous wife, our kids, and our cats Marco and Ivy.

Check out my other books on Amazon.com.

Want updates? Sign up for my author email newsletter now!

WWW.SUBSCRIBEPAGE.COM/FANTASY-READERS

Or find me on social media:

facebook.com/1benwolf
instagram.com/1benwolf
amazon.com/author/benwolf

Made in the USA
Las Vegas, NV
12 March 2024

87089810R00213